DOROTHY GARLOCK

The Edge of Town

A Time Warner Company

This book is a work of historical fiction. In order to give a sense of the times, some names or real people or places have been included in the book. However, the events depicted in this book are imaginary, and the names of nonhistorical persons or events are the product of the author's imagination or are used fictitiously. Any resemblance of such nonhistorical persons or events to actual ones is purely coincidental.

Warner Books, Inc., 1271 Avenue of the Americas, New York, NY 10020

Visit our Web site at www.twbookmark.com

A Time Warner Company

Printed in the United States of America

First Printing: April 2001

10 9 8 7 6 5 4 3 2 1

Library of Congress Cataloging-in-Publication Data
Garlock, Dorothy.
The edge of town / Dorothy Garlock.
p. cm.
ISBN 0-446-52769-6
1. Rural families—Fiction. 2. Farm life—Fiction. 3. Missouri—Fiction. I. Title.
PS3557.A71645 E34 2001
813'.54—dc21 00-050346

To a very special lady, my editor,

FREDDA S. ISAACSON

Fredda,

You have been my teacher and my guide during the 31 books we have worked on together. I could never have done it without you.

With this dedication goes my appreciation and my admiration.

Dorothy Garlock

The Edge of Town

Julie's Dream

There's loamy earth in Fertile, MO.
Men who seed, reap what they sow.
But where the dusty road grows narrow,
The rocky soil resists the harrow.
The yield is meager, profit down,
Farming on the edge of town.

If your name is Julie Jones,
You've learned to stifle inward groans,
Tending all your dead mom's brood
As a proper daughter should.
You must not let it get you down
Living on the edge of town.

But in the night by gaslight's glow
Your fears come rushing as you sew
That's when the dreadful mem'ries rise,
And bitter tears bedim your eyes.
You cut a patch and mend a gown,
Existing on the edge of town.

From children's beds comes dreaming laughter.
This farm is not "forever after."
You smile with hope that someone strong
Will someday, somehow come along
To smooth away your troubled frown
With loving on the edge of town.

F.S.I.

Prologue

March 17, 1918

For the past week she had felt an ache in her lower back but not as sharp as this one. When the muscles of her body relaxed, she lowered herself to the stool to start milking the cow. Her strong fingers grasped the cow's teats, and streams of milk hit the bucket. It was only half filled when a sharp pain knifed through her abdomen, and she realized she could no longer ignore what was happening.

Her time had come.

Clinging to the patient cow, she pulled herself to her feet and then, holding to the stall railing, inched her way to the barn door. An agonizing spasm of pain brought her to her knees and she feared that she would never make it back to the house. She tried to push open the barn door but had no strength.

Oh, Lord! It hurt so bad. She'd never dreamed that there could be such overpowering, racking pain. She fought to keep fear from clouding her mind. She was alone, and the baby inside her was tearing her apart.

"Remember," she muttered. "Remember to take deep breaths, remember to push down."

Oh, Lord, when it comes out, it will drop down onto the dirt floor.

Grasping the rail, she dragged herself back past the two big friendly workhorses, who neighed a greeting. In an empty stall covered with fresh straw, she shrugged out of her old sweater and quickly pulled the loose dress off over her head. When the cold air hit her damp body, she scrambled to pull the sweater back on again. First she got to her knees, then rolled over onto her back with her knees raised. She panted for breath and tried hard to remember everything she knew about childbirth.

Lord, help me!

"Help me! Somebody help me." She tried to shout, but her voice came out in a whimper

I can't breathe! She began to panic and rolled back onto her knees and, holding the stall post, positioned herself with her feet far apart. She remembered Mrs. Johnson, their neighbor, saying that Indian women gave birth in a squatting position.

The surge of water came first. From that moment on, her only reason for existing was to push from her body the thing that was causing the excruciating pain. She sobbed, she yelled, she prayed.

"Why me, Lord? What did I ever do to deserve this?"

She felt between her legs and realized the lump emerging from her was the baby's head.

She drew in quick, gasping breaths. Holding tightly to the railing to ease her cramping legs, she concentrated on pushing the child out of her. After what seemed an eternity, the wet, bloody lump dropped from her body.

Sweating, exhausted and relieved, she hung there until she could get her breath. Movement alerted her to the live bundle between her knees. She picked it up, dug into its mouth with her finger to remove the mucus and saw with relief that it was breathing. The cord was still attached. Having nothing to cut it with, she severed it with her teeth and wrapped the baby in her dress. Too weak to stand, she squatted there, having completely forgotten about the afterbirth until she felt the surge of liquid between her legs.

Not even checking to see the sex of the child, she hugged it in the dress against her body and pulled the sweater around it to keep it warm. She was cold and tired but knew that she had to get to the house and prayed that she had the strength to climb the slight rise.

Jethro Jones was standing at the cookstove when the door opened.

"It's about time. I was thinking ya hadn't gone to milk yet." He turned to look at her and saw her pale face and bloody clothes. "What the hell?" he exclaimed. His mouth remained open.

"There's a mess in the barn that's got to be cleaned up before the boys go out to do chores."

She walked stiffly through the kitchen and across the hall to the bedroom.

Chapter 1

Fertile, Missouri
July 1922

LILLIAN RUSSELL'S DIED!" Jill made the dramatic announcement and waited for her sister to comment. When Julie continued to wash the dishes and drop them in the rinse pan, she said, "All the wonderful women in the world are dying. First Nellie Bly and now Lillian."

"Where did you hear that?"

"Ruby May told me last night. Lillian was so beautiful, so elegant. All the men loved her." Jill lifted her arms in a circling motion. "I'm going to be just like her."

"You'll have to grow some," Julie said dryly. "She had quite a bosom. They were out to here." Julie held her cupped, wet hands out six inches from her slender body.

"And a tiny waist."

"Helped by a tight corset."

"She was beautiful—"

"And old enough to be your grandma. Dry the dishes while you're grieving for her."

Jill took a plate from the hot rinse water, dried it and set it on the table.

"The men who gave her diamonds must have liked a woman

with a big bust. Diamonds show up best lying on soft white flesh."

"Soft white flesh? Glory be! Well, don't worry about it. You've got a good start for a fifteen-year-old." Julie slid a greasy skillet into the sudsy water.

"Jack said they were like half an orange stuck up there."

Julie looked at her sister and frowned. "Why would Jack be making a remark about his sister's breasts?"

"I asked him."

"Justine Jill Jones!"

Jill rolled her eyes on hearing her full name. "I hate it when you call me that."

"It's the name Mama gave you."

"I'll never know why she added Justine to it."

"She didn't. She added Jill."

"Kids at school laugh about our names. They say if Mama'd had more kids, she'd probably have named them Jericho and Jerusalem."

"And what did you say to that?"

"Nothing. Kathy Jacobs said she should've named two of us Jenny and Jackass." Jill giggled.

Julie's shoulders shook with silent laughter. It didn't bother her that all their names started with a *J*. She rather liked it.

"I never asked Jack about my bosom," Jill said after she placed a stack of clean plates on the shelf. "I asked him if the boys at school thought I was pretty."

"And what did he say?"

"He said . . . oh, he was so mean!" Jill flipped her long blond curls over her shoulder and tilted her freckled nose. "He said only the dumb ones thought I was pretty. He said my hair was like straw, my nose was so turned up he was surprised I didn't drown when it rained."

Julie laughed in spite of the serious look on her sister's face.

"Never ask your brothers if you're pretty. If you were a raving beauty they'd not admit it."

"That's when he said my breasts were the size of a half an orange."

"It's a pact made between brothers to tell their sisters that they are ugly as a mud fence even if they are as pretty as Mary Pickford."

"I hate brothers!"

"Mable Normand is pretty."

"She's in *Molly O* at the Palace. I want to see it, but Papa said picture shows cost almost as much as a pair of stockings and I needed stockings more." Jill sighed heavily.

"Julie, Julie, guess what?" Ten-year-old Jason came into the kitchen, letting the screen door slam behind him. He always shouted when he was excited—and at times when he wasn't.

Since their mother's death four years before, Julie had become the person her brothers and sisters came to with news, hurts and needs.

Jason stumbled onto the back porch, yanked open the screen door and bounded into the kitchen, shutting the door just in time to keep the shaggy brown dog, his constant companion, from following him. Besides being small for his age, Jason had been born with a deformed foot that made it necessary for him to wear a special shoe.

"Julie, guess what?" He was breathless.

"Well, let me think for a minute. Is it something exciting?" Jason nodded his head vigorously. "Land-a-livin'! I think I know! Bananas are growing out of the old stump out by the woodpile."

"Ah, Julie, you're so silly sometimes." Jason stood as tall as his slight frame allowed. His muddy shoes were firmly planted on the clean kitchen floor.

"Ju-lie! Look at his shoes!" Jill sneered with sisterly disgust.

"Shut up." Jason turned on his sister. "Open your trap again and I won't tell ya!"

"What's your news, Jason?" Julie poured water from the teakettle over the dishes in the pan.

"Joe . . . said that we're havin' a baseball game tonight. The Birches, the Humphreys, and Roy and Thad Taylor . . . Jus-tine. Maybe the Jacobses and Evan Johnson. He helped at the Humphreys' today, though he ain't expecting no payback."

"Who cares about *him*?" Jill snorted.

Jason knew he would get the full attention of his younger sister when he mentioned the Taylors. Jill had been eyeing both Roy and Thad Taylor even though Thad was Joe's age.

"Joe told me to get out the bags we use for bases. I hope mice ain't chewed 'em up."

"Haven't," Julie corrected. "When was it decided to have a ball game?" She stopped working on the greasy skillet to give her full attention to her brother, who was inching toward the door, eager to be away.

"I dunno. They'll be done hayin' by midafternoon. Pa said to tell ya they'd noon at the Humphreys'."

"Then I'll go to town this afternoon. We'll have a light supper."

"Can I go?"

"No. You can help Jill watch Joy."

"That's . . . girl work!" Jason snorted.

"Just right for a sissy-britches," Jill said snippily and took a handful of forks from the rinse pan.

"Shut up, Jus-tine!" Jason drew out the hated name because he knew that it would irritate his sister. "You're so dumb, you stink. I gotta go."

Julie grabbed a towel to dry her hands and went to the door to see Jason hurrying across the yard.

"Jason," she called. "Where's Joy?"

"I dunno."

"Find her, please. She may have wandered off."

"Ah, Sis, I wanta go back."

"Honey, it's a good mile to the Humphreys'."

"I don't care," he shouted. "I told Joe I'd come back after I told ya. Jumpin' catfish! Here comes Joy. She's been in the mud. I ain't touchin' 'er."

Julie went out onto the back porch and looked at the small girl. The blond curls that she had dampened and brushed around her finger to form fat curls not two hours ago were speckled with mud, as was Joy's face. Mud covered her feet and legs up to the cuffs of her drawers, which came to just below her knees.

"Ah, Joy. You're a mess. You can't come in the house like that. Go to the pump. I'll come wash you off."

"I didn't mean to, Julie." The child's impish grin told her sister that she was not a bit sorry.

"I'll do it." Jill leaped down the back steps. "Come on, stinkpot."

"I ain't no stinkpot, Jus-tine." Joy's hero was Jason. She had learned from him a way to irritate Jill. "Jus-tine, Jus-tine, Just-tine," she said again and again, then stuck her tongue out and wriggled it.

Julie went back into the kitchen. At times her heart ached for Jason. He never complained about his foot, but she knew that he wished he could run like the other boys. Tonight at the ball game, he would bat and one of his older brothers would run the bases for him. She also wished that Jill would be kinder to him. The two were always hissing and snapping at each other like a dog and a cat.

Julie was finishing up the dishes when Jill came in, dragging Joy by the hand. The screen door slammed shut behind them.

"Here's this good-for-nothin' kid. I put her clothes in the tub on the porch."

Julie looked down at the small girl and shook her head. Joy's nakedness didn't seem to bother her at all.

"I don't know what we're going to do with you. You can't stay clean for a minute."

"Ya can shoot me." Big solemn eyes looked up at Julie.

"Shoot you? Where in the world did you get an idea like that?"

"Joe said it to Papa. Papa said, 'I donno what to do with ya.' Joe said, 'Shoot 'er.' "

"They were teasing."

"I'm not so sure," Jill said. "Come on, brat. We'll get you some bloomers, unless you want the boys to see your bare behind."

"I don't care," Joy replied sassily.

Julie rolled her eyes toward the ceiling. The name Joy was so right for the little one; she was the joy of the family. Her hair was curly, her eyes large and blue as the sky. Bright as a new penny and precocious, she was in danger of being terribly spoiled by doting brothers and sisters.

Julie put the kitchen in order. As she hung her apron on the back of a chair, Jill, with Joy in tow, came through the kitchen on the way to the front porch. Julie went upstairs to the room she shared with her sisters and changed out of her dress into a white blouse with a drawstring neckline and a blue skirt. Julie knew herself for what she was: a strong, slim woman with clear skin, a wide mouth and the responsibility of raising her siblings weighing heavily on her shoulders.

She looked at herself closely in the mirror as she braided, coiled and pinned her waist-length, wheat-colored hair to the back of her head. She had thought about getting a bob, but she feared what it would do to her already rather "unsteady" reputation. Her thick dark brows were slightly arched. Lashes, long and lush, framed light brown eyes that were both quiet and quick. Julie sighed. Nothing about her would cause a man to give her a second look. She was foolish, very foolish to dream that one would.

With a wide-brimmed straw hat set squarely on her head to shade her face as much as possible, she picked up the cloth bag she would use to carry home the few things she planned to get at the store.

On the porch she paused to give last-minute instructions to Jill.

"If I'm not back by the time Papa and the boys get here, tell them I'll be here by suppertime. Be nice, Joy, and pay mind to what your sister tells you."

"Do I have to?" The little girl's merry blue eyes twinkled up at Julie.

"Yes, you little imp." Julie smiled fondly at the child. "Come give me a kiss."

"Are you going to the library?" Jill asked.

"Is there something you need to return?"

"No. I'd love to read *The Trail of the Lonesome Pine* and *Girl of the Limberlost* again. If they're not in, get *Ramona* or *Freckles* or *A Knight of the Cumberland.*"

"You've read those books . . . several times. Why not try something new?"

"I'd rather read something I know I'll like. Old Miss Rothe made us read *Ivanhoe* and *Lady of the Lake.* She thought they were romantic. I thought they were boring!"

"Agnes Rothe is a good teacher."

"She's an old maid! Bet she's old as Papa."

"She's a good teacher even if she is *old*!" Julie retorted as she left the shade of the porch, stepped out into the bright July sunlight and walked down the lane toward the road. Sidney ran out from under the porch to follow. "You can't go, Sidney." Julie stopped and pointed a finger at the shaggy dog. "Why aren't you with Jason?"

"Jason didn't want him to go to the Humphreys'," Jill called.

"Why not? He always goes with Jason."

"There's a kid over there that's scared of him. The Humphreys have to keep their dog tied up."

"Go back and stay with Jill and Joy, Sidney. You can't go to town." She waited until the dog had settled down by the porch step before she was on her way again.

Julie breathed in deeply; the air was tinged with fresh-cut, sweet-smelling hay. Buttercups and broom clover grew along the edge of the lane. Bees buzzed amid wild honeysuckle. Beams of bright sunlight slanted down through the trees. The grove was alive with the cheeps and chirps and rustlings of the birds. A mockingbird scolded her from the high branch of a towering oak tree.

The summer day was serene and beautiful.

A pompous rooster was picking and scratching in the lane ahead. The chickens were confined to the chicken house only in the winter. The rest of the year they were as free as the wild birds to roam the farm wherever they wished. They never ventured far, however, from the security of the farmyard, where from dawn to dusk they could be found picking up grain, undigested tidbits from animal manure, grass and all the insects they could catch.

Julie had to smile when a rooster, upon finding a choice morsel, called his harem of hens with a "Tut, tut, tut, tut." A couple of gullible fat hens came running, but there was nothing left for them. The rooster made a great show of being a good provider and strutted away. Having the fluffy white hens at his beck and call seemed to do great things for his ego.

Julie had been born on this farm in the room across the hall from the parlor. She had walked the mile to town and the additional quarter mile through town to school from the time she was six years old. Living on the edge of town, she had been considered a country girl and had not been invited to the socials held by her classmates, even though she had been a favorite of the teachers and was one of the prettiest girls in school.

Her school days had come to an abrupt end the summer she was fifteen. She tried hard not to think of that terrible summer or the following winter at home taking care of the family and her mother, who had never fully recovered from influenza.

As she walked along the hard-packed road, Julie's mind roamed. Like all young girls, she had dreamed of a handsome man who would fall madly in love with her and take her away.

The dream was becoming dimmer and dimmer. Besides, the chance of finding such a man in Fertile, Missouri, was about as likely as waking up some morning and finding the sun coming up out of the west.

Was her lot to be the old-maid sister living out her life here on the farm? The boys would leave, marry and start families of their own. Jill was so pretty, she'd have no trouble finding a husband. Already the boys were eyeing her, even if Jack wouldn't tell her so. He'd told Julie he'd punched one boy in the nose for talking about Jill's bosom.

Julie walked the downhill road toward town and the river beyond. It was easy walking. Coming back up the road to the farm would require much more effort. She rounded a curve in the road and the town of Fertile, a huddle of buildings scattered along the bank of the Platte River, came into view.

Only the tall red-painted grain elevator and two white church steeples rose above the two-story brick shops and the wooden residences. The town sloped down to the river where the old mill stood. It had stopped operation several years before the Great War.

Julie crossed the railroad tracks. The train station was a one-room frame boxlike structure with a cattle pen on one side and the elevator on the other. The grass alongside the tracks was charred, deliberately burnt to keep the weeds from taking over.

A lumber wagon, its long box filled with large rolls of barbed-wire fencing and oak posts, rumbled past her and continued on down Main Street after the driver had tipped his hat politely. A Ford, rattling as if it were going to shake to pieces, rolled past and came to a stop in front of the drugstore, a building of heavy limestone that dwarfed the tiny jewelry shop next to it. In front of the shop was a large wooden clock that for as long as Julie could remember hadn't run.

A few automobiles were parked on the streets surrounding the county courthouse. Most merchants set aside an area for teams and wagons behind their stores. Fertile had a large and prosperous business area because it was the only town of any size in the county. The nearest large town was St. Joseph thirty miles to the west.

Behind the shops that lined the street sat neat cottages and some large comfortable houses surrounded by picket fences. Closer to the river, in the less prosperous part of town, the houses were unkempt, unpainted frame shacks, most with a cow or a horse staked out behind them.

Julie felt uncomfortable and out of place every time she walked alone down the main street of Fertile. A certain element of the population drew a discriminatory line between town people who "belonged" and those who lived on the surrounding farms and did not.

Next to the Palace, Fertile's movie house, was Carwilde and Graham's, the largest mercantile store in town. A clear glass window, installed just this year, displayed dresses and men's suits on mannequins that reminded Julie of corpses with painted faces.

"Good afternoon, ma'am. May I help you?"

Scott Graham, who stepped from behind the counter, wore his hair parted in the middle and slicked down, a high stiff collar and blue arm garters on his starched white shirt. Scott had been in Julie's class at school, but he never acknowledged that he knew who she was. Had she known that he would be the one to wait on her, she would not have come in.

"What can I do for you?"

"I need two spools of number fifty white thread."

"Right this way."

Her head held high, Julie followed him down the aisle as if she intended to buy out the store instead of two five-cent spools of thread. Scott opened a drawer on the thread cabinet and selected the thread.

"Anything else?"

"I'd like to look at the dress goods, please."

"This way," he said, as if she couldn't see the bolts of material piled on the table not six feet away.

Julie selected a blue and white check to make a new Sunday dress for Joy, who had outgrown the only one she had, and a length of white lawn to sew a new shirtwaist for Jill. She paid for her purchases and left the store, glad to leave the presence of the dandy who had waited on her.

When she passed the hotel, she glanced at a man sitting on the porch, his chair tilted back against the wall. His shirtsleeves were cuffless and he wore black arm garters, a linen collar but no tie. Their eyes met; his, friendly and appraising. He smiled and tipped his broad-brimmed hat. She felt his eyes follow her as she walked down the street to the grocery store.

She was greeted by name by the owner. The Joneses were valued customers of Mr. Oakley's. They had traded with him since he had come to town ten years ago and always paid their tab on time.

"Good day to ya, Miss Jones. Nice day for a walk into town, huh?"

"It was nice walking in, but I don't expect it to be so pleasant going back up the hill. How are the family?"

"Fit as fiddles. Little ones are growing like weeds. Wish they'd hurry up so they can give me some help here in the store." He laughed heartily.

"Don't wish your life away, Mr. Oakley. They will grow up fast enough."

"You're right as rain 'bout that. Jethro finished with hayin'?"

"They'll finish this afternoon. If we get some rain we should have a couple more cuttings before frost."

"It's been a good growin' year so far. Your corn looks good. Me'n the missus passed the field last Sunday when we drove out to visit her uncle."

"Papa and the boys got it in early."

"What can I get for you today?"

"I'm walking, so I'll just take a couple of things I can carry. Joe or Papa will be coming in with the wagon and a list in a few days. I need a can of baking powder and a small bottle of vanilla flavoring to get me by until then."

Julie waited while Mr. Oakley went to the back of the store. Her eyes roamed the neatly stocked shelves, the barrels of crackers, beans and rice and the bright red, big-wheeled coffee grinder that sat proudly on the counter. She breathed in the mixture of scents: coffee, spices, leather goods and overripe bananas.

The pucker-mouthed wife of the blacksmith waddled into the store, paused to look around, then greeted Julie.

"Ain't seen ya at church lately, Julie," she said in an accusing tone.

"I've been there almost every Sunday, Mrs. Yerby."

"I meant durin' the week. Been havin' good crowds fer the revival meetin's."

"I'm glad to hear it." Julie turned to Mr. Oakley and noticed the jar of peppermint sticks on the counter. "I'll take a half dozen sticks of peppermint. The kids need a treat once in a while." As she placed them in her cloth bag, the grocer pulled a thick ledger from beneath the counter, thumbed through the pages to the Jones account and added the purchases.

"Thank you," Julie murmured, then said more loudly, "Nice seeing you, Mrs. Yerby."

"Come to the revival, Julie. Ya just might meet a man lookin' for a wife. Ya ain't never goin' to get one jist stayin' out there on the farm takin' care of them kids."

Julie laughed nervously. "I'm not looking for a man, Mrs. Yerby."

"Pshaw! Ain't a woman alive who ain't lookin' for a man. Yo're better-lookin' than most."

"Thank you," Julie said dryly.

"Ya won't have no trouble a-tall if ya just spruce up and show yoreself some. That's if ya've not got yore sights set on one of them good-looking rich fellers like that William Desmond Taylor that got himself murdered out there in Hollywood." Mrs. Yerby's laugh was more of a dry cackle.

Embarrassed, Julie angrily turned and adjusted the items in her bag. Mrs. Yerby didn't seem to notice that she had made Julie uncomfortable and continued in a confidential tone.

"They ain't found out who killed him yet. I heard a feller say it on the radio. Bet it was that oh-so-pure Mary Miles Minter. Pshaw! Pure, my foot. Ain't nothin' *pure* in that wicked place."

Mrs. Yerby picked a raisin from the barrel and popped it quickly into her mouth when she saw Mr. Oakley wasn't looking. It didn't stop her from talking.

"That awful Johnson man came to the meetin' the other night and stood out in the dark lookin' in. I told 'em that they ain't ort to hold services in the pavilion with the sides raised up so that hill trash like Walter Johnson can see what's goin' on. But they went right ahead and done it, and look what they got."

"Did he disrupt the service?" Mr. Oakley asked.

"He was drinkin' and quarrelsome. When church was over he tried to pick a fight with Stan Decker. He called him a blank-blank hypocrite, but out of respect for the church Stan just walked off and left him. That Johnson is the meanest man I ever did see. He's too mean to live, is what he is. A person can see the devil right in him."

"I must go," Julie said. To the shopkeeper she added, "Tell Mrs. Oakley I'm sorry I missed her."

"Ya better watch that little sister of yores, Julie." Mrs. Yerby lowered her voice. "It's said that man's ruined more'n one young girl in this county. Wouldn't put it past him to waylay her out in the woods someplace and have his way with her. Now that his boy is back, there's two of 'em. I heard there's a girl down in Well's Point that was sent away sudden-like."

"Thanks for the warning, Mrs. Yerby."

Julie stepped out into the bright sunlight. She didn't want to hear anything more about the town bully or his son. Her intense hatred of the man could be the one thing that would keep her out of heaven. She couldn't remember when she hadn't hated and feared him.

Chapter 2

On her way to the library, Julie passed the barbershop and pool room. She glanced through the flyspecked window to see Mr. Clark, the proprietor, shaving a man whose face was covered with lather. Out front another young man held the cord of an awning while talking to an old farmer whose face looked like a piece of old leather. Both men nodded politely to Julie.

"Hel-lo, Julie." Zelda Wood came out of her papa's bank to call out.

"Hello."

Zelda's dark hair was bobbed and spit curls clung to her cheeks. She was short, plump and had extremely thick ankles. Her eyebrows had been plucked to a thin line, and her lips were painted in a cupid's bow. She had been a year ahead of Julie in school and always made sure that everyone knew that her papa owned the bank.

"I've not seen you for a while, kiddo."

"I've been busy."

"Doin' what?"

"A little of this and that. What have you been doing?"

"Going to parties, dances. Things like that. They're having dances three nights a week at Spring Lake. Want to come?" She continued without waiting for Julie to answer: "I might be able to find someone to take you."

"That's kind of you."

Zelda ignored or failed to detect the sarcasm in Julie's voice.

"We're doing the Charleston, the shimmy, the black-bottom and a whole bunch of other new dances."

"Have you heard that the Catholic Church has condemned the shimmy?"

"What do they know? Papa says those old Catholics are a bunch of heathens anyway."

Bet he doesn't mind those old heathens putting money in his bank.

"Do you do anything other than square dance? Well, they have sets for the old people," Zelda went on as if Julie had answered her question. Her eyes traveled down over Julie's plain skirt to her heavy shoes. "I'll even help you find something to wear if you want to go."

"I don't need you to find me something to wear, Zelda." Julie wanted to slap the girl, but she held on to her temper. Zelda appeared to be completely unaware that she had offended her.

"Do you see much of Evan Johnson? He's good-looking, but he thinks he's the cat's meow."

"Why do you say that?" Julie asked.

"He's . . . strange. Not very friendly. Papa said he'd been to college and to France."

"He was over there fighting the war. I doubt he did much sightseeing."

"I could fall for him. He's got money in Papa's bank and drives a real nice car. I wonder why he don't drive it to town. He was here yesterday on a *horse*!"

"He's a farmer. Surely you're not interested in a farmer."

"Of course not! Papa'd have a duck-fit if I had anything to do with him. I was thinking about you. It would be a chance to get out from under all that work. He's got money," she said again. "Papa said he'd be a good catch for me if he wasn't kin to Walter Johnson."

"Why did he say that? Evan hasn't done anything out of the way that I've heard about, even if he is Walter Johnson's son."

"For heaven's sake, Julie. Being that man's son is enough. Everyone knows what *he* is. How can his son *not* be trash?"

"Evan shouldn't be held accountable for what his father does." Julie was beginning to let her irritation show, even though she knew that Zelda was shallow and dumb and was only echoing what her father said.

"Mama says, 'blood will tell' and 'water seeks its own level.' He's got Walter Johnson's blood, hasn't he? Trashy blood, if you ask me."

"He's all right for me but not for you. Is that right?"

"Oh, shoot! You always did take everything I say wrong. I didn't mean it to sound like that, but I do have a position in town. My papa is the banker and—"

"I'm just a girl from the edge of town." Julie spoke as if speaking to a two-year-old. "Evan's mother was a dear, sweet woman. The best neighbor we ever had. He's got her blood, too, so he can't be all bad."

"She couldn't have been very smart, to marry a man like Walter Johnson," Zelda said with a grimace.

"He may not have been so bad when he was young. People change, you know."

Zelda rolled her eyes. "Why are you defending him?"

"I'm not defending him. I think it's wrong for you to blame the son for the father's deeds. But no matter. Folks have already made up their minds about him. I've got to be going."

Julie walked on down the street and, much to her chagrin, Zelda fell in step beside her.

"I don't know how you can stand being out there on that rocky old farm. Papa says it's dirt-poor land your papa's farming and he'll never get ahead. Don't you ever have any fun?"

"Of course I do, Zelda. I love butchering hogs and cooking the fresh heart and liver. Why don't you come out and I'll show you how to pull calves? Sometimes I have to stick my hand inside the cow and pull out the calf. I get awful bloody, but it's exciting. Then sometimes Joe shoots a mess of squirrels and I get to skin them. I nail their hind legs to a tree and split them down the middle—"

"Ugh! Here's where I turn off. 'Bye."

" 'Bye." Julie couldn't keep the grin off her face as she continued on down the street to the library. Zelda wanted more than anything to be a flapper, but she didn't have the looks or the personality.

By the time Julie crossed the railroad tracks and headed back up the rocky road toward home, there were rings of perspiration under her arms and her forehead was beaded with sweat. She enjoyed her forays into town but was always glad to get back to the sanctuary of the farm. Every time she came to town she grew more certain that she would never want to live there.

She trudged up the hill, shifting the bag from one arm to the other. The two books she had selected for Jill were heavy. Deep in thought, deciding what she was going to give the family for supper, she was unaware of the wagon coming up behind her until it was just a few feet away. She moved over to the side of the road and glanced back over her shoulder. Panic crept up her spine. She was deathly afraid of the man on the wagon.

Walter Johnson was big, whiskered and wore a straw hat on his head of gray-streaked hair. He spit a yellow stream of chewing tobacco out onto the dirt road. Julie choked down the panic that clogged her throat as he pulled the wagon up alongside her and stopped the team.

"Wal, looky thar!" He laughed as she continued to walk and passed the team. "If'n it ain't Miss Prissy-tail Jones. I ain't seen you fer a right long spell." He walked the horses until he was even with her. "Climb on up here and I'll give ya a ride home."

Julie tried to ignore him. There wasn't a house or a person

in sight. Her heart pounded with fear. The man moved the team so that the wagon forced her to walk in the grass that edged the road.

"If'n yo're right nice, I'll stop in that grove up ahead and pleasure ya some."

Fear kept Julie mute. She looked down and away from him while her mind grappled with what to do if he got down off the wagon seat.

"Seen ya in town a-switchin' that purty little ass around. Ya wearin' any drawers, gal? Be handier if ya ain't." His chuckle came from low in his throat. It was more like an animal growl.

Julie felt her face grow hot with humiliation and anger. Determined to defend herself, she switched the cloth bag to her right hand and prepared to swing it at him if he got down off the wagon.

"Ain't no need ya bein' so snooty. It ain't like ya ain't never had a man." He leered at her, lifted his brows and emitted a short guffaw of laughter.

Comprehending the meaning of the man's hateful words, Julie was terrified that he would force her off the road and into the woods ahead. She glanced behind her to see if anyone was coming. Not a soul was in sight!

Lord, help me.

Julie stopped. "Get away from me, you filthy scum," she yelled. "Touch me and I'll . . . kill you!"

"Wal, now. Ya finally got yore back up."

"I'll tell Papa and the boys—"

"Don't make no never mind. I'll have had my fun. Turn into that woods up thar, gal."

Julie spun around and ran as fast as she could back toward town. She wasn't going near those woods with Walter Johnson following her.

"It'll be you, the young gal or that gimpy kid. I ain't a bit choosy when it comes to gettin' my rocks off. Come back here, ya split-tailed bitch!" he yelled.

Oh, dear Lord. He's threatening Jason and Jill!

She heard a shout and looked back fearfully, thinking he was coming after her. A rider on a buckskin horse had come out of the woods and was racing down the road toward the wagon. He reached it, whirled his horse and lashed the team with the ends of his reins.

"You rotten son-of-a-bitch! Get the hell away from her!"

Evan Johnson lashed the team again, and they shot off up the road. Walter Johnson bounced on the seat, roaring with rage and trying to restrain the frantic mules.

Tears of relief rolled down Julie's cheeks. She stood in the middle of the dusty road and dug into her bag for a handkerchief to wipe her eyes. Evan Johnson rode up beside her.

"Did he hurt you?"

She shook her head, dabbing her eyes with a handkerchief. Turning her face away to hide her tears, she peered anxiously up the road to be sure her tormentor was gone.

"I'm sorry, Miss Jones. I'm real sorry."

Julie had to choke back a sob before she could say, "You didn't do anything."

"He had booze at home. I didn't think he'd go buy more." Evan swung down from the horse. "Let me take your bag. I'll walk with you to your lane."

"You don't need to do that. Just see to it that he doesn't come back."

"He won't come back. He'll go home and drink himself into a stupor." He lifted the bag from her hand and hung it over the horn on his saddle.

Julie looked up at him with tear-wet eyes. She had seen Evan only a couple of times since he had come home. She remembered that Mrs. Johnson had visited them often before she died and had talked about her son, whom she had sent to live with his grandparents when he was twelve. Julie's mother had said the reason the boy had been sent away was because he didn't get along with his father. Mrs. Johnson had said it was because she wanted Evan to have a better education. When he finished his schooling, he had enlisted in the army.

Mrs. Johnson had died of influenza during the war and Evan had stayed on in France for a while when the war ended. Then a few months ago he had come back to the farm.

Evan was a big man, both tall and broad. Everything about him was big: shoulders, arms, hands. His hair was light, his eyes slate-blue. His face matched the rest of him: big nose, prominent cheekbones and wide, thin mouth bracketed by indentations. His eyebrows and lashes were surprisingly dark for a person with light hair.

His eyes, shadowed with concern, were studying her with intensity. His rugged face was not exactly handsome, but it was . . . nice.

How could this man possibly be the son of such a despicable character as Walter Johnson?

From her brother Joe, she had learned that Evan Johnson was a quiet man who offered no apologies to him for his father's behavior and never talked about himself. He had a car—Joe had seen it in a shed—but he rode his horse wherever he wanted to go.

Walter Johnson didn't share work with the neighbors, but when Mr. Humphrey's baling machine broke down, Evan offered the use of his forge to repair the part that was broken, saving Mr. Humphrey the time it would take to go to town to the blacksmith. Jason had said that he had then helped put up the Humphreys' hay.

Joe liked him. Julie remembered her papa saying that the man was polite when spoken to but never smiled or laughed or joked with the boys. Evan didn't have a lot to smile about, Jethro had added. Being the son of the most hated man in the county wasn't easy.

"Thank you," Julie said, breaking the silence between herself and Evan. Reaction to her confrontation with his father had set in and she had to tense her lips to keep them from trembling.

"I'm sorry I didn't get here sooner. He was supposed to be back a couple hours ago with a barrel of kerosene. I'm glad I came looking for him."

"I . . . didn't see him in town or I'd not have started home."

"Has he bothered you before?"

Julie laughed nervously. "Who hasn't he bothered?"

"I can only say that I'm sorry and I'll try and keep closer tabs on him."

"Your mother was a good neighbor. My mother thought the world of her."

"She wrote to me about your family."

Julie glanced at him. He was looking straight ahead. Her mind went blank for a minute. When she began thinking again, she realized that he was having as hard a time making conversation as she was.

"She was there when most of my brothers and sisters were born." Julie spoke without looking at him.

"Mama would have made a good nurse."

"She talked about you. It worried her to death when you went to war."

"I'll not forgive myself for leaving her with *him*. She wanted me to go to my grandparents' long before I did."

"I'm sure that she thought it was best for you."

"Now she's gone."

"None of the neighbors knew when she took sick. We didn't know until the doctor came by and told us that she had passed away."

"Then he did call in a doctor?"

"Toward the end, I guess. He never asked for any help from the neighbors." When Evan remained quiet, she said, "Everyone who knew your mother liked her. There was a large turnout at her funeral."

"But her son wasn't with her."

"You were away fighting the Kaiser. She was very proud of you."

"When I received word she was gone, I decided never to come back."

"But you have."

"Yes. I got to thinking about how much she loved the farm. It was given to her by her grandparents."

"You're back to make sure that your father doesn't squander it." Julie didn't know why she had said such a thing. She glanced up to see him turn and look down at her.

"He has charge of it until he dies. Then, if there is anything left, it goes to me. I'm here to see that there's some of it left." She knew that he had revealed more about himself than he intended.

They had passed the grove. Julie looked into the dark, shady depths and shivered. Evan noticed.

"I'll keep an eye on him," he said firmly.

Julie shook her head. "I don't know how your mother lived with him."

"She had her reasons." His voice was quiet, soft.

They walked on in silence, broken only by the soft thud of the horse's hooves on the dirt road.

"Jason said you were coming to the ball game tonight."

"Joe asked me to come. Do you mind?"

"Heavens, no." She looked up at him with a puzzled frown. "The neighbors have been coming to our place to play ball for several years. The flat pasture between our house and the road makes a good ball diamond. You're welcome to come."

"Thank you." He almost smiled but didn't. "We Johnsons don't get many invitations."

They reached the lane leading up to the house. He stopped the horse and handed her the shopping bag. She looked up to see him gazing at her face.

"Thank you again."

Evan was not used to having such a strong and immediate

reaction to anyone. He looked at her more closely. She was not breathtakingly beautiful, but pretty. Her eyebrows were high, straight and heavy, her nose slightly pinched, her mouth wide and full. Huge, clear eyes, direct eyes, met his. She had no idea how utterly feminine and defenseless she looked. His breath caught for an instant. Suddenly he was stricken with an adolescent longing.

He was either hornier than he thought or he was reacting to more than her appearance.

He was shocked that he had an almost irresistible urge to kiss her brow, her eyes, the bridge of her nose, her cheeks, her chin and last of all her sweet mouth.

But all he said was, "I'll see how the work goes." Then, to himself, *I'll come if that old son-of-a-bitch drinks himself into a stupor and passes out.*

She smiled to let him know that she really had recovered from the ordeal with his father.

"My sister Jill plays sometimes."

"And you? Do you play?"

"I haven't for a long time. They usually have enough players without me. I'm better at running than batting. I keep in practice chasing after my little sister Joy."

She wanted to make him smile back at her because she was certain that his smile would soften his grave features, make him look younger and not quite so formidable. She almost succeeded. His eyes brightened but his mouth remained unsmiling.

"I'd like to see that." He wanted to stay and talk to her but didn't know how to prolong the conversation without making an utter fool of himself. So he turned and mounted his horse, looked down at her and nodded. "Good-bye, Miss Jones."

"Good-bye, Mr. Johnson."

Julie walked up the lane toward the house. She had already decided not to say anything to her papa and the boys about being accosted by the bully of the county. She wouldn't put it past Joe and Jack to catch him alone sometime when he was drunk, waylay him and work him over with their fists or a piece of stove wood. Not that she cared if he was beaten, but she didn't want the boys to get in trouble.

She had never given Evan Johnson much thought but had assumed that he probably thought he was too high and mighty for the farm folk around Fertile. After all, he had been to college, served as an officer in the army, and had lived in France. Today, however, he hadn't acted high and mighty. He seemed to be sincerely concerned for her and sorry for what she'd had to endure. His father's behavior was obviously an embarrassment to him.

The screen door banged and Joy came running down the lane to meet her.

"Julie, Julie. I been good. Did ya bring me somethin'?"

Julie felt an overpowering wave of love for the strikingly beautiful child coming toward her. She couldn't imagine life without her.

Chapter 3

EVAN RODE SLOWLY UP THE ROAD that curved over the hill to the high country above the river. When he'd decided to come back to Fertile, he had planned to keep himself aloof and focused on looking after his interest in the farm until Walter finally drank himself to death. When that happened, he intended to install a good tenant farmer on the place and go to St. Joseph, Kansas City or maybe even back to France. He'd been surprised to discover that he liked it here. He had taken to the land, and if Walter were not here, he could be happy and content on the farm.

Evan had not expected the hostility he had encountered from the townspeople when he returned to Fertile. The banker, Amos Wood, had given him a cool reception until he discovered the amount of money Evan planned to transfer to his bank. The man had then fawned disgustingly. Only the neighbors—the Jones family, the Taylors, the Humphreys and the Birches—had been able to separate him from Walter and treat him with civility.

The Jones property adjoined the Johnson farm on the west side. Evan had met Joe and Jack Jones on the property line when they came to repair a fence because one of their milch cows had strayed over onto Johnson land. Walter had gone out with the shotgun to accuse the brothers of letting the cow graze on his grass and of taking tree limbs from his land to use for fence posts.

Evan had arrived in time to smooth things over and had stayed to help Joe and Jack. He liked them both. They were hardworking, decent young men. They also seemed to take pride in their family farm. He had not noticed the Jones family when he was younger. He had been too busy keeping out of the way of Walter's fists. Later, he had learned about the Joneses from the letters his mother had written him. He especially knew about Julie. His mother had been fond of the girl, who had been forced to leave school to take care of her ailing mother and the rest of the family when she was just fifteen.

Now he had met her. He had expected her to be a rather dowdy, work-worn girl. He had found instead a warm, intelligent, pretty young woman.

Walter, in Evan's estimation, was little more than an animal. Evan could just imagine what he had said to Julie Jones. Walter thought of women as people to bully. When Evan came out of the grove and saw the woman running back toward town, he knew that Walter had been speaking indecently to her, and anger had made him want to horsewhip him.

Even now, as Evan approached the house where he had been born and had spent his early boyhood years, he could see in his mind's eye the girl's tear-filled eyes and the proud tilt of her chin when she looked up at him.

The wagon, with the team still hitched, was standing in the yard in front of the barn. He unsaddled his horse, rubbed him down and turned him into the pasture. After backing the wagon into the shed so that he could unload the barrel of kerosene, he unhitched the mules and turned them into the lot at the side of the barn, where they immediately rolled in the dirt.

At the pump, he put his head under the spout and let the cold water flow down over his head. After shaking off the excess, he ran his fingers through his thick sandy hair and then pumped water into the trough that flowed into one of the water tanks. He needed to work off his anger at Walter before he faced him.

Incredibly, Walter had not trashed the house during the time he lived there alone after his wife died. Evan had found his mother's belongings just as she had left them. Walter had lived in the kitchen of the big frame farmhouse: doing his drinking there, sleeping there on a couch at the end of the room. He was sitting at the kitchen table, drinking from a long-necked bottle, when Evan crossed the porch and entered the house.

Walter was angry. His face was red and he was well on his way to getting falling-down drunk.

"Goddamm ya fer the bastard ya are. I ort to whip yore ass."

"You've got about as much chance of whipping me as you have of pissing all the way to Kansas City," Evan retorted as he hung his hat on the peg beside the door.

He stood just inside the kitchen door, his hands on his hips, and looked at the man he had hated for as long as he could remember. His slate-blue eyes reflected that deep-seated hatred.

"Ya always thought ya was better'n anybody." Walter's lips were loose, his eyes bloodshot. He was downing rotgut whiskey as if it were water.

"You are a sorry excuse for a man. I should have taken the whip to you instead of the mules."

"Ya ain't got no right ter be tellin' me what to do. Ya try usin' that whip on me and I'll blow ya to hell and back."

"It's been tried by better men than you. You were talking nasty to that woman. You haven't an ounce of decency in your whole body."

"Decency? Ha!" Walter took a drink from his bottle and slammed it back down on the table. "Decency don't make ya feel good—don't empty yore balls."

"I don't care what makes you 'feel good.' Just keep away from decent women. Hear?"

"Ya got a itch fer Miss Hot-tail Jones? Hell, she's gettin' too old fer me anyhow. But she'd do in a pinch. I'd rather have that young one, or the gimpy kid. The girl must be twelve or thirteen—"

"Good God Almighty! You dirty old son-of-a-bitch!" Evan reached him in two strides, jerked him up out of the chair and slammed him against the wall.

"You stay away from those kids . . . any kids! Hear me? I'll kill you just as I'd kill a rabid dog if I hear of you molesting a woman or a kid. You'd better believe me because I mean every word of it. Do you understand me?"

"Yeah, I ain't deaf. Might be willing to chance it to get me a good piece of ass fer a change."

Evan shoved him away. Walter sat down heavily on the couch, his bottle still in his hand.

"You're not worth the dime's worth of powder it would take to blow you up."

"Ya ain't got the guts to do it nohow."

"I saw enough killing in France. When I think of the good men who died over there in the trenches and you not worth doodley-squat sitting over here warm and cozy with your belly full, I wonder if there is any justice. Why didn't you join up? You'd have made good cannon fodder."

"Ya know why I didn't. Yore maw needed me to work the farm. 'Sides, I was too old."

"You wouldn't have lasted two weeks in the army anyway. Someone, unable to put up with your mouth, would've put a knife in your back."

"Horseshit!" Walter yelled, getting tired of the verbal sparring. "Why don't ya go on over to St. Joe and waller 'round in that fine house that stingy ol' fart-knocker left ya? I ain't needin' ya here."

"Shut your mouth!"

"Shut yore mouth! Shut yore mouth!" he mimicked, his voice slurred. "I was good enough once."

Evan drew back his fist. "Say one more word and you'll be spitting out teeth."

"Ah . . . shit—" Walter lay down on the couch and put his feet up.

Evan retreated to the safety of his upstairs room. He didn't dare linger in the same room with the man for fear he would lose control and beat him to death.

Evan's small room was as sparsely furnished as it had been when he was a youth: a bed, bureau, wardrobe and trunk. Besides his army pistol, his rifle and a few mementos, he had brought with him only his clothes, a few favorite books, his Victrola and his collection of records when he came back to the farm.

The quilt his mother had made, piecing together leftovers from the fabric she had used to make his shirts and her dresses and aprons, lay folded on the humpbacked trunk. A large picture of a boy and a big yellow dog hung over the bed, and on the opposite wall was a picture of an Indian on a tired horse. This room had been his sanctuary when he was a boy. He had come here to escape Walter's drunken rages.

Evan wound his Victrola, put on one of his favorite records, *Una furtiva lagrima,* sung by Enrico Caruso, who had died the year before, and stood at the window. While listening to the soothing music, he pushed the curtain aside and looked out over the planted fields, the orchard, the cow lot and the wooded area north of the house.

He had not planned to spend the rest of his life here when he arrived, but the place had grown on him despite the detestable presence of Walter. Here he'd had a sense of belonging that he'd never had in the big house his grandparents had left him in St. Joseph.

Alerted by a dust cloud on the road, Evan watched as an open touring car turned into the lane and approached the house. It was a car he had seen parked at the courthouse in town and he knew it was the one used by the district marshal. Evan waited until the men got out of the car, then went down the stairs to open the front door as the marshal came up the walk, followed by his deputy.

"Hello, Marshal." Evan stepped out onto the porch.

"Mr. Johnson." Marshal Sanford held out his hand. "We've not met since you came back. I remember seeing you when you were a lad. You've grown up some."

"Fifteen years makes a difference."

"Yes, it does. Meet Deputy Weaver."

Evan extended his hand to the tall, whiplash-thin man with dark gray-streaked hair. A handlebar mustache curved down on each side of his mouth. He shifted a chew of tobacco to the other side of his cheek before he spoke.

"Glad to meetcha."

"Same here," Evan said. Then, "What can I do for you, Marshal?"

"Is Walter here?"

"He's here, but he may have passed out by now. Come in."

Evan led the two men to the kitchen, where Walter lay on the couch.

"Get up," Evan said roughly. "The marshal is here to see you."

Walter slowly sat up and swung his bootless feet to the floor. He clutched his whiskey bottle in one hand, forked the fingers of his other hand through his hair and looked up at the men with bloodshot eyes.

"Whataya want?"

"Where did you get this rotgut whiskey, Walter?" Marshal Sanford reached over and took the bottle out of his hand.

"None of yore business," Walter growled.

"I say it is. But I didn't come out here to find out where you get your bootlegged whiskey. I've got a pretty good idea about that."

"If hit ain't 'bout the whish-key . . . what's it?"

"I came to tell you that if I get any more complaints about your drunken rowdiness at the revival meeting, or anywhere else, I'm going to throw you so far back in jail you'll never find your way out."

"I ain't been to no revival meetin'."

"You've been hanging around outside trying to pick fights. Another thing, you've been out to the pavilion at Spring Lake causing trouble."

"What's that?" Walter's words were becoming more and more slurred. Evan wondered how he could even carry on a conversation after so much booze. "I went . . . danc-in', is all I done."

"I'm warning you, Johnson. Stay away from the revival meeting and the Spring Lake dance hall."

"I got rights to go where I want to. Ain't no business of yores."

"You have no right to disrupt a religious service or to disturb young folk having a good time. If you do, it's my business and I'll do something about it."

The marshal rocked back on his heels, and his sharp eyes went from Walter to his son.

"I'm not his keeper," Evan said stoutly, feeling that the man was conveying a message.

Sanford shook his head in disgust, set the whiskey bottle on the table with a bang and walked out of the room. The deputy followed. On the porch, Sanford turned to Evan, who stood with his back to the screen door.

"It's like talking to a stump." When Evan nodded in agreement, Sanford continued, "Drunk or sober, he's been trouble for as long as I can remember."

Evan nodded again.

"Ain't you able to do somethin' with him?" The deputy spoke for the first time.

"I didn't come back here to be a nursemaid for Walter. I came to see that my mother's farm wasn't run into the ground." Evan looked the cold-eyed deputy in the eye, wanting to make his position clear.

"The way he's goin', I ain't goin' to be surprised if someone ups and kills him." Deputy Weaver walked to the end of the porch and spit into the Rose of Sharon bush.

Evan shrugged. "If they do, they do."

"Be fine with you, huh? You'd have the farm. I reckon it's worth a pretty penny. Right?" The deputy came back, stopped within a few feet of Evan and eyed him through half-closed lids.

"I'll have it anyway," Evan replied, looking the deputy squarely in the eye.

"Yeah, but maybe you ain't wantin' to wait."

"What do you mean by that?"

Weaver shrugged, his eyes still on Evan's face, his lips curled in a sneer.

Marshal Sanford stepped in to break the tension between the two men. He held out his hand to Evan.

"I'd be obliged if you'd do what you can to keep him away from town."

"I appreciate the fact that it's your duty to keep peace in this county, but as I said before, I'm not Walter's keeper. He's a grown man—a poor excuse for one, I admit—but he'll have to take responsibility for his own actions."

"He's your pa, ain't he? Don't ya think it's your duty to look out for your pa?" Weaver taunted.

Evan decided that he didn't like the man's attitude and gave him a cold stare.

"No. I don't think it's my duty to look out for *him*. If he breaks the law, it's *your* duty to do something about it. It's what you're being paid for, isn't it?"

"That's clear enough," Deputy Weaver sneered. "You don't care if he disrupts church services, harasses young people or exposes himself to womenfolk. Did ya know that only about one in a hundred young ladies ever report being raped?"

"Damn you! Of course I care, but there's not much I can do about it."

"We'd best be getting on back to town." Sensing the antagonism growing between Evan and his deputy, the marshal stepped off the porch and headed for the car. With one last openly contemptuous look at Evan, the deputy followed.

Evan stood on the porch and waited for his temper to cool. He watched until the big touring car turned around in the barnyard and headed back down the lane to the road before he went back into the house.

One glance told him that Walter had downed what was left in the whiskey bottle. Dead drunk now, he was sprawled out on the couch, mouth open, spittle running from the corner. There was a big wet spot on the front of his overalls. It was a thoroughly disgusting sight.

Needing to get out of the house, Evan stepped onto the back porch and picked up the staff he used when he walked out into the pasture to drive in their three milch cows. Walking along the fence line, he pondered what that smart-mouthed deputy had said. Was he accusing Walter of rape?

Good grief! Walter had always talked nasty. His mother had said that he did it to shock folks and get attention. Evan remembered the fear on the face of Julie Jones. Had he just talked nasty to her or had he threatened her and her younger sister?

If he touches either one of them I swear I'll kill him!

Evan did the chores as quickly as possible, then washed and put on clean clothes. He was looking forward to going to the ball game and seeing Julie Jones again.

Chapter 4

WHERE'S JASON?"

The family had taken their places at the kitchen table for the light supper. Remembering Walter Johnson's threat, Julie became alarmed when she saw that Jason's chair was empty.

"Where's Jason?" Julie asked again, louder this time.

"He'll be along. Hurry up, Sis. Joe's gonna play catch with me." Jack, her sixteen-year-old brother, would rather play baseball than eat.

"Did Jason—"

"He's finishing his chores." As Jethro spoke, his youngest son came hurrying in through the back door. "Wash up, son. We're waiting for you."

Jason placed a basket of eggs on the workbench. "That danged old biddy pecked me."

"She doesn't peck me," Jill said smugly.

"Then you can have the job. It's woman's work anyhow."

"Sit down so Papa can say the blessing." Julie placed a platter of sliced bread on the table and took her place next to Joy.

While the family helped themselves to fresh bread, apple butter, jam and scrambled eggs, Julie debated with herself about whether to tell her father and the boys about her meeting with Walter Johnson. If she didn't and something happened to Jason or Jill, she would never forgive herself. She would talk to them later, she decided, when the younger kids were not around.

"I asked Evan Johnson to come play ball." Joe reached for the bread platter. "Reckon the neighbors will snub him?"

"Because of his pa?" Jack asked.

"You know how the Birches are. Pete and Clem can be stiff-necked at times, and they hate Walter Johnson like poison."

"Can't blame Evan for his pa." Jethro's eyes swept around the table.

"Just like folks can't blame me for mine," Joe teased and hit his father on the shoulder.

"Watch it, young scutter. You're not too old to whop."

"Joe's too big," Joy said seriously.

"*You're* not." Jill couldn't pass up the opportunity for the last word.

"I brought the cooler up out of the cellar," Julie announced during a break in the conversation. "One of you boys can fill it at the well and take it out to the ball field."

"Let Jill fill it. She can take it out in the coaster wagon—that is, if she gets through primpin' for the Taylor boys before dark," Jack said with a smirk.

Jason giggled.

"You shut up!" Jill rose up out of her chair and glared at her brother.

"Sit down, Sis," Jethro said. "Stop teasing her, Jack."

Joe, his dark eyes shining with amusement, winked at Julie. The handsomest of all the Jones siblings and just two years younger than Julie, he was her favorite, if she admitted to having a favorite. They had always been close. Lucky would be the girl who caught him.

"What kind of cake did you make for tonight, Sis?" Joe asked.

"Spice cake, and you stay out of it."

As soon as supper was over, the family scattered. Jill and Julie hurriedly cleared the table and washed the dishes. The neighbor women were sure to come into the house and Julie wanted the kitchen to be tidy. Her father came out of the bedroom wearing a clean shirt and a clean pair of overalls.

"You going to town?" Julie asked when he went to the wash dish and dampened his hair.

"Naw. Got splattered up with manure today."

She glanced at him. He was carefully parting his hair down the middle. It wasn't like him to take such pains with his appearance and especially for a ball game. Julie wondered what her father was up to.

"Jason, tie up Sidney or put him in the barn."

"Ah, Papa. Sidney won't hurt nothin'. He likes to chase balls."

"Mind what I said, son," Jethro cautioned sternly.

Julie emptied the dishwater and hung the pan on the porch. When she returned to the kitchen, her father had gone out to the front of the house and, with Jack's help, was placing an old wooden door on the sawhorses to serve as a picnic table. Every family would bring a dessert of some kind to eat after the ball game. There would be coffee for the grown-ups and milk for the children.

Clem and Pete Birch had adjoining farms and, with their families, arrived in one wagon. The women and children were sitting on bales of hay in the wagon bed. They were a lively, happy bunch. Between the two brothers they had six boys, three girls and both wives were expecting. After they piled out of the wagon, Clem unhitched the team and led them to the grass that grew alongside the lane. Pete was short and husky, Clem tall and thin.

Farley and Helen Jacobs had a girl and two boys. Ruby Jacobs was Jill's best friend. The two giggling girls vanished into the house.

Joy was anxiously waiting for the Taylors. Besides their two sons, Roy and Thad, they had three girls. Their little Sylvia was Joy's age. When they arrived the little girls paired off and went looking for mischief.

Ruth and Wilbur Humphrey were the last to arrive. They had five boys and two girls, ranging in age from seventeen to two years old; their twelve-year-old twins, This and That, had bright red hair and faces full of freckles. Their real names, Thomas and Thayer, were known to only a few people outside the family.

Ruth Humphrey, with her two-year-old on her hip, carried a dish wrapped in a tea towel to the picnic table, then came to the porch where Julie sat with the other women. A woman somewhere in her thirties and a girl about six or seven years old were with her.

"Hello, everyone. I want you to meet my sister-in-law, Birdie Stuart. She and Elsie have come to stay with us . . . for a while."

Julie got to her feet and extended her hand. "Glad to meet you. Come on up and sit down. When the game starts we can take some quilts and sit on the grass. Hello, Elsie."

The shy child bobbed her head but didn't speak.

The Humphrey girls yelled, "Come on, Elsie. Let's play on the sack swing."

The child shook her head and moved close to her mother. Birdie Stuart was a woman with hazel eyes and thick blond hair cut in a stylish bob. She had a lovely light peaches-and-cream complexion and full rounded breasts. She seated herself carefully on the edge of the porch after dusting it off with her handkerchief.

"Do you enjoy baseball, Mrs. Stuart?" Julie asked, trying to make the woman feel a part of the group.

"I don't know. I've never watched a real game." She spoke with a soft southern accent.

Julie laughed. "This is far from a real game. There's plenty of horseplay, and at times the rules are stretched a bit."

"Well, glory be," Grace Birch exclaimed. "Here comes Evan Johnson. What's a *Johnson* doing here? You never see him out anywhere, not even at church."

"The boys invited him to come play ball." Julie tried to keep the irritation out of her voice.

"Oh, well, of course. Guess you can invite anybody you want to your place."

"He came to eat some more of Birdie's custard pie or I miss my guess. Howard took him one for fixing our bailer." Ruth winked at Julie, making her wonder if Ruth was trying to make a match between her sister-in-law and Evan. Birdie Stuart must have been five or six years older than Evan, but Julie guessed that it wouldn't make all that much difference if they took to each other.

"He's not much on visitin'. Leastways that's what Pete says. He met him on the road and all he said was howdy." Iona Birch, standing at the end of the porch, placed her hand on the small of her back and stretched.

"Come up here and sit in the swing, Iona, and rest your back." Ruth Humphrey set her small son on his feet. "When are you due?"

"I figure in about six weeks. I'll be big as a barrel by then. The marshal was out at the Johnsons' today," Iona announced after she had settled into the swing. "I wonder what that nasty old man's been up to now."

"I know what it was," Helen Jacobs said. "He's been hanging around outside at the revival meetings, drinking, talking loud and nasty. My, my. I don't know how he's lived as long as he has. Twenty years ago, he'd have been lynched for pulling some of the stunts he's pulled. Folks now put up with most anything."

"Has anyone ever found out why Evan came back?" Ruth asked.

At the mention of his name, Julie's eyes turned to where Evan was playing catch with Joe. Most of the men were wearing overalls. Evan wore khaki-colored britches and a blue-and-white-striped shirt. He impressed Julie as an alert man who had a purpose for everything he did. Had he come to the ball game because he thought Birdie Stuart would be here with the Humphreys?

"A lot of gossip is goin' around. Some think he lost the money his grandpa left him and he had to come back. I don't think that for a minute. Amos Wood is falling all over him. There's got to be money involved for Amos to give a Johnson the time of day." This came from Helen Jacobs.

"The farm was Evan's mother's. It appears that she left it to Walter 'cause he's still there. Why in heaven's name would she do that? Mrs. Yerby said Evan was thrown out of the army for something he did in France." Grace closed her mouth with a snap, signifying her disapproval of the man.

"How would she know that?" Ruth Humphrey asked.

"Mrs. Yerby knows everybody's business in town. Ask her anything and she'll give you an answer."

"Looks like they are finally going to get down to business and choose up sides." Julie thought it was time to change the subject.

Jethro came from the side of the house. "I'll carry out chairs if you ladies want to watch the game."

"I'll take them, Papa," Julie said.

"I can do it. You bring a quilt, Sis."

Jethro picked up a chair in each hand and carried them out to the shade of the oak tree. He returned quickly and picked up two more. By then the women had come down off the porch. He walked alongside Birdie Stuart and her little girl. Julie couldn't hear what he said, but he was smiling first at the woman and then at the child. *Glory be!* Her papa was flirting with Birdie Stuart. She was the reason he had put on a clean shirt and overalls.

Julie was a little taken aback by the discovery. Her father had not shown the slightest interest in a woman since her mother's death. She had assumed he never would. But she realized that he was only forty-two years old. He had been twenty and her mother eighteen when they married. Nevertheless, it shocked her to think of her father bringing another woman into the family.

Without being obvious, Julie paid close attention to Birdie. She was quiet and soft-spoken and didn't appear to be paying more than normal attention to Jethro. Julie didn't think that she was a woman who would take to the hard work on a farm. Her hands were soft, her nails shaped and buffed. Her clothes were of good quality, indicating she had been well provided for. Julie wondered if she would be able to dress chickens, make head-cheese, wash overalls . . .

Feeling a little unsettled by her discovery, Julie went to the kitchen for another chair. Iona Birch was still in the swing on the porch.

"I'll get a cushion for the chair, Iona, if you want to come watch the game. We'll sit in the shade."

"I think I'll stay here for a while. I canned beans today. The girls help, but they're not like having a woman around. Lucky Ruth, to have Mrs. Stuart to help her."

"Ruth said Mrs. Stuart came to live with them. Is she a widow?"

"She just appeared on their doorstep and told them that her husband had died. Wilbur hadn't seen her in fifteen years. He didn't know that she was married or that she'd had a child. She said that her husband had been a traveling man and they had lived in many different places. What could they do but take her in?"

"If she's always lived in the city she may not be happy living on a farm."

"She's looking for a man to take care of her," Iona said bluntly. "I mean that she and Ruth are looking. Ruth thinks Evan Johnson would be a good catch. She's heard that he has a house in St. Joe and won't be hanging around here for very long. I think she's hoping that Evan or someone will marry Birdie and take her and the girl with him."

"How does she plan to accomplish this?"

"She's working on it. Started with the custard pie." Iona laughed. "Just watch her."

"Sounds to me like she's not too happy having a sister-in-law in the house."

"She's got her hands full over there without having extras piled on her. From the looks of Birdie Stuart, she's not too fond of hard work."

"The game's started." Jill and Ruby May came around the corner of the house on the run. Jill threw the words back over her shoulder. "Jack's gonna pitch."

"Game's started." Joy came out of the house on the run, her friend Sylvia Taylor behind her. "Mama, the game's started."

Julie looked quickly at Iona Birch and saw the puzzled look on her face.

"She does that sometimes when she's around other children who are talking about their mamas. She's asked me where *her* mama is."

"Poor little thing," Iona said sadly. "It's a good thing she has you, Julie."

Regardless of their age, everyone who came to the neighborhood ball games played if they wanted to. The men and the older boys were wonderfully patient with the younger players and divided them between the two teams. Julie was pleased to see that Jason was on Jack's team.

She sat on the quilt beside Myrtle Taylor and watched anxiously when it was Jason's turn to bat. Jack was set to run for him if he hit the ball. Pete Birch pitched. Jason swung and missed the first pitch but gripped the bat with determination. When Pete threw another ball, Jason's bat connected. The ball soared over the head of the outfielder and landed in the bushes that grew along the edge of the field. Knowing there was plenty of time for Jason to reach first base, Jack stepped aside so Jason could run.

With a victorious grin lighting his freckled face, Jason ran as fast as he could and stood proudly on first base as Evan came to bat.

"Hit a homer, Mr. Johnson," Jason called.

On the first pitch Evan hit the ball far out into center field. Jason ran the bases. Yelling encouragement, Jack urged him on.

"Come on, Jason! Run! You'll make it!"

When Jason crossed home plate, Jack caught him up and swung him around. The boy was so excited he failed to notice that Evan, running slowly along behind him, was forced to stop on third base.

"Did ya see that, Joe?" Jason yelled. "I made a score." When his excitement cooled down, he ran down the sideline to where Evan stood on third. "That was a whopper of a hit, Mr. Johnson."

"You didn't do too bad yourself."

"Mr. Taylor's comin' up to bat. He's a good hitter. We'll be ahead if you can get to home base."

"Then you'd better hang around and tell me when to go."

"You bet."

Julie's heart swelled with joy for her little brother, who tried so hard to be like other boys in spite of his crippled foot. He had been only six years old when their mother died. Not much more than a child herself, Julie had tried to fill the void.

The game was called after seven innings in order to give the neighbors time to get home before night settled in. Jason's team won and he was ecstatic.

Joe brought out the big granite coffeepot from the kitchen and filled cups while the women cut the cakes and pies and handed out the slices. Men squatted on the grass with cups of coffee and slabs of cake in their hands. The children gobbled down the first serving and came back for more.

"Wait until everyone has been served, then you can have more." Grace herded the Birch children, hers and Iona's, into a line.

Julie noticed that Evan had chosen a piece of Birdie Stuart's custard pie, as had her father, who had passed up the coconut cake and the raisin pie, which was his favorite. Evan had taken his pie and gone back to sink down on the grass beside Joe, but her father had stayed to talk with Birdie.

He's making a fool of himself by being so obvious, Julie thought when she noticed Ruth watching him as he lingered to talk to her sister-in-law. Then a thought hit her that almost sent her reeling. *What if Papa marries Birdie Stuart and brings her here to live?* She took a deep quivering breath. She knew that it was his right to marry whomever he pleased, but what would she do? The house and the children would no longer be hers.

Pushing these disturbing thoughts to the back of her mind, she loaded a plate with slices of cake and carried it to the men sitting on the grass. By the time she reached Joe and Evan, all that was left on the plate were pieces of her spice cake.

"Cake, Mr. Johnson?"

"Hold it, Evan." Joe grabbed Evan's wrist when he reached for a slice. "Julie made that cake. Ain't no tellin' what's in it. Could be mouse droppin's." His teasing dark eyes glinted up at Julie.

"Joseph Jones!" Julie kicked her brother's foot. "Mr. Johnson will think you mean it."

"I do mean it. She's sneaky, Evan."

"Guess, I'll just have to risk it." He reached for a piece of the cake, and for the first time she saw him smile. Julie's heart thumped until she saw his eyes shift past her and realized that Birdie was beside her holding out the last piece of custard pie.

"I saved it for you, Mr. Johnson." Birdie's voice was no more than a husky whisper. Julie caught a whiff of Lily of the Valley perfume.

Julie stepped aside. She felt big and awkward beside the petite woman.

"Well, thank you, but I've had my share of custard pie tonight. Joe was complaining he'd not had any." Evan took the pan from Birdie's hand and held it out to Joe.

"You sure?" Joe said, but he was already dipping his hand into the pie dish.

Julie moved away and offered cake to the circle of men seated on the ground. Their talk and the squeals of the children chasing fireflies prevented her from hearing what else Birdie Stuart had to say to Evan and Joe. Birdie didn't linger, Julie noticed. She was back at the picnic table when Julie returned with her empty plate. Her father had gone to squat down beside Wilbur Humphrey, Birdie's brother.

Julie was aware that none of this had escaped the attention of Ruth Humphrey.

Chapter 5

THE TAYLORS WERE THE FIRST TO LEAVE and the Humphreys the last, after it was decided to have another ball game on Sunday afternoon.

"We'll be here," Ruth called gaily as she lifted her two-year-old up onto the wagon bed.

"If you need help putting the roof on that cow shed, Wilbur, let me know, and me and the boys will be over to give you a hand." Jethro stepped forward to lift Elsie Stuart up into the wagon to sit beside her mother.

"It'll be a few days."

"Have you been to the revival, Julie?" Ruth asked.

"No. I'm not much for revival meetings."

"We're going Saturday night. If you want, we'll stop by for you."

"Thank you, but I don't think I'll go."

"The young people meet just before the service. This and That are going. They've got their eyes on a couple of girls," Ruth said with a wink.

"You ort to go, Sis," Jethro spoke up quickly. "I hear they got a hellfire-and-brimstone preacher."

"Then you go, Papa." Julie's words came out stronger than she intended and Jethro frowned.

"Maybe I will," he mumbled.

"We'll stop by anyway, Julie. We had a good time."

"So did we. 'Bye. See you Sunday if not before."

On Saturday morning Jethro and Jack loaded two hogs in the wagon and took them to town. The sale of the hogs would clear up the bill at Oakley's grocery store with money left over. Julie had sent a list with Jack to be filled at the store: sugar for canning, jar lids, salt and vinegar for making hominy and lye for making bar soap for washing. Julie and Jill worked in the garden after the kitchen was tidied, and Joe went over to help Evan work on his windmill.

Julie had decided to tell only Joe about her encounter on the road with Walter Johnson and about his threats to harm Jill and Jason. So far she'd had no opportunity to be alone with him. Her father had been quiet and moody lately, as if he had a lot on his mind. Julie decided not to add to his problems. He'd even been short with Joy and had made her cry, which was unusual because he doted on the child.

While Julie and Jill were setting the table for the noon meal, the wagon came down the lane.

"Jack's comin'," Joy yelled and raced through the house to the back porch. Joy never walked if she could run.

"Don't set a place for Joe. If he was coming for dinner he'd be here now," Julie said to Jill.

"I wouldn't want to eat at that old Mr. Johnson's." Jill placed the extra plate back on the shelf.

"Are you talking about the son or the father?"

"Old Mr. Johnson. Evan is . . . kind of handsome and not so old."

"But too old for you."

"Why do you always say that? I read that back in the olden days girls got married at twelve."

"And died during childbirth at thirteen."

"Is that what Mama died of? She had Joy, then died."

"Mama was weak from influenza. But tell me, has Walter

Johnson ever bothered you?" Julie was suddenly breathless as she waited for her sister to answer.

"No. Katie McDonald said he pinched her sister on the butt."

"Well, for goodness' sake. Isn't her sister the teacher over at Well's Point? What was he doing way over there?"

"It's where all the bootleggers hang out."

"How do you know so much about it?"

"I ain't deaf, Julie," Jill said disgustedly. "I hear things."

"You . . . ain't?"

"I'm not." Jill rolled her eyes to the ceiling.

"If that Walter Johnson comes near you, you scream your head off. Hear? Don't let yourself get into a place where he could catch you alone, like when you're walking over to the Jacobses. If you've got to go, ask Jack or Joe to take you on the horse."

Jill paused and put her hands on her hips. "You know what they'd say if I asked them to take me to the Jacobses? They'd say, 'You got two legs. Use 'em.' "

"You won't have to ask them. I will."

"Ruby May says that Mrs. Stuart has set her cap for Evan Johnson. Mrs. Humphrey will help her get him or any other man, for that matter."

"How does Ruby May know that?"

"She heard her mother and Mrs. Humphrey talking. Mrs. Humphrey wants her out of the house. The only way she's going to do it is get her married off. That kid of hers is a brat. Ruby May says she throws a fit if a dog comes near her."

"She probably can't help being afraid."

"Bullfoot," Jill snorted. "Mrs. Humphrey told Mrs. Jacobs that her sister-in-law was lazy and only worked when Mr. Humphrey came into the house."

"Ruby May shouldn't be spreading gossip."

"Ruby told me not to tell anyone. But . . . oh, poot! If I can't tell my very own sister—"

"Papa didn't come back with Jack," Jason announced from the back door. "Jack won't say where he went, but he's smilin' real big and keeps sayin', 'Just wait, just wait.' Make him tell, Julie."

"Open the door, stinkpot." Jack came in with a fifty-pound bag of sugar on his shoulder. "Where do you want this, Sis?"

"Leave it there by the door for now. Jill and I washed the big flour and sugar tins this morning, and they might not be completely dry yet."

"What are you grinning about?" Julie studied the smile on her brother's freckled face.

"You'll see. Want me to take the vinegar to the cellar?"

"No. That's my white pickling vinegar. I'm afraid someone will come along and dump it in with that old stuff in the barrel. When will Papa be back?"

"Soon."

"Shall I set a place for him or not?"

"I don't know." Jack winked at Jason and hurried out.

"See? Julie, make him tell."

"For crying out loud!" Julie exclaimed. "What's got into you two?"

"Car comin'. Car comin'." Joy pushed roughly past Jason, almost upsetting him, brushed against Julie and headed for the front of the house.

"That . . . that little . . . brat!" Jason sputtered.

"See who's coming, Jason. Lord, I hope it isn't someone we'll have to invite to dinner. This is a skimpy meal."

"It's comin' 'round—" Joy ran back through the kitchen. She was out the door and onto the porch.

"Grab her, Jason," Julie shouted. "She might run right out in front of it."

"Papa's drivin' a . . . car!" Jill squealed.

"Papa's . . . drivin' a car," Joy repeated in a shrill voice over the excited barks from Sidney.

"Whose car is it?" Jill moved off the back porch and into the yard.

Julie stood in the doorway, wiping her hands on her apron.

"Well, whatta ya think?" Jack's grin spread all over his face.

"Is it ours?" Jill asked.

"Papa bought it. So I guess it is."

Jethro stepped out of the car and screwed his old felt hat down on his head. He had a sheepish look on his face when he looked over the top at Julie, who had come out onto the porch.

"I didn't know you were thinking of buying a car."

"I . . . well, I hadn't thought about it much. Fred Olson down at the garage had it. It's in good shape. Well, maybe it needs a little fender work, and the top's kind of ragged, but it runs good." When Julie didn't say anything, he said rather defensively, "The boys need to know about cars."

"It's a Model T, Sis. The top folds back for good weather, but in case of rain you can snap on side curtains. The double windshield tilts out to let the breeze through. I bet we can get Evan to do some welding on the fenders." Jack lifted the engine cover on one side and Jethro lifted the other. As they stood gazing at the engine, Julie walked up beside her father.

"I didn't know that you knew how to drive, Papa."

"There's a lot you don't know about me," he said gruffly. "I don't have to explain to my kids when I buy something."

Julie backed away. "I haven't asked you to explain. Dinner is on the table." She went quickly back to the house.

The talk at the dinner table was about the car. Their father didn't say how much it cost or how he was going to pay for it. He did say that he had borrowed the money from Mr. Wood's bank.

"Can we go for a ride?" Jason asked.

Jethro gave him a broad smile. "I was planning on it right after dinner."

Not wanting to put a damper on the happy event, Julie left

the dishes in the dishwater and went out to the car. Jack and Jason sat in front with Jethro. Jill, Joy and Julie climbed in back. Jack watched anxiously as his father moved a lever beneath the steering wheel and took the crank from behind the driver's seat. The motor fired after a twist or two. Jethro hurried to get back behind the wheel. He adjusted the lever again and the engine purred softly. He set the car in motion and guided it in a big circle around the yard before heading down the lane toward the road.

Joy held tightly to Julie's hand. Her eyes were bright with excitement, and for once she was still. This was the first time since she was old enough to be aware of it that she had ridden in an automobile. The other time was when she was a baby and the doctor had come out because she was running a high fever. He had suggested that Julie and Joy return to town with him and spend the night in the spare room at his office so that he could keep an eye on the child.

Julie put her arm around Joy and hugged her close. She wanted so much for this precious little girl who had been thrust into her life.

"Where are we going, Papa?" Jill moved up onto the edge of the seat.

"Just up the road a piece."

"Can we stop and show Ruby?"

"We'll not be going that far, Sis," Jethro said as they approached the Humphrey farm. "We'll turn around here."

He's hoping that Birdie Stuart will see that he's got a car. The thought popped into Julie's head and immediately, she was ashamed of it. The Humphrey children and Birdie's little girl were playing in the lane. They stopped and watched the car turn around. Jill called out and waved. When Julie looked back, she saw the children running to the house to tell the news.

"Joe'll be surprised," Jack said as his father drove back home. "He's been wishin' we had a car."

When Jethro stopped the car in the area between the barn and the house, he didn't turn off the engine.

"I suspect he will," he said, pulling up on the emergency brake. "You all get out. I'm going to take it out for a little spin—"

"Can I go?" Jason asked eagerly.

"No, son. I'm going to see if I can get her up to about thirty-five and I don't want you kids in the car."

"Thirty-five what?"

"Miles an hour. They've got cars now that go up to forty or fifty."

"Fifty miles in an hour." Jack whooped. "I'm going to do it someday. Ride in an airplane, too."

"Not if I have anything to say about it," Julie said staunchly as she lifted Joy down from the running board.

"Ah, Sis," Jack said. "I wouldn't get hurt or nothin'."

"I might stop over and see what Evan thinks about welding the fenders." Jethro released the brake.

"Be careful." Julie grasped Joy's hand and backed away from the car.

As she stood in the yard and watched the automobile bounce down the lane toward the road and then turn right toward the Humphreys', Julie felt an anguished moment of fear and dread of what the future might hold for the family. She glanced at Jack and was surprised to see that the happy grin had left his face. The look in the boy's eyes as they met hers over the heads of their younger brother and sister told Julie that she wasn't alone in her concern that their father was enamored of the young widow. Should she return his affection, it could make a drastic change in their family.

The regular meeting of the City Council of Fertile was convened at five P.M. in the back room of the furniture store. Present were Amos Wood, banker; Ronald Poole, hardware and feed store owner; Frank Adler, druggist; Herman Maddock, furniture store owner and undertaker (or funeral director, as he'd rather be called); and Ira Brady, owner of the Fertile Telephone Company and mayor. Invited to sit in on the meeting was Marshal Sanford.

The minutes of the last meeting were read and approved. The town treasurer, Herman Maddock, reported a balance of $5,672.13, after an expenditure of $323.45 to repair the water tower.

"What did they do, for Christ's sake?" Amos Wood demanded.

"You know what had to be done, Amos," Ronald Poole, who was in charge of the project, explained. "You complained when the tank had to be drained so they could prop it back up. One side of the stand it's sitting on had sunk down until it looked like that tower they got over in France or Italy or wherever the hell it is. We couldn't leave it till it fell over."

"Seems like a lot of money. I suppose you sold the hardware to the town to fix it."

"Would you rather we had gone out of town to buy it? I made a profit, but a damn little one." Poole's face took on a hard look and he jutted his chin.

Mayor Brady cleared his throat. "Do we accept the treasurer's report?" There was a murmur of ayes and no nays.

"Report accepted," Ira said firmly. "Now we've got important business to settle today, business we've had hanging for damn near a year." A chair creaked. Ira glanced at Amos as the banker settled into a new position, indicating his displeasure concerning the topic to be discussed.

"You still on that kick, Ira?" Amos asked. "We've got a marshal. Don't you think he's doing his job?"

"Of course he's doing his job," Ira retorted sharply. "He's a *district* marshal. He covers a fourth of the state of Missouri. That's why we need our own police."

"Why spend the money for a policeman when all he'll do

is direct traffic on Saturday and arrest a drunk or two? Hell, Ira, we don't even have a county jail."

"Mr. Poole has an idea for that."

"More business for the hardware, huh, Ron?"

Ronald Poole stood. All six feet two inches towered over the banker.

"I've taken about all the slurs I'm goin' to take from you, Amos. You've got your ass over the line because, after I paid off my mortgage, I switched my account to Peterson's Savings and Loan. You've been ridin' my back ever since."

"Gentlemen, we have a guest. You can settle your personal differences outside this meeting. Amos, we passed a resolution almost a year ago that a policeman would be procured for Fertile. Unless you want to introduce a motion to repeal that resolution, this discussion is out of order." Ira waited a full minute, and when nothing more was said, he introduced the guest.

"You all know Marshal Sanford. I asked him to come today to explain fully the situation we face here."

Once the creaking of chairs and the scuffling of feet on the plank floor ceased and the room was quiet, Marshal Sanford leaned forward and put his elbows on the table.

"First let me speak on the matter of the jail. The town of Fertile should join with the county to put a jail in the basement of the courthouse. There's room down there and it would be handy. Wouldn't cost much."

"That was Ron's idea," Ira said. "We'll have to do it sooner or later as the population grows."

"It's a good idea," Frank Adler agreed.

"Well, I'll put in my two cents' worth and you can decide what you want to do." The marshal leaned back in his chair. "It's just as plain as the nose on my face, folks. I have so much territory to cover that, even with the help of my deputy, I can't possibly serve the town of Fertile as it should be served. I live thirty-five miles from here, right in the middle of my territory. I can't be running up here every time you have a neighborhood squabble or someone steals a watermelon. In my opinion anything that happens in Fertile can be handled by a man of good standing with the support of the council and my help, if needed."

Herman Maddock spoke up. "We have some petty crime here, not much traffic, but a few brawls down around Well's Point after we took it into the town limits. Any man with a good head on his shoulders and a ready fist should be able to handle the job."

"What do you plan to pay this . . . peacekeeper?" Amos Wood's voice was heavy with sarcasm.

Ira took a deep breath. "Marshal Sanford suggests fifty dollars a month and that we pay for his weapon."

Amos rolled his eyes toward the ceiling and his fat cheeks quivered as he gritted his teeth.

"Have you something else to say, Amos?" Ira asked.

"No. No. You'll just barrel on ahead. I thought I was the financial advisor on this council. When you bankrupt the town, you'll—"

"We won't come to you for a loan if I have anything to say about it," Ron Poole said firmly.

"Do you have anyone in mind?" the undertaker asked in his mild-mannered way of bringing the discussion back on track.

"Marshal Sanford has made a recommendation," Ira said. "We realized that we couldn't get an experienced man out of Kansas City or St. Louis without paying him considerably more money than we can afford. The man he recommends is from the southern part of the state, down around Joplin. He was with the military police during the war. That would make him qualified for a police job in the city, but he would rather settle down in a small town. He is a single man who lost his fiancée while he was away at war." Ira placed several pieces of paper on the table.

"I have here a copy of his army discharge, an evaluation

from his superior officer and several personal endorsements. The marshal tells me that he is twenty-six years old and an excellent marksman."

"You planning on having him shoot someone, Ira?" Amos asked.

"If your bank was being robbed, wouldn't you want the policeman you called to be able to shoot straight?"

Amos grunted and looked out the window.

Marshal Sanford's chair scraped the floor as he got to his feet.

"I'll bring the man in and you can talk to him. Nice seeing you again, Ira." He extended his hand, then shook hands with the rest of the council members. "If Appleby doesn't work out, let me know. I'll see what I can do about finding another man."

Marshal Sanford left the door open when he left the room. A short while later, he returned with a tall, lean but not thin, dark-haired man with broad shoulders and a scar that sliced across one eyebrow onto his cheek. It showed a pale, threadlike line through his summer tan. He carried a brown felt hat in his hand.

"Corbin Appleby, gentlemen." Marshal Sanford made the announcement, clapped the man on the shoulder, went out and closed the door.

Mayor Ira Brady extended his hand, introduced him to the rest of the council, then invited him to take a seat.

"Why do you want to move to a town the size of Fertile?" Amos Wood began the interview with the blunt question.

Corbin Appleby looked him in the eye. "Why not? Isn't it a desirable place to live?"

"It is," the banker answered quickly. "Fertile is a quiet, law-abiding town, prosperous—"

"Glad to hear it." Appleby turned then to Ira Brady. "I want you to know, Mr. Brady, that if I accept this job, I have my own firearm."

"If he *accepts* . . . listen to that." Amos chortled.

Appleby turned cold eyes on the banker. "Would you prefer we not lay all our cards on the table?"

"Of course I want honesty. But you don't seem to be aware that you're not the only man in the state qualified for the job."

"I never assumed that I was. I was invited here for an interview, but perhaps I'm wasting my time."

"Mr. Appleby," Frank Adler spoke up. "Mr. Wood is only one man on this council. The other four of us would like to continue the interview."

After a long silent moment, Mr. Appleby nodded his head.

Thirty minutes later, the chairman of the council said, "Thank you, Mr. Appleby. Will you wait outside, please? We will come to a decision and be with you shortly."

There was silence again while Corbin Appleby went out and closed the door behind him.

Herman Maddock, the undertaker, had not said much except to ask a question or two. Now he was ready to speak his piece.

"Mr. Appleby appears to be a responsible man. He seems intelligent, and the marshal feels that he'll not use the job to push anybody around."

"He pays his bills," Ron Poole added.

"We should have interviewed Evan Johnson. He was in the army and had a higher rank than this bozo." Amos made the statement defensively. Four sets of eyes turned on him.

"Bozo? Is that what you think of a man who fought on foreign soil for his country?" The undertaker's rarely shown temper was about to surface.

"He wasn't in the trenches, for God's sake!"

"How do you know? Who do you think took charge of the German prisoners? He didn't get that scar on his face sittin' on his fist leaning back on his thumb."

"I still think we should have talked to Evan Johnson."

"Evan Johnson wouldn't have touched this job with a ten-foot pole," Ron Poole said with conviction. "He's not hurtin' for money, as you probably know. He's not going to risk his life for fifty a month."

"All right." Ira Brady slapped the table with his palm to bring order. "Let's get back on track. Anybody else have anything to say about Appleby before we take a vote?"

"I think we're being hasty." This from Amos Wood.

"I think the man would give us his best." Ron Poole glared at the banker.

Herman Maddock spoke. "I move that we hire him."

"So moved," Ira said without hesitation.

"Seconded," said Frank Adler.

"All in favor, say aye."

There was a collective aye from everybody but Amos Wood.

"All opposed?"

"Nay," said the banker. "I think you are giving too much authority to a man we don't know."

"The motion is passed." Ira slammed his hand down on the table again. "Someone move we adjourn."

"I so move."

"Seconded."

"All in favor?"

"Aye."

"Go out and welcome the new policeman to our town."

"I hope to hell he can do something about Walter Johnson before he kills someone," Herman Maddock said.

"The marshal didn't do anything about him." Amos slammed his hat on his head. "Don't expect this bird to do anything, either. He'll collect his fifty a month, strut around with a star on his chest and get free meals at the restaurant. That's as much as he'll amount to."

When Corbin was told that he was hired, he shook hands with each of the council members. Then, not wanting to stay and chat, he crossed the street to the hotel to sit on the porch and watch as each of them came out of the furniture store. He didn't have long to wait.

Mayor Ira Brady, who had told him the swearing-in ceremony would take place at nine the next morning, was a man in his late forties with thinning dark hair. He was small, neat, and would probably be overlooked in a crowd, yet he projected an aura of competence and trustworthiness.

Corbin watched him pass the banker without speaking and walk on down the street. Amos Wood, Corbin suspected, had a low self-image. The only way he could make himself feel important was to be against things the other members were for. His short legs supported an overweight body. There appeared to be no neck at all between his head and his shoulders. His jowls hung heavily and the brows above black-button eyes grew together over his nose. He was not a likable fellow.

Ronald Poole, the youngest council member, seemed the most pleasant of the five. He impressed Corbin as being intelligent, efficient and capable. His face, unremarkable though handsome, was framed by a mop of unruly blond hair. His clear green eyes were warm and friendly. His shoulders were broad, his arms heavily muscled. He was a man who could take care of himself.

The druggist, Frank Adler, had drooping eyelids and pale skin. He was nearly six feet tall, gaunt, a man in his late thirties and not as easily led, Corbin suspected, as he allowed others to believe.

Herman Maddock, undertaker/furniture store owner, reminded Corbin of a hound dog. His face was long and thin. Even the corners of his sad eyes drooped like those of a hound. His shoulders were narrow, his ears were large and his head jutted forward when he moved his tall, stooped body. Strands of dark hair were carefully combed over his near bald pate. Corbin could see him operating as an undertaker but could not imagine buying a sofa or a bed from him.

The council was as mixed a group as Marshal Sanford had

described them. The mayor, Ira Brady, was the brains and Ronald Poole the brawn. Wood was the pain in the butt and the others went along with the majority.

It was a good assessment.

Now, Corbin thought, *let's see what happens next. Someone in this town is a goddamn murderer. When I find him, I'll prove it. If I can't, I'll kill him.*

Chapter 6

YOU'RE NOT GOING TO THE REVIVAL MEETING?" Jill put the leftover biscuits in the warming oven.

"Joy and I will stay here."

"Jack isn't going."

"Jack's old enough to know what he wants to do."

"He wanted to go to town with Joe."

"Joe will be home pretty soon and they can go. You and Jason go with Papa."

"Why don't you want to come with us?"

"I don't want to, and that's that."

"You don't have to be mad about it."

"I'm not mad, Jill. I'm tired. I don't feel like sitting for three hours on a hard bench at a revival meeting. I'm not going to do something I don't want to do just to please you and Papa."

"Well, all right. Papa won't like it. He thinks you're going."

Julie didn't bother to answer. She tilted the pan of water into the tin sink and watched the water flow down through the hole. Joe had run the pipe from the sink down the wall and outside. It had saved her many steps, as had the red iron hand pump on the side of the sink.

Joe could do about anything he set his mind to. He was handier with tools than her father and no doubt was delighted to have the car to tinker with.

"You'd better get Joy cleaned up, Sis. We'll be leaving in a little bit."

Jethro had come into the kitchen from his room across the hall. He wore his good black pants, a white shirt and a perky bow tie. He went past her to the mirror over the wash bench, dipped his comb in the water in the basin and carefully parted his hair.

"Joy and I are not going."

Jethro turned to frown at her. "You said the other night you were. The Humphreys were going to stop by for you."

"No, I didn't. They offered to stop by *if* I was going. Joy and I will stay here, take a bath and wash our hair. We'll go to church tomorrow."

"I wish you'd go," he said slowly.

"Why?" Julie asked, then silently answered her own question. *You want to use me as an excuse to be with Birdie Stuart and . . . you want to show off the car.*

"Well, I told Mrs. Humphrey that you were and that we'd come by and give them a ride."

"Without Joy and me, there'll be more room in the car."

Her father put the comb in the tin box that hung by the mirror and went out onto the back porch. *He'll sulk for a while,* Julie thought, *but I can't help that. I need time to get used to the idea that he wants to court a woman, possibly marry her and bring her here. It's his right to do that, but I hope and pray that he'll not rush into it.*

Julie tried to imagine her father as another woman would see him. He was a nice-looking man. Hard work had made him lean and muscular. His hair was dark and curly. He had a wide mouth and his teeth were nice and white, not tobacco-stained as some men's were. He was a gentle man and . . . he loved his children. His farm was almost paid for, proving that he was a good provider.

On the downside, he had a grown daughter to contend with, and his three younger children would be at home for a long time. Julie decided, even with that burden, some unattached females would consider her father a good catch.

Papa, be careful . . . be careful. There's something about that woman that bothers me.

As soon as the car disappeared down the road, Jack took a teakettle of hot water and went down to the barn to bathe while Julie soaped and scrubbed Joy in the tub in the kitchen. By the time she had washed the child's hair and rubbed it almost dry with the towel, Joy was yawning and ready for bed. Julie took her upstairs and tucked her into the bed they shared.

"Good night, honey. I'll be up soon."

"Night." Joy tucked her hand under her cheek and was almost instantly asleep.

Julie looked down at the child, who was so precious to her, and remembered the day she was born: so tiny, so helpless. The baby had been crying lustily when she placed her on the bed beside her mother.

"Oh, you darlin' little thing. You're just a kickin' and a rearin', ain't ya? You're a joy, is what you are," Julie's mother had crooned to the child and she had become quiet. "Let's call her Joy, Julie. That's what she is, a joy to behold."

Julie closed the door now and hurried back down to take her bath before Jack came up from the barn. Times were rare when she was alone in the quiet house. She had put her clothes back on and was rinsing her hair over the tin sink when her brother came in.

"Smells like vinegar in here."

"I'm rinsing my hair in it, nut-head," Julie said from beneath the swirl of dark blond hair. "Hand me my towel."

"Nut-head? You called your sweet little brother a nut-head?" Grinning, Jack put the wet cloth she used to wash the dishes in her outstretched hand.

"Ja-ck—" she sputtered and dropped it. "Hand me the towel. If I drip water all over the floor, I'll box your ears."

"Say please."

"Please, please, pretty please with sugar on it."

"That's more like it. Here you are."

Julie grabbed the towel. "Just wait until I get my hands on you!" she threatened as she wound the towel around her head.

When she straightened, Jack was giving her a taunting grin from the other side of the table.

"Bet you can't catch me."

"I'm not even going to try. There are other ways of getting even."

"Like what? You'll pee in the tea?"

"Jack Jones!" Julie stared at her brother. "What in the world caused you to say such a nasty thing?"

"I'm a poet and don't know it." He dodged behind a chair. "Rhymes, doesn't it?"

Jack wasn't as tall as Joe, but he was heavier. He had an engaging smile and was the prankster of the family. Furiously protective of his brothers and sisters, he was ready to fight at the drop of a hat for any of them, including Jill, whom he teased almost constantly.

"I'll empty your bathwater if you'll make a batch of fudge."

"It uses up too much sugar."

"Please, pretty please."

"I don't know why I should do anything for you . . . you imp . . . but we all deserve a treat."

"Whoopee!"

"Fire up the cookstove while I change out of this wet dress and dry my hair."

By the time the fudge, bubbling on the stove, had tested ready by forming a firm ball when dropped into a cup of cold water, night had begun to fall.

"Light the lamp, Jack." Julie lifted the heavy skillet off the stove and onto a wooden breadboard. "You beat the fudge and I'll butter the platter."

Julie seldom had a chance to be alone with one of her brothers and she was enjoying Jack's company. He had a cheerful disposition. He was always happy, especially if there was a chance to play baseball. He had loved the game since catching his first ball at the age of two or three.

"Darn, that handle's hot." Jack wrapped the dish towel around the handle on the iron skillet so that he could tilt it. "Sis, do you think Pop likes that Stuart woman over at the Humphreys'?"

Julie's heart stilled for a second or two. Her eyes went quickly to her brother. His young face was serious. She put the lid back on the butter crock before she answered.

"Why do you ask?"

"Oh, I don't know. He went out of his way to be nice to her at the ball game. Even This and That noticed it. I had the feeling that he drove up to the Humphreys' today to show off the car."

"Would you object to him remarrying?"

"Maybe. I've heard too much about wicked stepmothers." His endearing grin was back when he looked across the table at her. "It'll not matter so much to me. I'm almost grown. In a couple years I'll be gone from here."

"Oh, I hope not!" The distress in Julie's voice wiped the smile from Jack's face.

"I'm not a baby anymore, Julie."

"I know, but—it's hard to think of the family breaking up."

"Ah, Sis . . . it's so damn unfair. You've been stuck here taking care of us and haven't had a chance to go anywhere, do anything or meet anyone."

Julie was surprised that her happy-go-lucky brother had such serious thoughts.

"I might be forced to, if Papa remarries and his new wife doesn't want me around."

"He'd not stand still and let her run you off!"

"She could make it so unpleasant for me that I'd want to go."

"Joe and I would have something to say about that. If it

happened, I'd get a job and take care of you. You'd not just up and leave, would you?"

"Not unless I had someplace to go. I'd take Joy and Jason. They were so little when Mama died. It would be hard on them to be left. I'd hate leaving Jill."

"Pop wouldn't want you to leave."

"His first concern would be for the woman he married. But maybe we're worrying for nothing."

"Lord, if he gets it in his head to marry someone, I hope it isn't that Stuart woman."

"Why do you say that?"

"I've heard plenty about her from This and That. This told me that she don't know beans from bull-foot about anything and complains that she isn't used to working in the garden and washing fruit jars in a tub or clothes on a rub board. The boys don't like her much."

"She knew her brother lived on a farm. Surely she was aware that the work on a farm never ends."

"I don't think she planned on workin' for her keep. Mrs. Humphrey is tryin' to team her up with Evan." Jack stuck his finger in the fudge, then into his mouth. "She invited him to supper, and they've taken pies and pickled beets over to him. Mrs. Stuart even offered to mend his clothes. Joe teased Evan and asked him how come he hadn't taken the bait."

"What did Evan say?"

"He laughed and said that when the time came, he'd pick his own woman. Evan's too smart to be taken in by a pie and a jar of pickled beets." Jack lifted the spoon from the fudge. "Is this about ready to pour in the platter?"

"After I put in the vanilla, give it another dozen strokes to mix it in." Julie watched the spoon slice through the rapidly thickening candy. "Now hold the skillet over the platter and I'll scrape it out."

The iron skillet was heavy. Jack had to use both hands.

While Julie smoothed the thick dark fudge with a wet knife, Jack licked the spoon, then scraped the skillet.

"This is good. Want a bite?"

"I'll lick the knife. Humm . . . it is good."

"Smells good."

Julie turned at the sound of Joe's voice to see him in the doorway. Evan Johnson was behind him, his eyes on her as her tongue swept the chocolate from the knife.

"Jack and I . . . made fudge."

"Pop said you were going to the revival meeting." Joe ran his finger along the edge of the platter, then put a dab of fudge in his mouth.

"Well, I didn't. Keep your dirty fingers out of the fudge. Come in, Mr. Johnson. Joe, where are your manners?"

"Lost 'em a long time ago, little sister." Joe stood a head taller than Julie and liked to refer to her as his *little* sister. "When will this be ready to eat?"

Julie swatted his hand. "I said, keep your dirty fingers out of the candy. It'll be ready in a little bit." She poured water from the teakettle into the skillet to have something to do. Good Lord, her hair was hanging down her back and she had fudge on her face. *Evan had caught her licking a knife!* He must really think she was a backwoods clod.

What Evan was thinking was that she was as pretty and as fresh and as natural as any woman he'd seen for a long time . . . probably ever. Not in London or Paris or in New York, where the women wore bobbed hair and skirts just to their knees, had he seen a sweeter-looking or a more desirable woman. Julie Jones was a woman as women were meant to be. The realization hit him with the force of a fist on his chin: Here on this rocky farm on the edge of town was a treasure, a real honest-to-God treasure.

"Evan and I were going to play a couple games of checkers while everyone was gone," Joe said while washing his hands.

"With you two here, we could play a couple hands of pitch. Course it'd be a runaway, 'cause you're both lousy players."

Deep in his own thoughts, Evan vaguely heard what Joe was saying. Since meeting Julie on the road and seeing her at the ball game, he had been thinking about her a lot. Today he coaxed more information about her from her unsuspecting brother. She didn't have a steady beau, in fact no beau at all. What was the matter with the men around here? He had not seen another woman worth looking at twice since coming back to Fertile.

Knowing that Evan's eyes were still on her, Julie felt her cheeks grow warm. She became suddenly and uncomfortably aware of the faded gingham dress she wore, but she couldn't do anything about it now. He would think that she was primping for him if she did anything about her hair. Julie was careful to keep her features deceptively calm, masking her swirling thoughts.

"I suppose you think that you and Evan will team up against me and Julie." Jack gave a vigorous shake of his head. "Not fair. You and Julie against me and Evan."

"That's not fair! Evan's the best player. He can have Julie."

Julie turned with her hands on her hips. "Thank you, brothers mine, for the confidence. I can remember when Papa and I skunked you two. Three games out of three, and you didn't even come close to winning any of them."

"That was because I was sick with a cold and couldn't think straight and you tallied the score." Joe clapped his hand down on Julie's shoulder. Over her head he winked at Evan.

"I've not said that I'll play," Julie replied haughtily, with her chin tilted so that she appeared to look down her nose at her brother. "Besides . . . how dare you give me away like . . . like an old shoe."

Julie looked up to see Evan staring at her intently. A muscle stood out in the hard plane of his cheek and his mouth was grim. Then, in the flash of an eye, he smiled. His expression changed drastically. His smiling eyes caught hers and held them captive. She couldn't have looked away if the house had been on fire.

"Shall we take on these two scamps? They'll lose, and I've got a pile of wood over at my place that needs working up. It wouldn't take them more than a couple of days with me cracking the whip."

"How about if they wash dishes here for a week?"

"Wait a dadgummed minute," Joe said heatedly. "What do we get if we win?"

Still smiling at Evan, Julie said, "You won't."

"Bull-foot!" Jack dropped a deck of cards on the table, sat down and began to shuffle them. "Let's show 'em, Joe."

"Yeah. Our little sis is gettin' a mite too feisty. We'll put her back in her place."

Evan watched Julie as she teased with her brothers. She looked younger with her hair down. Joe had said that she was two years older than his eighteen years.

"I'll play, but I'll keep score." Julie looped her hair behind her ears and sat down. "I don't trust either of you."

Joe passed the tablet to Julie. "You think we'd *cheat*? Jack, our little sister thinks we'd cheat."

"Cuts me to the quick that she'd think that," Jack said and dealt the cards.

Julie snorted. "The only thing that cuts you to the quick is missing a meal." She threw away two cards. "Give me two."

"One," Evan said when his turn came to bid.

The hand ended with Evan taking all five tricks.

"What do you think now, little brothers?" Julie crowed.

Jack overbid and was set on the next hand.

Julie and Evan won the first game. Joe and Jack won the next game and wanted to quit while they were even. Evan and Julie insisted on playing another game, which they won.

"We won two games out of three!" Julie looked across at

Evan. His smile matched hers. "We showed them, didn't we?" She was breathless, excited and felt young and giddy.

"We sure did. Do you think they should have any of the fudge?"

"If I don't give them a little, they'll not be fit to live with for a month." Julie brought the platter to the table and cut the candy in squares.

"You're sure doing a lot of crowing. It'll be different next time," Joe said, reaching toward the platter. "I was just getting warmed up."

"Company first." Julie swatted his hand with the flat of the knife and pushed the plate across to Evan.

Evan couldn't recall having spent a more enjoyable evening and he hated to see it end. He watched Julie and listened to her good-natured banter with her brothers. There was a great deal of affection between them. Not having had a sibling, Evan couldn't help but feel a twinge of envy.

"Take another piece, everyone, then I'm putting it away so there'll be some for the kids." Julie wrapped a cloth around the platter and was placing it on a shelf when she heard Sidney's bark, then the sound of a car. "Papa's back."

The car came to a stop and a little later turned around in the yard and headed back down the lane. Jill came across the porch and into the kitchen. Jason was close behind. Never one to hide her feelings, Jill had a mutinous look on her face.

"Have a good time?" Julie asked.

"No."

"No?" Julie quirked a brow at her sister's grumpiness. "Wasn't Ruby May there?"

"She was there."

"Where did Papa go?"

"To take *her* home." Jill slumped down in a kitchen chair. "Her and her whiny . . . brat."

Evan sat back, watching the family. Julie's wide mouth, its lower lip fuller and softer than the upper one, turned down at the corners, told him that she was less than happy at the news her sister had imparted. The grin had left Jack's face, and Joe had turned his head to watch his older sister.

"Would a piece of fudge cheer you up?" Julie brought the platter from the shelf. "Jason, honey, come have some."

"I didn't even get to sit in front with Papa."

"You got to sit in front on the way to town." Julie put her arm around the boy and drew him to the table. He leaned his head against her for a moment.

"No, he didn't," Jill blurted. "When we got to the Humphreys' he had to get in back with me and the four Humphrey kids. Mrs. Stuart got in front with her . . . brat."

"Didn't Mrs. Humphrey go?"

"They went in the wagon so the kids could ride to town in the car."

"Well, let's not be grumpy about it. Tomorrow is Sunday. Maybe Papa will take us for a ride."

"I don't like her. She never said one word to me or Jason. Papa treated her like she was . . . Queen of the May." Jill popped a piece of fudge in her mouth. "He helped her get in the car and lifted the brat up to sit by her. I don't like her," Jill said again.

"It isn't important whether you like her or not. Papa was just giving her a ride."

A quick spate of words broke from Jill's lips. "If you believe that . . . then there's a cow sitting out in the oak tree chirping like a robin."

"Don't talk with your mouth full." Julie stood still, head tilted back, arms folded. She looked at her sister with a mixture of exasperation and desperation.

"Evan was their first choice," Jill continued with the brashness of youth. "He was too smart to be taken in. I thought Papa was smarter, too. He's not thinkin' straight or he'd not—"

"Watch your mouth, Jill," Joe said sharply.

"I'm not saying anything that isn't true, am I, Mr. Johnson?"

Julie darted a glance at Evan. His narrowed gaze was on her. His eyes held a combination of sharp intelligence and quiet strength. Embarrassment reddened her cheeks. He turned his head slightly toward Jill.

"Young lady, I'd say that you have a pretty good handle on the situation."

"See? I'm not so dumb."

"I wondered why Papa was so eager to get a car. He hadn't mentioned it before." Jack sat quietly with his hands clasped on the table.

"Arrr-woof!" Sidney had his nose pressed to the screen door.

"Can I let him in, Julie? He's not muddy or nothin'." Jason looked imploringly at his sister.

"Honey, he's been in the cockleburs. They'll be on the floor and Joy will be getting them in her feet. You should be in bed. It's almost ten o'clock."

"Arrr-woof!"

"Oh, all right," Jason said dejectedly. "Ever'thin's goin' wrong 'round here anyhow."

"It'll be better tomorrow. You'll . . . see." Julie's voice was not quite convincing.

Jill raised her eyes to the ceiling. "You guys are so dumb! You'd better do somethin' before she gets her hooks deeper into him."

"And what do you think we ought to do?" Joe reached out a hand, clapped it on the top of Jill's head and gave it a gentle shake.

"How do I know? You're always tellin' me that I'm just a kid. You think of somethin'." Jill glanced at her sister's frowning face, then down at the table.

"You and Jason head on up to bed. I'll see if the quilt I put on the line is dry." The stress lines between Julie's brows deepened and her mouth tensed as she hurried out the door.

"You've upset Julie with all this talk about Papa and that woman," Jack said. "I hope you're satisfied."

Evan got to his feet. "I'll be going. Tell your father I'll see what I can do about fixing the fenders on his car."

"Can I ride in your car someday, Mr. Johnson?" Jason asked.

"I didn't know you had a car." This from Jill.

"Sure, Jason." Evan headed for the door. "The next time I get it out of the shed."

"Why do you ride that horse if you've got a car? That's dumb." Jill failed to see the annoyance on her older brother's face.

"That's enough out of you, Jill." Joe followed his new friend out the door. "Sorry about that, Evan. Jill's mouth runs away with her, and Julie will be put out with us for airing our family problems in front of company."

"There's nothing to be sorry for. Maybe you're worried over nothing. Your father may not be interested in Mrs. Stuart after he gets to know her better."

"I hope you're right."

"Night, Jack. I'm going to say good night to your sister." Evan stepped off the porch. In the darkness he could see Julie was struggling with a heavy quilt on the clothesline. As he approached, a low growl came from Sidney, who stood stiff-legged beside her. "Will the dog take my leg off if I help you with that?"

"Sidney, it's all right." She spoke calmly to the dog. Then to Evan: "I've about got it turned. I washed it this afternoon. I thought it would be dry by now."

"There was a lot of humidity today and it looked like we were in for a good rain." Evan easily lifted the quilt and flung it over the line. "It's clear tonight. That moon looks like someone hung a yellow ball in the sky."

"Or a balloon." Julie took extra pains seeing that the quilt was straight on the line because she didn't know what else to say.

Evan knew what he wanted to say, but he couldn't blurt it

right out. *Damn my heart for beating so fast and making me feel like a callow youth.*

"Joe is standing on the porch keeping an eye on me," he said and chuckled.

"What does he think you're going to do?"

"I admire him for watching over you," he said instead of answering her question.

"He's very dear to me. All of them are, but Joe is special."

A breeze came up and wrapped strands of her long hair around her neck. She gathered it in her hands and brought it all forward over one shoulder.

"You're lucky to have brothers and sisters." His words came out slowly and fell into the quiet pool of silence.

"You might not think so if you could hear them squabbling all at once. It was tame tonight. They were united against . . ." Her voice trailed.

"I understand their concern."

"Papa is a levelheaded man. He'll not do anything to hurt the family."

Evan made no comment. He was trying to think of a way to keep her out here in the dark with him a little longer. Worry that her father might be driving in at any minute forced him to blurt out what he had come to say.

"Julie . . . would you go with me to the picture show or out to Spring Lake some night?"

His head was tilted to the side. Julie could feel his eyes on her face. She couldn't move, couldn't speak, could scarcely breathe. They were alone in the dark. Her thoughts were so muddled that she couldn't remember exactly what he had said.

"If you don't want to go, I'll understand. It's Walter, isn't it?"

"You're not like . . . your father," she said quickly.

"God, I hope not. Walk with me over to the pen to get my horse." He reached for her hand, holding it lightly to give her a chance to withdraw it. When she didn't, he drew it up into the crook of his arm, holding the back of it pressed to his side. She slipped her hand from his arm when they reached the pole corral and he missed the warm touch.

Had he gone too fast, been too intimate?

"Joe asked me to come to the ball game tomorrow afternoon."

"You don't have to be invited. It's open to anyone who wants to come."

"How about going out with me next Saturday night?"

"All right." Julie wondered what he would think if he knew that she had never been asked out on a date.

"We'll go wherever you want to go, to the picture show or to the dance."

"May I decide later?"

"Sure. I'll have to give Jason a ride in the car before we go. I promised him."

"He'll not let you forget it."

"Thanks for the fudge."

"You're welcome," she said softly.

Evan opened the gate. "I hear your father coming. I'll let myself out the back gate. Good night, Julie."

"Good night, Evan."

Chapter 7

THE RED LIGHT WAS ON. It was the signal for Chief Corbin Appleby to call the telephone operator or come to the office. Hung in the center of the line stretched across Main Street from the telephone office to the hardware store, the light shone for only the second time since Corbin's swearing in three days ago.

Diane Ham, the telephone operator, had turned the signal on yesterday when the county supervisor wanted the chief's input on the room they were remodeling in the basement of the courthouse to use as a temporary jail while a more permanent facility was being made ready.

Chief Appleby hurriedly passed the people milling around on the sidewalk in front of the stores. The revival meeting had just ended, and a number of cars were parked along the street. To the folks who came to town only on Saturday night, it was a chance to visit with friends and get caught up on the news. The crowd parted to allow the new police chief to pass, then their eyes followed him to the telephone office.

Mrs. Ham looked up when the chief came in the door but continued to talk into the mouthpiece that hung around her neck.

"Chief Appleby is here now, Mrs. Reynolds. I must hang up so I can tell him what you've told me." Mrs. Ham, a petite blonde, widowed by the war, pulled the plug from the switchboard. "Mrs. Reynolds says that something is going on in the house across the street from hers. Otto Bloom and his wife are fighting. Their little boy ran over to tell her that his papa was beating his mama. Mrs. Reynolds says hurry. He has hurt her before and could kill her this time."

"Where do they live?" the chief asked on the way to the door.

"Two blocks toward the river from the corner and a half block north. Mrs. Reynolds will be waiting in the yard," Mrs. Ham called as Corbin shot out the door, letting it bang shut behind him.

Corbin could run a half mile without breaking into a sweat. He liked to run. During his high school days he had been state champion in the mile and long-distance races and had considered training for the national competition, but his need to hold a job had prevented that. However, to stay fit he went out into the country once a week, usually on Sunday, and ran a mile or two.

He trotted effortlessly down the middle of the darkened street, holding the gun on his hip to keep it from bouncing. He had just turned and slowed when a woman, clutching the hand of a small boy, stepped out from behind a tree.

"Hurry! She's crying and begging." Then they heard clearly the sound of a crash coming from the house.

Corbin hardly paused to hear what the woman said. He bounded up the porch steps and flung open the door. He could hear a woman sobbing and pleading in the next room. Long strides took him to the doorway.

"Don't . . . Otto. Please—"

"What's going on here?"

A man was holding a woman by the hair. She was on her knees and he was slapping her with his free hand. He looked up at Corbin with bloodshot eyes.

"Who . . . the hell are you? Get outta my house!" The words were slurred.

"I'm the police. Let her go."

"This's my woman. This's my house." The clean-shaven man wore a white shirt splattered with blood. He jerked on his wife's hair. She cried out and he drew back his fist.

"Hit her again, and I'll beat you to a pulp." Corbin sprang across the room and grabbed the man's arm. "Let go of her hair, you spineless worm, or by God, I'll break your damn arm."

Yelping at the pressure, Otto released his grip on his wife. She fell back sobbing. With each sob, blood spurted from her nose. The apron that covered her dress was soaked. The thin brunette, who may have been pretty once, scrambled to her feet and stood back against the wall.

The chief jerked the abuser's arm behind his back. The man began to struggle.

"Ya got no right to be messin' in my 'ffairs—"

Corbin had had plenty of experience in dealing with tough drunks while he was in the army, and he subdued and handcuffed the pudgy man easily. In the process Corbin's foot kicked something solid. He looked down to see a large chunk of coal on the floor.

"Did he hit you with that coal?" he asked the cowering woman.

"He threw it. It hit me on the back."

Corbin jerked the cuffed hands up between the man's shoulder blades. He yelped in pain.

"Yeow! Ya . . . son-of-a—"

"Call me that and I'll throw both your damn shoulder bones out of joint. A man that'd beat a defenseless woman isn't fit for crow bait."

"He's . . . drunk," the woman said between sobs.

"You need to see the doctor, lady. I'll put this pile of dung away and send the doc down."

"You're takin' him?"

"Yeah, I'm taking him. He can sober up in jail."

"Now, listen here"—Otto was becoming agitated again—"ya got no right to take me nowhere. I work for Mr. Wood—"

"I don't care if you work for the Lord Jesus Christ. You're going to jail. Not because you're drunk, but because of what you've done to this woman."

"Couldn't you . . . just tie him up here . . . till he sobers up?" The woman's muffled voice came through the cloth she was holding to her nose. "He could lose his job."

"No. He's going to jail." Corbin shoved the man against the wall. "Stay there," he commanded. He took the woman by the arm and led her to a chair. One of her eyes was swollen shut and would likely be very black in a short time. Corbin began to grow angry when he looked over at Otto Bloom. The man's expression was one of an outraged child who had been picked on by a bully.

Corbin took a minute to look around. The house was surprisingly neat except for the smashed dishes and food on the floor. The table had been set for supper when the fight began.

"Your boy is with the lady across the road. I'll ask her to come stay with you until the doctor gets here—"

"No. I don't want . . . her to see me—"

"Ma'am, your nose is broken. You could be bleeding inside. You'd better get tended for the boy's sake."

"She's not hurt. She's puttin' on, like she always does."

Corbin turned on the man. "Shut your mouth," he snarled. "If I hear another word from you, I'll take out this blackjack and do to you what you've done to her."

Anger did to Corbin what running didn't. He was breathing very fast. Even in his drunken condition, Otto Bloom knew he was in danger of being beaten with the blackjack. When the tall angry man grabbed his arm again, Otto scrambled to his feet and let himself be pushed out of the house, onto the porch and out into the yard.

"Mrs. Reynolds," Corbin called from the front yard and waited for the woman and the boy to appear. "Will you stay with Mrs. Bloom until the doctor gets here? I'll have the telephone operator send him down."

"Doctor? I'm not payin' no doctor," Otto started to protest.

Only the wide frightened eyes of the boy stopped Corbin from hitting the drunk. With one hand he clamped Otto's arm, fingers pinching so tightly the man yelled; with the other, Corbin patted the child on the head.

"Go on in and help your mama, boy. She needs to know that you're all right and that there's one real man in the family."

The boy made a wide circle around his father and ran into the house. Mrs. Reynolds followed.

Corbin propelled Otto down the middle of the street. He debated about marching him down Main Street in full view of the Saturday night crowd but changed his mind and took him in the back door of the courthouse. Otto began to threaten.

"You'll lose your job. Mr. Wood's not going to like it."

Corbin pushed him into a room that held only a cot and a slop jar. A dim light from the street came through a small window near the ceiling.

"You can't leave me here," Otto said, suddenly becoming aware of his situation.

Corbin didn't bother to answer. He took the key from his pocket and unlocked the handcuffs.

"I'm . . . not staying here."

Corbin went to the door without answering. "I'll be back in the morning." He closed it and twisted the key in the lock.

"Mr. Wood will fire you for this!" The yell reached the chief as he was walking up the stairs.

The next morning Amos Wood and Mrs. Bloom were waiting on the courthouse steps when Corbin came to check on his prisoner.

"We're here to get Otto. Let him out," Wood demanded without so much as a greeting.

"That's up to Mrs. Bloom." The pair followed Corbin down

the stairs. At the door of the locked room, he turned and looked at the woman. Both her eyes were black, a strip of tape crossed her nose, her lips were puffed and her cheeks were bruised.

"Get on with it," Wood snarled. "I've not got all day."

"Look at her, goddammit!" Corbin snarled. "Don't you care what this man did to his wife?"

"What happens between a man and his wife is no concern of mine . . . or yours."

Corbin eyed him with contempt before turning to Mrs. Bloom and speaking to her gently.

"Ma'am, you've got a right to press charges against him for what he did to you."

"I can't. He was . . . drunk—"

"The next time he could hurt you real bad."

"I can't—" Came the whispered response.

"You heard her, Appleby. She'll not press charges. She knows what side of the bread her butter's on."

"What's your interest in this, Wood?"

"He works for me. I look out for the men who work for me," Wood answered belligerently.

"How about their families? Do you look out for them, too?

"I pay a good wage. That takes care of them."

Corbin gave him a disgusted look and turned to the woman.

"Are you sure you want me to let him out, Mrs. Bloom?"

She nodded, and Corbin knew that she would not listen to any argument. She had been beaten down until she no longer had strength to stand up for herself. And Wood, the fat toad, for some reason, owed something to Otto Bloom.

Corbin Appleby was furious as he unlocked the door.

"I didn't want to ride in his old car anyway." Jill reached the end of the lane, turned and marched off down the road toward town.

"I wanted to ride," Joy whined.

"Honey, the car wouldn't start this morning and if we waited much longer we'd be late for church," Julie explained.

"We could've gone in the wagon. Jack said he'd hitch up." Jason was sulking. He had wanted to stay and watch Joe and his father work on the car.

"It's only a twenty-minute walk to the church. We'll be there by the time Jack could hitch up. Besides, it's all downhill." Julie tilted her hat to keep the sun off her face.

"I'll be all sweaty by the time we get there," Jill called over her shoulder.

"We've had the car only one day and already you've all gotten lazy," Julie teased. "If we didn't have it you would have walked to church without a complaint."

"I wish we didn't have it." Jill's bad mood of last night had carried over to this morning. "*She'll* ride in it more than we will."

"Joe said that if they got it started, he'd be at the church at noon to take us home. Joy, stop kicking your toes in the dirt. You're getting your stockings dirty."

"Papa won't let him drive it," Jason said.

When they turned a bend in the road, Julie's saw a man running up the hill toward them. What in the world? Had something bad happened?

"What's he running for?" Jason asked the obvious question.

In his shirtsleeves and wearing lightweight shoes laced up over his ankles, the tall, lean man kept up a steady pace as he ran toward them. His elbows were bent and his arms moved in conjunction with each stride. Dark hair flopped down on his forehead.

He moved over to the far side of the road as he approached them but never broke stride. His eyes flicked quickly over the children, then settled on Julie. He smiled.

"Mornin', ma'am."

"Mornin'." Julie hardly had the word out of her mouth by the time he passed. Astonished, she and the children turned to watch him. They had never seen a grown man running along the road. She wondered where he was going.

"Do you know him?" Jill asked.

"No. I don't think I've ever seen him before."

"He's crazy. He running away from the asylum?"

"There's not an asylum within a hundred miles. He didn't look as if he'd run that far."

"I wish I could run like that," Jason said, and Julie's heart lurched painfully for her little brother. "My teacher said that some Indian tribes could run almost as fast as a horse. Reckon he's a Indian?"

The white frame church sat on the outskirts of town. It had been a country church at the turn of the century. Now the town of Fertile had spread out until the church was within the town limits. Julie's grandfather had been the mason who had laid the foundation for the New Methodist Church. On the other side of town was the Lutheran church and nearer to the river, the Southern Baptist.

Julie and the children entered the church and slid along one of the pews to sit near the open windows. It was so hot! Her dress was sticking to her back. She removed Joy's straw hat and swished it back and forth to create a little breeze. Her thoughts wandered when the preacher settled into his sermon.

She hadn't told anyone about her date this coming Saturday night with Evan. Oh, Lord. She was glad now that she hadn't. He might just have asked her on an impulse and wouldn't show up. She had lain awake last night and thought about him, remembering every word he had said to her.

His face was sharply etched in her memory. His blue eyes beneath dark, level brows had seemed to see right into her mind while they were playing cards. His mouth was firm and unsmiling—most of the time. It and his eyes set the tone of him, hard and rough and capable of taking care of himself in any situation; yet she could sense the loneliness and vulnerability in him.

The idea that a man who had seen much of the world would be interested in a country girl was ridiculous. He must have met many attractive worldly women. Julie was perfectly aware of how countrified she was—*and then there was the other thing*! The more she thought about it, the more miserable she became.

"All stand for the final hymn."

The words interrupted Julie's thoughts. The service was drawing to an end. She took the hymn book from Joy, who was seated between her and Jill, and nudged Jason, who was almost asleep.

When the hymn ended, the Joneses filed down the aisle to the door of the church where the Reverend Meadows waited to greet them. He shook hands with each of the children before greeting Julie.

"How are you, Julie?"

"Fine. I didn't see your wife here this morning. Is she well?"

"She stayed with Mother this morning to give Eudora a chance to come to church."

"Give my regards to both Mrs. Meadows and your mother."

"I'll do that."

Julie followed the children out into the bright sunlight, where the congregation mingled in the area in front of the church, visiting and exchanging bits of news.

"There's Miss Meadows," Jill exclaimed. "Hello, Miss Meadows." The preacher's sister had been Jill's first Sunday school teacher, and Jill had formed an attachment to her.

"Hello, Jill."

"I was hoping I'd see you." Jill wrapped an arm around Eudora's waist. "You weren't here last Sunday."

"Mama wasn't well. Hello, Julie."

"Nice to see you, Eudora."

In her middle thirties, Eudora was not quite as tall as Julie and was a little more rounded. Her beautiful chestnut hair was coiled and piled high atop her head. She had pearly white skin and luminous brown eyes. As always, she was handsomely dressed; her skirt was a soft gray, her blouse was sparkling white, with three rows of tiny tucks and pink embroidery that disappeared into the waistband of her skirt. Everyone liked Eudora. She was pretty not only on the outside, but on the inside as well.

Julie had often wondered why such a sweet, dainty woman had never married, but she was told that a love affair that ended badly had destroyed Eudora's interest in cultivating another relationship.

"How are you, Joy?" Eudora enjoyed little children and always took time to talk to them.

"Papa got a car."

"A car? My, that's exciting."

"It broke down and we had to walk."

"Goodness' sake!"

"We saw a man running," Joy blurted, loving the attention the pretty woman was giving her.

Eudora looked questioningly at Julie.

"On the way to town we met a man running. He didn't seem to be in any trouble or—anything."

"It must have been the new police chief. Mayor Brady told my brother that Mr. Appleby runs a mile or two a couple times a week."

"What for?" Jill asked.

"Fertile has a policeman?" This from Julie.

Eudora answered Jill first. "He runs to keep fit, and he must like it. And yes, Mayor Brady said the council had hired a policeman."

"I guess it's time Fertile had its own policeman. The town is growing. I remember when there wasn't anything but woods between the church and the town."

"Then old Mr. Johnson had better watch out," Jill said, then switched the subject suddenly, as was her habit to do when she had things to say. "The neighbors are comin' to play ball in our pasture this afternoon. I wish you'd come."

Eudora laughed. "I'm not much of a ball player."

"Not to play! You came and watched one time . . . a long time ago."

"Do come, Eudora," Julie said, extending the invitation.

"We'll see. I'd have to make arrangements for someone to stay with Mother."

"If the reverend brings you out, one of the boys will take you home. Now, where is Jason?" Julie had suddenly realized that her brother was not with them. She looked around and found him standing on the edge of the road beside . . . Evan Johnson. Evan's head was tilted toward Jason, but his eyes were on her. Julie felt her heart thump in a strange and disturbing way. As she vaguely listened to Jill begging Eudora to come to the game, she watched people who ordinarily spoke to everyone pass Evan as if he weren't there. Anger accelerated her heartbeat even more.

"Jason's with Mr. Johnson," Joy shouted when she spied her brother. She pulled away from Julie's hand and ran to them.

"Eudora, will you come meet Mr. Johnson?" Julie said on impulse. "It looks like the good people of Fertile are not going to the trouble of finding out that he isn't at all like his father."

Eudora gave Julie a curious glance. She'd never heard her friend speak with such intensity of emotion.

"I'd like to meet Mr. Johnson. I've seen him around town a few times."

The two women and Jill crossed the churchyard to where Evan stood with Jason on one side and Joy on the other. The pounding of Julie's heart warmed her face. She hoped Evan would think the reddening of her cheeks was caused by the sun.

"Hello. I didn't see you in church," Julie managed to say.

"I wasn't there."

"Miss Meadows, I'd like you to meet our neighbor, Mr. Johnson."

Eudora held out her hand and gave him a friendly smile. "Glad to meet you."

"Same here." Evan took her hand and smiled down at her.

"Eudora's brother is the pastor of our church," Julie said to fill the silence that followed.

"And my Sunday school teacher," Jill added. "Are you coming to the ball game?" She looked up into Evan's serious face. "Miss Meadows might come," she said as an added inducement.

For once Julie blessed her sister's ability for never being at a loss for words.

"I may not be able to get away, Jill," Eudora said quickly.

"Evan . . . ah, Mr. Johnson came to take us home," Jason announced. "We're going to ride in his car."

"His car?" Jill looked around.

"It's there on the other side of the church," Evan said. Then, to Julie, "I went by your place and Joe asked me to give you a ride home. It's pretty hot walking up that hill this time of day."

"Oh, he shouldn't have—"

"Goody! Goody! We get to ride in the car." Joy grabbed Evan's hand and jumped up and down with excitement.

Julie started to reach out to the child, but then she realized that Evan was grinning down at Joy with obvious enjoyment.

"Stop jumpin', Joy," Jill said impatiently. "Your stockings are comin' down."

"I don't care." The child's sparkling eyes twinkled up at Evan as she swung on his hand. "I like him."

Julie glanced quickly at Evan. The smile he gave her spread a warm light into his eyes. He was beaming with pleasure, not in the least uncomfortable with Joy hanging on to him.

"I must be going." Eudora gave Jill a hug. "It was nice seeing all you Joneses and meeting you, too, Mr. Johnson."

"It was nice meeting you, ma'am."

"Come out this afternoon . . . if you can," Jill called.

Eudora lifted her hand, waved and hurried down the street.

"Are you ready to go?" Evan asked.

"W-well, yes," Julie stammered. "But . . . well, Joe shouldn't have asked you to stop by for us. I'm sure you have things to do."

"Nothing more important than this."

To Julie's surprise, he lifted Joy up to sit on his arm. Joy laughed delightedly and put her arm around Evan's neck. He glanced at Julie. The happy light in his eyes did strange things in the area around her heart.

"The car is just around the corner."

Chapter 8

EVAN'S CAR WAS A SHINY BLACK enclosed sedan with cloth-covered seats. He opened the back door and deposited Joy on the seat.

"Holy cow!" Jill exclaimed, getting into the car. "This puts that old rattletrap Papa bought to shame."

"Jill . . . please—" When Julie moved to follow her sister into the back seat, she felt Evan's hand on her elbow holding her back.

"Hop in, Jason," Evan said.

"Is this the ride you promised me?"

"One of them. We can arrange for you to have another one sometime soon."

Evan closed the door behind the boy and opened the front door. After Julie stepped up onto the running board and slid onto the seat, Evan closed the door and went around to slide in behind the wheel. He turned the key, pushed on a button and, after a grinding noise, the motor started.

"Golly-bill!" Jason was leaning over the back of the front seat. "Ya didn't even have to get out and crank it."

"It will start automatically if the battery is up to full strength."

"Lordy-mercy! Look at this." Jill rubbed her hand over the plush upholstery. "You must be rich!"

Julie closed her eyes against the embarrassment that washed

over her and missed seeing Evan's amused glance at her flushed face.

"I'm a long way from being rich, Jill." Then, to Julie: "Do we have time to drive down through town before heading home?"

"Say yes, Julie, pl-eese," Joy squealed and slid off the seat to wrap her arms around Julie's neck from behind.

"We can take a few minutes if . . . you want to bother. Sit down, Joy." Julie turned in the seat. "Sit down and keep your feet off the seats."

"They're all right, Julie. They can't hurt a thing."

Evan drove down the main street of Fertile happier than he had been in a long, long time. Being with this woman and giving pleasure to these children with something as simple as a ride in the car delighted him. He had been alone for so long. His mother and his grandparents had been the only people who cared for him, and they were gone. Until now it had not bothered him. He had been content with his solitary life.

Was this, in some small part, what it was like to have a family of your own?

On the way home Evan patiently answered the questions Jason and Jill fired at him.

"How fast will it go?" Jason asked.

"I don't really know. I've never had it up to top speed."

"Will it go twenty-five?"

"Easily. Back in 1910, not quite twelve years ago, a fellow named Barney Oldfield drove a car a hundred and thirty-one miles an hour."

"Holy cow! Are you kiddin'?"

"It's true." Evan chuckled and glanced over his shoulder at the wide-eyed boy. "I'm not kidding."

"Was it a car like this?"

"No, it was a Benz. This car is a Hudson."

"I thought all cars were Fords."

"Almost half of the cars made are Fords. The Hudson is a heavier car."

"I'm going to drive a car . . . someday."

"I don't doubt that a bit, Jason. In the meanwhile, if you're interested, you can learn about what makes a car run."

"Will you show me?"

"I'll show you what I know. While I was in the army I had a driver who was a whiz at keeping the truck going. In our spare time we tinkered with motors."

"Golly. I don't reckon I'll ever get to go to the army," Jason said wistfully.

"I hope you never need to," Evan said as he drove the car into the lane leading to the house and stopped beside the back porch. The yard was empty.

"Your father must have gotten the car started." Evan slid out and opened the door for Julie.

"Thank you. Won't you stay and eat dinner with us? I'll have it on the table in about thirty minutes. Papa and the boys should be back soon."

"No, thanks. It's hard to turn down a good meal, but I'd better get on and . . . see to things."

"Thanks for the ride, Mr. Johnson." Jill climbed out of the car on the other side. "Are ya comin' to the ball game?"

"I'm planning on it."

To Julie's embarrassment, Joy stood on the seat and held her arms out for Evan to lift her down. When he bent to lift her, she wrapped her little arms around his neck and kissed him on the cheek.

"Well, now. I don't know when I've been kissed by a prettier girl." He had a pleased grin on his face as he set the child on her feet, grabbed her hands and swung her around several times.

"Come on, brat." Jill took the giggling child's hand. "Let's go change our clothes before Julie tells us to."

"That's a switch." Julie smiled up at Evan, then stood hesitantly, a slim woman in a blue dress with a wide ribbon sash around her narrow waist. Her flushed cheeks made her eyes seem all the warmer. "Thanks again for bringing us home." Her voice was scratchy. It was hard to get enough air in her lungs.

"You're very welcome, Julie. I have a block of ice in the trunk of the car. It's my contribution to the picnic. Where shall I put it?"

"How nice. There's a tub on the porch. I'll get it."

"Never mind. I can carry it that far."

"I'll cover it with an old quilt to keep it from melting so fast. We've got lemons for lemonade."

"I'll see you this afternoon," Evan said when he was ready to leave.

"We'll be looking for you."

He waited until she had walked up onto the porch before getting in the car. She had disappeared into the house by the time he turned around and started back down the lane.

Confused by his feelings, Evan asked himself how things had ever come down to this. Both last night and today he had felt as if he and Julie were sharing something warm and intimate. It was ridiculous how the mere thought of seeing her made his heart beat faster. He was sure of one thing. He had not felt this good in a mighty long time.

Jill, bubbly as a fountain, monopolized the conversation at the dinner table during the noon meal.

"Mr. Johnson said almost twelve years ago a man drove a car a hundred and thirty-one miles an hour. I don't believe it. Oh, I believe Mr. Johnson, but I don't believe the man who said he did it. I bet he cheated. Mr. Johnson has a nice car. Riding in it is like sitting on a sofa. When we went down Main Street, I saw Gracie Lee Gibbs. She's such a stuck-up flitter-head. I hope she saw me in that car." Jill paused only long enough to take a breath.

"Did I tell you that Miss Meadows may come out to the ball

game? Julie told her that if the reverend brought her out, one of you boys would take her home. Isn't that right, Julie? Maybe Mr. Johnson will take her in his car. Reckon your car will start, Papa?" She darted a glance at him. "Maybe you could take her home. She's nice. We all like her. Everybody likes Miss Meadows. She's not afraid of work. She takes care of her—"

"Jill, do you ever run down?" Joe interrupted his sister.

"Why should I? Nobody else is sayin' anythin'."

"Thunderation! No one else has had a chance. Once your mouth gets going, it doesn't stop long enough for anyone to get in a word."

"What did you want to say?" Jill put her elbow on the table and waved the slice of bread in her hand. "Go ahead. Say something. I'm all ears."

"Papa," Joe said, turning his head toward the end of the table, "do you think the moon is made of green cheese?"

"Wha-at? What are you talking about?" Jethro, lost in his own thoughts, looked around the table to discover that everyone was looking at him. "What are you talking about?" he asked again.

"Nothing." Joe bent his head over his place. "We were just funnin'."

"I like him," Joy blurted in the quiet that ensued. Seated on the stool between Jill and Julie, the child seemed unaware that her mouth and chin were smeared with the butter that had been put on her bread.

"Who are you talkin' about, little piggie?" Jack wrinkled up his nose. "Oink, oink."

"I ain't no piggie."

"Your face looks like it."

"Does not."

"Who do you like, sugarfoot?" Joe asked.

Jason answered: "She likes Mr. Johnson. I like him, too."

"Julie likes him," Joy announced.

"Is that right?" Joe's laughing eyes settled on Julie and watched the color come up her neck to flood her face.

"Of course I like him." Julie rose to bring the bread pudding to the table. "I'd like the devil himself if he saved me from walking up that hill at high noon." She set the warm pudding in the middle of the table and went back to get the pitcher of cream.

"He's smart enough not to let that sticky-sweet Mrs. Stuart get her claws in him." Jill helped herself to the pudding, then reached for the cream when Julie brought it to the table. "She'd sure like to get herself a man who'd—"

"That's enough!" Jethro glared at the girl. "You've been runnin' off at the mouth quite a lot lately."

"I was only sayin'—"

"Enough!" Jethro's booming voice reached into every corner of the farmhouse.

Startled by her papa's anger and his unusually loud voice, Joy began to whimper, Jill's eyes filled with tears, Jason looked as if his papa had struck him. The older boys silently helped themselves to the pudding.

"It'll probably not be as fancy as something *she* brings to the ball game."

Jill sifted sugar and cinnamon on top of the Everyday Cake Julie took from the oven. The cake was a family favorite. The recipe had been passed down from Julie's grandmother, who, with her husband, had come to Missouri from Wyoming.

"She'll bring custard pie," Julie said absently, knowing perfectly well whom Jill was talking about. "Be careful what you say about her in front of Papa."

"Why'd he get so mad all of a sudden?"

"I'm not sure, but I think he may like her and doesn't want to hear her criticized."

"Think he likes her? Bull-foot. I know he does. What'll we do if he marries that . . . that—"

"Watch it, Jill. We'll cross that bridge when we come to it. But the way it stands now, each time we say something against her, it makes him defend her all the more."

"I don't understand *that* at all. I wish Mr. Johnson liked her. If he did, Papa wouldn't stand a chance."

Ever since Evan had asked her to go out with him, Julie's heart had fluttered each time she thought about it. He hadn't mentioned it when he brought them home from church. He hadn't really had a chance, she reasoned. What if he didn't mean it . . . or forgot about asking her? What if she got ready and he didn't show up? Oh, Lord, would she be able to stand the humiliation? Well, she'd not make plans to go if she didn't hear something more from him between now and then. She had to get him out of her mind. There were things to do.

"Maybe we're making a mountain out of a molehill," Julie said, in an effort to bring her thoughts back to the present.

"If Miss Meadows comes, try to finagle it so that Papa takes her home. Maybe he'll see the difference between a nice lady and a floozie."

"A floozie?" Julie rolled her eyes. "You're a schemer, but it might work."

"If he's got to have someone, why can't it be someone nice like Miss Meadows?"

"I doubt that Miss Meadows would be interested in Papa. She isn't looking for a home, and she has her mother to take care of."

"Her mother isn't going to live forever."

"Don't let your dislike for Mrs. Stuart ruin your afternoon. Go make yourself pretty for Roy Taylor—or is it Thad you like?"

"I don't like either one of them. I'm going to marry a man like Mr. Johnson who's been someplace and done something important. Why are folks giving him the cold shoulder?"

"You noticed?"

"Sure. I may be just a kid, but I'm not dumb. Only one person spoke to him besides Miss Meadows."

"Who was that?"

"Old Mrs. Patrick."

"She was a friend of his mother's."

"The Birches don't like him and Mrs. Taylor said something silly like 'blood will tell,' whatever that means. Ruby's papa said, 'An apple don't fall far from the tree.' "

"Evan got blood from his mother, too. She was a nice person. Everyone liked her."

"Julie! Ya better come get Joy," Jason yelled in through the screen door.

"What's she doing?" Julie dried her hands on a towel.

"The little stinkpot's on Papa's car."

"She can't hurt it."

"She's . . . on the top!"

"Oh, my goodness." Julie hurried out the door.

A breeze came up in the middle of the afternoon just before the neighbors began to arrive for the ball game. Jason had put the base bags on the field and Jack and Joe had set the door that served as a picnic table on the sawhorses.

When a Ford coupe came up the lane, it was immediately recognized as belonging to Reverend Meadows. Jill let out a whoop.

"Miss Meadows is coming!" Jill was at the door of the car the instant it stopped. "I'm so glad you came."

Eudora got out of the car. Julie came from the house and greeted Eudora, then spoke to the reverend, who sat in the car with the motor running. "Can't you stay awhile?"

"Not today, Miss Jones. Mrs. Meadows and I will stay with Mother and give Eudora a little time to enjoy herself."

"We'll see to it that she gets home, Reverend."

"I'll appreciate it. Good-bye." The small car turned around in the barnyard and headed back down the lane.

Eudora was wearing a blue-checked gingham dress with a white collar. Just what a woman would wear to a picnic, nothing fancy. She was not one to put on "the dog," Julie mused, and she was able to fit into any situation. She could afford to dress as stylishly as any woman in town if she chose to. Her father had left her and her mother well provided for. They lived in a small neat house next door to the church parsonage.

"I'm so glad you came." Jill was so excited she was fairly dancing. Julie hoped that her exuberance would not be overpowering and make Eudora uncomfortable.

Sidney, dirty and stinking from a chase across the hog lot and with his fur full of cockleburs, waited at the porch step. When Eudora paused to pat his head, the dog's tail swung back and forth so hard his hind legs almost left the ground.

Julie led her guest through the kitchen to the front of the house and out to the porch swing. Jill came out with a couple of cardboard fans the furniture store had given out as advertising. She sat on the edge of the porch and proceeded to tell Eudora in detail about the neighborhood ball games, forgetting that last summer Eudora had been out when they played.

Jethro and Joe appeared, carrying a big heavy bench. Jethro was wearing his duck britches and a fresh shirt. He had shaved while Julie and the children were in church. He came to the porch and greeted Miss Meadows.

"Howdy, ma'am. I take it that was the preacher's car that turned around in the yard. I was just coming down from the loft. I'm sorry I missed him."

"Hello, Mr. Jones. Brother had to hurry back or he would have stayed to watch the game."

Jethro chuckled. "The Baptists frown on our Sunday games. At the revival last night the preacher said something about how folks who fail to keep the Sabbath holy will find themselves in the fiery furnace. I'm glad to know that the Methodists are a little more broad-minded."

"The Baptists get pretty radical at times, but they mean well."

Joy darted from around the house chasing the big red rooster. As she went to pass Joe, he caught her up in his arms.

"Come here, you little bugger! That rooster is goin' to turn on you one of these days and peck your legs good."

"He was eatin' . . . chicken do-do," Joy shouted as Joe held her above his head.

"Maybe he likes it."

"It's nasty! Put me down—" Joy's legs were churning up and down.

"I see Joy's drawers. I see Joy's drawers." Jack had appeared, carrying several baseballs and a couple of bats.

"I don't care," Joy shouted her favorite words. "Put me down—you old . . . poot!"

"Not till you promise to behave yourself."

"I'll bite you."

"I'll bite you back."

"Put her down, Joe." Julie had qualms about what Joy would say next.

The instant Joe stood Joy on her feet, she ran. He took a few steps after her. She shrieked and disappeared around the side of the house.

Julie noticed that her father was smiling. Her heart lifted. He loved his children, and she was sure that he wouldn't do anything to hurt them.

Jethro was still smiling when he said, "Boys, take the bench over to the shade so the ladies can watch the game." Then, to Miss Meadows, "That child is a handful. The older kids spoil her rotten."

"Little girls are supposed to be spoiled." Eudora laughed as if she were truly enjoying herself.

"Here come the Taylors." Jill flounced down the steps. "Joy," she called. "Sylvia's comin'."

Two wagonloads of Birches came next, and then came the Jacobses. The Humphreys were the last to arrive. Wilbur stopped the wagon in the lane beside the porch. Jethro went to help first Ruth Humphrey down, then Birdie Stuart. Ruth reached into the wagon bed for her two-year-old and Jethro lifted Mrs.

Stuart's girl down. The girl immediately grabbed her mother's skirts.

Ruth Humphrey wore an everyday dress that appeared to have gone through many washings, but Birdie looked as if she were headed for church or to a social event. Her dress was made of pink-flowered voile with rows of ruffles around the neck and on the bottom of the calf-length skirt. She wore white stockings and white shoes with small heels and pointed toes. Her hair was combed back and held with a flat ribbon on the top of her head. Strands of hair formed flat curls on her forehead and spit curls on her cheeks.

Julie had seen the style in *Collier's* magazine on very young girls. In her opinion Birdie was too old for such a hairstyle, but she promised herself that she would say nothing critical of the woman . . . today. She noticed that her father's eyes lingered on Birdie, who was laughing up at him in a flirtatious way. He was almost beaming as, his hand in the middle of her back, he ushered her to the porch. Julie's heart sank.

She was as sure as this was Sunday that her father was smitten with Birdie Stuart.

Determined to keep her anxiety to herself, Julie went to the end of the porch and called out to Ruth after Ruth had directed her redheaded twins to take their picnic basket to the table.

"Ruth, the children are out back playing on the swing."

The Humphrey girls took off around the house after a word from their mother. The Stuart child peeked around from behind her mother and shook her head when asked to go.

Jethro lingered until he saw that Birdie Stuart was seated on a chair on the porch before he went to join the men who were tossing the baseball back and forth.

The Humphreys didn't attend church often except when a revival meeting was in town. But Ruth knew Eudora Meadows and, after speaking to her, introduced her to her sister-in-law.

"How nice that you could come visit your brother and his

family," Eudora said after she was told that Birdie and Elsie had lived in such places as St. Charles, St. Louis and Memphis.

"Yes," Birdie said softly. "They've been wonderful to me and Elsie . . . in our sorrow." She smoothed the skirt of her dress out to keep it from wrinkling and listened while her daughter whispered in her ear.

"If you plan to be here for a while we would love to have you visit our Do Your Bit Club at the church. We do a little of everything, from making baby quilts to canning food for the poor."

"I'd like that, but . . . it's hard to get to town from way out here." Birdie sighed dramatically. Elsie whispered in her mother's ear again. Birdie whispered back. The whispered conversation between mother and daughter went on and on.

Julie glanced at Ruth to see how she was taking her sister-in-law's rude behavior. Poor Ruth. Her head was bent and she was busy pulling down the legs of the britches on the small boy on her lap. How long was she going to be able to put up with Birdie Stuart and her annoying child? Jill was right about this one. Julie could imagine what Elsie would be like when she was Jill's age.

"Do you have a lot of cucumbers this year, Ruth?" Iona Birch asked.

"Quite a few. I've put up thirty quarts of dill pickles."

"I've extras if you can use them."

"Thanks, but I'm saving my canning jars for green beans."

"I'm already canning beans," Myrtle Taylor said. "Haven't yours put out yet?"

"Oh, yes, the vines are loaded, but I've only got two hands." A slight tone of irritation tinged Ruth's voice. "The girls help pick and the twins have helped some, though they carry on about it being woman's work. Birdie is afraid she'll get a freckle if she goes out in the sun."

Julie's eyes shot to Birdie. She wasn't paying the slightest attention to the conversation going on around her. Her eyes were on the men getting ready to start the game. Evan was among them. Julie had not been aware that he had arrived. He must have come across the field on his horse and left it in the back lot. She looked back at Birdie and felt a sharp stab of foreboding.

The woman had to be terribly thick-skinned not to care about what Ruth was saying. She acted as if she were superior and far above the fray. She was polite and answered when spoken to but never made any overtures to be friendly with Julie or the other women.

She was strange and she was . . . awfully pretty.

Chapter 9

THE WOMEN, except for Ruth Humphrey and Iona Birch, moved from the porch and out under the oak tree to watch the game. Iona's baby was due in a few weeks. She settled herself in a chair with a cushion at her back and Ruth sat in the swing holding her sleeping child. Julie and Eudora occupied the bench with Birdie Stuart and Elsie, while the other women sat on the kitchen chairs.

The game started after a lot of joshing back and forth while choosing sides. During the first inning, Jack hit a home run. Joe hit a high ball caught by Thad Taylor, who let out a whoop and waved the ball at Joe. Evan hit a line drive. One of the Humphrey twins, it was hard to tell which one, tagged him out.

The game was played for the fun of it. When an eight-year-old hit the ball, Joe fumbled it to allow the boy to reach first base, then threw the ball that tagged him out on second.

Neither Jack nor Joe was on Jason's team and when he came up to bat, Jethro got into position to run for him. Jason hit a ball out into center field and Jethro barely made it to first base. Julie glanced over to see if Birdie was watching her father and saw that her eyes were on Evan in left field.

"Good hit, Jason," Eudora called.

The inning ended without Jethro making a score for Jason.

Evan came off the field and headed for the water cooler. Birdie, with Elsie in tow, left the bench and went to intercept him.

"She's not goin' to miss a chance, is she?" Grace Birch murmured to Myrtle Taylor.

"I hope she gets someone soon or poor Ruth will go to the crazy house. Imagine having her in the house day after day. I'd go mad and bite myself."

"That woman and Evan Johnson are two of a kind, if ya ask me."

"My Oscar thinks he's a good sort. Thad likes him, too."

"Myrtle, he couldn't be all right and be the son of Walter Johnson. I'm thinkin' he's a mite smarter than his pa and don't let folks see what he is."

Julie's ears were burning and she had to bite her lip to keep from butting into the conversation she was overhearing. She had to tell herself that the Birches had had rough dealings with Walter Johnson and hadn't taken the trouble to get to know his son. She glanced toward the water cooler, where Evan was handing the dipper to Birdie.

"It's a real treat watching you play ball." Birdie fanned herself with her handkerchief. "I just couldn't wait another minute for a drink of water." She drank daintily, then held the dipper for Elsie. After the girl took a sip of the water, she tossed out what water remained and handed the dipper back to Evan.

"I hope you'll be hungry after the game. I brought an extra custard pie for you."

"I'm sure that I will be." Evan drank thirstily from the dipper. He was letting it sink back in the crock when Joy ran up and grabbed him around the legs.

"Whoa, little sweetheart." He reached down and she grabbed his hand.

"Can I have a drink?"

"Sure." Evan brushed the damp hair back from the child's smiling face. He brought out a dipper half full of water from the crock and held it for Joy. She gobbled it, letting it run out her mouth and over her chin and onto her dress.

Elsie made a squeamish noise and wrinkled her nose.

"Swing me . . . pl-ease, pretty pl-ease—"

Evan laughed. "All right. Since you asked me so nicely."

He took hold of the small wrists and whirled around several times until Joy's feet left the ground. The little girl giggled happily and when she was on her feet, she grabbed him around the legs. Her pixie face grinned up at him.

"I like you."

"I'm glad, because I like you, too."

"When can I ride in your car?"

"We'll figure out a time."

"I gotta go tell Sylvie." She broke away and ran to the children playing on the swing, leaving Evan to wonder if the child ever walked.

"Poor little thing," Birdie said, her eyes following the little girl.

"Why do you say that?"

"I'm afraid she'll have a hard life."

"Why so?" Evan frowned.

"The child's mother died right after she was born. Julie is the only mother she has ever known and she . . . she won't be around much longer. She's . . . ah . . . well . . ." Birdie lowered her eyes.

"Go on, Mrs. Stuart. What are you trying to say?"

"I'm not saying anything that hasn't been said before. I'm repeating what's talked about by the neighbors. I've heard that she meets someone in the woods . . . someone from town that she doesn't want her father to know about."

Evan would have walked away, but he wanted to know just how far the woman would go to damage Julie's reputation.

"Everyone around here seems to know a lot about other folks' business."

"She's probably lonely and it's exciting to meet someone

that's reckless and . . . fast. The little girl will be the one to suffer when she leaves." Birdie had moved a step closer to Evan and lowered her voice to keep Elsie from hearing what she was saying. She looked up at him with round, sorrowful eyes.

"Are you telling me that Julie Jones is a loose woman? How would you know that, Mrs. Stuart?"

"I don't really *know.* I'm just telling you what appears to be common knowledge among the neighbors here and even the people in town."

Evan looked down at the woman, his face closed and tight. He had met her type before. He didn't believe a thing she had said. She was a conniving bitch. If she thought to win favor with him by slandering Julie Jones, she was barking up the wrong tree.

"Mrs. Stuart, I have only one thing to say to you. You'd be smart to refrain from making slanderous statements about Julie Jones or any other woman."

"They were not slanderous, Mr. Johnson. I'm not saying it's wrong for a woman to try to better her lot in life. I'm merely telling you what I heard the first week I was here. I feel sorry for the girl."

"Excuse me," he said abruptly

Birdie watched Evan walk away. It had irritated her to learn from one of the twins that Evan had brought Julie and the kids home from church. She had decided to plant a seed of doubt in his mind, in case he was interested in the farm girl.

She wasn't pleased with his reaction to her news about Julie, but she wasn't displeased. It would take a while for the facts to sink in and then he would realize that Julie wasn't a woman he'd want to introduce to his friends over in St. Joseph. Ruth and Wilbur were sure that he was here only to look after his interest in the farm and before fall he would return to the home his grandparents had left him. Birdie intended that she and Elsie would go with him.

The game ended. The winning team was the one that the

Humphrey twins and the Taylor boys were on. Jill and Ruby May, keeping score on a tablet, came in for a lot of teasing.

"How come my team never wins? Huh? Huh?" Jack asked, belligerently.

"'Cause you're a rotten player," Jill answered sassily.

"I bet ya cheated," he yelled.

"I didn't cheat, Jack. There it is on the tablet. You made four scores and that is all."

"I made five scores," Jack insisted to annoy his sister. "You didn't count one of my home runs. Were you watching Roy and Thad and missed it? I made five scores, didn't I, Ruby May?"

Ruby May, who had a terrible crush on Jack, didn't know what to say. She nodded numbly.

"Come on, Ruby May." Jill stomped her foot in angry frustration. "Next time my smart-aleck of a brother can keep score. Oh . . . he makes me soooo mad!"

Ruby May's heart was thumping wildly because Jack had winked at her.

Julie asked Joe to bring out to the front porch the big crock she usually used to soak pickles in. Today she had used it to make the lemonade. When he returned, Evan was with him carrying the tub of ice. Evan chipped the ice and dropped large chunks in the crock, leaving the small pieces for the children who stood waiting with their hands out. Julie brought out the sack of tin cups they used when feeding thrashers. Eudora filled them with lemonade and Joe carried them to the table.

When the food was laid out, Julie noticed that Birdie stood at the table behind her custard pie and dished it out when it was asked for. Her father had already taken a piece and had gone to join the other men, where Pete Birch was talking and gesturing.

"Booze is pretty easy to get down along the river. Somebody up in the hills is makin' a powerful white lightnin' and the marshal is lookin' the other way."

"Anybody had any trouble with Walter Johnson lately?" Oscar Taylor asked.

"I don't see much of him, thank God," Farley Jacobs said. I heard he was down at Well's Point the other night raising Cain. He got into a fight with that old river rat he hangs out with. I heard both came out with bloody noses. When they sober up, the fools forget that they were ever mad at each other."

"Does the new policeman cover Well's Point?"

"Hell, I don't know. He don't have enough sense to cover anythin', to my notion. He's touched in the head. Damn fool runs as if he was bein' chased but he ain't goin' nowhere but up the road and back. Can you beat that?"

"He was out by our place this mornin'," Wilbur Humphrey said. "Queerest sight I ever did see." He snorted. "A grown man running down the road."

"Thad met him in town the other night," Oscar Taylor remarked. "He said they visited a minute, and he told 'im he liked the town just fine. Thad thought he was all right."

"If the man ain't got nothin' to do but run up and down a road, I can't see they need to pay him for that."

"He turned around just above our place and headed back to town, runnin' like he's just knocked down a hornet's nest and they was after him."

"Might be he'll throw Walter in jail next time he gets to actin' up. That's if they got a jail to throw him in."

"They got one. It's downstairs at the courthouse. They've needed a jail. It's the one good thing the council's done that I can see."

"How long do ya think Evan's goin' to hang around?" Wilbur Humphrey asked, looking directly at Jethro.

"I've not heard him say."

"He hangs around here a bit, don't he?"

"Not much. Joe goes over there some. I don't understand what brought him back here but figure it's none of my business. He's good about helpin' out a neighbor when he can. He come over and fixed a fender on my car." Jethro stopped talking as Julie approached with a pitcher of lemonade to refill their cups.

"There's plenty of cake and pie left. Better come get second helpings."

"Think I'll do that." Jethro got to his feet.

Birdie was alone at the picnic table.

"Any more of that pie left?"

"There sure is." Birdie looked into his eyes and smiled. "I saved a big piece, just for you."

"I like hearin' you say it even if it ain't so."

"How do you know it's not so, Mr. Smarty Jones?" She let her lower lip protrude as if she were pouting.

"I just know, that's all." Jethro felt like a schoolboy each time he talked to her. She was the prettiest thing he'd seen in a long time. He hadn't realized how much he'd missed a woman's company until he met her. Jethro managed to croak out the words he was determined to ask before the afternoon was over. "Would, ah . . . you like to go to the picture show Saturday night?"

"How sweet of you to ask!" she gushed. "But . . . I don't know if I can. Ruth said something . . ." Birdie let her voice trail. "Can I let you know later? I've not been anywhere since I came here except here to the ball games and to the revival meeting. Gracious! That wasn't any fun. I'd like to go, Jethro, and I will—if I can."

Jethro saw the women coming back to the table and murmured, "Let me know."

"I will, Jethro. I sure will. It was so sweet of you to think about me."

Birdie lowered her head, pretending to be scraping a pan, so that she'd not have to talk to the women as they moved along the table selecting food for the children. She had no intention of hooking up with a man who had six children at home and especially not the father of Julie Jones. Birdie had taken an instant dislike to the girl that Ruth applauded for stepping into her mother's shoes and taking over the responsibility for her brothers and sisters.

Julie might know about cleaning, canning and slopping hogs, Birdie thought as she watched her. *She can prance around with the pitcher of lemonade, but she doesn't know squat about attracting a man or making kids mind. If I had that little four-year-old brat and that mouthy Jill for a few weeks, I'd teach them to act like ladies damn quick.*

Birdie continued to watch Julie with a critical eye. The dress she wore was limp as a rag. She'd attempted to brighten it with a white collar, which did nothing but make her face look all the more sun-browned and brought out the freckles on her nose. Didn't she know that buttermilk would remove them and lighten her skin?

Now that she thought about it, she didn't think that Julie was competition for her. A man like Evan who had left this god-forsaken place and seen some of the world wouldn't, couldn't, be interested in an ignorant farm girl who didn't know anything but how to wash clothes, can beans and put up chow-chow.

Lordy mercy! How long am I going to have to live in that awful house where Ruth lets her kids run wild, where there isn't an indoor toilet or electric lights and all there is to do all day long is work, work, work?

Birdie cautioned herself to be careful and keep her options open. If things didn't work out with Evan Johnson, she might have to settle for Jethro Jones . . . for a while. She'd have to take it a step at a time.

Birdie had been trying to save a piece of custard pie for Evan, but when she went to get lemonade for Elsie, one of the Taylor boys reached into the pie pan and took it. Birdie was furious but smart enough not to let it show. She wrapped the empty plates in a towel, put them in Ruth's picnic basket and went to sit on the porch swing. Evan was on the porch with

Joe and Thad Taylor, who was a year older than Joe but not quite as tall.

Joe asked Thad, "Have you met the new policeman?"

"Last night. He seems all right. We shot the breeze for a while. Roy and I went to town to see what was goin' on and to gawk at the girls."

"See anythin' interestin'?"

"Wanda Landry. She's the hottest thin' around . . . painted face, short skirt, bobbed hair, earrings down to her shoulders. She had red beads twisted around her neck that hung all the way to her knees. Her hair's red now."

"Wow! Did you talk to her?"

"A minute or two. She's too fast for me."

"The Hollingworths are havin' a dance when they finish their new barn. Why don't you ask Wanda to go? Bet she'd jump at the chance."

"She'd wear a dress up to her butt and cause a stampede. Hell, if I go to a dance I don't want to spend my time fightin' the yokels off her. I want to have some fun. You goin'?"

"Sure. Ever'body's invited. How about it, Evan? Want to go to a barn dance?"

"When?"

Evan was leaning against the porch post and thinking about moving out into the yard to put some distance between himself and Birdie, who was looking at him each time his eyes passed over her. Elsie, her daughter, was sitting so prim and proper in a chair while the other children were running and playing in the yard. The girl was a miniature of the mother. Pity the man who got the two of them.

"A week from Saturday night. Will said the barn would be ready by then."

"A barn dance?" Birdie leaned forward eagerly and clapped her hands. "How exciting! Oh, I'd love to go."

"Have you ever been to a barn dance, Mrs. Stuart?" Thad asked.

"No, but it sounds like fun!"

"If you've not been to one," Joe said, "you may not like it. Sometimes they get down and dirty."

"Down and dirty? What do you mean?"

"Ah . . ." Joe hesitated. "You tell her, Thad. You've been to more of them than I have."

"I don't know if I should."

"She needs to know, if she plans to go. It'd be a shock to her to get there and find out—"

"I guess you're right." Thad put his foot up on the porch and leaned his forearm on it. "Well, Mrs. Stuart, in this area everyone wears old clothes to a barn dance."

"I can understand that . . . in a barn, of course they'd not dress up."

"And they dance barefoot. Shoes are left at the door."

"Barefoot? Hummm . . . that's strange."

"Not so strange if you knew what they put on the floor to make it slick for dancing." Birdie was wide-eyed and interested. Thad continued in a serious voice. "City folk wouldn't understand this . . . but country folk like to get back to how things were done in the olden days. What do they call it, Joe?"

"Fiddle, I don't know. Old ways are born and bred in folks livin' around here. You'd better tell her, Thad."

"Mrs. Stuart, you need to know that fresh cow pies are brought in to slicken up the dance floor. Best ones are after the cows have fed on fresh green grass. Isn't that right, Joe?"

"You bet. Green grass makes the manure wetter—doesn't dry out so fast. It not only makes a better dance floor, but it's good for feet. Cures itching and scales between the toes."

"Why, I never heard of such a thing!" Birdie sputtered.

"It's true. Old-time doctors will tell you that fresh cow manure cures itchy feet," Thad said without hesitation. "My granny said so, and I read it in one of those old-time medical books. Sometimes, after a hard day, folks put it in a dishpan and soak their feet in it, that is if it's fresh and the cows have fed on fresh grass."

"I . . . I meant that I never heard of dancing in that . . . stuff."

"I'm not surprised." Thad nodded his head gravely. "Some of our traditions never leave this area. I don't suppose you ever heard about mixing the white on chicken droppings with a spoonful of sugar and taking it for lung congestion. Works like a charm, don't it, Joe?"

Joe nodded gravely. "Papa took it once. Saved his life, Mama said."

Thad continued, "Our ways are strange, I'll admit it. You know what we do to get rid of warts? Rub them with the hand of a corpse three mornings in a row. They'll vanish slick as a whistle. I swear it." Thad put his hand over his heart.

"A dead . . . person?" Birdie's eyes reflected her horror.

"Yup. Newly dead, if there's one handy. That's one of my granny's remedies. Hers were best. Another one that she swore by was that if a baby kissed a red rooster's behind before the age of one year, it would never have whooping cough. Folks in this area hold on to that one. That and slickin' up a dance floor with cow manure is right at the top of the list."

"That's . . . so nasty!" Birdie exclaimed.

"Maybe so," Joe said, "but it serves two purposes. Folks around here like to kill two birds with one stone."

No longer able to contain the laughter rumbling in his chest, Evan left the porch, walked quickly around the side of the house to the back porch and ran head-on into Julie. He grabbed her shoulders to keep her from toppling over.

"Sorry." He began to laugh. "Sorry, Julie."

A smile was spread charmingly on his usually serious face, rearranging his features until he was . . . handsome as sin.

"What's tickled your funny bone?"

His hands still gripped her shoulders. His eyes shone as he laughed. Julie couldn't take her eyes off his face.

"It's . . . that brother of yours and Thad Taylor. I'll tell you about it sometime. Lord, it's funny how they can spin a yarn." Then, realizing he was still holding on to her shoulders, he dropped his hands.

"Hey, Evan." Joe came down the side of the house. "Why'd ya run off?"

"How could you keep a straight face?"

Joe grinned broadly. "It wasn't easy. I don't think we'll have to worry about Queeny wantin' to go to the barn dance."

"Queeny? What in the world are you two talking about?" Julie asked.

"You're too young to know the ways of men of the world and how we have to connive to get along, little sis."

"Oh, you. The two of you have been up to something. I hope it wasn't anything to do with Eudora."

"No. No." Joe held up his hands, palms out. "Nothing to do with Miss Meadows. *She's* a nice lady."

"All right, then." She looked up at Evan. He was smiling into her eyes and tides of warmth washed over her. "I'm going to hold you to your promise to tell me later."

"You'll have to remind me."

"Don't worry about that." Her silly heart was fluttering like that of a caged wild bird. Her eyes refused to leave his face. "I don't like the pleased look on my brother's face. He's pulled a shenanigan. I know it."

"I never said a word. But I enjoyed every minute of it."

"You could have helped us out a little." Joe clapped Evan on the back.

"You were doing fine without any help from me."

"Thad was just getting warmed up when I left."

Still grinning, Evan shook his head. "I'd better get on home. Thanks, Julie, for the cake and lemonade."

When had he stopped calling her Miss Jones? Julie hoped that he didn't know how her insides were acting.

"'Bye, Evan." Julie's throat tightened as she said his name.

With a final smile, she walked away from the most pleasant few minutes of the afternoon, of the week . . . of a lifetime?

Joe and Evan headed for the back lot, where Evan had left his horse.

"Now Thad's telling her about the hog roast they'll have after the dance and that a prize is given to the one that can stuff the longest string of hog guts with mashed pumpkin." Joe could hardly contain his laughter. "He already told her about the horseshoe games they play with cow pies instead of horseshoes, and about the contest to catch the greased pig and twist its tail off. Thad can sure spin a windy story."

"You're no slouch yourself, Joe."

"I can't hold a candle to Thad. He used to have a big thing for Julie. I think he's got over it. She didn't give him any encouragement at all. They were in the same grade at school when Julie quit to take care of Ma and the rest of us."

"She doesn't get out much, does she?"

"She goes to town now and then and to church. She's tied down with the kids." Joe sighed with regret, then dug his hands down in his pockets and rocked back on his heels. "Back to Mrs. Stuart. Do you think she'll tell Wilbur?"

"Is he the kind to blow up if she does?" Evan settled the saddle on his horse's back and cinched it.

"Up to now I'd have said no. But she's his sister and she knows how to make herself pretty and helpless. I hope Pa don't find out about it. He'd be the one to blow up."

"He may be a little bit infatuated with her now. But it won't last. Your pa is too smart."

"Dammit, I hope you're right. Come over one night and we'll play a game of cards."

Evan nodded and put his heels to his horse.

Evan rocked gently in the saddle as the horse passed through the woods. His senses swarmed with details of the afternoon's events. He had only to close his eyes to see Julie's laughing face:

soft mouth, high cheekbones, magnificent light brown eyes. He drew in a deep breath, thinking that he could still smell the warm, woman scent of her.

She was not indifferent to him. He was almost sure of that.

A moment he would always remember was when little Joy looked up at him and said, *I like you.* The sincerity of the child's spontaneous words and the grin on her small face when she said them had been one of the most pleasant experiences of his life. Unknowingly, he smiled while thinking about it.

He had never known people like the Jones family. Poor but proud. Hardworking but fun-loving. They were loyal to each other and united in all things that mattered. Lord, he hoped that Jethro Jones came to his senses before he got more involved with Birdie Stuart. The woman could tear his family apart.

As he rode into the farmyard, Evan wondered if Julie had told her family about their date Saturday night. There were only two places they could go: the picture show or the dance at Spring Lake. How did she feel about being seen in public with the son of the notorious Walter Johnson?

Evan unsaddled his horse, wiped him down and turned him loose in the pasture. He was glad to see that the old nag Walter rode was not in the lot. He'd have the place to himself for a while. On the way to the house, Evan stopped in the middle of the yard and took a deep breath.

The scent of honeysuckle was in the air. A hummingbird was dipping its long beak into the blossoms on the bushes his mother had planted long ago. Evan looked up at the clear blue sky, then toward the pasture at the side of the house where the milch cow was grazing contentedly. The windmill creaked; the hogs rooted in the pen beside the barn; a chicken wandered to the edge of the porch, flapped its wings and pecked at something on the ground.

He loved this place. He wanted to raise a family here. He wanted to love and be loved here—and to be accepted by his neighbors as Evan Johnson and not known as Evan Johnson, son of the town drunk.

In the kitchen Evan looked around at the mess of dirty dishes and cooking pots on the table, the filthy clothes on the floor and the unmade foul-smelling cot. This was Walter's domain. He ate here, slept here, drank himself into a stupor here.

A vision flashed through Evan's mind of the neat kitchen at the Joneses' farm, filled with the aroma of fresh-baked bread, table set for the family meal, a girl with laughing eyes, hair hanging down her back, teasing with her brothers and sisters.

It was a glimpse of the kind of family life that had always eluded him.

An idea had been playing over and over in his mind since shortly after he came back to the farm: *How much money would it take to buy Walter out and get him off the farm, out of the county, out of his life?*

Evan heard the clang of the gate, then a curse. He went to the door. Walter had returned and he was drunker than a hoot-owl. Evan went up to his room. Now was not the time to offer to buy him out.

Chapter 10

JULIE, LOOK. I FOUND A BIG ONE." Jason held up a cucumber that was already turning yellow with age.

"It's too ripe, Jason. Throw it away."

After the breakfast dishes were cleared away, most mornings were spent in the garden. It was an everyday chore to pick beans and cucumbers. The root vegetables such as beets, potatoes and turnips would be ready by the time pickles were put up and the beans were canned. Then it would be time to shred the cabbage and pack it down in the crocks to make sauerkraut.

Julie had given Jill her choice of going to the garden or ironing yesterday's wash, which they had sprinkled with water the night before when they took the clothes off the line. Jill chose the ironing.

"I gotta pee-pee." Joy backed up to where Julie was searching the cucumber vines and turned around so her sister could unbutton the fold-down flap on the back of her drawers.

"Go squat down behind the bean vines where Jason won't see you." Julie gave the child a gentle push.

"He's seen me pee-pee."

"That was when you were little. Mind me and don't argue."

"I want to do it here."

Julie looked at the child with an exasperated frown. Joy was a stubborn child with a strong personality.

"You're asking for a spanking. I said go behind the bean vines. You're too big to be doing your business in front of Jason."

"I didn't ask for a spankin'," she said sassily.

When Julie reached for her, Joy darted out of the way, ran down the row a short distance and squatted down. She returned to stand a few feet away from Julie.

"You goin' to spank me?"

"Do you think you deserve spanking?"

"No. Jason didn't see me."

"He didn't see you because he was looking the other way. I told you to go behind the bean vines."

"I had to go . . . bad."

"Come here and let me button your drawers."

"You like me, Julie?"

"Of course I do, puddin', but I want other people to like you and they won't if you're sassy."

"Mr. Johnson likes me. He said so."

"When was this?" Julie finished with the buttons and pulled Joy's dress down.

"At the ball game. I like him."

"You do, huh?" Julie stood, straightened her aching back and looked down at the child. "When we get to the house, you're going to sit in a chair for an hour. If you had told me you had to go so bad, I'd have found a closer place for you to do it. Instead you were sassy and defiant."

"I wasn't de-fant."

"Defiant. Yes, you were. We'll talk about it later. Let's go in, Jason," Julie called. "I've got about all I can carry."

At the edge of the woods, on the rise behind the farm, a man with a pair of binoculars watched the garden. The little tad was growing like a weed. She was cute as a button. He chuckled when she turned her bare little butt up and squatted to pee. Lately he'd had an urge to see her. Why, he didn't know.

Hell, he'd not wanted to see any of the rest of them. Just knowing they were there had been enough.

He watched until the woman and the two kids disappeared in the house before he lowered the glasses and hung the strap over his shoulder. After looking carefully around, he retraced his steps back through the woods to the rocky path leading to the river.

Corbin Appleby left the rooming house on E Street where he had taken up residence in Mrs. Shamblin's upstairs room. It was a pleasant room across the front of the house giving him a view of the Courthouse Square. Dressed neatly in duck pants, a silver star pinned to his white shirt and a tan felt hat on his head, he walked quickly toward Sparky's Eatery, where he went every morning for breakfast.

Corbin had a lot on his mind this morning. He had not gone to bed until long after midnight. Then, as tired as he was, the events of the night had robbed him of his sleep. The same words floated through his mind over and over. *I was not wrong in coming here, I was not wrong in coming here. I was not—*

"Mornin'," Sparky called when Corbin entered the small eatery and hung his hat on one of the pegs along the wall.

"Mornin'." Corbin adjusted the gun belt around his slim hips before he straddled a stool at the counter. "It's goin' to be a scorcher today."

"Startin' out like it. What'll ya have, Chief? The woman's takin' out a fresh batch of biscuits."

"I'll have gravy with them."

Sparky was a thin man with a big, bald head and buck teeth. If a prize were to be given to the ugliest man Corbin had ever met and liked, Sparky would win hands down. But he was easygoing, intelligent and if there was one man in town whom Corbin could depend on to back him should he need it, that man would be Sparky. He slapped a heavy mug down on the counter and filled it with coffee from a granite pot with a cloth wrapped around the handle.

"Gonna want to take somethin' to your prisoner?"

"Yeah. Somethin' not over ten cents. The town will pay a quarter a day for his eats. I might have to come back for his supper."

"How about a few biscuits, a piece of sowbelly and a jar a coffee?"

"I doubt he can chew sowbelly. He was busted in the mouth last night."

"Fightin's taken serious down there at Well's Point."

"They can fight each other all they want, but when they start destroying property, I'll step in."

Sparky set a plate of biscuits and a bowl of steaming sausage gravy on the counter. Corbin put two split biscuits on his plate and covered them with the gravy.

"I heard he set fire to a boat. S'that right?"

"Among other things. Tell your wife these are damn good biscuits."

Corbin ate quickly, drank his coffee and placed a dime on the counter for his meal. He reached for the sack Sparky had prepared for his prisoner.

"Put this on a tab. If the judge don't let him out, I'll be back for his supper."

Corbin passed the hardware store on the way to the jail. A woman was sweeping dirt from the store out onto the sidewalk.

"Morning," she said with a shy smile.

"Morning." Corbin tipped his hat and walked on.

He had been surprised when he met Shirley Poole, the wife of Ron Poole, the owner of the store and a member of the town council. The two didn't seem to go together. Ron was a big, well-built man whom even Corbin considered rather handsome. His wife was small and shy, while he was large and seemed never to meet a stranger. Mrs. Poole was neat and had a pleasant way about her. Long ago, Corbin had given up on trying to figure out what attracted a man and a woman to each other, especially Ron and Shirley Poole.

Frank Adler was rolling down the awning in front of the drugstore when Corbin passed. They exchanged a greeting and Corbin crossed the street to the courthouse. He had a feeling that the druggist was watching him. At the door to the courthouse, he turned slightly to see the man standing in the doorway of his store staring at him and continuing to do so even with Corbin looking at him. Corbin thought about staring back, but decided that it would not be wise to irritate the man.

The prisoner was lying on the cot, his hands behind his head, when Corbin opened the door. He swung his feet off the cot and sat up.

"It's 'bout time. When do I get outta here?" he growled through puffed, split lips.

"That's up to the judge. I'll take you up to see him when he comes in."

"When's that gonna be?"

"In about an hour or so. Here's some breakfast. You've got water there and a towel. My advice is to use it and make yourself as presentable as possible before you see the judge."

"Why'd I take yore advice for? I'd not be here if not for you."

"You'd not be here if you hadn't set fire to the man's boat. I wouldn't care if you beat each other's brains out down there. The fire you set could have spread to the dock and destroyed a half dozen boats."

"I was goin' to cut it loose and let it drive downriver."

"That would have been smart. Were you wanting to set the woods on fire? I'm not going to argue with you. I brought you in, it's up to the judge how long you stay."

Corbin went out and locked the door. On the sidewalk he took out his pocket watch and glanced at it, then walked down the street to the telephone office.

"Morning, Mrs. Ham. Are you on day duty this week?"

Corbin had removed his hat when he came in the door. During the past week he had come to know and like the telephone operator. He had learned that her husband had been an officer in the infantry who had been killed in the Argonne Forest in France. Sergeant Alvin York, most decorated hero of the war, had been in his battalion.

"I'm just filling in for Gertrude. She's come down with something or the other. I hope it isn't that influenza starting up again."

"I'm with you on that. Is Mr. Brady in?"

"He's in his office. Go on back."

The mayor was standing when Corbin reached the door. "Morning, Chief. Come on in and have a seat."

Corbin took the chair in front of the desk and placed his hat on the floor beside him.

"How's things goin'?" the mayor asked and reached into a box on the desk. "Cigar?"

"No, thanks. I find they cut down my wind."

"I heard that you were out running the other day." Ira chuckled. "Folks around Fertile think it odd to see a grown man running. No one runs around here unless someone's chasing him or his pants are on fire."

"I started running in school and continued when I went to the army. It came in handy a time or two when I had to chase someone down. I can work off some of my frustrations by running."

"The job is frustrating you?"

"I've a few things I'd like to discuss if you've got the time."

"What's on your mind?"

"For one thing, I'm curious to know why Wood resents having a lawman in town."

"Has he been giving you trouble?"

"I guess you heard that I put Otto Bloom in jail. The man was drunk, beat hell out of his wife and hit her with a chunk of coal. Bloom was arrogant and sure that Wood would get him out—which he did. Mrs. Bloom refused to file charges against her husband. Instead of defending the man, you'd think that the banker would have fired him."

"Otto Bloom works on the ledgers in the bank. He and Wood are thick. However, they don't socialize outside the bank. It could be that Amos thought he'd not be able to get along without him."

"It could be that Wood doesn't want someone else handling the books."

"That's a thought. I've heard that there's a lot of bank fraud going on nowadays, not that anyone has complained about Wood's bank. He lost a few depositors when the other bank came to town. Ron Poole switched, but that was because he and Wood seldom see eye to eye on anything."

"Once a wife beater, always a wife beater. If Bloom beats that woman again, he might kill her. How will Wood feel about that? If I hear of Otto hurting her again, I'm putting him back in jail. I wanted you to be aware of it."

"It's what we're paying you for. Don't let Wood intimidate you. He's only one of five on the council."

"There's no danger of that. I'll do what I was hired to do."

Corbin studied the face of the man on the other side of the desk before he spoke again. "There was a rape down at Well's Point last night."

Ira Brady's mouth opened, then snapped shut. "Ah . . . law. I hate to hear that."

"I was looking around down there after we'd put out the boat fire, and a kid came up to me and said a man had hurt his sister. He wanted my gun because he was goin' to kill him. The kid was crying. He couldn't have been over ten years old. After talking to him for a while he finally took me to a shed where his sister was trying to get herself together before she went into the house."

"Did you get a name?"

"Holstead. The kids' mother is dead. Holstead hauls coal for the railroad. From what I gathered, the girl was scared her pa would find out and blame her for being out at night. She and the boy had heard the fight and had gone down, like a lot of other folks, to see what was going on.

"The way they explained it to me, the boy wandered off, leaving the girl alone. She said there were some other folks around and she hung back, not wanting them to see her and tell her pa she was there. A man—a big man, she said—put his hand over her nose and her mouth and dragged her backwards into the woods. He wrapped something around her head so she couldn't see and stuck the ends of it in her mouth to gag her."

"The . . . dirty son-of-a-bitch! Any man would seem big to a kid like that."

"He threw her on the ground and went inside of her. She didn't want to tell me that. Hell, she's just a fourteen- or fifteen-year-old kid. When he was finished, he turned her over on her stomach, took the cloth off her head and pushed her face down on the ground so she couldn't see him and said that if she told anyone, he'd find her and really hurt her.

"The poor kid was afraid to move for fear he'd come back. Finally she heard her brother calling her. She said she called out to him, but it was so dark it took him a while to find her."

"Did you talk to Holstead?"

"No. The girl begged me not to tell her pa or anyone. She was in a panic, and I figured she'd been through enough for one night. I asked her if she wanted to see the doctor. She got scared and began to cry and shake. All she wanted to do was get in the house and in bed before her pa came home."

Ira Brady leaned back in his swivel chair, rocked back and forth a time or two, then put his elbows on the desk and looked directly at Corbin.

"Doc Curtis told me that during the past five years or so there have been eight or ten young women that he's pretty sure have been raped. Only one came forward and told him outright. Others, he suspects, have ended up pregnant and were sent away to have their babies in secret. He's a reliable source in such matters because folks tell doctors things they don't tell anyone else."

"I'd like to talk to him. Do you think he'd tell me anything?"

"You can try. Doc is getting up in years. He's crotchety, but loyal to his patients. I don't think he'll name names."

"Think about this. It could be that this man has raped dozens of young girls and the only ones the doctor knows about are the ones he made pregnant."

"Doc won't talk about this. A woman would be ruined for life if word got out she had been raped. You're up against a stone wall. None of the girls that I've heard about have been . . . ah . . . hurt in any other way except for . . . you know . . ."

"Sooner or later he'll kill one of them. He'll do it if she finds out who he is," Corbin said quietly.

"I can see that he would." Ira leaned back in his chair and drummed his fingertips on the arm. "He knows that he'd be hanged, if not by the law, then by a lynch mob. What do you plan to do?"

"Keep my eyes and ears open. I'd like you to do the same."

"Of course I will. How are things going otherwise? Have you had any run-ins with Walter Johnson?"

"A few times. He's mean and mouthy and drunk most of the time when I see him."

"Could he be the one?"

"I'm not ruling out anyone at this point."

"Liquor is flowing pretty free down at Well's Point."

"Some of it's coming down from Canada, some more from stills in the hills and there are folks here making their own. Fertile is a river town. It would take an army of men to stop the bootlegging. Prohibition is a stupid law."

"Yes, but it is the law."

"It's the law for poor folks. You can bet the rich folks in

town have their booze. It flows like water in the speakeasies in Chicago and breeds men like Al Capone and his gang."

"Give it a few years and the law will be repealed."

"I hope so." Corbin pulled out his pocket watch, looked at it and got to his feet. "I'd better get my prisoner up to see Judge Murphy."

"Ron Poole tells me that your office and the new jail will be ready in a week or two."

"I'll be glad to have headquarters and a decent jail. Right now I have to let one prisoner out in order to put another prisoner in. Marshal Sanford will be here at the end of the week."

"Will you consult with him about the rape?"

"I've not decided. I don't have anything to go on except the girl's word, which I don't doubt for a minute. But the fewer people who know about this, the better. Marshal Sanford's deputy, Weaver, has a loose tongue. For some reason, he's got it in for Walter Johnson's son, who came here from St. Joseph."

"I've met Evan Johnson. He isn't what you'd expect, knowing his old man. He was an officer during the war and stayed for a while in France doing work for the government. I can't understand why he came here, except that the farm belonged to his mother and he wants to see that Walter doesn't run it into the ground."

"From what I heard, it's one of the more prosperous farms in the area."

"Walter may be a genuine asshole, but he's worked that farm."

Corbin grinned at the earthy expression that came from the dapper little mayor, then stooped and picked up his hat.

"I've met a few of the neighbors up that way. They spoke well of Evan Johnson. No one has a good word for his pa."

"It's always been that way around here. When I came here back in '14, he was about the same then as he is now. He's got an ironclad stomach and a hide like an elephant, or he'd have been dead long ago."

"I plan to buy a car," Corbin said, abruptly changing the subject. "What can I expect from the town in the way of expenses?"

"Wood would go up in smoke if it's suggested the town buy you a car."

"I'll buy it myself; but it's only fair that if I use it for city business, I have help with the expense of running it." Corbin spoke firmly, letting the mayor know that he would not be taken advantage of by a tight-fisted council. "I may be the only police chief in the state who has to buy his own car."

"I realize that. I'll see to it that you are provided with a license tag and gas money."

"Thanks." Corbin headed for the door, then turned to ask, "How many new businesses have come to town during the past five or six years?"

"New businesses? Let me see. The new bank, Star Mercantile, Sparky's Eatery, the automobile mechanic. There may be a few more that have come and gone. Most of the Main Street businesses were here before the war. Why do you ask?"

"Just curious."

"Fertile hasn't grown much, but hasn't lost much, either. The railroad helps to keep it going. It'll not die out, because it's the county seat."

"I'm glad to know that I'll not be out of a job anytime soon." He grinned. "Unless Wood fires me. Good day to you, Mayor."

"He'd have a hell of a time doing that by himself. Come in again, Appleby. I like to know what's going on."

Ira sat quietly after Corbin left. He heard the chief speaking to Mrs. Ham, then all he heard was the faint sound of her voice at the switchboard. Thinking over the conversation, Ira decided that there was more to the new police chief than he had first believed. He was definitely overqualified for the job of police chief of a town the size of Fertile.

Why had he come here? Who or what was he looking for?

Chapter 11

AFTER AN AFTERNOON of picking up rocks in a field that his father wanted to plant with winter wheat, Joe announced at the supper table that he and Jack were going over to help Evan pull down an old wamper-jawed lean-to shed.

"What's he doin' that for?" his father asked without looking up from his plate.

"So he can build a decent shed for his car."

"Then he's stayin' the winter?"

Joe's eyes caught Julie's before he answered. "He's not said anything about leaving."

During the quiet that followed, Julie put green beans on Joy's plate and buttered a square of corn bread for herself.

"You boys are getting pretty thick with Evan. Ain't he a mite old for you to be hangin' out with?" Jethro looked up briefly, letting his eyes pass over Joe and Jack, then back to his plate.

"We're not really hanging out with him, Pa. We've given him a little help now and then."

"When did we ever get any help from Walter Johnson?"

"You said yourself that Evan couldn't be blamed for his pa. I thought you liked Evan," Jack said. "Besides, he fixed the fenders on the car."

"I never said I didn't like him, but just 'cause he fixed the fenders don't mean I've got to kowtow to him." Jethro's voice was gruff. "Dammit, you should be chummin' with the Taylor or Humphrey boys, not with a man who's been over the mountain and around the bend. Ya don't know what kind of life he's led up to now."

"He learned a lot about motorcars while he was in France," Jack insisted. "He's going to show me and Joe how to put in spark plugs, change belts and—"

"He may know all that, but if he's so all-fired smart, what's he doin' on a two-bit farm when he could be livin' high on the hog in the city? Somethin' 'bout him don't ring true."

"Their farm is hardly two-bit," Jack mumbled.

It was the habit of the two older boys to keep silent when they didn't agree with their father on a matter. They did that now. Jill, however, had no qualms about giving her opinion at any time on any subject.

"Evan isn't like old Walter. He's nice as pie. He's been all over and done a lot of things. I like him. I hope I meet a man like him someday."

"What do you mean, 'done a lot of things'?" Jethro's eyes zeroed in on his next-to-eldest daughter.

"He's . . . been across the ocean, gone to stage shows and to fancy eatin' places. He saw girls doin' the cancan dance in Paris and he even rode on a streetcar. He's not just a . . . farmer." Jill, blissfully unaware that she had just expressed contempt for her father's occupation, continued to fork potatoes into her mouth. "Ouch!" she cried. "Who kicked me?"

Julie could tell that her usually mild-mannered father was angry . . . instantly, seethingly angry. He held his knife and fork clenched on each side of his plate. The muscle in his jaw twitched.

"You don't know horse hockey from apple butter, Miss High and Mighty. It's the labor of a *farmer* that puts the food in your mouth and the clothes on your back. It's the labor of a *farmer* that keeps a roof over your head and a quilt on your bed." The first words that left Jethro's mouth were equally spaced to give emphasis. The last words were rushed and shouted. He ended his declaration by pounding a fist on the table.

Jill looked as if she had been hit by a thunderbolt.

Jethro's outburst was so loud and so sudden that Joy began to cry, and Jason leaned closer to Julie.

Julie saw the stricken look on her young sister's face. She knew that Jill often spoke without thinking.

"Jill didn't mean that the way it came out, Papa. She wasn't—"

Jethro's frosty eyes turned to Julie. "Hush up!" he snarled. "This is between me and her. I'm tired of the know-it-all's smart mouth. She's got an opinion about ever'thin' and ever'body." He glared at Jill's crumbling face.

"I didn't mean . . . I didn't mean—"

"You don't know diddley-squat about how to scrape out a living or anythin' else. Everythin' you need is handed to you. It's about time you were taught to keep your mouth shut when you don't know what yo're talkin' about," he shouted. "Leave the table."

Never had their father been so harsh; never had he ordered one of his children to leave the table. They stared at him in astonishment. When Jill moved her chair back to obey, Joe and then Jack got to their feet. Jason followed the older boys. Jill ran up the stairs to her room and the boys went out the back door, leaving only Julie and Joy at the table with their father. Julie hugged the crying child to her, keeping her eyes on the top of Joy's head.

"Oh, hell!" Jethro's chair scraped the floor as he got to his feet. He stomped out of the kitchen, crossed the hall and went into his room, slamming the door behind him.

Julie was too numb to do anything but sit at the table holding the small girl. She stared at the uneaten food, the fresh green beans she had snapped and cooked with pieces of leftover ham and the small new potatoes. The platter was still full of the warm, neatly cut squares of corn bread. The gingerbread she had made for a special treat waited on the counter uncut.

Her father had been moody for the past couple of weeks. He had taken Eudora Meadows home after the game Sunday. Jill and Jason had ridden along, while Julie washed Joy and got her ready for bed. Jill reported that the only thing her father said to Eudora was you're welcome, when she said thank you after getting out of the car.

Was he in love with Birdie Stuart? Did he think that she would reject him because of his children? Julie wondered if he resented Evan because he was free to come and go as he pleased without the burden of a family. Evan was obviously better off financially than her father. Maybe he worried that Birdie was attracted to Evan.

Goodness gracious! If her father got it into his head to marry Birdie Stuart and bring her here, the family would be torn apart. She wanted him to be happy. He had been the best father a girl could have, and she could understand that maybe he was lonely for a woman to share his life. After all, kids grow up and leave the nest. *All but me,* Julie thought. *I've grown up and I'm still here.*

How was she going to tell her father that she had promised to go out with Evan on Saturday night? She wondered if he would be angry. On second thought, he might be glad that she and not Birdie would be with Evan. Finally Julie decided that she couldn't take a chance on another scene like the one tonight. She had to get to Joe and have him tell Evan that she couldn't go.

After putting a piece of warm buttered gingerbread on a plate for Joy, she went to the back porch. The boys were at the windmill, where Jack was pumping water into the conduit to fill the watering tanks. When she called out to Joe, he came to the porch.

"Whataya think got into Papa?" he asked.

"I don't know. He's been moody lately. Jill just said the wrong thing."

"The kid didn't mean it the way he took it. We all know

that she spouts off without thinkin'. I've never seen him blow up like that."

"Joe, I've not told anyone this, but when Evan was here the other night, he came out to the clothesline before he went home and asked me to go to the picture show with him this Saturday night."

"You've got a date with Evan? That's great. Don't worry about the kids, I'll be here."

"I can't go. You've got to tell him when you go over there."

"Ya can't go? Why?" The smile faded.

"I just can't. Papa may cause some . . . unpleasantness. I thought he liked Evan, but I guess he doesn't." Julie put her hand on her brother's arm. "Please, Joe. Tell him I can't go . . . that I'm sick or something."

"I'm not goin' to lie and say you're sick—"

"Of course not. I'm sorry I put it that way. Just tell him that I changed my mind and I don't want to go."

"Aren't you bein' hasty? This is only Thursday. Papa may cool off by Saturday."

"Tell him tonight. I don't want to be worryin' about it."

"Do you like Evan?" Joe asked bluntly.

"I don't know him very well, but he's . . . been nice."

"Were ya lookin' forward to goin'?"

"I guess so. He said we'd go to the picture show or to the dance, but—"

"Don't break the date, Julie. You've got a right to go out with anyone you want. Good Lord, you've been stuck here takin' care of the kids and the house and you deserve to do things like other girls. I'd bet my life that Evan would treat you with respect. I'd not let you go with him if I thought different."

"I'm not worried about that. I may be getting the cart before the horse. He didn't mention anything about it when he was here Sunday. He may have forgotten about it."

"Hold off until Saturday morning, Sis. If Pa hasn't cooled off and you still don't want to go, I'll ride over and tell him."

"I don't want to get dressed and have him not show up."

"He'll be here. But I'll do whatever you want if you'll wait until Saturday morning."

"I'll wait if you promise to go tell him not to come."

"I promise. I wouldn't want him to come over and catch Papa . . . like he was tonight. I've seen him get mad, but he's never been downright mean as he was to Jill."

"She'll be heartbroken that Papa talked to her like that. She says things without thinking. We all know it. I thought Papa did, too. He's got something on his mind, Joe. I've been thinking that he may be . . . really smitten with Birdie Stuart."

"I've thought the same. Lord, I hope he gets over it before he does somethin' foolish."

"Do you think he'd marry her?"

"She's lookin' for a place. She had her sights set on Evan. He saw through her right away. Maybe if she can't have him, she'll go after Papa. She's worn out her welcome at the Humphreys'. The kids don't get along with her kid. Mrs. Stuart complains to Wilbur that they pick on her. Mrs. Humphrey is cross as a bear. The boys said Mrs. Stuart is sweet as pie when Wilbur is around, and when their mother complains about her, he gets all mad and stomps away."

"Ruth's patience will run out. I wonder what will happen then."

"I'm done, Julie." Joy came out of the house and grabbed Julie's skirt. "Is Papa still mad?"

"He's not mad at you, honey. I'll come and wash you off. Joe, do you boys want to come back in and eat? Papa went to his room."

"I'm not hungry now. We'll take Jason along with us over to Evan's. He can ride with me on Blackjack."

"Keep your eye on him. I don't want him anywhere near Walter Johnson." Julie placed her hand on her brother's arm. "Promise?"

"Of course, I promise. We seldom see the old coot when we're over there. He steers clear of Evan."

"Come to the house before you leave. You might as well take along the pan of gingerbread."

On Friday morning the family was subdued when they gathered at the breakfast table, although their father acted as if nothing unusual had happened the night before. He talked with the boys about weaning the piglets and about clearing out some timber at the far corner of the farm and dragging it to the house to saw into firewood.

Jill's eyes were swollen from crying and Jason was strangely quiet. He kept looking at his father as if he hadn't known him before. Julie had let Joy sleep. During the meal she came downstairs in her nightgown and crawled up onto Jethro's lap.

"My little sleepyhead finally got up."

"Uh-huh." Joy's small hand stroked her father's cheek, feeling the rough whiskers. "You still mad at Jill, Papa?"

Julie held her breath and waited for her father to reply. He breathed deeply before he spoke.

"No, puddin'-pie," he said softly and kissed her forehead. "You better get over there on your stool so Papa can finish his breakfast."

Julie brought a wet cloth to the table and wiped Joy's face and hands before putting a spoonful of scrambled eggs on her plate. This was the papa they had always known, kind and gentle.

As soon as the men were out the door and headed for the barn, the resentment Jill had held in check erupted in a spate of words.

"I wish I didn't have to live here. I hate it. I hate *him*! He's mean and ugly. He doesn't care about us anymore. All he cares about is that floozy over at the Humphreys'. He wants to get in bed with her. Don't look so shocked, Julie. I'm not so dumb that I don't know about things like that. Ruby May said that men have got to have . . . *it* . . . or they get mean. He'll be sorry. I'll run away—"

"Jill Jones! Hush that talk right now."

"I take that back. He'd not be sorry, he'd be glad to be rid of the know-it-all he hates so much. I'm almost fifteen. I'll go someplace and get a job."

"Jill, honey, I know you're hurt. I was mad at Papa, too, for the way he talked to you. I bet he's sorry this morning. We all do and say things we don't mean."

"He meant it. He hates . . . me—" Sobs clogged Jill's throat.

Julie put her arms around her. "He doesn't hate you. The boys left the table when you did last night. You know that when Joe and Jack leave food, they're riled up. They'll not say so, but they love you. You're their little sister." Julie lifted the end of her apron and dried Jill's face. "Don't you dare go off and leave me here. I don't know what I'd do without you." Julie wrinkled her nose at her sister and hugged her one last time. "There's one good thing came out of what happened last night. We've got leftover food for dinner today."

"There's a watermelon out in the patch that's about ready," Jill said, wiping her eyes on the tail of her dress. "Let's put it in the tank to cool and cut it for supper."

Late in the morning a car came down the lane. Joy was first to see it and ran to Julie with the news.

"Julie, Julie, car comin'."

"All right, honey. Calm down."

Julie looked out the window to see a man in a white shirt and tan felt hat get out of an enclosed car that had stopped in the lane beside the front porch. She had never seen him or the car before. When he stepped up onto the porch, she opened the screen door and stepped outside.

"Hello."

"Ma'am." He immediately took off his hat, and she recognized him as the runner they had met on their way to church. He looked different with a hat on. Her eyes were drawn to the big silver star pinned to his shirt. This was the new lawman. Oh, my goodness, what was he doing here?

"Mrs. Jones?"

"Miss Jones. Our mother passed away several years ago."

"I'm sorry to hear it. I'm Chief Appleby."

"How do you do?" Julie extended her hand. His grip was firm as he shook her hand briefly. "We heard that Fertile had its own police. We saw you last Sunday . . . on the road."

"I remember." His smile crinkled the corners of his eyes. "You were on your way to town and I was having my weekly run."

"You do that every week?"

"Sometimes twice a week, if I can work it in. Strange, huh?"

Julie laughed. "Will you be insulted if I say . . . yeah, I think so?"

"Not at all." For a long moment he looked at her. Then he remembered why he had come here. "Is Joe Jones or Jack Jones here?"

"They're out with Papa clearing timber. They'll be here in a little while for the noon meal."

"Are they working very far from here? Could I walk out there?"

"It would be a rough walk through a nettle patch. You're welcome to come in and wait—that is, if you'll be able to endure Joy's curiosity." Julie put her hand on the child's head.

The man smiled down at the little girl, who grinned at him. Joy had never met a stranger.

"I can wait in the car, ma'am."

"No need of that. Come around to the back porch. It's shady there and I'll bring you a cool drink."

Joy took the man's hand. "I'll show you. What you got that pin on your shirt for? I like to run. Can I run with you sometime? We're goin' to have a watermelon for dinner. You can stay and have some."

He looked at Julie as if to ask, *What do I do now?*

Julie smiled. "You're on your own."

As soon as she turned back into the house, the smile faded from her face. What would a lawman want with Joe and Jack? She knew for a fact that neither one of them had been to town since a week ago Friday. Thank goodness Jill was upstairs or she would ask him a hundred questions.

Julie came out of the back of the house as Joy and the police chief came around the corner. The child was looking up at him and talking a mile a minute.

"Our dog's name's Sidney. Julie don't let him in the house when he's rolled in cow-do. He's nasty and he stinks. Do you have a little girl?"

Corbin saw Julie and reached for the cedar water bucket she carried.

"I'll get it, ma'am."

"Did Joy talk your arm off?"

"I picked up quite a bit of information about the family on the way around the house. Sylvia comes to the ball games, your dog's name is Sidney. He sometimes gets nasty, and Papa isn't mad at Jill."

"Oh, dear. I'm afraid to ask what else she told you."

"I like him, Julie." Joy's forefinger went up her nose and Julie hastily pulled it down.

Corbin went to the pump and Joy followed. Julie waited on the porch and opened the door when he returned with a full bucket of water.

"Put it here on the table and help yourself." She handed him the dipper.

"Good well water," he said after plunging the dipper into the cool water and drinking thirstily. He could smell and taste the sweet flavor that cedar wood gave to the water.

"We're partial to it."

"Whose car's out there?" Jill's voice reached the kitchen before she did. She came into the room and stopped.

"This is my sister, Jill. Mr. Appleby, the policeman from town."

"Her name's Justine," Joy said loudly. "But she don't like it."

"I can't say that I blame her. Jill is a much prettier name." Corbin smiled at the young girl. "I'll wait out on the porch, Miss Jones."

"Papa and the boys should be here anytime now. I can usually count on them not being late for a meal. Will you stay and eat with us, Mr. Appleby?"

"Oh, no, ma'am. I'd not put you out. I'm sorry I came at mealtime."

"You wouldn't be putting us out. We've having green beans, new potatoes and corn bread. Nothing fancy."

"Pl-ease! Julie made green-tomato pie," Joy coaxed with her head cocked to one side.

"I hate it," Jill said scathingly. "If you stay she might open a jar of pickled peaches."

The man's eyes were going from one girl to the other. Julie felt the heat of embarrassment on her face. Then she heard the sound of the men coming into the farmyard.

"Papa and the boys are here." She went out onto the back porch and Corbin followed.

As they watered the mules, the Jones men observed the stranger on the porch. They herded the animals into the fenced enclosure next to the barn, then came to the house.

Corbin stepped off the porch to meet them. He spoke to Jethro first.

"Mr. Jones, I'm Chief Appleby from Fertile." He held out his hand and Jethro took it.

"Howdy. These are my boys, Joe and Jack."

Corbin shook hands with each of them. "I stopped by to ask if you boys were at the Johnson farm Wednesday night."

"We were there," Joe spoke up quickly. "Something wrong over at Johnson's?"

"No. Not that I know of."

"We helped Evan pull down an old shed."

"I was there, too." Jason, with Sidney at his heels, came around the end of the porch.

"Yes, you were, you brat!" Joe picked him up and hung him in the crook of his arm like a gunnysack and rubbed his head with his knuckles.

"Put me down, you . . . you, pootknocker!"

"Watch what you say, brat, or I'll dump you in the horse trough."

"Stop horsin' around, Joe." Jethro had a worried look on his face. "Is Johnson in some sort of trouble?"

Corbin ignored the question and spoke to Joe. "Did you see Walter Johnson while you were there?"

"No, but he was there."

"I saw him," Jason said. "He was on the porch. Julie and Joe told me to stay away from him, so when he came out I ran to where Joe and Jack were working on the shed."

"How long did you stay?"

"We came home about an hour after dark."

"Was Walter still there?"

"The light was on in the kitchen. If he went anywhere he walked. His horse was in the barn."

"That's what his son said. I just wanted to verify that he was at home. Thank you—"

"Has there been trouble in town?" Jethro asked.

"The usual. Fights down at Well's Point and a boat set on fire."

"I'd be surprised if Walter wasn't mixed up in it."

"I guess he's in the clear this time."

"Why wouldn't you take Evan's word that he was home?" Joe asked. "He'd not lie about a thing like that."

"Mr. Corbin," Julie called before he could answer. "Jill has set another place at the table. You're welcome to stay and eat."

"Thank you, Miss Jones. That green-tomato pie is mighty tempting."

"Tell her you like pickled peaches," Jill called, then scooted into the house.

"Wash up there on the porch, Chief," Jethro said. "You're welcome to stay."

"Gol-ly," Jason exclaimed. "A real live lawman is goin' to eat dinner with us."

"All the lawmen who've eaten with us before were dead," Jack explained in a loud whisper and grabbed his younger brother by the back of the neck.

Chapter 12

CORBIN ENJOYED HIS DINNER more than any he'd had in a long time. He had not only been hungry for a home-cooked meal, but he found he genuinely liked every member of the Jones family. Jethro, the head of the family, was rather quiet. Jill, the younger daughter, was sulky, but the others made up for it with their constant friendly chatter.

"I tell you, that blasted mule dragged me and the plow all the way to the holler without breaking a sweat. The only thing that slowed the sucker down was the bog."

"I remember that, Joe." Jason reached across Joy for a piece of corn bread, only to have Julie lift the plate from under his hand and pass it to him.

"You ought to, you little pea brain. You started it all by coming out waving that blasted flag you got on the Fourth," Joe replied, grinning.

"That's not the worse thin' he ever did," Jack said gleefully. "Don't you remember when he threw rocks at that hornet's nest and knocked it to the ground? They took out after Pa and he had to dive in the horse tank."

"Hey, wait a minute," Julie spoke up. "Stop picking on Jason."

"We'd better stop it right here." Jethro passed the pickled

peaches to their guest. "The boys are windy when they've got a new listener," he said by way of apology.

"I'm enjoying it, and the meal."

Corbin liked the way Julie treated her brothers and sisters. She didn't prod or scold, but corrected the younger ones gently and without fuss. He tried not to stare at her, but she was just across the table and every time he looked up from his plate her face was within his view. She was pretty—not flashy pretty, but in a soft, natural way.

"We have baseball games on Sunday," Jason said. "One time I hit a ball that got Jack on third."

"That must have been some hit."

"Jack runs faster than I do."

"You're welcome to come to the games," Jethro said. "It would be a way of getting acquainted with some of the neighbors."

"Do you have to work on Sunday?" Jill asked.

"I'm on duty all the time, being the only lawman in town, but I can take time off if I let the telephone operator know where I am."

"We don't have a phone," Jill said and looked quickly at her father.

"They haven't run the lines out this way." Julie rose from the table. "If everyone is finished, I'll get the pie."

"Have you had many run-ins with the Johnsons?" Jethro asked in the silence that followed.

"With Walter Johnson a time or two. Nothing that amounted to much." Corbin's eyes followed Julie.

"You will. He's been trouble around here for the past twenty-five years."

"I was surprised to meet his son. He's nothing like his father."

"Yeah, well, who can tell?" Ending the subject, Jethro turned to his younger daughter. "Help your sister, Sis."

When the meal was over, Corbin thanked Julie before he left the kitchen.

"Best meal I've had in a while, ma'am. Thank you very much."

"You're welcome. We Joneses think it's best to stay on the good side of the law." She smiled and a dimple appeared in one cheek. "Not that we've got anything to hide," she added quickly.

Out on the porch, Jack, the one with the freckles, asked him why he liked to run.

Corbin explained that when he was a kid he helped his father chop wood and got used to exercise. When he went away to school, he was on the track team and discovered he liked to run.

"I want to play baseball with a big league. Do you think running would help me?"

"It wouldn't do any harm, that's sure. But you probably get more exercise working here on the farm than I get walking the streets of Fertile. Did you know that a league is coming to town for an exhibition game?"

"When?" Jack's eyes lit up.

"I'm not sure of the date. The advance man came though the first part of the week. In a few days they'll be putting up notices."

"Who's the league gonna play?"

"A team from right here in Fertile. Ron Poole is in charge of the team. Why don't you get in touch with him and try out? He's got a bunch of fellows together and they've been practicing a couple nights a week."

"Do you think I could?"

"You never know until you try."

After the lawman left, Joe and Jack came back into the kitchen to get a mason jar to hold water to take to the field. Julie went to the pantry to find a lid.

Julie had been proud of the family during the meal. For the most part they had used the manners she had tried to instill in them. Even Joy's exuberance hadn't risen to the high pitch it usually did when a stranger was present. Jill had been careful to not irritate her father who was as edgy this morning as an old tomcat with a burr under his tail.

Yeah, well. Who can tell?

Her father's words about Evan reverberated in her mind. He didn't like Evan! What was she going to do? She had to tell him by this time tomorrow that she had agreed to go out with Evan. Julie dreaded making the announcement and was anxious to get it over with.

The only bright spot on the horizon was Jack's excitement about the minor league baseball team coming to play in Fertile.

"Here's the lid. Wet that old piece of blanket on the porch and wrap it around the jar. Jack, you should go to town and talk to Mr. Poole at the hardware. Ask him to let you try out for the town team."

"That's what I been telling him."

"Will you go with me, Joe?"

"Sure. I'll even go to the game if you play," he teased.

"If you play, we'll all be there, proud as punch," Julie assured him.

She smiled fondly at her two brothers. Joe was the handsome one. Jack, less handsome and charming than his brother, needed to excel at something. Baseball was his love. She hoped that he would be allowed to play on the Fertile team.

"I'm going to town tonight with Evan," Joe announced. "Sissy-britches can come along and we'll stop and see Mr. Poole."

"Watch out who you're callin' sissy," Jack sputtered.

Surprised, Julie looked quickly at her brother, who avoided looking at her.

"You didn't tell me Evan was coming by."

"I didn't know until this morning. I met him out along the fence line. Guess he'd been riding down by the river."

"Papa?"

"Papa and Jack were up in the woods."

Jack's interest perked up. His eyes traveled from his brother to his sister.

"What's going on?"

"Nothin' you'd be interested in, ball-brain." Joe grinned and hit his brother on the shoulder.

"I would, too. What's goin' on?" he repeated.

"Julie thinks Papa has it in for Evan for some reason."

"He's jealous," Jack said quickly. "He's got a crush on Mrs. Stuart, and he's afraid Evan will beat his time with her."

"Well, what do you know, Sis? Our brother isn't so dumb after all," Joe exclaimed.

Julie looked around quickly to make sure the younger children were not in hearing range and cautioned her brother.

"Be careful what you say, Joe. Jason and Joy have big ears."

"And bigger mouths," Jack added.

"I hope Evan does beat his time with her. The Humphrey boys say that she's a pain in the butt. They can't wait to get her and her brat out of there. Why couldn't Papa like someone like Miss Meadows? She's a nice woman."

"You boys goin' to lollygag in there all day?" Jethro called from the yard.

"Comin'," Jack answered and went out the door.

Julie put her hand on Joe's arm. "Tell him tonight that I've changed my mind."

"Not until noon tomorrow," Joe said firmly and went out onto the porch.

Corbin was glad circumstances had forced him to stop at the Jones farm. When Ira Brady had given him a rundown on the families living on the farms surrounding the town, he had merely mentioned the Joneses as well as the Humphreys and the Birches. He had spoken at length about Walter Johnson, as had Marshal Sanford. Not much had been said about the son.

Evan Johnson was a surprise. Why would an educated, world-traveled man be satisfied to spend his time laboring on a Missouri farm? Corbin couldn't see that the father and son had a single thing in common. Or had they? He had the impression that Jethro Jones had his doubts about the son.

Corbin's thoughts lingered on Julie Jones as he parked the car in front of the telephone office. He had liked looking at her, liked her lack of pretension. She was a girl, yet she was a woman, too. He doubted that she was even aware that she was warm, pretty and fresh as a summer breeze. He wondered if she had a steady beau and how long she had been tied down taking care of that family.

Inside the telephone office, the mayor was talking to Frank Adler, the druggist, and old Doc Curtis. The doctor was stoop-shouldered, cantankerous and tired.

"Doc went down to see Mrs. Bloom's little boy this morning and says Mrs. Bloom has two black eyes. The woman was so crippled up she could hardly get up off her chair."

"There's nothing I can do if the woman won't file charges," Corbin said angrily. "I'd like to get that man of hers behind a barn somewhere and give him some of what he's been giving that woman."

"He's Wood's man," the druggist said quietly.

"What's the matter with Wood that he lets him get away with beating his wife?"

"I asked her why she stayed with him. She says she has no place to go." Doc threw up his hands.

"She'll be going to the cemetery if she isn't careful." Corbin wiped his brow with his handkerchief. There wasn't anything that riled him as much as a man beating a woman or a child.

"What's the matter with her boy?" Ira asked.

"I'm pretty sure it's diphtheria. I'm going back when I leave here. I came back to the office to get some antitoxin."

"Good Lord, Doc. Could we have an epidemic on our hands?"

"Could be several cases before it's done. Seldom have I seen a single case without others popping up." Doc Curtis shrugged.

"I'm putting a quarantine sign on the house." He went to the door. "By the way, I've got a young fellow coming in today or tomorrow. If he likes it here he might stay and give me a hand until I kick the bucket. Then he'll take over."

"I didn't know you wanted to retire, Doc," Frank said.

"I didn't say I was goin' to retire. I said I was going to get some help. By jinks damn," he snorted, "I'm not ready for the grave yet!"

The druggist followed Doc Curtis out, and Ira asked Corbin, "Find out anything at the Johnsons'?"

"Walter's son, Evan, and three of the Jones boys said he was home."

"Hell. I'da sworn it was him."

"I'm reasonably sure it wasn't him this time. I want to talk to Doc Curtis about it but not in front of Frank."

Corbin had his chance to talk to the doctor when he followed him down to the Blooms', where he tacked a red quarantine sign on the front of the house. Corbin stood in the yard with his foot on the edge of the porch and watched the doctor.

"How about Bloom?" he asked.

"If he goes into the house, he stays."

"I'd better go up to the bank and tell him."

"Good idea."

"Doc, a girl was attacked down by the river the other night."

Doc Curtis turned. His sharp eyes caught Corbin's. "Raped?"

"Yeah. She's about fifteen, I'd say."

"Son-of-a-bitch," Doc swore. "Who's the girl?"

"Holstead. Her father hauls coal for the railroad."

"I know her. Name escapes me—"

"Fern. She was really scared—said her father would blame her."

"Ignorant shit-head. Guess there's no chance that the girl will come to see me."

"None."

"I'll go by there today—talk about the diphtheria, and maybe she'll tell me something."

"He came on to her from behind, covered her eyes and her mouth and threw her to the ground. When he left, he took whatever he had used as a blindfold."

"It's the same. He's done it four times before . . . that I know of. No telling how many I don't know about."

"Four times that you know of? Gol-damn, Doc. How long has this been going on?"

"I suspected it . . . 'bout six years ago, but what the hell could I do about it? Pregnant girls hustled out of town and folks depending on me to keep my mouth shut."

"Do you reckon it's one man, or is this the horniest town in northern Missouri?"

"He likes 'em young . . . fifteen or sixteen. One was fourteen. None had a clue as to who he was."

"I'd no more than hit town when I heard of Walter Johnson. Could it be him?"

"Could be, but I doubt it. Walter isn't smart enough to get by with it all this time."

"Thanks for the chat, Doc. I'd better get up to the bank and tell Bloom about the quarantine."

During supper Joe casually mentioned that he was going into town with Evan and suggested Jack should come along and that they would go see if he could try out for the Fertile baseball team.

Julie held her breath when her father asked, "What'er ya goin' to town for?"

"Kick up my heels." Joe laughed. "I'm not a kid anymore, Pa."

"I forget about that, son. Look out for your brother."

"Can I go, Joe?" Jason spoke up.

"Not this time, birdbrain. We might play a few games of pool, and the billiard parlor is no place for a squirt like you."

"I'd wait in the car."

"Can I go, too? Ple-ase, Joe—" Joy smiled her sweetest smile.

"You're too little," Jason said with disgust.

"So are you, so there!" Joy stuck her tongue out at Jason.

"Julie," Jill wailed. "That's disgusting! She's got food in her mouth."

"Who would like a slice of watermelon?"

When the meal was over, Julie desperately wanted to be finished with the cleanup and be upstairs when Evan came to pick up Joe and Jack. She went to the porch to call Jason to come take the watermelon rinds to the hogs and heard the sound of his car coming down the lane. It rounded the side of the house and he was looking directly at her. She managed a wave before darting back into the house.

"Can you finish here, Jill? I'm going upstairs for a minute."

"I know what you're up to. You don't want Evan to see you in that faded old dress."

"Oh, hush," Julie said irritably. She closed the door to the stairs, something they seldom did in the summer, and hurried up the steps to the room where she could look down on the yard behind the house.

Evan wore khaki pants, left over from his army days, and a blue shirt. His blond hair was combed back. He was neat as always. Now he was talking earnestly to Jason while Jack and Joe stood by. Joy came running and screeching from the barn. She ran straight to Evan. He scooped her up, unmindful or unknowing that she'd been playing in the dirt.

Julie grimaced to think of Evan's clean shirt being soiled. Joy wrapped her arms around his neck and planted a kiss on his cheek.

Joe tried to peel Joy from Evan. Evan laughed and turned away, much to Joy's delight. Julie's glance caught her father standing in the doorway of the chicken house watching the horseplay. He hadn't come forward to greet Evan. Julie turned her eyes away; and when she looked back, he had gone inside.

Julie watched until Evan carried Joy to the porch and set her down. Jason went to take her hand and held her there until the car had turned around in the farmyard and started back up the lane.

In the room she shared with Joy, Julie sat down on the edge of the bed and pressed her palm to her chest. Her heart was beating like a drum. If she had just refused the invitation the night he asked her to go out with him, she wouldn't be in this dilemma. She had hardly slept a wink that night. Her mind had gone over each word he'd said from the minute she had looked up from licking the fudge knife and had seen him watching her.

Then on Sunday, when they had met at the side of the house and he had put his hands on her shoulders to steady her, she had been thrilled to the center of her being. Thinking about it now, could she go against her father's wishes if he forbade her to go out with Evan?

Oh, Lord. She hoped she wouldn't be forced to make that decision.

Julie was in bed but not asleep when the car came down the lane and stopped beside the back porch. She heard male voices, then the car doors slam. The car lights momentarily lit the bedroom as Evan turned it around and started back down the lane. Joe and Jack came up the stairs to their room.

Soon all was quiet.

"We're closing down, Walter. Go on home."

"I ain't ready to go." Walter chalked the end of his pool cue and lined up a shot on the table.

"It's twenty minutes past closing time."

"Then close up an' go on. I ain't stoppin' ya."

The proprietor of the billiard parlor looked at the glass clock, the hanging lamp with the stained-glass shade and the pool cue in the hand of a dangerous, unpredictable man and sighed.

"I'll wait until you finish the game."

Harvey Knapp had come to Fertile five years before and

opened Knapp's Billiard Parlor. In the years he had been here, the only trouble he'd had had been with Walter Johnson. He tried to run a good, clean place where men could come in, shoot a game of pool and have a drink of near beer without a hassle.

"I want a beer."

"Can't do it, Walter. I can't sell beer after midnight."

"Who says?"

"The town council says."

"And ya kowtow to 'em?"

"It's the law."

"I ain't askin' to *buy* one." Walter took a bottle from the bib of his overalls and drank several big gulps.

"It's closing time, Walter. I've been here since noon today and I'm tired. I want to close up and go home."

"Ya got pussy waitin' at home?" Walter asked casually and shot a ball that went into a pocket.

"I don't like that kind of talk." Harvey's face reddened with anger.

"I ain't carin' if ya like it. I seen yore woman. She's got a old pussy—all stretched outta shape. I like young, tight pussies. Ain't ya ever had a hankerin' for a young, tight puss, Harvey?"

"Get out of here, you nasty-minded pervert!"

"Well, la-di-da. Ain't nothin' nasty 'bout pussy."

Harvey went to the phone in the back of the parlor, picked up the earpiece and twisted the crank to ring for central.

"I heared that s-some folks what calls in the law on other folks s-sometimes gets their house burnt down. Ss—right, ain't hit, Harvey?" His words were becoming slurred.

The threat registered slowly. Fear for his family held Harvey silent when the operator answered.

"Number, please." Then: "This is the operator. Is someone on the line? Is that you, Mr. Knapp?"

"I'm sorry. I rang by mistake."

Harvey slowly hung up the receiver and, ignoring Walter,

walked to the front of the building and opened the door. He stood breathing in the warm night air. Lights were off in every store building along Main Street. Not a car was in sight. Harvey stood there with his hands in his pockets, wondering what to do.

He'd had small problems with the town bully, but Johnson had never threatened him before. This was the first time he'd ever been alone with the man, and the nasty talk about his wife had almost caused him to do something foolish.

Harvey was about to turn and go back into the parlor when he saw the police chief come around the corner, checking doors as he did each night. Harvey glanced nervously over his shoulder. Walter was still at the pool table.

"Isn't it late for you to be open, Mr. Knapp?"

"Well, yes. I have a customer who wanted to finish his game."

Corbin glanced inside. "Evening, Mr. Johnson."

"Howdy-do." Walter didn't look up.

"I'll be getting along. Evening to you, Mr. Knapp." Corbin winked as he passed Harvey.

"Evening, Chief."

Harvey lingered at the door long enough to see Corbin step into the recessed doorway of the building next door before he went back into the parlor. Walter had put his cue stick in the rack and was walking with his feet spread wide to keep his balance.

"I'm gone," he said as he passed Harvey and went out the door.

Harvey breathed a sigh of relief and quickly turned off the lights. He looked up and down the street for a sign of Walter Johnson before he stepped out onto the sidewalk and locked the door.

Chief Appleby appeared swiftly and silently. Harvey jumped sideways.

"Lord, Chief, you scared me."

"Having trouble with Johnson?"

"The man's no good to himself or anyone else." Harvey put his keys in his pocket. "He said folks that call the law get their houses burnt down." He wiped his forehead with his handkerchief. "Can't something be done about him?"

"Not until he does something I can jail him for."

"He was drunk as a skunk, but he holds his liquor."

"He's conditioned to it."

"I'd like to smear his nasty mouth all over his face."

"Talkin' nasty, was he?"

"Real nasty."

"I'll see that he leaves town. I saw his horse down by the depot and knew that he was around someplace. Good night, Mr. Knapp."

Chapter 13

JULIE COOKED BREAKFAST FOR HER FATHER, Joe and Jack. They planned to cut down a large oak tree that had been split by lightning the summer before. They would drag the huge logs up behind the barn. Then, with a two-man saw, they would cut them into lengths suitable for the cookstove and the Acme heater but would wait until cold weather to split and stack them close to the house.

Joe and Jack took turns milking. This morning it was Joe who brought in the pail of fresh milk, set it on the bench on the porch and stuck his head in the kitchen door.

"When I take this to the cellar do you want me to bring up last night's milking?"

"Yes, please. And Joe, cover it tightly. Yesterday I found a fly floating on top."

"You're too fussy. Flies don't eat much."

Joe avoided looking at his sister during the meal and was careful not to be left alone with her. Julie wanted to kick him. He must have known how anxious she was to hear if Evan had said anything about taking her out tonight. Maybe he'd forgotten about it! Oh, Lord, how humiliating it would be if she got dressed to go and he didn't show up.

The talk during breakfast was about Jack going to town to try out for the Fertile baseball team.

"If you can't play better than that stuck-up bird from the Carwilde and Graham Department Store, I'll disown you as a brother," Joe teased.

"Scott Graham plays baseball?" Julie asked. "In his high starched collar?"

"I guess so. I've not seen him without it. They must be pretty hard up for players. I bet Jason could make the team."

"Why don't you try out?" Julie asked and removed Joe's empty plate.

"I don't want to show up my little brother. They'd be sure to take me and leave him bawling on the bench. Come on, Babe Ruth"—he swatted Jack with his hat—"let's go get Pa's tree cut down."

While she was waiting for the younger kids to get up, Julie dipped water from the rain barrel and washed her hair. She told herself that washing it had nothing to do with whether or not she was going out with Evan Johnson. She usually washed it on Saturday.

Last night, while she waited for Joe and Jack to come home, she had thought that if she did go—and it was a big if—she would wear her blue scoop-necked dress with the puffed sleeves. It would probably need washing and ironing.

Julie sat down on the edge of the porch in the sun and toweled her hair. She bent over and with it hanging from the top of her head ran her fingers though it, then raked it with the big-toothed comb. The sun felt warm on her back. *When I finish here,* she thought, *I'll wash the voile dress and hang it on the line. Jill will think I'm getting it ready for church.*

"Let me do that."

The male voice and the comb suddenly taken from her hand startled Julie so much that she jumped to her feet, her forearm scooping her hair back from her face.

"Evan! You . . . scared me."

"I didn't mean to frighten you. I thought you heard me ride up." His next words were whispered as if to himself. "Your hair is beautiful. It looks like a ripe wheat field." He stood holding the comb awkwardly.

"Thank you."

The silence stretched. Julie felt a knot of anxiety forming in her stomach. *Say something, you nitwit,* she told herself. She tried to smile, but her smile faded as the seconds ticked by and as Evan, looking at her as if he'd not seen her before, said absolutely nothing.

"I didn't . . . know anyone was . . . around," she stammered. She had to tilt her head to look up at him.

"I left my horse there beside the barn."

Julie's eyes darted to the horse, then back to Evan.

"I didn't hear you ride up. Papa and the boys are down by the creek."

He reached out, almost as if he couldn't help himself, and ran the comb through the ends of long dark-blond hair hanging on her arm.

"There's an awful lot of it. Are you going to cut it into a flapper bob, shingled in the back like a man's?"

"Why do you think I'd do that?" Julie lifted her hand and threw the strands back over her shoulder.

"I don't know. Women in the cities and some here are cutting their hair."

"It would be easier to take care of if it was short. It's so long and thick, it takes a while for it to dry."

"I hope you don't cut it."

Evan didn't understand himself. He had talked to rich women, poor women, slutty women and nuns. Why was he so tongue-tied around this sweet, innocent farm girl? He had convinced himself that when he had asked her to go out tonight, it was because he had felt sorry for her being tied down taking care of the family and only wanted to show her a good time, talk to her. Hell, he not only wanted to talk to her, he wanted to hold her in his arms, kiss her all over and feel her arms curl around his neck in sweet surrender.

He had never been so enamored, so completely captivated by a woman before. It was scary as hell.

"You've not forgotten about tonight?" he asked hesitantly.

Their eyes held for a timeless moment. What Julie saw in the blue depth of his gaze barely registered with her. Later she was to decide that it was loneliness, fear of rejection.

"Well . . . you see, I was going to . . ." Her voice trailed off and she became lost in the anxious look she saw on his face.

"Yes? You were going to what?"

"I wasn't sure if you were . . . serious . . . about it."

"Of course I was serious. Oh, yes, I almost forgot. I've a note for Jethro. One of the Humphrey boys was coming down the lane when I went past their place and said that it would save him a trip if I would stop and give this to Jethro." He took a small envelope from his pocket and held it out.

Julie felt a quick stab of anxiety and shook her head. "You'd better give it to him. It must be from—"

"Mrs. Stuart?" He held the letter to his nose. "I was thinking that it was. I doubt that Mr. or Mrs. Humphrey would send him a letter that smelled like rose petals." He put it back in his shirt pocket. "I'll take it to him. I'll be here at seven-thirty. Is that all right?"

"I'll be ready."

Julie watched him walk back to his horse, mount and ride toward the creek. The note to her father from Birdie Stuart had decided for her that she would go out with Evan whether her father liked him or not. She couldn't understand why a sensible man like her father would be interested in a feather-head like Birdie Stuart. But if he had a right to choose his friends, so did she. She was an adult. She would go out with Evan, and if her father pouted and sulked . . . so be it.

The morning went fast. Julie put a pot of vegetables on for the noon meal: cabbage, onions, new potatoes and carrots. She seasoned the vegetables with slices of ham from the smokehouse.

The sun was directly overhead when the men washed on the porch and trooped into the kitchen. Joe and Jack were rowdy, as usual.

"Joy can lift as much as you can, sissy boy." Joe constantly teased Jack. Jack took the teasing good-naturedly and gave back as good as he got.

"Hush up . . . pea-brain. He made sure I got the heavy end of the log, didn't he, Pa? He thinks he's so all-fired smart."

"Yeah, and you held up your end." Jethro was smiling.

"I *am* smart, boy. I've got something up here besides hot air." Joe tapped on his temple with a forefinger.

"Yeah, Jack," Jason chimed in. "They'll be glad to have you on the Fertile team. You're the best player . . . in the whole town."

Jethro laughed again. "He's good, but that might be stretchin' it a bit, son." He ruffled Jason's hair. "It's good that you're loyal to your brother."

Julie glanced at her father and away. A change had come over him since morning. Gone was the grumpy mood that had been on him for days. Was the note from Mrs. Stuart the cause of his good humor? Julie was determined to tell him before he and the boys went back to the field that she was going to the picture show with Evan . . . and she didn't much care if he liked it or not.

Jill had been subdued and moody since their father had ordered her from the table. In Jethro's good mood, Julie hoped that he would tease her a little, put his arm across her shoulders and maybe even hug her as he used to do.

He did. When the meal was over, Jethro lingered in the kitchen when the boys went to the porch. He threw his arm around Jill as she passed him on her way to get a cloth to wash Joy's face.

"How's my pretty girl? The first thing I know, I'm going to have two grown-up daughters."

Shocked, Jill looked up at him, then grinned and leaned her head against him for a moment.

"Ah . . . Papa . . ."

Julie was watching, hoping to have a minute alone with her father.

"Evan tells me that he's taking you to the picture show tonight," Jethro said, smiling at Julie.

"Ah . . . yes. He asked me a week ago." Julie was so surprised she could hardly speak.

"I'm going out tonight myself. Joe wants to go to town with Jack when he tries out for the ball team, but he said they would be back before dark. Will you be all right with the kids until then, pretty girl?" His arm tightened around Jill's shoulders.

"Sure," she said and moved away to grab Joy before she scrambled out the door. Jethro failed to see the smile fade from Jill's face and the anxious glance she sent her sister.

Jethro went to the porch and called to the boys.

Jill wiped Joy's face and hands. As soon as the child was out the door, she returned to the table, put her head on her arms and burst into tears.

Julie stood by helplessly. She was still in shock from her father's announcement that Evan had told him he was taking her out, shocked more that he appeared to have no objection. Mrs. Stuart was the reason for his good mood. Jill knew it, too. Julie went to her sister and put her hand on her shoulder.

"Ah, honey. Don't cry."

"Nothing will be the same . . . now," Jill sobbed. "He'll marry her and bring her here. It'll be her house and we'll have to jump every time she hollers."

"I don't think that she would marry him even if he wanted her to. She wants something more than a man with six children all at home."

"She'll get rid of you, Joe and Jack, and there'll only be three of us left for her to boss around."

"Papa needs the boys to help him. He couldn't do all the work by himself and Jason isn't big enough to help."

Jill looked up with teary eyes. "I'm trying not to hate him."

"Oh, honey. Don't say that."

"Why didn't you tell me Evan had asked you to go out with him?"

"I hadn't planned to go. I didn't think Papa liked him, and I didn't want to create a fuss here at home."

"But . . . now you're going?"

"Yes. Do you mind staying with Joy and Jason until Joe comes home?"

"Papa's relieved that Evan wants to take you out and not *her.*"

"We don't know that. Evan might take her out next time."

"He doesn't like her. He saw through her right away. Papa is too . . . dumb to see that she's nothing but a . . . a put-on."

"What a thing to say. Papa is not dumb!"

"He is where women are concerned or he would have liked Miss Meadows."

"Eudora Meadows may not have liked him . . . in that way."

"Are you going to marry Evan and move away?"

"For goodness' sake! I'm just going to the picture show with him."

"Don't leave us with . . . her, Julie." Jill wrapped her arms around her sister's waist and hugged her.

"Jill, honey, you're upset over something that probably will never happen."

"I can't help it. I just know Papa's changed since that *Birdie* woman came. Do you think he's in love with her?"

"I don't know. Mama's been gone almost four years. Papa is only forty-two. Some men don't even marry until they are that age."

"It isn't that I don't want him to have someone. Someday we'll all be gone. I just don't want it to be *her.*"

For Julie the suspicion that their father was going out with

Birdie Stuart dulled the anticipation of her date with Evan. Still, at times she was so excited she could hardly think. What would she say to him? He had been to college and to war. He'd traveled in Europe. She had not been more than fifty miles from home and had not even been able to finish high school. What in the world would they talk about?

Supper was hot buttered corn bread covered with cream gravy or crumbled in sweet milk. Jack and Joe were in a hurry to eat and left for town as soon as they finished. When Jethro got up from the table, he picked up the teakettle, which was sending a plume of steam from its spout.

"If you have enough hot water in the reservoir for dishes, I'll take this out to the barn."

Julie nodded and watched him go out the door. The men bathed in the barn in the summer, and no doubt he wanted to take the chill off the well water.

"See there?" Jill said as soon as their father left the porch. "He's going to get all spruced up for *her.* He'd better not ask me to iron his good shirt."

"He won't. It's ironed and hanging in his room."

"He knows we don't like her. Nobody does. It would serve him right if she takes that whiny kid with her."

"Shame on you."

"If I'm so bad, why are you smiling?" Jill asked and giggled.

"Will you give Joy a bath while I'm gone?"

"I'll wash her good, but I'm not putting that wiggle-wart in the tub. What time is Evan coming?"

"In about an hour."

"Then we'd better get a move on. I'm glad you're goin' out with Evan. I think he's nice even if he is related to old Walter."

"Oh, gosh." Julie had a stricken look on her face. "You and the kids will be here alone for a couple of hours. If Walter Johnson or any man you don't know comes on the place, you take the kids and hide in that hidey-hole off the boys' room. Understand?"

"I understand. But old Mr. Johnson never comes here."

"I'm just saying if he does."

"Why are you so jumpy all of a sudden about Mr. Johnson?"

"I just know that he isn't a very nice man. I doubt that he would come here. He won't know that you kids are here alone. Joe said that he would be back before it's completely dark and Joe usually does what he says he'll do."

"I'd like to be a little bird and go along with you and Evan. Are you going to let him kiss you?" Jill's eyes sparkled.

Julie's face turned a dull red.

"What a thing to say! I'll swear to goodness, Jill. At times you are the limit."

"I'd let him kiss me. He'll probably never want to, but if he did, I'd let him."

"Jill Jones, you are scaring me!"

"Scaring you? Why?"

"I don't want you to grow up to be . . . fast."

"Fast? This is 1922, Julie. Ruby May has already kissed two boys. I've not kissed any yet."

"Yet? You plan to kiss boys?"

"Sure, if they want to."

"Good Lord. What have I been doing wrong?"

"Oh, Julie. I'm teasing. You've done nothing wrong. You're the best sister in the world. I'd rather have you for a sister than old Mrs. Yerby or *Birdie*!"

Julie laughed. "If that's a compliment, I'm flattered . . . I think."

Julie took her time dressing. After she washed herself from head to toe in the wash pan she had taken up to the room she shared with Joy, she put on her clean underclothes, then her dress. She took down her hair and brushed it. Evan had said her hair was pretty. The thought popped in her mind as she twisted it in a rope and fastened it in a long roll to the back of her head with her big celluloid hairpins. Keeping it loose, she had parted it in the middle, allowing it to dip down on each side of the part. Using the hand mirror, she inspected the back.

Satisfied she had done the best she could, she dabbed a little toilet water on her neck. Then, as an afterthought, she looped the blue beads Joe had brought her from St. Joseph around her neck.

It was hard for her to believe that she was dressing to go out alone with a man. This was her first date. What would Evan think if he knew that no boy or man had ever asked her out before?

Oh, Lord. Don't let me make a fool of myself.

Chapter 14

AFTER HE HAD FINISHED WORK FOR THE DAY, Evan bathed in the tub of water he had drawn that morning and left sitting in the sun beside the new shed he was building. Walter, of course, had something derisive to say when he came by to see Evan immersed in the tub.

"What ya doin' that fer? Goin' to the Joneses or to see that stuck-up bitch at the Humphreys'?" When Evan ignored him, he continued, "Women ain't carin' if a man stinks as long as he's got a good thick stick 'tween his legs." He waited for Evan to say something. When he remained silent, Walter went on as if determined to get a rise out of him. "Bet yo're goin' to the Joneses. That's where I'd go if I was cravin' puss. Which one ya got yore eye on? Ya can have the old one. Leave that young one be."

At that, Evan's temper flared.

"You rotten old son-of-a-bitch! Touch one of those kids . . . any kid, and I'll blow your damn brains out."

"Haw, haw, haw! I'm thinkin' ya ain't got the guts to even try. Yore ma had more guts than ya got. She come at me more'n once with a stick a stove wood." He grinned proudly.

"Shut up. I don't want to hear her name coming from your filthy mouth."

Walter walked on to the house, leaving Evan cursing under

his breath. How much longer was he going to be able to stand the man? He had put up for sale the St. Joseph house his grandparents left him. He planned to offer Walter money for his interest in the farm and get rid of him. He hesitated about speaking about it, wanting to be sure that the old man was completely sober before he laid out the proposition.

Evan ate his supper, washed his dinner plate and put it back on the shelf behind the curtain. He had cooked a pot of green beans earlier in the day and, judging by the amount left in the pot, Walter had helped himself before he took off through the woods in the direction of the joints on the river at Well's Point.

Evan made a real effort to put Walter out of his mind. Right now he wasn't going to let anything interfere with his enjoyment of the evening with Julie.

Julie had hoped her father would be gone by the time she came downstairs. He stood at the kitchen sink, dampened his hair, carefully parted it in the middle and combed it back on each side. He had on his good trousers, the freshly ironed shirt and a bow tie.

"Thanks, Sis, for ironing my shirt . . . and don't you look pretty," he exclaimed when he turned to look at her.

"Thank you. I really shouldn't leave the kids here by themselves."

"Why not? They'll be all right until Joe gets here. He said he would leave in time to get home before dark even if Jack stayed longer."

"I know, but it makes me uneasy for them to be here alone."

"Ah, don't worry about it. Go on and have a good time. You deserve it." With his hand on the door, he turned. "I'm not sure what time I'll be home."

Julie nodded. She wanted him to be happy, but all she could see ahead for him was heartbreak if he had fallen in love with Birdie Stuart.

Jill was sitting in the porch swing with Joy and Jason when Evan's car came up the lane. Julie was in the house trying to keep her nerves under control.

"Mr. Johnson's here," Jason shouted.

Evan stopped beside the front porch rather than at the back as he usually did. Joy ran to meet him as soon as he stepped from the car.

"Swing me, swing me," she yelled.

"Hello, sugar bunch." He reached for her hands and swung her around a few times.

"Jill said you're takin' Julie on a . . . on a—"

"I'm taking Julie out for a while. Is that all right with you?"

"Why can't I go?"

"You can go another time. This is my time with Julie." He held on to her hand as they stepped up onto the porch. "Hello, Jason, Jill."

"Jill said she'd let you kiss her if you wanted to," Joy blurted.

"Joy! Hush up!" Jill put her hands over her face to hide her embarrassment.

About to step out onto the porch, Julie stayed inside the screen door. Mortified, she closed her eyes.

"If I wanted to? A man would have to be out of his mind not to want to kiss a pretty girl like Jill."

"Would he want to kiss me and Jason?" Joy asked.

"You, I'm sure." Evan lifted the child up and kissed her on the cheek. "Men shake hands." He gave Jason's hand a manly shake.

"Are you going to kiss Julie?" Joy shouted.

Julie came out onto the porch. "That's enough out of you, Joy," she said sternly. Her face was red and her heart was pounding a mile a minute.

"Hello, Julie." She was so pretty. It made Evan smile just to look at her.

"Evan, may I speak to you for a moment?"

"Sure," he said slowly and followed her to the other side

of the car, where she stopped and faced him. He had a moment of dread thinking that she was going to tell him she had changed her mind about going.

"I'm worried about leaving the kids here by themselves. Joe said that he'd be home before dark, but that's a couple of hours away. Would you mind . . . ah . . . if we stayed here for a while?" She realized in her nervousness that she was talking too fast.

"Course not," he said looking into her worried eyes.

Was it Walter she was afraid of? Had he told her that day on the road that he would come after Jill and Jason? Dear God! The man wasn't worth the shot it would take to kill him.

"Thank you." Julie felt a warm flood of relief.

"Are you afraid Walter will come here? He left home a couple of hours ago. He'll be in one of the joints on the river by now."

"I'd just rather not . . . leave them."

"It's all right. We'll stay for a while. It'll be too late to go to the picture show, but we can go out to Spring Lake for a while. We'll go to the picture show another time."

Julie's heart leaped. The smile he gave her filled her with tenderness for this gentle man who was so understanding yet who had the misfortune to be the son of the man she most hated and feared. He reached down and took her hand when he saw the serious look on her face.

"Don't worry about it."

"I know that Joy is . . . sometimes . . . a little pesky. We've all spoiled her a little."

"Don't apologize for Joy or any of the others. I've never been around a little girl, but aren't they supposed to be spoiled a little? She's a little scamp, all right, but bright as a new penny." A smile spread across his lips. "She makes me feel"—he rubbed his chin while he thought of the right word—"special, as if she likes me."

"Of course she likes you. That's the problem. She likes you

a lot. Not many men, other than the family, pay attention to her like you do."

"I do it because I'm selfish. I like her attention, too. Julie, I understand your not wanting to leave them here alone. Why don't we take them for a ride?"

"Oh . . . you don't have to do that." Julie's hand went to her throat. He gently removed it and held both her hands in his.

"I want to. Don't deprive me of the pleasure." He pulled one of her hands into the crook of his arm and they stepped up onto the porch. "Is there anyone here who would like to go into town for an ice-cream cone?"

"Me," Joy screeched and ran to grab Evan's other hand.

"You mean it?" Jason slid out of the swing.

"That's two of you. How about the pretty girl with the yellow hair ribbon?"

"Well . . ." Jill rolled her eyes as she stood. "I guess I'll have to go along and look after the kids. It's plain you've only got eyes for Julie."

"Oh, Lord." Julie thought she had muttered the words under her breath, but Evan heard them, looked down at her and smiled, then hugged her hand to his side with his arm.

Evan was acutely aware that when he was with the Jones family he was happy. Happier than he had been in a long, long time. He could toss caution to the wind when he was with them, say and do things he wouldn't have thought of doing six months ago. The Joneses, from Julie to Joy, accepted him. He wasn't sure yet about Jethro. It gave him a queer, quivery feeling around his heart when little Joy ran to him with her arms outstretched.

This is how it would be to belong to a family.

"You can't go, Sidney," Jason was saying sternly to the shaggy dog. "Stay here on the porch and don't let anyone in the house while we're gone."

Sidney made a few whining sounds, then went to lie down on the porch beside the door.

Jill got into the back seat. Evan swung Joy in beside her, then stepped back, not wanting to embarrass Jason by offering help. He waited as the boy climbed into the car, then closed the door and opened the front one for Julie. With his hand beneath her elbow, he assisted her up into the car, making sure that her dress was tucked in before he closed the door.

"He is sooooo . . . nice," Jill hissed as Evan made his way around the car.

"I like 'im," Joy shouted.

Evan was smiling when he opened the door. "I hope it's me you like." He settled behind the wheel.

"I love ya." Joy jumped up and wrapped her arms around his neck from behind.

"Joy, sit down." Jill pulled the child away from Evan and down on the seat.

Julie darted a glance at Evan. He was smiling, beaming, as if someone had given him the world. His laughing eyes met Julie's.

"Don't you dare apologize," he muttered as he started the car.

Julie felt as if she were in a dream. *What could be better than this? Is this what it feels like when a woman meets a man she likes very much?* Evan Johnson was the last person she ever thought she would fall in love with. *Oh, Lord, why am I thinking these thoughts? He's just being kind to the kids.*

Julie and the kids waited in the car while Evan went into the drugstore. He came out with five ice-cream cones fitted into the round holes of a cardboard.

"Evan, they'll mess up the car," Julie exclaimed.

"Hold the cones. We'll go to the ball park and see how Jack is doing. The kids can get out there."

Julie laughed. "Hurry, or I'll have a lap full of melted ice cream."

The kids poured out of the car the instant Evan stopped a

short distance behind home plate. The cones were passed around and all were licking happily when Joe approached.

"What have we here? Is this one for me?" He attempted to take the cone from Joy. She shrieked and ran. "I'm sure Jack has made the team," he said excitedly. "He's hit two home runs. Scott Graham's nose is out of joint. He objected to Jack playing because he isn't a town boy."

"Wesley Philpot is playing. He lives down south of town along the river." Julie leaned over so that the melting ice cream didn't fall on her dress. She looked up to see Evan watching her lick the cream from her lips and dab them with her handkerchief.

"They'll not pay any attention to Graham." Joe's eyes were busy going from Evan to his sister. "He's a lousy player, and they're wanting to make a halfway decent showing at the game. He can't throw a ball past third base and will lose his catching position to Jack. Hey, I thought you two were going to the picture show."

"Another time," Evan said, glancing at Julie. "We'll drive out to Spring Lake after we take you and the kids home."

"Hey, I'll like that. I wasn't looking forward to that uphill walk."

"Look! Jack's goin' to bat." Jason was so excited he forgot to lick his cone and melting ice cream was running down over his fist. "Hit it, Jack. Hit a homer."

Jack hit a line drive and beat it to first base. Ron Poole, playing first base, hit him on the shoulder and teasingly tried to push him off base.

Julie watched her brother with a tender smile on her face, then turned her glance to Joe.

"He's having such a good time. Oh, I hope he gets to play."

"Mr. Poole seems glad to have him," Joe said with a hint of pride in his voice. "I heard him ask Jack if he could practice tomorrow afternoon and again Monday night."

The next man up struck out. Jack stole second base and

Jason was beside himself with excitement. Evan nudged Julie and tilted his head toward the boy who had forgotten to eat his ice cream.

"He thinks the sun rises and sets on Jack, even though Jack teases him unmercifully," Julie explained.

On the next play the batter hit the ball into right field. Jack rounded the bases and slid safely home as Jason, Jill and Joe shouted encouragement.

Evan looked down at the smiling girl at his side.

"Isn't this better than an old picture show?"

"You bet. And . . . thank you for thinking of it, although I'm going to have to do something about Joy's face and hands before we let her get back into the car."

"I've already got that figured out." He pulled a handkerchief from his pocket. "I'll wet this over there at the water cooler."

After he walked away, Corbin Appleby drove up and got out of his car.

"I see Jack's got his own cheering section."

"He hit two homers," Jason said.

"Will he make the team?" Jill asked.

"That'll be up to the team manager."

Evan felt a stab of jealousy when he saw the Jones family gathered around the police chief. Joy had stuffed the last of the ice-cream cone in her mouth, so he took first one of her hands then the other and wiped them with the wet handkerchief.

"Don't you think we'd better wipe the ice cream off your face?" he asked.

"I don't care." Joy repeated her favorite phrase with twinkling eyes.

While wiping her face, Evan looked up to see Corbin watching.

"Now you're pretty again."

"Mr. Johnson says I'm pretty again," Joy announced. "Hello." She looked up at Corbin with her mischievous grin.

"Hello."

"Ya ate with us."

"I sure did."

"Are ya goin' to do it again?"

"I might." Corbin grinned down at the child, then spoke to Julie. "I saw your father a while ago. He said Jack was coming in to try out for the team, so I thought I'd come by and see how he was doin'."

"Are you going to play?"

"No. The team wouldn't be able to depend on me. Something could come up and I'd have to leave. How about you, Johnson? Are you a ball player?"

"Only on a very low level."

"Looks like the practice is over," Corbin said, his eyes shifting out to the ball field.

"Jack made the team," Joe announced enthusiastically. "Look at that grin on his face. There'll be no livin' with him now."

"Congratulations, Jack," Corbin said when the boy joined them.

"Thanks for telling us about it." Jack grinned at Julie. "That was fun, Sis. I could hear the kids yelling for me."

"I just knew you'd make the team," Julie said proudly.

"Now he'll be pestering me to throw balls at him morning, noon and night," Joe complained, but he was beaming.

"When he's playing at Wrigley Field, you can say you had a hand in his training." Evan held out his hand to Jack. "Congratulations, Jack."

Ron Poole came toward them, wiping sweat off his face with a white handkerchief. He was with a man in duck pants, a striped shirt and wide suspenders.

"Chief," Ron called, "thanks for sending Jack. He may save

us from making complete fools of ourselves when we play the league team."

Julie glanced at her brother. He was beaming.

"You may have the next Babe Ruth here," Corbin replied.

"Welcome to the team, Jack." Ron stuck out his hand.

"Thanks." It was all Jack was able to say.

"Dr. Forbes," Ron said. He turned to the man beside him. "Meet Chief Appleby and the Jones family. This is Miss Jones," he said, indicating Julie. When she extended her hand, the young doctor shook it. "Another Miss Jones, Joe and Jack the young ones."

"Don't forget me. My name's Joy." The child looked up at the tall man and grinned.

Ron put his hand on her head. "No one could forget a pretty little girl like you. How old are you now? Seven? Eight?"

"I'm four." Joy held up four fingers.

"Only four?" Ron said and winked at her. "I thought you were old enough to get married. I was coming courting."

"You're silly," Joy shouted and giggled happily.

Ron introduced the doctor to Evan.

"Pleasure to meet you," Evan said as the two men shook hands.

The young doctor was a stocky man with broad shoulders and legs as sturdy as tree trunks. His sandy hair was thick and needed trimming. He had friendly light green eyes and a constant smile.

"Dr. Forbes is here to lend Doc Curtis a hand," Ron said. "He's from a small town in Tennessee about the size of Fertile. We're hoping to keep him here when Doc Curtis retires."

"Where in Tennessee?" Corbin asked. "I've been there a time or two."

"Harpersville in the eastern part of the s-tate." The doctor had a definite southern accent and a slight hesitancy in his speech.

"I've not been east of Nashville. Welcome to Fertile."

"Thank you. My father was a s-small town doctor. It's what I always wanted to be."

"Doc's going to play shortstop for us. He played while he was in school in Knoxville."

Julie noticed that Ron Poole directed his conversation to the police chief, seeming to ignore Evan after the introduction. It irritated her. Evan, however, stood with arms folded, appearing to be totally at ease. His eyes went often to Julie, who stood between her brothers. Joy sidled over and took his hand. The gesture was noticed by both the police chief and the councilman.

"I've got to be going," Corbin said. "Anyone need a ride uptown?"

"Doc and I will take you up on that. See you tomorrow afternoon, Jack."

"Yeah and . . . thanks."

After Corbin left with the doctor and Ron, Joe helped the kids get into the back seat, then got in and pulled Joy onto his lap. Julie moved close to Evan to make room for Jack.

"You look pretty tonight, Sis. I'll get you dirty. Why don't I stand on the running board?"

"No," Julie said quickly. "That's too dangerous. If you get my dress dirty, it will wash."

"Get in, Jack, so she'll have to sit close to me." Evan winked at Jack, and Julie's face reddened.

"There's Papa's car," Jill said as they drove through town. "I bet he took *her* to the picture show. I hope she took that whiny brat of hers with her. Serve him right."

"Whoa. Our little sister's got her stinger out tonight." Jack glanced back over his shoulder at Jill.

Joe laughed, but there was no mirth in it. "I'm goin' to be careful and not get on your bad side. When you get down on someone, you stomp on 'em."

"I don't care. I hate her."

"I hate her, too." Not knowing whom they were talking about, Joy was sure she would hate whomever Jill hated.

"Who do you hate?" Jason asked in a quiet voice. He, too, was in the dark as to Jill's meaning. "Miss Meadows said we're not to hate people."

"Miss Meadows is nice. I wish Papa liked her."

"Why don't Papa like her?"

"Papa likes her, but . . . oh, you're too young to know about these things."

"When do you practice again, Jack?" Julie hoped to change the subject. She was conscious that her shoulder was tucked behind Evan's and her hip and thigh against his. If she tilted her head the slightest, her cheek would be against his shoulder.

"Tomorrow afternoon. Scott Graham didn't want me on the team. He said I lived on the edge of town so I wasn't eligible to play. Mr. Poole said it didn't matter."

Evan turned the car up the lane and stopped beside the porch. Sidney stood wagging his tail in greeting. Jack got out, opened the back door and took Joy off Joe's lap. With her straddling his hip, he stepped up onto the porch. Joy put her arms around her brother's neck and laid her head on his shoulder.

"Thank you for the ice cream and the ride, Mr. Johnson." Jill nudged Jason.

"Yeah, thanks, Mr. Johnson."

"You're very welcome. We'll do it again sometime."

"This little gal is all tuckered out." Jack nuzzled his nose in Joy's tangled curls.

"Wash her feet before you put her to bed," Julie called as Jack carried his sister across the porch to the door.

Joe closed the door, stuck his head in the window and winked at Julie. "Have a good time. Sir," he said to Evan, "I trust your intentions toward my sister are honorable."

"Joe!" Embarrassed, Julie pressed her palms to her hot cheeks.

"Honorable?" Evan leered and twisted the end of an imaginary mustache. "It depends on what you consider to be . . . honorable, young sir."

"Oh, you two. Cut it out."

Grinning, Joe backed away from the car and waved when it headed back down the lane.

Julie had moved over until she was no longer touching Evan. Alone with him in the close confines of the car, she could feel the pounding of her heart. She glanced at him and saw that he was looking at her.

"Are you scared to be alone with me?"

"Goodness' sakes! I wouldn't have come out with you if I were."

"You look like a frightened little bird ready to fly out the window."

"I . . . didn't bring my wings," she said with mock dismay, and he laughed, delighted with her.

"I envy your having brothers and sisters," he said quietly after he turned the car and headed back toward town. "It wasn't much fun growing up alone."

She took a deep breath. "I can't imagine life without them. Joe and I have always been close. I couldn't have managed without him."

"You don't mind having the responsibility of the house and seeing to your brothers and sisters?"

"No. It was just something that had to be done when my mother died."

"How old were you?"

"Sixteen and Joe was fourteen."

As they passed through town, Julie saw her father's car parked near the picture show.

"Are you worried that your father will become interested in Mrs. Stuart?"

"He's already interested."

"It may not come to anything. She's not the type to settle down on a farm."

"Then why is she leading him on?"

"Because there isn't anyone else handy."

"You're handy."

"I've made it clear to her that I'm not interested."

Evan glanced at her profile and wished for a way to wipe the worried look from her face.

Julie Jones was too honest to ever understand a devious, self-centered woman like Birdie Stuart.

Chapter 15

"You promised to tell me what Joe and Thad Taylor were up to last Sunday at the ball game," Julie said as they headed down the road toward town.

"Didn't Joe tell you?"

"No. But I think he told Jack. They were snickering about something . . . regarding Mrs. Stuart. Joe said if I didn't know, I'd not get in trouble with Papa."

"Thad and Joe are quite a team when it comes to spinning a windy."

"You had no part of it?"

"Not directly. Thad, with help from Joe, was telling Mrs. Stuart about the barn dances that are held in this part of the country and how they make the floor slick for dancing."

"I've not been to a dance where they made the floor slick. What did he say they used?"

"You don't want to know."

"Now you've got me curious."

"It's something a farm has plenty of and readily available." He glanced at her again, with more laughter in his eyes than she'd seen before. When he saw her eyes widen as she realized what he was talking about, laughter rumbled in his chest.

"No! He didn't tell her . . . that!" A giggle burst from her lips. "Thad wouldn't—"

"He sure did. Joe chimed in, too."

"Did she believe it?" Julie asked between gasps of laughter.

"She did. I almost believed it myself, to hear Thad and Joe tell it." It was such a pleasure to see and hear her laugh.

"Oh, my. How could anyone be so . . . I wonder if she'll tell my father. Surely by now she knows a joke was played on her. He'll be angry at Joe."

"If she's smart, she won't tell him how dumb she was to believe it."

"Oh, she'll make herself out the victim of a cruel prank." Julie lapsed into silence, wishing she hadn't made the remark. It made her sound petty.

A mile beyond town, Evan turned on a well-used road that would take them to the area known as Spring Lake. The lake was not large, but it was clear, had a sandy beach and was popular for swimming and picnicking. Right after the war a pavilion had been erected for dancing.

Tonight the large shutters on the sides and back of the building had been pulled up and fastened for an open-air effect. A string of light bulbs was hung around the pavilion. A railing surrounded two sides of the dance floor, leaving a space for benches along the wall.

A sign on the outside of the building read:

10 CENTS A DANCE OR 3 FOR 25 CENTS.
TUES and THURS 2 FOR 15 CENTS.

Evan found a place to park the car facing the building so that they could watch the dancers. A dozen or more couples were dancing to the music of a five-piece band.

Julie leaned forward, her lips curved in a smile. He studied her profile, enjoying her obvious pleasure as she watched the dancers.

"There's Ernie Price." She turned to look at him with shining eyes. "He works at the feed store."

"Do you want to go in and dance?"

She turned quickly and shook her head. "Oh, no. I . . . can't dance. Do you mind if we just watch?"

"I won't mind a bit if I can hold your hand." His eyes teased her. She laughed. It seemed so natural to hold out her hand. He enclosed it in his big one and held it on the seat between them. The music ended and the couples left the floor. "If you want to learn how to dance, I'll teach you."

"Oh, I couldn't. I would be embarrassed for anyone to see me." The band started up again. They were playing "The Sheik of Araby." Couples passed through the gate where a man took their tickets.

"They all had to learn at one time."

"I'd rather not . . . go in."

"Then let's walk down by the lake. There'll be no one down on the beach and we can still hear the music."

He opened his door before she could protest. Around on her side of the car, he took her hand and helped her out. Still holding her hand, he folded his arm under hers and laced her fingers through his. As they walked away, they heard the sound of breaking glass as a bottle fell from one of the cars. Then a muttered curse and a girlish giggle.

"Someone is boozing it up," Evan whispered.

"There are almost as many people on the outside as on the inside."

"It's early yet."

"Have you been here before?"

"I drove out one night to see what was going on."

"Did you dance?"

"No. Watch out for those rocks. Hold it. I'll help you down."

Evan jumped down, turned and with his hands at her waist lifted her down.

"Oh, no! I'm too heavy!" Her hands had automatically gone to his shoulders.

"Too heavy?" He held her for an instant longer than was necessary. "I went over the side of a ship with a pack and a rifle that weighed more than you do."

"Thank you," she said as soon as her feet touched solid ground. "The water is all sparkly." She hoped that her voice didn't sound as breathless as she felt.

"The moon will be up soon."

They walked along the sandy beach until the dense trees and bushes hid the lights from the pavilion, although they could still hear the music. The band was playing "I'll See You in My Dreams." Evan turned her toward him, took her hand in his and lifted her free hand to his shoulder. With his hand at her waist, he began to sway.

"Just sway to the music. You've square-danced, haven't you?"

"Yes. Joe and I have waltzed . . . some."

"That's a good start."

"I can't dance the Charleston or the shimmy."

"You've not missed much. I'd rather waltz." He made a turn and she followed. "Did you say you couldn't dance?" he teased and made another turn.

"Not the way they were dancing in there."

His hand moved to her back and he pulled her so close her breasts were touching his chest. Her heart beat in a strange and disturbing way as she struggled to get sufficient air into her lungs. She felt the hardness of his chest and his breath on her cheek. She moved her feet automatically, praying that he didn't feel the thumping of her heart.

Evan was sure that Julie was enjoying herself. Her feet were light, her head high, and from time to time, when she stumbled a bit in the sand, a small excited laugh came from her. He stored her laughter in his mind to bring out and enjoy when he was feeling lonely.

"You smell like roses," he murmured into the hair at her

temple just as the music stopped. He released her waist but held on to her hand. "We'll have to go to a barn dance sometime. If we can dance in the sand, think what we could do on a slick dance floor."

"The moon is coming up," she said, her voice slightly shaky. "Isn't it pretty, shining on the water?"

"Yes, very pretty." He murmured the words with his eyes still on her face, then looked out over the lake.

The band began to play a fast tune and a female voice sang "Ma, He's Making Eyes at Me."

"I don't think we want to dance to that," Evan said. "We'll wait for the next waltz."

"Where did you learn to dance?"

"In college. When I was in the army, officers were expected to go to social events, and those of us who couldn't dance very well practiced with the other officers. It's much more formal in Europe than here in the Midwest. The officers had to attend teas and spit-and-polish balls where everyone got dressed up as if they were going to call on the queen."

Julie felt, as never before, the distance between her life and his. He was an educated gentleman who knew about such things as teas and balls, and she was a farm girl who had not even graduated from high school.

When she didn't say anything, Evan wanted to kick himself for running off at the mouth about that flimflam that he'd despised. He was searching his mind for something to say when she spoke.

"Why did you come back here? Oh, I know you came to see your father, but why are you staying?"

"I didn't come to see Walter. I came to see my old home again and found out that I like working the soil."

"Was he like . . . he is now when you were little?"

"I don't remember much about him until I was about Jason's age, then I despised him. My mother sent me to my grandparents' because of him. But let's not talk about Walter. I don't want to spoil the evening. The music has started again. Shall we dance again? 'I'll be with you in apple blossom time,'" he sang the words to the popular tune.

Evan held her lightly, as if fearing she would bolt if he tried to pull her close to him. They had danced for several minutes when he tilted his head and placed his cheek against the hair above her temple. Julie's heart was racing a mile a minute and her mind had shut down. She didn't even hear when the music stopped. He released her and reached up to brush her hair.

"We'd better get back to the car. The mosquitoes are coming out in full force. I just brushed one off your hair."

They walked back toward the pavilion. Evan held her close to him by hooking her arm beneath his and holding tightly to her hand. The crowd around the pavilion had almost doubled in size. Cars and buggies with horses tied to trees and shrubs filled the area at the side of the dance hall.

Young people lounged against the cars or sat in them watching the dancers. As they approached Evan's car, a girl called out, "Julie, is that you? Well, as I live and breathe, it's Julie Jones."

Zelda Wood stepped away from a group that leaned on the car next to Evan's. She was wearing a sleeveless dress with a beaded front and a skirt edged in fringe that danced around her knees when she walked. Huge spit curls were plastered to her cheeks. Julie was shocked to see that she was smoking a cigarette in a long holder.

"Hello, Zelda."

"Good Lord. I thought that was you." Zelda's eyes went to Evan. "I see you took my advice."

"Uh . . . what advice?" As soon as Julie uttered the words, she wished that she could take them back.

"You know." Zelda took a puff from her cigarette and rolled her eyes up at Evan beneath the highly arched, thinly plucked brows.

"Do you know Evan Johnson?" Julie asked, embarrassment making her voice tremble.

Evan answered. "We've met. Evening, Miss Wood."

"I'm surprised to see you out here with . . . her."

"Why are you surprised?" Evan asked with a lift of his brows. "There aren't many places around Fertile where a man can take his girl out for an evening."

"Bee's knees! His girl? Fast work, Julie. I didn't know you had it in you. You can't tell about these quiet types." She tossed the last words over her shoulder toward her friends leaning on the car and gestured with the cigarette holder.

"You're wrong, Miss Wood," Evan said quickly. "The chasing was on my part. It took a lot of persuasion to convince Miss Jones to come out with me. It won't be the last time if I have anything to say about it." His tone more than his words caused Zelda's face to redden and lose its smirk, but she wasn't about to back down in front of her friends.

"She is amusing, isn't she? Different from what you're used to."

"Very different. Very refreshing. I had begun to fear that all the sweet, *wholesome* women had been taken."

Afraid to look up at him, Julie felt as if the breath had been sucked out of her.

"Well, I've got to get back to my chums. We're here every Saturday night to keep up on the latest dances. Next time you bring your eggs to town, Julie, stop by the bank."

Evan opened the door for Julie. She got in and stared straight ahead while Evan rounded the car and got behind the wheel. She knew that Zelda and her "chums" were watching her. Some of them, along with Zelda, had been in her class at school.

"What else could he say?" The male voice reached Julie. "Being who he is, he'd have to go out with someone like her . . . if he went out."

"Of course she'd go. I don't think the poor girl has ever

been to a dance hall. Did you know all the names in that family start with a *J*? Isn't that the cat's meow?"

Julie's face was still burning as they left the lake and headed toward town. The silence was thick and heavy. Julie felt as if she were in another world. Wondering what Evan could be thinking after the encounter with Zelda, she was filled with misery.

"Are we going to let that silly little twit spoil our evening?" Evan asked quietly. "She's trying so hard to be a flapper, she makes a fool of herself." He reached for Julie's hand and held it lightly, giving her the opportunity to pull away. When she didn't, he tugged gently. "Come sit close to me. I hear that it's what people do on a date. I've not been on many, so I have to take their word for it."

He looked at her when he could take his eyes off the road. His nearness confused her and weakened her willpower. She moved until her shoulder and thigh were touching his.

"That's much better. Forget about what the jealous cat said. She's ill-mannered, rude, and not worth our giving her a second thought."

"She was in my class at school." It was all Julie could think of to say as she swallowed an assortment of lumps in her throat.

Evan stopped the car on Main Street in front of the drugstore. He looked at Julie. Her lips were slightly parted as she breathed through her mouth. The flush on her cheeks and the vein that throbbed in her neck were signs of her discomfiture. He wanted badly to cradle her in his arms and rest his chin on the top of her head. He didn't dare, for fear he would damage her trust in him.

"How about another ice-cream cone?"

She turned to him and immediately the corners of her mouth tilted.

"Oh, no. But thank you."

"I want to get some tooth powder. Do you mind waiting while I run in?"

"Of course not."

"Be right back."

Julie watched him go into the drugstore. *He uses tooth powder,* she thought, with growing concern. Another difference between them. She'd never used tooth powder. All of her life she had cleaned her teeth with soda and salt.

Was Zelda right? Was he just giving the poor country girl a break from her dull life?

There were quite a few people on the street. They strolled along, either on their way home from the picture show or gathering in groups to visit. Several people looked pointedly at her, or was it Evan's nice car that had drawn their eyes?

Julie hadn't thought to check if her father's car was still on the street. The picture show was over. Miss Dahlstrom, the round-shouldered spinster who played the piano to accompany the movie, had gone by.

She was surprised to realize that she hadn't thought of her father or Birdie Stuart since she and Evan had laughed about the joke Thad and Joe had played on her. The fear that her father had become infatuated with the woman was still there even if she had forgotten about it for a while.

She watched Evan come out of the drugstore. He was a good-looking man, half a head taller than most of the men on the street. He moved with such assurance that people automatically moved out of his way.

A man like Evan would never be seriously interested in a girl like me.

Evan opened the door, got in the car and placed a box on her lap.

"What's this?"

"What does it say?"

Julie tilted the box up to the light. "French Chocolate Creams?"

"Open it," Evan said, smiling. "I've got a fondness for sweets."

"Oh, you! You're like a little kid." Excitement made her cheeks rosy as she broke the paper seal and opened the box. Inside were three rows of small round pieces of chocolate. Evan reached for one and held it up to her mouth.

"Open up," he commanded laughingly.

When she opened her mouth, he popped the chocolate inside. The instant she bit down on it, a burst of delicious cherry-flavored cream filled her mouth.

Her eyes, alight with pleasure, met his. "Oh, my," she said. "Good."

His eyes still holding hers, he popped one into his own mouth.

"Oh, my, you're right." He lifted his arm to position it on the top of the seat behind her. Their heads were close.

"I've never had candy so good."

"I think I'll have another. How about you?" Without waiting for her to answer, he held the chocolate to her lips. She took it, being careful not to touch his fingers.

Their eyes held. She was the girl of his dreams, even more wonderful than he had imagined. Her hair was the rich color of ripened wheat, her mouth wide and sweet, her eyes like stars. The desolate look on her face when she heard the cruel remarks by the tart at the dance hall had cut him to the bone.

Sweetheart, somehow I've got to make you want me. I'd give you the world if I could.

Julie stared at him for a long silent minute. He was so close she could see the small squint lines at the ends of his eyes and the cowlick that stood up next to the part in his hair. She was afraid that if she moved, he would be sure to know how happy she was, being here with him. When she finally spoke, her voice caught, then came out in a husky whisper.

"Thank you for the treat."

"The entire evening has been a treat for me."

"It's nice of you to say that."

"I mean it. I hope you've enjoyed it and we can do it again."

He was looking past her down the walk. "It's time we moved on. I see Walter and a couple of his cronies coming this way. I sure don't want to give them a ride home." Evan started the car, backed out and turned toward the road leading out of town.

The extraordinarily wonderful evening was almost over.

Chapter 16

WHEN EVAN STOPPED THE CAR at the side of the front porch, Julie wasn't sure what to do.

"Thank you. I've had a good time." She placed her hand on the door handle.

"Will you stay for just a little while? I don't want the evening to end."

"I . . . ah . . . really had a good time," she stammered, not knowing what else to say.

"I'm glad. I'd like to do it again sometime."

"Go to Spring Lake?"

"Or the picture show. Just be with you."

"All right."

"I like being with you . . . and your family."

Julie laughed nervously. "I'd think that we're rather dull compared to what you're used to."

"You're anything but dull, Julie." His hand on the back of the seat moved to her shoulder, then to massage the nape of her neck. "Do I make you nervous?"

"A little bit."

"I make myself nervous. I'm so afraid I'll make a mistake and scare you away from me."

"I don't scare easily," she whispered and turned to look at him. His face was closer than she expected.

"I hope not, because before you go in, I'd like to kiss you."

"You . . . would?"

"Will you scream for Joe if I do?"

A smile tilted the corners of her mouth. "I imagine it would be over by the time he got here."

Evan chuckled. She was fun, intelligent . . . soft. She was all a woman should be.

"He could drag me out and punch me in the nose."

"He might—if I yelled real loud."

"To kiss you would be worth a dozen punches in the nose." His voice was husky and rawly disturbed, like his deep, quivering breaths. "But I won't do it if you don't want me to. . . ."

The hand at her nape brought her face toward his, then slipped down to cup her shoulder to allow her to turn away if she chose. She felt the caress of his warm breath on her cheek before, with the utmost tenderness and caution, his lips, warm and soft, settled on hers.

Oh, my! This is what I've heard about, read about, but it's a thousand times more wonderful. The thought floated through Julie's mind during the brief kiss. A warm tide of tingling excitement washed over her. Her heart beat wildly and her mind whirled giddily.

Evan moved his head and placed his cheek against hers. His arm tightened. His heart was drumming; he was stunned with happiness. Neither of them spoke for long minutes. He was content holding her and she was content resting against him. Finally she stirred and gently moved away from him. For an instant he feared her sweet surrender was all a dream, then she uttered a little laugh so soundless that it was no more than an exhalation of breath.

"I've not had much experience . . . kissing—"

"I'm glad." He laughed with relief and pure happiness. "Maybe we should practice," he teased.

"I could volunteer for the kissing booth at the county fair. I'd get a lot of practice there."

"You don't have to go to the fair. You can practice on me . . . right here." Then he laughed, intimately, joyously, and his arm tightened around her. "The only thing that would have made that kiss better was if you had put your arm around my neck. Shall we try it again?"

"If you want to."

He heard her voice quiver. His relief was so profound that he thought his whole being would dissolve, that his heart would cease its beating. Too moved for words when her hand crept up over his shoulder and around his neck, he kissed her lips softly, gently, so as to not scare her away. Their lips caught and clung, released and smiled, and caught again.

"You're getting the hang of it," he whispered against the side of her mouth, then kissed her again. "After a few hours of this, you might get to be an expert."

She squirmed and turned her mouth away from his. Her hand slid from around his neck.

"My goodness. I don't know what came over me. I shouldn't be doing this. I don't . . . I never—"

"Thank God that you don't and you never. You're a rare treasure, Julie Jones." So much tenderness was in his voice that Julie blinked several times, then leaned back so that she could look into his face. Her hand went up to cup his cheek.

"I'm no treasure! I'm terribly ordinary, Evan. I've lived on this farm all my life and not been more than fifty miles from it. I've not ridden on a train and very few times in a motorcar. I can count on my fingers the times I've been to the picture show, and tonight is the first time I've been to Spring Lake. I'm what Zelda and her chums called me, a country girl, and I'm not ashamed of it. I'd rather be what I am than what they are.

"There." She drew in a deep breath and let it out slowly. "I've said it."

"You've not said anything I didn't know. It isn't where you've been that matters. It's what you are on the inside—what you care about. I like what you are, Julie: untarnished, unaffected and innocent. You've got more integrity in this little finger"—he stroked her finger with his thumb—"than the banker's daughter has in her whole body. I'd like for us to go out again, get to know each other . . . that is, if you don't mind being seen with the son of the man they call the meanest in the county."

Innocent? Lord, what would he think if he found out?

"You're not like Mr. Johnson," Julie said quickly, hoping to rid her mind of unpleasant thoughts.

"I can't help what people think. I just want you and your family to know that I have Walter's name, but that is as far as the kinship goes."

"Do you remember Miss Meadows? You met her at the ball game. She once told me that you can choose your friends but not your relatives."

"Words of wisdom," he said quietly. "Did it bother you when the jelly bean said I asked you out because I couldn't get anyone else to go out with me?"

"No." She spoke without hesitation. "I know it isn't true. Zelda and any number of her crowd would jump at the chance to go out with you."

"That will never happen." He tilted his head and took a deep breath. There was a decided firmness in his voice.

Uneasy silence hung between them for a long moment before Julie spoke.

"I . . . should go in."

"Shall we go out somewhere next Saturday night?"

"If you want to."

"I do. I was afraid to ask for fear you'd turn me down."

Julie laughed. "I can't imagine you being afraid of anything."

"You'd be surprised at what I'm afraid of."

Evan got out of the car and came around to open the door for her. She got out, leaving the box of chocolates on the seat. He reached in and put the box in her hands.

"You forgot these. They were for you."

"All . . . for me? You shouldn't have—"

"I wanted to." He took her elbow and walked with her to the door.

"Thank you for the candy and . . . the cones for the kids and for everything."

"Thank you, Julie. I'll be looking forward to next Saturday night." He desperately wanted to kiss her again but feared to press his luck.

"Me, too. Good night."

"Good night, Julie."

Evan waited on the porch until she was in the house, then went back to his car. He had met women of all types, from St. Joseph to London and Paris: flappers, courtesans and society dames. Not one of them had even come close to tying him in knots as Julie was doing. There was a freshness about her that caused him to want to be with her every moment. Every night for the past week he had lain awake thinking about her.

He was reasonably sure, he thought as he drove home, that she felt something for him. She had melted against him. Her mouth had clung sweetly to his. A woman like Julie wouldn't kiss a man as she had done if there wasn't some feeling involved.

Happier than he could remember being in a long, long time, he parked the car in the shed and headed for the darkened house.

Chief Corbin Appleby and the young doctor, whom he had met at the ball park, stood on the street corner near the telephone office. Dr. Forbes had come uptown with him after they took Ron Poole back to his store.

"You're the second man I've met in my life who likes to run. When I was a kid back in Harpersville, Tennessee, I knew a boy who would rather run than eat. He was a colored boy my brother-in-law had taken in to raise. His dream was to race in the Olympics."

"Did he make it?"

"No. He went to school down in Tuskegee, Alabama. His love for running was replaced with love for learning. He's not only one of the fastest but one of the smartest men I ever met. He's passionately interested in gardening now and working with his people to produce food not only for their families but to sell. He would have been good at anything he set his mind to."

"He never ran after he went away to school?"

"Not that I know of." Dr. Forbes grinned. "He gave the fastest man in the county a fifty-foot head start and still beat him in the Fourth of July footrace. And he was only a fourteen-year-old kid at the time. Raised a stink in town . . . that's sure."

"I gave up thinking about competition when I went into the army. Now I run for the fun of it."

"There was a stupid law in Harpersville that forbade coloreds being in town after dark. One night just at dusk, Jodie ran right down the middle of Main Street and thumbed his nose at the marshal. Lord, that was funny. The old banker almost had apoplexy. He wanted the marshal to arrest him. But the marshal was a good sort, he—"

"Uh-oh. Light's on. I'm wanted." Corbin hurried to the telephone office. Dr. Forbes followed.

"Otto Bloom is acting up again," Mrs. Ham said, as soon as Corbin entered the office. "He's down at the house shouting at his wife. She's locked the door and won't let him in."

"The house is under quarantine. If he goes in, he can't come out until the doc lifts the quarantine."

"The call came from one of the neighbors."

"I'll go right down."

"Mind if I go along?" Dr. Forbes asked.

"Not at all, if you can keep up. I can run there in less time than it would take me to get the car. It's two blocks down and the third house on the right. You'll hear a commotion."

Corbin was off running down the middle of the street before the doctor could answer.

At the Bloom house, Otto was pounding on the door and shouting obscenities.

"Let me in, ya damn whorin' bitch! This is my house!"

"Please, Otto. Dennis is sick—"

"Open this goddamn door or I'll strip the hide off your back when I do get in."

"I don't think so." Corbin stepped up onto the porch and with a heavy hand on his shoulder spun the obviously very drunk man around.

"Whater ya doin' here? Get off my porch."

"You've got a very sick kid in there—"

"It's my kid. Ain't yores."

"If you go in, you can't come out. The house is under quarantine." Corbin wanted more than anything to put his fist in the man's mouth, but he held on to his patience.

"Who says I can't come out?"

"I say so."

"Your say-so don't mean shit. Your say-so didn't stand up to Mr. Wood when ya put me in jail. He told ya how important I was. Can't run that two-bit bank without me." He turned and pounded on the door. "Edith, ya ugly bitch, you're goin' to get it good if you don't open this door."

"Go away, Otto. You woke Dennis and he's crying."

"Damn kid is always cryin'," he shouted.

"Do you mind if I talk to him?" Doc Forbes had arrived, slightly out of breath.

"Go ahead. I can't keep him from going into his own house. It'll be hell for the woman if he can't come out again."

"Mr. Bloom, I'm Doc Forbes. I'm here to help Doc Curtis during this epidemic."

"He's a old quack. Not lettin' a man in his own house ort to be 'gainst the law."

"Maybe. I noticed that you have a cut on your cheek and thought I should warn you."

" 'Bout what?"

"About diphtheria germs getting into an open cut. Kids can survive diphtheria . . . sometimes. Grown-ups are g-goners if they get it. The germs are very active and float around in the air seeking open wounds. I'd not go in there if I were you. I've seen men—women, too—die within three days after a germ gets into even a small open place on the skin."

Otto backed away from the door. "Why didn't that old quack tell me?"

"He probably thought you knew. Most people do."

"How'd I know? I ain't no doc." Otto stepped off the porch then turned. "How long will it be till I can get in my house?"

"Until the child no longer has a fever and the house is fumigated."

"I hope to hell that ugly bitch's got a cut. I've had all a her I can stand." Otto lurched off into the darkness, talking to himself.

"I'll get even with that so-called lawman who's come to town actin' like he owns it, and I know just the man to help me do it. I'm not goin' to be walked on. I'm important to Mr. Wood. The fat turd will back me 'cause I know what to do to stop his clock. Oh, yes. I know what to do to make the fat fart squeal."

Otto continued to mutter as he headed for Well's Point.

"N-nice fellow," Dr. Forbes remarked after Otto left.

"Pretty good tale you spun there."

"If it hadn't worked, I had one in reserve." Dr. Forbes grinned and rapped on the door. "Mrs. Bloom, I'm Dr. Forbes, I was here this afternoon with Doc Curtis. Your husband is gone. I'd like to speak to you about your boy."

The door opened a crack and Mrs. Bloom peered out. "He's gone?"

"He's gone. I scared him off. I don't think he'll come back. May I come in and see Dennis?"

Edith Bloom held the door open in invitation.

"I'll be going back uptown," Corbin called and walked out into the yard.

Otto and Walter Johnson had gotten into a scuffle down at Well's Point the night before and both had come away with bloody noses. But, according to the bartender, they were drinking together again before the night was over.

Walter Johnson was back in town tonight. Corbin had told Harvey Knapp at the billiard parlor that he would keep an eye on his place in case the bully again refused to leave at closing time. Corbin headed up that way, his mind busy. He had thought quite a bit about Julie Jones since the day he'd eaten dinner at her house and had felt a stab of disappointment tonight seeing her with Walter Johnson's son.

When he saw the entire Jones family at the ball field, he hadn't thought much about Johnson's being there, but then he had seen the two of them sitting in the car in front of the drugstore. It made him wonder if Johnson was seriously courting Julie.

Corbin had asked Ira Brady, the mayor, about Evan Johnson and had learned that the man had left Fertile as a twelve-year-old kid and returned here a few months ago after serving in the military during the war. Why would a college educated, world-traveled man with a sizable inheritance from his grandparents come back to a one-horse town like Fertile?

Corbin slowed his steps as he reached Main Street. He bet folks wondered the same thing about him. But he had a damn good reason for being here. He was reasonably sure that a man in this town was responsible for the death of a girl he had loved all his life and he was determined to find him. When he'd come home from the war and learned that Elaine was dead, grief had brought him to his knees.

Corbin had learned that three other girls from the area had been raped that summer, all blindfolded and dragged into the woods. Elaine had fought her rapist. The tiny scrap of paper found clutched in her hand was torn from a sale bill. The paper was wet, but the printed words were easy to read: *Fertile, Mo.*

April—. Elaine had seen and recognized the rapist and he had killed her.

Businesses along the street were closing. Corbin nodded a good-night to Frank Adler, the druggist, when he came to lock the front door. He had made it his business to find out as much as he could about the council members. Frank was the only one who wasn't married. He lived in rooms over the drugstore. To Corbin's way of thinking, Adler was an unlikely man to be in the retail business. He wasn't very friendly.

Corbin stopped to chat with Albert Boyer, who, with two helpers, ran the only barbershop in town.

"Night, Chief. Don't forget the free cut you got coming for dragging that drunk outta my shop."

"That's what I'm paid for, Albert. You owe me nothing."

"It eases my mind knowin' you're around, Chief."

"Thanks. I'll tell the council. Maybe they'll raise my pay." Corbin grinned, tipped his hat and moved on.

As Corbin moved on down the street, he realized that he liked this town and the people in it. Most of them, anyway. Maybe after his mission was completed he would settle here with a nice girl, like Julie Jones, and raise a family. With that thought, he decided to make a run out past the Jones farm in the morning.

Julie opened the firebox on the stove and shoved in another stick of wood. She had come down to the kitchen this morning after her father had gone out to do the morning chores.

She heard the sound of boots coming down the stairs. Then Joe came in, pushing his shirt down into his pants, and headed for the washbasin.

"Have a good time?" he asked when Julie came to fill the teakettle from the hand pump.

"Pretty good," she replied, looking into his grinning face, her own lips twitching to keep from smiling.

"Pretty good? Guess I'll have to ask Evan."

"Jack Jones! Don't you dare! I'm glad I went. There, are you satisfied? I'm . . . going out with him again next Saturday night," she said with a rush.

"Well, whataya know? You'll probably turn out to be a regular gadabout." Joe splashed water on his face and reached for the towel. "It was an eventful night for the Joneses. You and Papa had dates and Jack made the baseball team."

"Papa didn't come in until late." The smile vanished from Julie's face.

"I know. I heard him."

"Well, what's to come will come. Are you and Jack going to church with us this morning?"

"Ah . . . Sis, I purely hate sittin' in that hot church for hours. I'll ask Papa if I can take you in the car, then come get you when it's over. It's too hot for you and the kids to walk up that hill."

Hearing the sound of boot heels clanking against the wooden stairs, Julie was ready to scold Jack when he entered the kitchen.

"I swear, Jack, you and Joe sound like a couple of mules in a tin barn. You don't know the meaning of the word *quiet*. You're determined to wake up Joy. I was hoping she would sleep until I got breakfast on the table."

The scolding rolled off Jack like water off a duck. He had a wide grin on his face.

"Did ya have a good time with Evan last night? Where'd ya go? What did ya do? Ya like him, don't you? Yeah, ya do." He answered his own question, then added, "I can tell."

"Yeah, she likes him," said Joe. "She's going out with him again."

"No kiddin'? When?"

"This coming Saturday night," Joe said before Julie could answer.

"Don't be spreading that around," Julie said quickly. "I don't want Papa to know yet."

"Sis, when Evan's our brother-in-law, will you put in a good word for me so he'll let me drive his car?" Sparks of mischief glittered in Jack's eyes.

"Get out of here, you . . . you miserable rascals. Get your chores done. Breakfast in thirty minutes." Julie waved a dish towel at them and they scurried to the door.

"Ain't it funny how a woman gets all bossy when she's got a beau?"

"Yeah. She's frisky as a calf full of beans and vinegar this mornin'." Jack let the screen door slam behind him as he trailed his brother out the door.

Julie watched them laughing and teasing each other as they headed for the barn. She loved her brothers very much and knew that they loved her and wanted her to be happy.

Lord, don't let me make too much of what happened last night, even though it was the most exciting night of my life. Let me enjoy Evan's company while it lasts.

A little of the happy glow left her when she remembered that she had no right to dream of a life with any man as long as Joy, Jill and Jason needed her to take care of them.

Chapter 17

JULIE LIFTED HER GAZE from the pancake batter she was stirring when her father came into the kitchen.

"Mornin', Papa."

"Mornin'. Jack didn't cover the milk very good when he took it to the cellar last night. A mouse fell in and drowned. I used it to slop the hogs."

"I wish you hadn't told me that."

Julie knew from his tone that he was not in a very agreeable mood, and it wasn't because of the milk. A bucket of milk was no great loss. His outing with Mrs. Stuart might not have gone well. Julie was thinking this when he left the kitchen, crossed the hall and went into the room he'd shared with Julie's mother for seventeen years. She heard the door close.

When breakfast was ready, except for the frying of the pancakes, Julie hurried up the stairs to wake Jill and Jason. Normally she would have called to them, but she didn't want her father to become aware that Jill had not come down to help prepare the meal.

When she left the boys' room, she met Jill going down the stairs. After looking in to see if Joy was still sleeping, she followed Jill to the kitchen.

The first thing Jill said was, "Did you have a good time?"

"Yes, I did."

"I like him. He's nice and he doesn't treat me like I was a little kid. Did he kiss you?" Jill put her hand over her mouth in an attempt to stifle a giggle and watched her sister's cheeks turn rosy.

"That is none of your business." Julie put her fingers to her lips. "Papa's grouchy this morning, so don't mention Evan."

"He didn't come home until after midnight. I heard the clock strike. I hope he had a miserable time."

"Oh, honey—"

Jill tossed her head. "I don't care." When she said Joy's favorite words, Julie smiled in spite of the dread that breakfast was not going to be pleasant this morning.

"Wash up. The boys will be here in a minute."

Julie fried pancakes in a large shallow skillet while the family was settling at the table. Jethro had come in when he heard the boys at the wash bench. Julie put the platter on the table, then sat down between Jill and Jason.

"Do I have to go to church?" Jason grumbled.

"Do you have anything better to do?" Julie asked.

"Joe and Jack don't have to go."

"They did when they were your age."

"When I'm sixteen, I'm not going."

"You've got a way to go before then. Eat your breakfast and go get cleaned up."

Julie glanced at her father. The only words he had uttered since coming to the table were, "Pass the butter." Joe and Jack had their heads bowed over their plates and Jill had turned sulky. Only Jason seemed unaware of the tension. Julie tried to catch Joe's eyes, but he evaded hers. Was he aware, as she was, that their father was wound tighter than a drum this morning?

When he had finished his breakfast, Jethro got up and filled his coffee cup from the pot on the cookstove. He sat back down and, with his forearms on the table, his big hands around his cup, looked directly across the table at Julie.

"This is my house." The unexpected words fell into a silence. His next words were almost belligerent. "I have the right to invite anyone I want to come here."

Julie knew that his words were directed to her. She couldn't have said anything if her life had depended on it.

"I have invited Mrs. Stuart and her daughter to come and stay here for a while."

Julie's spine sagged; her heart suddenly felt as if it were going to jump out of her chest. She sat there stupidly, her emotions like a crazy seesaw. Her gaze clashed head-on with her father's. She blinked. Oh, sweet Jesus! She took a deep breath and held it.

"I'll remind you again that I am the head of this house, and any guest I invite here will be made to feel welcome."

No one said anything. The others were as shocked as she was.

"This is a . . . surprise." Julie's throat was tight, and she just barely managed the words. *Surprise* wasn't the right word. It sounded so trite, when she felt as if she had just fallen off a cliff or been hit by a tornado.

"I guess it is, but it's done." Jethro's eyes roamed the faces of his children, resting longer on Jill than the others, as if daring her to question his decision.

Julie's mind grasped the situation. He was being defensive because he knew the family didn't like Birdie. He would have to have been deaf not to have heard the remarks made about her, not only by his family, but by the neighbors.

"We don't have an extra . . . bed." Julie's words filled the void.

"Birdie and Elsie can have my room. I'll take Jill's bed and she can sleep on the canvas cot in your room."

Julie held his gaze. She felt tears close to the surface now. How long would she be able to hold them back?

"I don't like that girl," Jason blurted. "She's nasty and spoiled."

"It doesn't matter if you like her or not. You'll be nice to her." Jethro's eyes turned on his youngest son. "And you'll keep Sidney tied up. If he bites her, I'll shoot him."

"Sidney won't bite her if she don't hit him with a stick. It's what she done to Blackie over at the Humphreys'." Jason's voice trembled and tears appeared in his eyes. Julie grasped his hand under the table and held it. She knew how much he loved Sidney and how he hated to cry in front of his brothers.

"She's afraid of dogs like you're afraid of lightning. You'll keep Sidney in the barn and tied up. That's my final word and you'd better heed it."

"I . . . hate her." Jason got up and hurried out onto the back porch.

Seeing her little brother slump down on the edge of the porch and put his face in his hands made Julie angry. She stood and braced herself. Her slender fingers whitened as they gripped the back of the chair. Her father also stood.

"When is she coming?"

"I'm going to get her and Elsie this morning. She'll be here for the noon meal. She'll be a help to you, Julie." He said the last in a softer tone.

You'll not convince me of that in a million years.

"Before Mrs. Stuart takes over your room, I'd like to take out some of Mama's things."

"Your mother's been gone for nigh on five years—"

"I want her comb and brush set, her crocheted dresser scarves, her trunk and her pictures," she insisted.

"Then take them." He glared at her and swore. "Dammit to hell!" After surveying the others with an angry glance, he stomped out of the room and down the hall to the front porch.

Julie put her hand on her sister's stiff shoulder when she heard the groan of pain that came from her. Jill looked straight ahead as if she were in a daze.

"Oh, honey!" Julie hugged Jill's head to her. Jill made no response.

Joe and Jack got up from the table. "Need help, Sis?" Joe asked.

Julie nodded and led the way to the room across the hall.

"Joe, the pitcher and bowl set was a wedding present to Mama and Papa from her folks. Take it up to my room and bring down the one I've been using."

Julie took the comb, brush and mirror from the bureau and opened the top drawer to get the hair saver that matched them. She placed them in Jack's waiting arms, then folded a scarf and took two more out of the drawer. Working calmly and swiftly, she removed from the wall a picture of a girl standing beside a garden gate. She and Joe had given it to their mother the last Christmas of her life. She took several family pictures from the wall, then lifted the lid on the humpbacked trunk and placed them and the other things inside.

"Take the trunk to my room," she instructed when Joe returned.

While the boys were struggling to get the heavy trunk up the stairs, Julie surveyed the room. The bed was unmade and her father's clothes were scattered about. So be it; she'd be damned if she would clean it. She went out and shut the door.

Jill was still sitting at the table when Julie went back to the kitchen. She was staring off into space. It was as if all the emotion had been drained out of her. She didn't acknowledge Julie as she began clearing the table and piling the dishes in the dishpan.

Joe and Jack came down and went to sit on the edge of the porch with Jason, who was scratching the ears of a grateful Sidney.

"Julie." Jill's voice came from behind her and she jumped. "I'll not stay here. I'm going to ask Ruby May's mother if I can stay there for a while. If I can't stay there, I'll run away to Iowa. Aunt Blanche would want me."

"Oh, Jill. Don't do anything foolish. I couldn't bear it here without you. Wait it out with me and see what happens." Julie blinked the tears from her eyes.

"I won't stay here with her. She's a rotten, two-faced bitch!" Jill went back to the table and put her head on her folded arms.

Joy came down and climbed onto a chair beside Jill and helped herself to a cold pancake.

"You want butter on that, honey?" Julie asked.

"Uh-huh. Is Jill sick?" Joy's little face screwed up in a frown. "I don't want Jill to be sick."

"I don't, either. Maybe if we don't bother her she'll feel better."

Julie buttered a pancake, spread it with jelly and rolled it so that Joy could hold it. She set a glass of milk on the table and went back to stacking the dishes in the pan.

"Julie." Jethro stood in the doorway. "I'd like to talk to you."

Julie took her time drying her hands. She glanced at Jill, who sat as still as before.

"Eat your breakfast, Joy. I'll be right back."

Julie reached the porch and stood with her back to the screen door while she waited for him to turn and say what he wanted to say. When he did turn to face her, she saw anger on his face.

"Why don't you like Birdie? Why are you acting as if I don't have the right to invite her to my home? Birdie has no other place to go. She lost her husband, for Christ's sake, and the Humphreys are treating her as if she and her daughter are taking the food right out of the mouths of their kids. She needs a place to stay until she can get her affairs in order." Julie said nothing and was shocked at the bitterness in his voice when he added, "I've worked for twenty-five years on this farm to make a living for my family; and when I invite someone to my home, I have to take shit from my kids."

"What do you want me to do, Papa?"

"I want you to make her welcome. Set the example. The others will follow your lead."

"How long will she stay?"

"I don't know. She's going to get in touch with her in-laws in Tennessee and see if she can go there."

"Why didn't she go to them in the first place instead of coming here?"

"I don't know about that."

"She could get a job and work for her keep. Other widows do."

"Christ on a horse, Julie. Birdie has always had someone to take care of her. She doesn't know the first thing about working and taking care of herself."

"She could learn. I'm sure there are a great many things she could do."

Jethro shoved his hands down into his pockets and paced the porch, seeming not to have heard what Julie said.

"The Humphreys have made her life miserable for the last few weeks. Birdie can't do anything to please Mrs. Humphrey. She complains constantly to Wilbur about his sister being there. Poor little Elsie is picked on by the Humphrey kids until she's scared to leave her mother's side."

"Ruth Humphrey has her hands full taking care of her own family, without taking in extras to wait on," Julie murmured.

Jethro stopped pacing. "I thought that you, of all people, would understand that things can happen beyond a woman's control. And at that time a woman needs the support of family and friends to help her weather a rough time."

The words were said slowly and whipped Julie like a lash. Julie felt as if her father, her beloved father, had kicked her in the stomach. She took a deep breath and braced her thin shoulders. Her eyes glazed over as she gazed at the back of his head as he stared out across the field. Determined not to let him know how much he had hurt her, she looked him straight in the eye when he turned to face her.

"Do you plan to marry her?"

"Would it be so bad if I married . . . someone?"

"It's your right." She switched her gaze to some point behind him.

"Birdie thinks that you don't like her."

"I've not given her a reason to think that."

"She says that when she tries to talk to you, get to know you, you turn away and give her the cold shoulder."

"That's not true. She's never tried to get to know me, or Jill, or Joy, for that matter."

"If you're afraid she'll set her cap for Evan Johnson, you can rest easy. She said for me to tell you that she has no interest in him because of Walter, and as far as she's concerned, you have a clear field with him."

"Evan isn't good enough for her, but he's good enough for me. That's very generous of Mrs. Stuart." Julie's voice was heavy with sarcasm.

"Don't be nasty!" Jethro said sharply. "Birdie thinks that you like him, and that as long as he's here, you might as well go out with him. That doesn't mean she would approve of you marrying him."

Julie stared at some point beyond his head for a long moment before she answered.

"You've discussed me with her. Have you shared all the family secrets with Mrs. Stuart, Papa?"

"Don't be ridiculous! Birdie thinks you should get out more and mix with other young people—that it isn't fair that you be tied down here. She suggested that you cut your hair and dress suitable to the times. She's promised to help you."

"Are you ashamed of the way I look, the way I dress, of what . . . I am?"

"You know damn well I'm not!"

"Do you want me to leave, to make it easier for Mrs. Stuart to be here?" Julie felt as though someone else were speaking the words for her. She heard them but couldn't feel them in her mouth. An incredible numbness had settled over her like a heavy cloak.

"Leave? Hell, who said anything about you leaving? Where would you go, for God's sake?"

"Women who find themselves in a situation beyond their control usually call on family and friends to help them weather a rough time." She was glad to see the sparks of anger glitter in his eyes when she repeated his words. She wiped the swath of hair from her forehead and turned to open the screen door.

"She wants to be a help to you, Julie."

It was the second time he'd said that. Julie looked at her father as if she had never seen him before. His words hung in the air between them. Anguish worked in her face, threatening her control.

Birdie Stuart knew exactly what she was doing. She had him so infatuated with her that he would believe whatever she told him and would turn against his own family in order to have her.

"Julie? Can I count on you to make Birdie and Elsie welcome?"

"As long as I'm living in your house, eating your food, I'll not disgrace you. I owe you that, Papa." She trembled with the force of unreleased emotions and backed away from the cold fury in his eyes that her words had provoked.

"Julie! Julie! Come quick. Joy cut her hand with the butcher knife."

Julie threw open the door and ran down the hall to the kitchen. Jill had Joy astride her hip and was holding her hand over the wash dish. Joy was screaming, "Julie, Julie!"

"Let me see." Julie worked the handle on the water pump until water gushed out. After the water washed the blood away, Julie could see only a small slice on the end of the child's thumb. "It's isn't bad. Just a little cut."

"Blood," Joy shrieked. "It hurts!"

"We'll have to put iodine on it, honey. It will sting for a minute."

"Come to Papa, pumpkin." Jethro crowded in behind Jill

and lifted Joy from her arms. He sat down and cuddled the child on his lap.

"It hurts, Papa."

"It won't hurt long. Julie will put iodine on it, then wrap it in a bandage. You're a big girl."

Julie got out the iodine and a strip of clean cloth. She was so wrung out from the emotional scene on the porch that she couldn't even look at her father while she bandaged Joy's finger. When she finished, she put away the iodine, took the little girl up into her arms and headed for the stairs.

"Julie." Her father's voice stopped her, but she didn't turn. "What am I going to do with my things?"

"There are boxes in the attic," she said and continued on up the steps.

Out of breath from carrying the child, she sank down on the edge of her bed when she reached it. She cuddled Joy to her and rocked back and forth. She wished that she could lie back on the bed and give way to her grief. She felt as if her heart had been pounded to a pulp. Her father's infatuation with Mrs. Stuart was tearing the family apart.

Julie abandoned any notion of going to church. The thought uppermost in her mind was that she had to get herself together. The others were depending on her to help them get through this. But was it something that would end? Was Birdie going to be a permanent part of their lives?

It wasn't until Jethro got into his car and left that Julie had a chance to talk to Joe. He and Jack came to the house as soon as the car turned from the lane onto the road.

"Jason's sick about having to keep Sidney tied up." Jack set a couple of ripe cantaloupes on the counter. "That dog trails him everywhere."

"What do you think, Sis?" For once her brother Joe was not teasing. He and Jack looked dead serious. "I saw you and Pa on the porch."

"He wants us to make her welcome. Joe, I don't know if I can do it. If it was anyone else, I'd be happy for Papa."

"I'm not stayin' here to wait on her. I'm going to write Aunt Blanche and see if I can go stay with her." Jill was so angry her voice was shrill. "To hear the Humphreys tell it, she's sweet as pie when her brother is around and mean as sin when he isn't. It's how she'll be here."

"Now, hold on," Joe said and put his arm across Jill's shoulders. "She'd like nothin' more than to get rid of us. Then she'd have everything her own way. Jack and I have been mulling this over, and we think that her coming here is the best thing that could have happened."

Jill jerked from under his arm. "Are you crazy?"

"We'll give her the rope to hang herself. With her here day after day, Pa will finally see what she's really like. We'll have to be careful and be polite and give her nothing to use against us. It'll be hardest on you, Julie and Joy. Jack and I will keep our distance and try and figure out a way to keep Jason from clobbering her brat."

"Jack?" Julie's questioning eyes went to her younger brother.

"It's the best we can do right now. Let's hope Pa comes to his senses before he marries her."

"She's told Papa the Humphreys were mean to her and that I wouldn't talk to her."

"She's a big fat liar," Jill said angrily. "She told Mr. Humphrey that This would sic the dog on Elsie whenever she was outside and she wanted him to give This a whipping. They hate her over there."

"We've got to be smarter than she is, Jill," Joe said patiently. "Don't let her see how much you hate her. It'll just make Pa feel sorry for her."

"Where did you learn so much, Joe?" Julie asked, hugging his arm.

"Why, Sis, I've been smart all along and you just haven't noticed it."

"Can I give you a hug?"

"Hadn't you better save your hugs for Evan?" he said laughingly and threw his arm around her shoulders when her cheeks reddened.

"That's another thing—Mrs. Stuart told Papa that she couldn't be interested in Evan because of who his father is, and would step aside and give me a clear field with him. Wasn't that nice of her?"

"Name of a cow! Wait till I tell Evan she's lettin' him off the hook. He was on to her from the start. He calls her a piranha."

"Whatever that is, I hope it's bad," Jill said.

"I asked him what it was and he said it was a fish with powerful jaws and razor-sharp teeth. It kills animals or humans and eats them."

"Don't tell Evan," Julie said quickly. "Please. It's embarrassing to think that Papa discussed me with her."

"Why not tell him? He'll get a laugh out of it. But I won't tell him if you don't want me to."

Julie felt a little better after talking to her brothers. Joe's reasoning had made sense. If they criticized Birdie, their father would be forced to take her side. Julie took comfort in knowing that she and Jill were not alone in their dislike of the woman.

The front screen door slammed. Seconds later Joy burst into the room.

"Julie, Julie. The runnin' man's comin'."

Chapter 18

CHIEF APPLEBY?"

"The runnin' man," Joy shouted again and raced back down the hall to the front door.

As the others followed, Julie asked, "Where's Jason?"

"The last I saw of him, he was on the back porch with Sidney."

"Go on and meet Mr. Appleby. I'll talk to Jason."

Julie had been unable to voice the fear of Walter Johnson's threat to anyone but Joe. He believed that the man was just being mean and trying to scare her; but she knew that his threat could be real, and with that thought she went out into the yard and called to Jason.

When she didn't receive an answer and there was no sign of him or Sidney, she went down the slope to the barn.

"Jason? Are you in here?" She walked between the silent stalls. "Jason." She reached the open doors at the end of the barn and scanned the cow lot and the pasture beyond. After going back through the barn and up the ladder to the hayloft, she called him again, then hurried to the shed where the plows and other equipment were kept. "Jason!" She continued to call as she went to the tack room attached to the barn.

Julie's anxiety was escalating by the time she finished searching the outbuildings. Jason always answered if he was within hearing distance of her call. She made one more trip to the barn, then ran around to the front of the house.

The oak water bucket was on the porch, and Corbin Appleby had just poured a dipper of water over his head to the shrieks of delight coming from Joy, who sat astride Jack's hip.

"I can't find Jason," Julie gasped. Then, remembering her manners: "Hello, Chief Appleby."

Joe stepped off the porch. "Isn't he in the barn?"

"No. The only place I haven't looked is the cellar, but he couldn't lift the door, then close it behind him."

"Don't worry, Sis. Joe and I will find him." Jack set Joy on her feet.

"I'm afraid he's taken Sidney and run off."

Jill stood on the porch holding tightly to Joy's hand to keep her from following Joe and Jack.

"I just knew something like this would happen," Jill blurted. "I hope *he's* satisfied."

"Tell me where to look." Corbin ran his fingers through his hair to shake out the water. His sharp ears had caught Jill's words and wondered who the *he* was.

"Jason may have gone over to the Humphreys'," Jack said.

"He wouldn't have gone there, knowing that Papa would be there. He may have gone toward town," Jill said.

"Is Jason lost?" Joy pulled on Jill's hand.

"We just don't know where he is," Jill answered patiently.

"I don't want Jason to be lost." Joy began to cry.

"I didn't meet anyone on the road," Corbin said.

"Jack, why don't you take the lane through the woods that comes out at Well's Point?"

"I'll get a bridle and grab a horse as I go through the pasture." Jack darted into the tack room.

Julie clutched Joe's arm. "Joe, I'm afraid of . . . you know."

Corbin saw the fear on Julie's face and heard her whispered words to her brother. Was she afraid the boy would fall in the river or was there something else frightening her?

"He hasn't been gone long enough to get far. I'll get my horse and search the timber between us and the Johnsons' where we cut the dead trees; and Chief Appleby, if you don't mind, take a look in the patch of woods between here and town. He may have decided to go that way," Joe said.

"Sis, you stay here with Jill and Joy; and if he comes back, pull on the lever that starts the windmill. If we see the blades turning, it means he's been found."

"Hurry, Joe. Please hurry."

Julie was afraid that Walter Johnson had come across Jason out in the woods. Would Sidney be able to protect him against a man Walter's size? This spring the dog had set himself between Jason and a mean bull, giving the boy time to roll under a fence. But a man could pick up a club and knock the animal senseless.

Corbin lingered to speak to Julie. When he had met her before, she had been as tranquil as a harbor in a storm. Today, she was different. She was on edge; her eyes were never still. He sensed that there was something troubling her in addition to not being able to find her brother.

"Are there any pits or wells or areas of quicksand around here the boy could have fallen into?" Fear flickered across her face and he added, "It's a question that's asked when a child is missing."

"There are no pits or wells that I know of. I've heard that there's quicksand down by the river."

"How far are you from the river?"

"About a mile and a half. Jason . . . can't walk very fast."

"I noticed that he wore a special shoe. Do you think he's had time to get to the river?"

"I'm trying to think of the last time I saw him. It couldn't have been more than an hour ago that he was sitting on the porch with Sidney."

"Sidney is his dog?"

"Papa told him that he had to keep Sidney tied in the barn,"

Jill said angrily. "Jason hardly ever goes anywhere without Sidney tagging along."

"I suppose your father has a reason for wanting the dog tied in the barn."

"You can bet your sweet patoot he does!"

"Jill, please don't," Julie scolded her sister, while her eyes continued to scan the edges of the woods surrounding the homestead.

"I'll look for him between here and town, Miss Jones."

"Thank you."

Corbin took off across the pasture that was used for the ball games. Julie watched him running easily, but her concern for her little brother overwhelmed any further interest. *Oh, God, please don't let Jason be with Walter Johnson.*

Thoughts of Birdie Stuart had fled to the back of Julie's mind. Jason was hurting, feeling he had been shoved aside by his father in favor of a spoiled little brat he detested. Julie feared that he might have gone to Evan and had encountered Walter instead.

"Julie." Joy came to lean against Julie. "Did the buggerman get Jason?" Julie looked down at the little tear-streaked face.

"No, honey. He just went off somewhere and forgot to tell me where he was going. Joe and Jack will bring him back."

"And the runnin' man?"

"If he finds him, he'll bring him back."

"I like Mr. Johnson better'n him."

"You know Mr. Johnson better. Chief Appleby is a nice man."

"He didn't pick me up or swing me like Mr. Johnson does or take me for a ride in his car or buy me ice cream."

"You shouldn't like people only for what they do for you."

"I hope *he* comes back before they find Jason." Jill, with a mutinous look on her young face, folded her arms across her chest. "It would serve *him* right to see how bad *he* hurt Jason. But I guess *he* don't care as long as *he* gets what *he* wants."

"Jill, please." Julie rolled her eyes down to Joy, who was listening intently to what Jill was saying.

"Is Jason hurt?" Joy asked, eyes filling with tears.

"No, honey. Jason is—" Julie stopped when she heard Sidney's bark. "Oh, thank goodness," she breathed when she saw Evan riding along the side pasture fence with Jason sitting in the saddle in front of him. Joe was riding beside them. "Jill, run pull the lever to start the blades turning so that Jack and Chief Appleby will know we've found him."

"Here comes Papa and *her*."

The car had turned into the lane and stopped beside the front porch by the time Jill pulled the lever and ran back to wait with Julie for the horse bringing Jason home. Thinking it great fun to be following the horses, Sidney ran around them and barked. Joe came on ahead. When he saw the car beside the porch, he knew that the dog would run and bark a greeting. Jumping off his horse, he caught Sidney just as the dog spied the woman and girl getting out of the car.

Joy broke loose from Julie and ran back toward the house. Visitors were more exciting than Jason coming home on a horse. At Julie's nod, Jill ran to catch up with her.

Evan got off his horse and lifted Jason down.

"Honey, I was so worried." Julie hugged the boy to her. Looking over Jason's head to Evan, she said, "Thank you for bringing him home."

Evan nodded. "He'll be all right. We were on our way here when we met Joe."

"Oh, honey, did you run all the way to Evan's?"

"No. He met me . . . in the woods. That girl's here," Jason said accusingly. "I hate her."

"It's your right to dislike her, but try and not let it show in front of Papa. Now go help Joe find a good cool place in the barn for Sidney." As soon as the boy left them, Julie turned her back to the house and looked up at Evan. "He's bringing her here to stay until she can go to her in-laws'." Her lips trembled. Evan wished they were out of sight of the others so that he could put his arms around her.

"Jason told me. He's torn up about having to keep his dog tied up."

"That's why he ran off."

"He wanted to know if he could live with me."

"Oh, Evan. The poor little boy. Papa doesn't know what he's doing to the family. Jill wants to go the Jacobs' and stay with Ruby May until she can write to our aunt in Iowa. Papa has demanded that we welcome Mrs. Stuart and her daughter. I don't know if I can do it."

"Ah, sweetheart. I wish there was something I could do to help." The endearment slipped out without either of them noticing it. "All you can do is play her game. She'll be all sweetness when Jethro is around. You can do the same and then it'll be her word against yours when she complains about you."

"That's what Joe said to do. I don't know how Jill and Jason will manage that. Jack is supposed to go practice this afternoon. Maybe he'll take Jason with him."

"Why don't I take all of you to watch the game?"

"Evan. You don't have to. I'll—"

"I want to. It'll keep you away from her for a while and give you a little breathing space." He glanced over her shoulder and saw that Joe was helping his father carry Birdie's trunk into the house. Evan reached out and squeezed Julie's hand. "We'll plan our strategy. It's what we did during the war." He smiled, attempting to lighten her mood.

"All right." Her eyes were still misty bright, her mouth was taut and there was an air of unconscious dignity about her poised head.

"Please. Never hesitate to ask me for help." He rubbed his fingertips back and forth across her arm. "Remember this, Julie. Mrs. Stuart can't hold a candle to you. Don't let her make you feel that you are in any way inferior to her, because believe me, you're not." He longed to kiss the bleakness from her eyes. "Promise me?"

"I promise." She turned her hand over and gripped his. "I'd better go get dinner on. You're welcome to stay."

He laughed. "And make matters worse? I'll get on home, but I'll be back to take you to the ball game."

Jack came riding into the yard. "You found him?"

"He was on his way over to Evan's. Evan brought him home."

"Hellfire," Jack swore as he got off his horse. "I don't know what Pa's thinkin' of. Jason is just a little kid and he loves that dog."

"Jason is afraid the girl will hit Sidney; and if she does, the dog will bite her." Evan held on to Julie's hand even when she tried to pull it away.

"Pa said he'd shoot him. I can't believe he'd do that, but Jason thinks he would."

"I'd better go see what Jill's up to." Julie tugged on her hand again. "Thanks again, Evan."

"What time is your game, Jack?"

"Mr. Poole said to be there about three."

"I'll be back here at two-thirty, Julie." Evan reluctantly let go of Julie's hand. He and Jack watched her hurry toward the house.

"She'll have a rough time with that woman here." Jack's gaze flicked to Evan's. "You like my sister, don't you?"

Evan betrayed no surprise at the question. "Yes, I do. Do you mind?" He sensed, rather than heard, the boy sigh.

"I'm glad," Jack said slowly. "She'll never leave the kids here. You need to know that."

"I know it. If she'll have me, she'll not have to leave them."

Jack's head whipped around. "Are you shittin' me?"

"No." Evan laughed. "It's early for me to say anything, so keep it under your hat."

"It's a relief to know she'll have someone after Joe and I

are gone. Joe'll be glad, too." Jack's young face lost its grin. "I don't know what the hell's wrong with Pa. There are several nice women in town he could have courted. Miss Meadows, the preacher's sister, is one of them. There wouldn't be the ruckus there is now if he'd chosen her."

"There's a saying in the army that when a man's pecker get's hard, his brain gets soft. Let's hope that while that's going on, your pa doesn't marry Mrs. Stuart."

Determined to keep her dislike for Birdie under control, Julie went through the kitchen and crossed the hall to stand in the doorway of her father's room. Birdie was taking clothes out of her suitcase. Her daughter was lying on the bed. Joy leaned against it, trying to get Elsie to go out and play.

"I'll push you in the swing," Joy coaxed. "I'll show you where my red hen lays her eggs."

Elsie ignored Joy's pleadings.

"I'm sorry I wasn't here when you arrived," Julie said, louder than she had intended.

"Hello, Julie. I hope we'll not be an inconvenience. Jethro insisted that we come here."

"It will take some adjusting for both of us, Mrs. Stuart. Is there anything you need?" Not waiting for an answer, Julie continued, "If not, I'll get dinner on. Come help me, Joy."

"Call me Birdie, dear."

"I can't do that, Mrs. Stuart. I try to set an example for the younger children by not calling older people by their first names."

Julie beckoned to Joy and failed to see the tightening of Birdie's lips. As Julie and Joy turned to go down the hall to look for Jill, she heard Elsie's whiny voice.

"Ma . . . Ma. I don't like it here."

"She doesn't like me," Joy said and sniffed back tears.

"Don't worry about it. I like you more than any little girl

in the whole world." Julie opened the screen door and looked out onto the vacant porch.

"Why don't she like me? I didn't do anythin' to her."

"I'm sure you didn't, honey. Try to not pay attention to what she says. Do you know where Jill is?"

"Upstairs."

"Then you've got to help me by setting the table."

Jethro was in the kitchen combing his hair. He moved back away from the wash dish when Julie poured water to wash her hands.

"Where's Jill?"

"Joy said she went upstairs."

"She'd better get herself down here and act decent."

"She's fixing herself a place to sleep." Julie wet a cloth and washed Joy's face and then her hands.

"What's for dinner?"

"Chicken and dumplings, peas, carrots and . . . corn bread. I baked it right after breakfast. It only needs warming up." She looked at him and away. "There'll be nine at the table. We only have seven chairs and Joy's stool. You'll have to bring in the short wash bench from the porch."

When Jethro went to the porch, Julie whispered to Joy, "Go up and tell Jill to come down."

It was a quiet group that gathered on the back porch waiting to be called in for dinner. Normally they would have been in the kitchen, nagging Julie to hurry. When Julie set the large bowl of chicken and dumplings on the table, Jethro knocked on his bedroom door.

"Birdie, dinner is ready."

The door opened immediately. Birdie, wearing a soft pink dress as if she were going to church, came into the kitchen. Elsie, in a white skirt and middy, white knee-high stockings and black button slippers, clung to her hand. Long fat curls hung over her shoulders. Across the top of her head was a white, flat bow. The thought crossed Julie's mind that Birdie's late husband had been a good provider.

"Something smells delicious." Then, eyeing the table, "Goodness' sakes, it looks like a regular feast. I've heard that you're a wonderful cook, Julie."

"Sit here, Mrs. Stuart. Elsie can sit on the bench beside you."

The boys filed in. Joe and Jack nodded to Birdie. Jason walked around the table and took his place next to where Julie sat between him and Joy. Jill took her place, then Jethro. The family bowed their heads and Jethro prayed aloud in a clear, calm voice.

"Dear Lord, we thank Thee for the provisions Thou hath provided for us, your children. Bless this food for the nourishment of our bodies. We ask Thee to bless this family and our guests. Amen." He looked at Birdie. "Pass your plate, Birdie. This bowl is too big to pass around."

"Oh, my, it looks just scrumptious, but don't give me very much and give Elsie just a tiny bit until we see whether or not she likes it."

There was silence until all the plates were filled. Julie tried to think of something to say and finally said, "This is the last of the fresh peas."

"They are certainly delicious. You are a good cook, Julie."

"Thank you, but it doesn't take much skill to boil peas."

"Everything is so good."

Elsie tugged at her mother's sleeve. Birdie tilted her head toward her daughter.

"I don't like this," Elsie said in a loud whisper and pushed the dumpling around on her plate with her fork.

"Then eat your chicken and corn bread."

"I don't like the chicken either. It's . . . tough."

"She's a finicky eater." Birdie looked at Julie with an apologetic smile. "She doesn't like peas or carrots. There aren't many things she likes."

"Why don't she like peas and carrots, Julie? I like 'em." Joy's voice overrode Birdie's last words.

"I like ice cream," Elsie said, and looked up at her mother for confirmation.

"We don't happen to have ice cream today, Elsie." Julie smiled. "You'll have to make do with milk and corn bread."

"Chief Appleby came by on his morning run, Pa." Joe edged in to change the subject.

"He poured water on his head," Joy added. "Then he went to find Jason."

"Why?" Jethro asked. "Where was Jason?"

"He was riding with Evan on his horse. Joe was with them," Julie spoke matter-of-factly. "Save room for bread pudding, Joy."

"Bread pudding?" Birdie smiled down at her daughter. "You like bread pudding."

"Not if it doesn't have raisins," Elsie whispered, but loud enough for everyone at the table to hear.

"Does it have raisins in it?" Joy asked.

"No, honey, it doesn't," Julie replied quietly.

Jethro asked Jack about the baseball practice and who was on the Fertile team. Jack gleefully told him how he had edged out Scott Graham as team catcher.

When the chicken and dumpling bowl was empty, Jill removed it from the table and brought the pan of bread pudding and a pitcher of cream.

"You'll like this, sugar, even without raisins." Birdie added a generous amount of cream to the pudding in her daughter's bowl.

Julie's eyes met Joe's briefly, then went to her father, whose face seemed anxious. He was watching Birdie serve her daughter.

Julie was relieved when the meal was finished. She had eaten automatically. When the boys pushed back their chairs and left the table, Jason rose, too.

"Finish your pudding, Jason." When his father spoke, the

boy slumped back down on the chair and spooned the pudding into his mouth at a fast pace until the bowl was empty. He looked at his father, then left the table and hurried outside.

After Julie lifted Joy from her stool and washed her face and hands, the child went to Elsie.

"Come play with me, pl-ease!"

"You're gettin' me dirty." Elsie pushed Joy's hands from her dress.

"I am not. My hands just got washed." She held her palms up.

"I don't want to play with you. You're too little."

Joy backed away. "I don't like you, either. So there!" She turned and ran toward the door. Jethro caught her up in his arms before she could go outside.

"She'll play with you later, punkin. This place is strange to her now."

"I don't like her. She's mean. Jason don't like her, either." Joy wriggled, trying to get down. Jethro set her on her feet and she ran out the door.

Julie caught Jill hiding a smile behind a dish towel.

"Oh, Jethro. I'm so sorry. Elsie has been alone so much that she doesn't know how to act with other children."

Jethro always insisted the children eat what they put on their plates. Julie wondered how he would react to the chicken and dumpling Elsie left on her plate and to the half-filled dish of pudding when she left the table to go stand beside her mother.

"What can I do to help, Julie?" Birdie began gathering dishes from the table.

"You can scrape any food left on the plates here in the slop bucket for the hogs and stack the dishes on the counter. Jill and I will start washing."

"Honey, go sit down," Birdie said to Elsie, "while Mommy helps Julie."

"No," Julie said quickly when Birdie dumped the peas in the bucket. "Just throw out the food left on the plates. The corn bread and pudding still left in the pan can be eaten later."

"I'm sorry. I didn't realize you wanted to save the peas."

Jethro watched from the doorway, then went down the hall to the porch.

Chapter 19

SUNDAY WAS A SLOW DAY IN FERTILE. Corbin finished his run, bathed and put on a freshly ironed pair of tan pants and a white shirt. He headed for Sparky's Eatery, the only place that served food on Sunday.

Yesterday Corbin had circled around to go back to the Jones farm when he saw the blades on the windmill spinning, the signal the boy had been found. He had been relieved. A small boy lost, expecially in the vicinity of quicksand, was not a pleasant thought.

Something was going on out there that had the younger Jones girl riled up against someone. Corbin keep seeing in his mind's eye the worried look on Julie's face. Christ on a horse! When had he started thinking about Miss Jones as Julie?

Well, hell. Why not? She was a pretty woman and he liked the way she had taken on the care of her younger brothers and sisters. She reminded him a lot of Elaine, although Elaine was much smaller, more fragile.

Goddamn the son-of-a-bitch that killed her!

"Been to church already?" Sparky asked when Corbin entered the eatery.

"Naw. Went for a run. Is the missus cooking flapjacks this morning?"

"Sure is. Want a stack?"

"Yeah. And coffee."

"That goes without sayin'. Hear that, honeybunch?" he called toward the kitchen. "Chief wants a stack." Sparky set a cup of steaming coffee on the counter in front of Corbin. "Otto Bloom was in here last night raving about how he was going to get even with you for keeping him out of his house."

"Otto doesn't know his ass from a hole in the ground," Corbin muttered.

"Hey, that's good." Sparky laughed, showing a mouth of gold-filled teeth.

"His kid has the diphtheria. The doc's keeping Otto out so he won't spread the germs around town. Otto's too dumb to understand he could help spread the epidemic."

"He's hangin' out with Walter Johnson."

"Two of a kind."

"I'd not want to tangle with the two of them when they get boozed up. Watch your back around Otto—he's sneaky. Walter is mean as a ruttin' moose, but he'll come at you straight on."

"Mornin', Chief." Young Dr. Forbes came in and slid onto the stool beside Corbin.

"Mornin', Doc."

"Your landlady said I'd find you here."

"What's on your mind?"

"Maybe nothing. Maybe I just like your company." Dr. Forbes grinned at Sparky. "How about coffee?"

"Comin' up."

While Corbin finished his breakfast, he listened to the banter between Sparky and Dr. Todd Forbes and decided that the young doctor could shoot the bull with the best of them.

"Missouri watermelons can't compare to Tennessee watermelons. Tennessee watermelons have the nicest, biggest, flattest seeds for spitting. I can spit one darn near twenty feet and I'm not even the champion."

"Come on, Doc. I'm not talkin' seeds. I'm talking about size. Missouri grows watermelons big around as a water barrel—"

"Yeah. Tennessee grows 'em as big around as a wagon wheel."

Corbin stood. "I don't know if I can wade through all this bullshit to get out of here." He placed some coins on the counter, held up his pants legs and walked carefully to the door.

"Prissy, isn't he?" Dr. Forbes said over his shoulder to Sparky as he followed Corbin out. They walked to the street corner before they spoke.

"Doc Curtis sent me to tell you that a girl was grabbed last night but managed to break away. He thinks it may be the same man who raped the girl down at Well's Point a week or two ago."

"Thank God she got away from him."

"This girl left the house to go to the privy. It sits well back of the house among some bushes. When she came out someone grabbed her from behind, slapped his hand over her mouth and attempted to drag her back into the heavy brush. The girl had her mouth open when he covered it, a finger went inside and she chomped down on it hard. He muttered a curse. She broke away, screamed and ran. She was almost to the house when she fell, cutting her leg on a piece of glass.

"The girl's father and brother searched the area but failed to find a sign of anyone. Her folks brought her in this morning to have Doc sew up the cut in her leg."

"Does Doc think she'll talk to me?"

"She's a brave little girl. He thinks she will, and he thought you might want to look around."

"Let's go."

Birdie settled Elsie on the bed in their room for a nap and escaped to the front porch as soon as she had made a show of helping with the cleanup. Jethro had heard her offer to help and had seen her trying to please Julie.

"It's nice and peaceful here, Jethro," she said and sat down in the porch swing beside him. "Thank you for letting us come here for a while."

"You're welcome to stay as long as you want, Birdie. I couldn't stand to think of you going somewhere and feeling like you were putting folks out."

"Your boys didn't have anything to say to me," she said with a small pout to her lips.

"They're bashful around a pretty woman. They'll get used to you."

"Do you think I'm pretty, Jethro?" She tilted her head inquiringly toward him.

"You're the prettiest woman I've seen in a long, long time," he replied thickly.

"You're sweet, that's what you are." She reached over and placed her hand on the back of his. "I hope I can make Julie and Jill like me. I'm going to try real, real hard. You'll see."

"Give them a little time, Birdie." He turned his hand over and clasped hers tightly. "It's a shock to them to have another woman in the house."

"Oh, I understand. Truly I do. It's difficult for us, too . . . not having a ho-me." Her voice broke and she pulled her hand from his. "Don't be mad at poor little Elsie for not playing with Joy. She had a terrible time over at Wilbur's and she's scared it'll be the same here."

"No one here will mistreat her, or they'll answer to me. Jason is sulking because I told him to tie up his dog, but he'll get over it."

"Elsie and I don't want to be a bother. Oh, my, you don't know how wonderful it is to be here. It's so nice and quiet and . . . safe. All that hubbub over at Wilbur's just kept me on edge all the time."

The screen door slammed behind Joy. She ran to the swing and climbed up into Jethro's lap.

"Papa, guess what?" Her small hands framed his face so he had to look at her. "We're goin' to town to see Jack play ball. Mr. Johnson is comin' in his car."

"When was all of this decided?"

"I don't know." Joy wrapped her arms around his neck and planted a wet kiss on his cheek before she jumped off his lap and raced around the side of the house, scattering the white hens who were busy pecking and scratching among the grass and other greens that edged the lane.

"She's a pistol." Jethro laughed and wiped his cheek. "We've all spoiled her."

"I've noticed," Birdie said dryly. "Aren't you a little worried about the younger children being . . . so familiar with the Johnsons?"

"What do you mean?"

"Well, you know the reputation *they* have."

"Walter has the reputation, not Evan."

"There's an old saying, an apple doesn't fall far from the tree."

"You seem to think it all right for Julie to go out with Evan."

"Julie is a grown woman and can take care of herself. Jill is the one I'd worry about. She's at an age where she's susceptible to the flattery of a worldly man with a nice car and money to spend."

"She's only a kid. She'll be fifteen in a week or two."

"That's what I mean, Jethro, dear. Some men like them young. Evan could be paying attention to Julie in order to be near Jill. You must admit, as lovely as *we* think Julie is, she's not the type a man who has been all over the world would be attracted to. As sad as it is to have to say this, he could be just using her. I'd watch Jill around him if she were my daughter."

"I hadn't thought of that."

"You're such a good, dear, sweet man, Jethro Jones." She patted his thigh. "A thought like that wouldn't enter your mind. You haven't had to face the sorry side of life as I've had to do."

"I reckon not, but I thought Evan was a decent sort. Joe and Jack think so, too."

"I'm not surprised that the *boys* would like him. *Boys* admire a man of the world . . . one who has a car and can tell tall tales."

"Joe is pretty sensible, and he'd raise holy hell if anyone misused Jill or Julie."

"Jethro, dear, all they know about Evan Johnson is what he's told them. How do you know he was in the army? He could have been in prison, for all we know."

"He was in the army. I'm sure of that."

"I've learned to trust my own instincts, Jethro. Some people are just not what they seem to be. My husband's own brother tried to get me in bed not a month after Bobby died. Can you imagine? He had been so nice, helping me with the funeral and all."

"And you want to go back there?"

A small sob escaped her. "It isn't that I want to. We don't have anywhere else to go."

Jethro patted the hands clasped in her lap and Birdie gloated to herself. *If I told him black was white, he'd believe me.*

They were silent for a while and during that time Birdie's mind was busy.

You'll be sorry for slighting me, Evan Johnson, you low-down bastard. If it's the last thing I do before I leave here, I'm going to make sure your name is mud in this town, and people will spit on you when you walk down the street.

When Birdie went to the bedroom to see about Elsie, Jethro went to find Julie. He found her in the kitchen. Joy stood on a kitchen chair stripped down to her underpants. Julie was washing her. Joy was chattering as usual.

"Will Mr. Johnson buy us an ice cream?"

"I don't know, sugarfoot. It wouldn't be nice to mention it."

"I won't. Can I ride in front? I'll be still."

"We'll have to wait and see. You'll be nice. I know you will." Julie lifted Joy off the chair. "Run up and put on the clean dress I laid out for you." Julie poured the water from the wash dish into the tin sink and watched as it drained down the pipe and into the yard while she waited for her father to speak.

"Joy said Evan was coming by to take you and the kids to the ball park. Do you think it's the thing to do . . . leave when we have company in the house?" He eyed her keenly.

"I didn't realize that Mrs. Stuart was company. I thought you were providing a place for her to stay for a while."

"She's company. I invited her here," he said belligerently.

"If she's a guest, Papa, she's your guest. I don't think we should deprive the kids of an outing because she's here. Do you object to us going to the ball game?" She looked at him with a puzzled frown.

"No, but I want you to keep an eye on Jill. I don't want Evan Johnson alone with her for one second. Is that understood?"

"What in the world are you hinting at?" Julie stood ramrod straight, chin tilted so that she could look up at him. Her eyes locked with his, her temper in danger of flaring out of control. *What has Mrs. Stuart been telling you?*

"I'm not hinting at anythin'. I'm tellin' ya to keep an eye on Jill and keep her away from Evan Johnson."

Julie took a deep breath, refusing to look away from her father's narrowed eyes.

"What's brought this on? Has Evan given you a reason to think he's interested in Jill?" she asked, but she was sure she knew who was behind his suspicion.

"Jill's just a kid. She's goin' over fool's hill and can be swayed by pretty words from a man like Johnson."

"Good grief, Papa. Do you think Evan is going to force himself on Jill?"

"I'm saying we don't know much about him. Girls Jill's age are easily swayed, and some men get ideas about them. Heed what I say, and you can take the kids. That's my final word on the matter."

Jethro went out onto the back porch and stood with his

back to the door looking off toward the orchard, where Jason sat in the shade of a gnarled old apple tree holding the end of a rope tied around Sidney's neck.

Joe and Jack were playing catch. Jethro was proud of Jack for making the Fertile team. He would like to see him in action. When Elsie woke up from her nap, he might ask Birdie if she would like to go watch the practice.

Why in hell did things have to be so complicated? Why couldn't the kids have been happy that he had found someone to be a companion to him? In another few years they would be gone and he would be alone. If Julie married, she would take Joy. Thoughts of the lonely years ahead were scary.

Birdie wasn't suited to life on the farm, and he feared that she never would be. He was uncertain about how he would making a living for her if they left the farm after the children were gone. His hope had been that Birdie would get used to it and be content to stay here.

It occurred to him suddenly that he was thinking about marrying her. Reason kicked in, and he realized that it was too soon for that. He didn't want to rush her into anything just because, at the present, she didn't have anywhere to go; but Lord, how his heart pounded when he was near her.

Upstairs, Julie only had time to run the brush through Joy's hair and she was out the door and down the stairs. She combed her own hair and put on a clean dress.

"Do you think Papa would have a fit if I cut my hair?" Jill preened before the mirror.

"I don't know, honey. Mrs. Stuart has short hair. But you're kind of young to have a flapper cut."

"I hate her. I hate her kid. I hate her guts."

"I'm not real fond of her myself."

"Did you see how she tried to be helpful while Papa was around? And she threw out a half a bowl of peas. I had to shell those darn peas."

"It's easy to see why Ruth Humphrey wanted to get rid of her."

"That kid of hers is a brat. *I don't like this. I'd like it if it had raisins in it. The chicken is . . . tough.*" Jill mimicked Elsie's whiny voice. "Papa made Jason finish his pudding, but he didn't say anything about the *brat* leaving hers. I'd like to wash her ugly, pinched face with a fresh cow pie."

"It's best to stay away from her. Don't give Birdie an excuse to complain to Papa. It'll just make him feel sorry for her."

"If you married Evan, would you take us with you?"

"Honey, I'm not going to marry Evan. I've just gone out with him one time." *Oh, Lord. How can I tell her Mrs. Stuart has planted a seed in Papa's mind that Evan is like Walter and that I'm not to let her be alone with him?*

"I'm afraid that if you married him, you'd go to St. Joseph. Mrs. Jacobs said he has a fine big house there."

"Evan isn't wanting to marry me. He's being kind to us. He doesn't have any friends here and he gets lonesome. Don't make more of it than there is."

"I think he likes you . . . a lot. Jack thinks so, too. Why else would he buy you candy? Do you have any left?"

"A piece or two I'm saving for Jason and Joy." Julie's cheeks were flushed. "Come here and I'll tie this blue ribbon in your hair."

They went down the stairs and out through the kitchen to the back porch, hoping to avoid Birdie, but she was on the porch with Jethro.

"My, goodness. Don't you girls look pretty? Your Papa is so proud of you."

"Thank you. I don't think Jason has washed." Julie, feeling the eyes of Birdie stabbing her in the back, escaped to cross the yard to where Jason sat with Sidney.

Jill followed. "*My goodness, don't you girls look pretty,*" she mimicked as soon as they were out of hearing range.

Seeing Jason slumped dispiritedly with eyes so sad tore at

Julie's already bruised heart. She knelt down beside him and put a chocolate in this hand.

"Thanks, but I've already had one."

"You've got another. Evan will be here pretty soon. Why don't you put Sidney back in the barn?"

"He don't like to stay in there all the time. He . . . cries."

"There's a big ham bone in the smokehouse. I was saving it for soup, but let's get it. It'll give Sidney something to do while we're gone."

"Ya mean it?"

"Course I do. Come on."

Julie and Jason were coming out of the barn when Evan drove into the yard. Jill ran to the car to meet him. On the porch Birdie gave Jethro a knowing look and clicked her tongue sadly. Joy, riding on Joe's shoulders, squealed when Joe swung her to the ground and ran toward the car. Jill and Jason got into the back seat on one side, Joe on the other. He pulled Joy up onto his lap.

Jack, carefully holding his freshly oiled glove, waited for Julie to get in beside Evan. She waved her hand at the two on the porch, then slid across the seat to make room for her brother. Jack got in and closed the door.

"All in?" Evan said cheerfully, loving being in the midst of this family, loving more the feel of Julie's shoulder and thigh against his.

"Better hurry, or *she'll* want to go." Jill sat on the edge of the seat and spoke close to the back to Evan's head. She was still leaning toward him when the car passed the porch.

Birdie put her hand on Jethro's arm, pleased to see that he had noticed and was frowning. Her little seed had taken root.

"I'm sure there's nothing to worry about . . . yet. Why don't you have a talk with Julie?"

"I already did. I warned her to keep Jill away from him."

"How did she take it?"

"She was mad as a wet hen."

"Of course. Oh, poor girl. She has hopes Evan is interested in her. How sad."

"Would you and Elsie like to go for a ride? We can go to the ball park and watch the practice."

"Oh, goody! I'd love to go. It's sweet of you to think of it."

There were several dozen spectators milling around at the ball field when Evan stopped the car well back of the batter's box. Julie could feel Jack's excitement and placed her hand on his arm before he got out of the car.

"Good luck. We'll be cheering for you."

"Thanks, Sis."

Jill got out of the car the minute it stopped. She had spied Ruby May and went over to where she sat on a quilt with her mother. The others piled out of the car, Joe holding on to Joy, giving Julie a minute alone with Evan. She moved away until they were no longer touching.

"Things going all right?" he asked.

"I . . . think so. At least we got through the noon meal. School starts tomorrow. Jill and Jason will be gone all day. That will help. Mrs. Stuart isn't sending Elsie. She said she is so far ahead she can sit out a year and still be at the head of the class."

"Good for Elsie," Evan said dryly. "How about Jack?"

"He doesn't want to go back, but Papa is making him go. All he can think about is playing baseball."

"Very few make a living playing ball. You have to be exceptionally good."

"After he plays with the traveling league, he may realize that he isn't good enough. He's dreamed about it since he was a little boy. I hope he isn't disappointed."

"He'll have his family. He'll handle it." Evan reached over and took her hand. "Having Mrs. Stuart in your home is hard on you. I wish that there was something I could do to help."

Julie turned to look at him and suddenly a bubble of laughter came from her smiling lips.

"If you want to help, you can court her, invite her to stay at your house."

Evan's lips spread in a wide grin and he laced his fingers with hers.

"Anything but that . . . or murder."

Julie's smile was beautiful. Her lips tilted upward, her eyes shone. She held tightly to his hand. His eyes roamed her face, taking in every detail to remember later.

"I'm glad I met you, Julie Jones." The words came out as he was thinking them.

"I'm glad I met you, too, Evan Johnson." Julie was surprised at how easy it was to say the words. Her eyes searched his face. He was smiling; his eyes were bright pools of happiness. His face looked younger than it had been when he first came home. How could her papa think that he'd do anything so terrible as to hurt Jill?

"Speaking of courting, I've picked out the girl I want to court." Hungrily, his eyes devoured her face.

Julie's heart fluttered and her cheeks reddened. His fingers went to her chin so that she couldn't turn her face away.

"Julie . . . do you have any objection to spending time with me while we get to know each other?"

"Not . . . if you want to."

"I want to. Believe me, I do."

"I'd better see to the kids."

"They're all right. Jill has found her friend. Joy and Jason are with Joe."

"Joy is a handful. She might dart out onto the field."

"She's a crackerjack, all right, but Joe can handle her."

"She's very dear to me."

"I know that," he said simply.

Her eyes searched his for a hidden meaning to the statement, but found nothing but genuine sincerity. How could her father possibly think him a dishonorable man?

"We'd . . . better get out."

"Do you mind if people think that you're my girl?"

"Oh, I don't think people think that." She looked away from him.

"Would you mind if they did?" With his fingers beneath her chin again, he turned her face toward him.

"I wouldn't mind." Her voice trembled a little. Her eyes were wide and clear and honest as they looked into his.

They were so close, their breaths were mingling when they became aware that a car had pulled up beside them. Julie turned to looked into the eyes of the police chief, who was staring at them. Beside him was Dr. Forbes. Julie smiled and nodded. He tipped his hat.

Julie got out of the car; and on her way to where Jill sat on a quilt with Ruby May, she glanced over her shoulder to see that the chief had stopped Evan in front of his car.

"A word with you, Johnson."

"Sure. What's on your mind?"

"Was your father home last night?"

"No. He left about dark. I think he was heading for Well's Point."

"When did he return?"

"I'm not sure. It was quite a while after I got home."

"When was that?"

"Midnight, or a little after."

"You were with someone until then?"

"You know I was. You saw us in town."

"I thought you might have taken Miss Jones home and gone out again."

"No. I was with her until I headed home. Why all the questions?"

"Is your father home?"

"Sleeping off a drunk. I doubt if you'll be able to wake him for another couple of hours, but you're welcome to go out and try."

"I'll come out later." Joe walked up and Corbin said, "I didn't come back to the house when I saw the windmill blades turning. I see the boy's here, so no harm was done?"

"Evan found him in the woods and brought him home. He's sorry for the trouble he caused."

Corbin glanced at Evan. He liked the man; couldn't help it. It was too bad he had such a disreputable character for a father and had a head start with a girl Corbin would like to know better himself.

Dr. Forbes was leaning on the hood of the police chief's car when Ron Poole came to speak to him.

"Come on, Doc. I'm not letting you weasel out of playing shortstop." He tossed a ball to Dr. Forbes. "Would you rather play first base?"

"No. I'd rather play short. Got an extra glove?"

The game was well under way when Julie saw her father drive in and park. She was sitting with Helen Jacobs, Ruby May and Jill. Evan, Joe and Jason were sitting in the shade on the running board of Evan's car. Joy was inside turning the steering wheel, pretending that she was driving. Evan had turned the car so that they were facing the ball field.

"He bought that brat an ice-cream cone!" Resentment vibrated in Jill's voice.

"Maybe Mrs. Stuart bought it," Julie said.

"Yeah, and maybe pigs can dance the Charleston."

"I talked to Ruth Humphrey this morning at church." Mrs. Jacobs glanced around to be sure no one was within hearing distance. "She said Wilbur was going to buy Mrs. Stuart a train ticket and send her back to Memphis. Then this morning, out of clear blue sky, Mrs. Stuart announced that Jethro Jones wanted her to come there and take over when Julie left."

"I'm not going anywhere." The words exploded from Julie's mouth

"Birdie told Ruth that Jethro is afraid you'll just up and leave, and he doesn't know what he'll do with the younger kids. Jill isn't old enough to take over."

"Did Ruth believe her?"

"Ruth wouldn't believe anything she said if she swore on a stack of Bibles as high as her head."

"That's the craziest thing I ever heard. Papa wouldn't have told her that. It's not true."

"Tell her the rest, Mama," Ruby May urged.

"She's a smooth one, all right. Ruth said that Mrs. Stuart saw you meeting a man in the woods. She was sure it was someone from town."

"Another . . . lie." Julie almost choked on the words. "Why would she say such a thing?"

"Ruth said she had wanted Evan Johnson real bad and tried to turn him against you," Helen Jacobs went on in a low tone. "But he gave her a cold shoulder, and she's turned against him now. She hasn't a good word to say about him now."

"I wonder if she told him that I was meeting a man in the woods."

"I'd not put it past her."

"He saw through her right away, but Papa—"

"Shush, Jill. Papa will come to his senses."

"He won't if she gets him in bed!" There was a sob in Jill's voice.

"Jill, honey! What a thing to say." Julie looked apologetically at Helen Jacobs.

"Jill is right, Julie. You'd better get prepared for it."

The man's eyes kept straying to the two young girls sitting on the blanket. The one with the light hair and long legs reminded him of a young filly in heat. His sex began to harden just thinking about the fight she would put up when he threw her to the ground. She'd pretend not to like it, just like the others, but she would love having him conquer her, make her a woman; just like the others.

An offspring out of her would be a sight to behold.

Chapter 20

JULIE HANDED JASON HIS LUNCH BUCKET and promised for the tenth time that she would go to the barn several times during the day and make sure Sidney had water.

"And talk to him a little. He'll be lonesome sittin' in that old barn all day."

"Joe will be in and out. Sidney will be glad to see you when you get home. You can take him out in the pasture and play with him."

"Come on," Jill commanded her brother when she came out onto the porch. They were to meet Ruby May Jacobs at the end of the lane and walk with her to school.

"Jason, don't drop your pencil and new tablet. Jill, come home with Jack and Jason after school."

"Oh, all right. You've said that a dozen times."

"I don't want you to forget."

"How can I forget when you keep harping on it? I don't know why Jason couldn't have ridden on the horse with Jack. Ruby May and I like to talk about things we don't want him to hear."

"Jack wanted to go early and Jason wasn't ready. Jason can ride home with him. Jack said that he'd wait for you. That should please Ruby May."

"Yeah. All she'll do is look ga-ga at him and won't hear a

word I say." Jill made a disgusted noise and her lips turned down. She finished securing two books with a strap and flung them over her shoulder.

Hating to see them go, Julie watched her brother and sister walk down the lane toward the road. She wasn't looking forward to spending the day with Birdie and Elsie. Breakfast had been almost over when Birdie came out of the bedroom dressed as if she weren't expected to do a lick of work.

"I intended to help you with breakfast, Julie. I overslept. I got up as soon as I heard someone stirring around."

She'd have to have been dead, Julie thought, not to have heard Jill tromping down the stairs. Jill had grinned at Julie wickedly when she slammed the stairway door.

"Sit down, Birdie," Jethro said. "I'll pour you some coffee."

"This is the first day of school, isn't it?" Birdie had said after she sat down. "What grade are you in, Jill?"

"Ninth."

"Ninth? Did you get a late start, dear?"

"Why? Do you think I'm dumb and failed a grade? I didn't. I'm right where I'm supposed to be for my age. As a matter of fact, I'm younger than some."

"No! How could I possibly think that you were dumb? Country schools usually run a little behind city schools. Anyway, you look awfully pretty this morning. I just bet the boys will think so, too." Birdie turned a smiling face up to Jethro when he brought her coffee. "You're going to have to watch her, Jethro. The boys will be swarming all over the place in a few years."

Julie looked at Joe and almost laughed when he made a gagging sign behind Jethro's back. Last night she had gone to her brothers' room; and, after making sure Jason was asleep, and whispering because their father was sleeping in the next room, she had told them of their father's suspicion of Evan and what she had learned from Helen Jacobs.

"That old bitch," Joe whispered angrily. "Evan is as decent

a fellow as I've ever met. I'd not have let you go out with him if I'd heard the slightest bad thing about him."

"Why is she saying that?" Jack asked.

"She's getting even with him because he wouldn't have anything to do with her," Joe answered.

"Why would she tell such lies?" Julie asked. "Do you think she told Evan I was meeting a man in the woods?"

"We'll ask him. Won't we, Joe?"

"Don't do that. It's too embarrassing."

"Why not, Sis? Evan's smitten with you." Jack turned to his brother for conformation. "Ain't he, Joe?"

"Yeah, and only God knows why," Joe teased and leaned down to peek into his sister's face.

Julie had shrugged off her brother's words even as her heart did a fancy dance in her chest. She had gone back to bed feeling better for having shared her concerns with them.

They had discussed their father's infatuation with Birdie and the tactics she was using to turn him against Evan. Both boys were angry that their father would believe that Evan had designs on Jill.

The breakfast dishes were still on the table when Julie went back to the kitchen after seeing Jill and Jason off to school. There was no sign of Birdie. Joe and her father had decided to dig potatoes today. The potatoes would lie out in the sun for a day. After the dried dirt was shaken off, they would be put in the cellar. Most years they had enough potatoes to last until spring.

Julie put the soiled dishes in the dishpan and covered them with hot water. The leftover biscuits went into the warming oven and a clean cloth covered the necessaries in the middle of the table. When Joy and Elsie got up, they could have biscuits and apple butter for breakfast.

Julie went into the yard, where Joe had filled the big iron pot with water and had built a fire beneath it. The water was already steaming. As long as Julie could remember, Monday had been wash day, and on Tuesday she ironed.

This morning the clothes were already piled on the back porch. The wash bench was set up in the shade of the house and on it were the two big galvanized tubs, one filled with warm water, one with cold for rinsing. The extremely dirty work clothes would be boiled in the iron pot.

Although it was backbreaking work, Julie didn't mind wash day when the weather was nice. She buried her arms in the warm suds and let her mind wander as she worked.

She was worried that Birdie Stuart had told Evan the tale about seeing her meet someone in the woods. If she had, it must have been before they went out last Saturday night. He had treated her with the utmost respect, not at all as if she were a loose woman who met men in the woods, although she had let him kiss her. Because of that, did he think she was . . . fast?

In her mind Julie went over every single word they had exchanged Saturday night and on Sunday afternoon. Had he really said, "I've found the girl I want to court"? She didn't think Evan was the type to joke about something like that, yet it was hard for Julie to believe that he could have meant it.

Joy, knuckling her eyes, came out onto the porch holding up her nightdress.

"I wanta biscuit with jam on it."

"Mrs. Stuart is in there. Ask her to give you one."

"She won't."

"She won't?"

"She said I wasn't nice."

Julie brought her hands out of the wash water and dried them on her apron as she stepped up onto the porch. She opened the door and ushered Joy in ahead of her. Elsie, dressed in a fresh ruffled dress, and with her hair arranged in the fat curls, sat beside her mother at the table. On Elsie's plate were biscuits and a generous serving of strawberry jam. Birdie had taken the jar from the bottom shelf of the pie safe and gouged out the sealing wax. Without a word, Julie lifted Joy to her stool.

"I told her that nice young ladies didn't come to the breakfast table in their nightclothes," Birdie said.

"She isn't a young lady, she's a child." Julie's voice was not friendly. "And you have no business telling Joy to do anything."

"Well, if you want her to grow up . . . countrified—I don't think Jethro will agree with you."

"He hasn't had any complaints so far." Julie was so angry her hands were shaking.

"Not that he's told you about," Birdie said smugly.

Julie put a generous amount of the strawberry jam on Joy's biscuit before she spoke.

"If you've got something to say, Mrs. Stuart, say it and stop beating around the bush."

"All right. Jethro wants me to teach Jill and Joy some manners. He thinks they should know how to act like ladies. We both realize that it's too late for you."

"Is that right? I guess I'll have to ask him about that. Joy, come out to the porch and eat. You can get dressed later."

For a minute anger blurred Julie's vision. She carried Joy's plate to the porch and settled the child down by it. Back at the washtubs, she was so agitated that she rubbed the soiled clothes viciously on the scrub board, wrung them out and tossed them into the rinse water.

The nerve of the woman, to help herself to the jam Julie had saved to put on Jason's birthday cake and to tell Joy she couldn't eat until she was dressed.

If she wanted a war, she would get one!

Jethro came into the yard with a wheelbarrow full of potatoes that he dumped on the ground near the root cellar.

"You just now eating breakfast, sleepyhead?" He stopped at the edge of the porch and patted Joy on the head.

"Julie got me a biscuit . . . and jam."

"I see she did. You've got it on your face, punkin."

"She didn't want me to have one, said I wasn't nice. Julie said I am, too, nice."

Julie felt her father's disapproving eyes on her. She knew with certainty that she would be blamed for any confrontation with Birdie. She didn't look up from the washtub until he went into the kitchen. The low murmur of voices went on long enough for Julie to wash three shirts and Jill's petticoat. When Jethro came back out onto the porch, Birdie was with him.

"Dear," she called to Julie. "Would you mind if I add a few little things to the wash? I'll wash our good things separately."

Birdie dropped a bundle on the porch. Out of the corner of her eye, Julie saw her father's steps hesitate as he went to the wheelbarrow.

"I don't mind at all, Mrs. Stuart. You can leave your wash right there on the porch." *And it can stay there a hundred years before I'll wash it.*

"Thank you, dear. I'll put the breakfast dishes in the pan. Is there anything else I can do to help?"

"You can wash the dishes . . . if you don't mind?" Julie said, loud enough for her father to hear. Birdie gave her a smug smile and went back into the house.

Julie let Joy play on the porch in her nightdress until after she had hung the first tub of clothes on the line. As they passed through the kitchen to go upstairs, she noticed that the dishes had been cleared from the table and piled unwashed in the dishpan. Before going back to her outside chore, Julie added fuel to the cookstove and put on a pot of turnips and greens for dinner.

When Jethro and Joe came in for the noon meal, Birdie and Elsie were in their room and Julie was washing dishes. Joe's eyes caught Julie's as their father washed at the wash bench.

"Need help with the dishes, Sis?"

"Thanks, but I'll just wash enough to get us through the noon meal."

"I was going to empty the wash water, but I see that you still have clothes to wash."

"Don't empty it. Mrs. Stuart hasn't washed her things yet. You might tell her that dinner is ready, Papa."

Jethro crossed the hall and, shortly after, Julie heard the door close. She and Joe exchanged glances. They were ready to sit down at the table when Jethro came out.

"Birdie hopes that you will excuse her and Elsie. She said . . . Elsie didn't feel very good." He pulled out his chair and sat down.

"What's the matter with her?" Julie asked and took her place beside Joy. "She seemed all right earlier."

"She didn't say."

"She don't like me," Joy blurted.

Jethro, his hands in his lap, made no attempt to fill his plate. He looked across the table at his eldest daughter.

"You shouldn't have made Birdie feel bad about opening the jam."

"I never said a word to her about opening the jam. I had been saving it for Jason's birthday cake. That's why it was at the bottom of the pie safe."

"She didn't know that."

"While we're on the subject of Mrs. Stuart, Papa, did you ask her to teach Jill and Joy some manners?" Julie's suppressed temper was causing her cheeks to burn.

"She said something about the children lacking social graces and offered to help them. What's wrong with that? Do you want them to be laughed at because they're . . . countrified?"

"Countrified? I never thought it was so bad to be countrified. I suppose she wants to teach Jason manners, too. It's too late for the rest of us. Is that right?"

"Now, don't be getting your back up. You should appreciate that Birdie is willing to help instead of bucking her every step of the way."

Julie didn't trust herself to answer. Instead she spoke to Joy. "Eat, honey. Greens are not good after they get cold."

Joe and Jethro had finished digging the potatoes and Jethro was at the grinder in the shed sharpening the plow blades.

"You might as well empty the wash water, Joe," Julie called from the porch. "It's cold by now. I guess Mrs. Stuart decided not to do her wash today."

Julie had taken the clothes from the lines as soon as they dried and was folding them on the porch. It had been a long, lonesome day for Joy. The kids would be home from school any time now, and she was on the front porch watching for them.

"They comin'." Screen doors slammed as Joy raced through the house with the news. "They comin' on the horse with Jack."

Minutes later Jack's horse, with Jason and Ruby May cradled in front of Jack and Jill holding on behind him, walked around the house and stopped. Jack held Jason's arm while he slid off over the horse's neck. Jason ran to the barn to see Sidney. Joy was at his heels.

Joe came around and lifted Jill from the horse. Jack, a foolish grin on his freckled face and holding the reins with his arms around Ruby May, announced that he'd give her a ride home.

"Well, get going and get back so you can do your chores." Joe clapped the brown mare on the rump and she headed back down the lane.

"'Bye, Jill. See ya tomorrow," Ruby May called.

"She wasn't any fun at all," Jill complained when she met Julie on the porch. "All she did at dinnertime and recess was talk about Jack as if he were somethin' grand."

"You might think he was grand, too, if he wasn't your brother."

"My drawers and stockings are dirty from that old horse. They hogged the horse blanket."

"Your skirt is clean. Change clothes, honey, and help me sprinkle down the clothes. You can tell me about school."

"It was all right." Jill moved closer to Julie and whispered, "Is *she* still here?"

Julie nodded.

"Poot! Poot! Poot! I was hoping a tree had fallen on her or something."

"How about if she sat down on a red anthill?"

Jill giggled. "Now, that would be a sight worth seeing." Impulsively, Jill threw her arms around Julie. "I worry that you'll go and leave us here with *her,*" she whispered.

"Don't worry, honey. I promise I'll never go off and leave you with Mrs. Stuart or anyone like her." She kissed her sister on the cheek.

At supper, Jethro asked each of the children about school. Birdie appeared to be interested in what each of them had to say.

"Sammy Bowen brought a frog to school," Jason said. "He kept it in his pocket until Miss Davis left the room, then he put it in her desk drawer."

"What did she do when she found it?" Julie asked.

"Nothin'. She held it in her hand and rubbed its head. She likes frogs."

"The boy should have been spanked." Birdie put potatoes on Elsie's plate, mashed them with her fork and dotted them with butter. "There, sugar. Eat now for Mommy."

"I know a few kids who should be spanked," Jill said and winced when the toe of a shoe connected with her leg under the table.

"It wasn't a bit nice of that boy. Boys should learn to be respectful and protective of ladies."

The family retreated into silence during the remainder of the meal.

Again, Birdie made a showing of helping to clear off the table.

"Mrs. Stuart, would you rather wash or dry?" Jill asked bluntly with a twisted little smile.

"I don't know where things go, dear. I'll just do this little bit that I know will help. Oh, there you are," she said when Jethro came to the kitchen door. "I'll help the girls and be out in just a minute."

As soon as Jethro went to the front porch, Birdie and Elsie went out back to the outhouse.

"That's the first time today she's gone to the privy. I bet the chamber pot is full."

"Is she waiting for one of us to empty it?"

"If she is, she'll wait until it snows on the Fourth of July," Julie said, causing Jill to giggle.

When Birdie and Elsie came back to the house, Birdie picked up the bundle of clothes that she had expected Julie to wash and took them to the room she now occupied. Then she and Elsie went to the front porch and sat down in the swing beside Jethro. Unusually quiet, Joy slid off his lap and went into the house.

Julie and Jill were finishing the kitchen chores when Jason came in.

"Are you looking for something to feed Sidney?" Julie asked.

"No. Joe fed him the corn bread you'd saved for him."

Without saying more, Jason went through the kitchen and down the hall to look out the front door. A few minutes later, he scurried back through the kitchen and out to the barn.

Ordinarily the family would have gathered on the front porch during the twilight hours and everything that had happened on the first day at school would have been discussed.

Tonight Joe and Jack had not returned to the house after the evening meal. Jason was in the orchard with Sidney and Joy. Julie and Jill were in the kitchen. The front porch was occupied by Jethro, Birdie and Elsie.

It was almost eight o'clock when Julie lit the lamp and placed it on the table. She sat down to darn socks and Jill brought out a book to read.

"What did she do all day?" Jill asked.

"She set up the ironing board and ironed a few things she'd rinsed out in the wash dish. She spent the rest of the time in Papa's room."

"The brat, too?"

"Joy begged her to come and play. She refuses to have anything to do with her."

"I wish Joy wouldn't beg her."

"Joy's just a little girl, honey. She doesn't understand why Elsie won't play with her. Elsie is just a little girl, too. She's being shaped by her mother's influence."

"Where did you learn all that?"

"It's common horse sense." Julie grinned at her sister and put her darning back in the basket. "I've got to get Joy and Jason in. The mosquitoes will eat them up."

Later, after Jason had washed and been sent up to bed and Julie was washing Joy, Birdie and Elsie came into the kitchen, followed by Jethro.

"I don't see how you girls can stand to stay in this hot kitchen." Birdie smiled rather tightly and fanned herself and Elsie with a feathered fan. "Thank goodness our room is cooler." She pumped a quantity of water into the tin sink with the hand pump before filling a glass for Elsie. "Say good night to the girls, sugar. Wake me in the morning, Julie, so I can help with breakfast."

Julie looked from Birdie to her father, who stood behind Birdie, and nodded her head.

The pair went to their room and as soon as Birdie lit the lamp, the door closed.

Jethro stood for a moment looking from one daughter to the other, then, with sagging shoulders, went out onto the back porch.

Just as Julie lifted Joy down from the chair after running the wet cloth over her legs and feet, a piercing scream came from the bedroom. The door was thrown open and Birdie, yelling for Jethro and clutching Elsie, burst from the room.

"What's the matter?" Jethro came hurrying in from the porch.

"Sn-ake! In there . . . under the pillow. Oh, God! It was two inches from Elsie."

"A snake in the house?"

Jethro went into the bedroom and came out holding a green snake just below the head. The snake, about six inches long, was trying to curl itself around his hand.

"It's just a harmless little old grass snake, Birdie. Nothing to be afraid of."

"Oh . . . keep it away! How did it get in? Are there more?"

"I've never found one in the house," Julie said. "I imagine it came in with the clothes she left lying on the porch."

Jethro went to the porch and flung the snake out into the lilac bushes.

"Did you kill it?" Birdie asked when he returned.

"It's gone."

"I don't know if I can sleep in there tonight."

"I'll come in and look around. Like Julie said, it probably got into the clothes you had on the porch and you carried it in."

As soon as their father and Birdie went to the bedroom, Jill looked at Julie with a happy grin and mouthed, "Jason."

"Why's she scared?" Joy asked. "Jason—"

Julie clamped her hand over the child's mouth and whispered in her ear.

"We'll talk about it upstairs."

After Joy was tucked into bed, Julie took the lamp and went into the boys' room. Jason's eyes were wide open and he was grinning.

"She yelled loud, didn't she?"

"Jason Jones, you rascal! You put that snake in there, didn't you?"

"You didn't see me."

"No, I didn't, but I know you did. Papa better not find out."

"I wish it'd been a great big rattler."

"No, you don't. You scared her good. That's what you wanted, wasn't it? Don't do anything like that again, or Papa will catch on. Promise?"

"Promise, and . . . thanks for not telling."

Julie's fingers made a twisting movement against her lips. "My lips are locked."

"You're the best sister in the whole world." Jason wound his arms around Julie's neck. "If Papa marries her, will you stay here? You'll not go off and leave us?"

Julie kissed him on the forehead. "If I go anywhere at all, you'll go with me. That's a promise."

"Cross your heart?"

"Cross my heart, hope to die, poke a needle in my eye and cut my throat if I tell a lie. Satisfied?" She kissed him again. "Now, go to sleep."

It was a promise Julie swore to keep should it become necessary for her to leave.

Chapter 21

"WHEN IS DOC GOING TO LIFT THE QUARANTINE on Bloom's place?" Chief Appleby dropped his lanky body down in the chair beside young Dr. Forbes's desk.

"The boy is no longer contagious, but Doc is going to keep the quarantine on until next week." Dr. Todd Forbes's eyes held a roguish twinkle.

"Giving Mrs. Bloom an extended vacation, huh?"

"Something like that."

"Any new cases of diphtheria?"

"None, thank God. Four is too many for this small town." The young doctor leaned back in his chair. "Do you think Bloom could be our rapist?"

"No, but I could be wrong. In the first place, he's dumb as a stump. In the second place, he's usually drunk. Neither of the girls I've talked to have mentioned that they smelled liquor."

"Logical reasoning."

"I'd appreciate it if, while you're visiting around, you would mention Springfield or the southern part of the state and see if anyone admits to having been there. Our fellow may have gone down there during the war and done the same thing he's doing here."

"Doc mentioned that you're from down around Springfield."

"The girl I was going to marry was raped and murdered

while I was in France. I figure she knew who he was and he couldn't let her live. The same could happen here."

"And you've traced him to Fertile."

"I wasn't sure until Doc told me that two or three girls a year were showing up pregnant and being sent away. No telling how many he's raped who didn't get pregnant. I've been told that once a man starts raping and gets away with it, he doesn't stop."

"Anyone special you want me to nose around?"

Corbin pulled a paper from his shirt pocket and laid it on the desk. Dr. Forbes picked it up, scanned the names and then folded the paper and put it in his pocket.

"I've not had much experience in this sort of thing."

"Neither have I. All the police work I've done was in the army and this is far different." Corbin stood. "How's the ball team shaping up?"

"Not bad. We've got two pretty good hitters on the team. I don't think we'll get skunked."

"Practice again tomorrow night?"

"And again Sunday afternoon." Dr. Forbes grinned. "The banker, Amos Wood, has been after me to come to Sunday dinner. So far my excuse has been I can't play ball on a full stomach. When this game is over, I'II have to think of something else."

Corbin laughed. "Trying to reel you in for Miss Zelda? Thank God he and I got started off on the wrong foot. He avoids me like poison."

"Some fellows have all the luck."

On Friday, after an early supper, Jill and Julie washed fruit jars in the big tub on the back porch. By dark, three dozen shining mason jars were turned upside down on a clean cloth on the porch. Early Saturday morning, Joe and Jack picked the ripe tomatoes and washed and stemmed them, while Julie and Jill sterilized the jars with boiling water.

After removing the skins of the tomatoes by dipping them in very hot water, Julie packed the jars and made them ready for the hot water bath that would seal and preserve them for future use. It was a family project, with everyone doing his or her part, from Jason, who carried the skins and culled tomatoes to the hogs, to Joe and Jack, who kept the fire going under the copper boiler in the yard.

Jethro went to herd their milch cows to the alfalfa pasture; and when he returned, he took a crate of eggs to town. He had asked Jason and Joy if they wanted to go; but when they learned that Birdie and Elsie were going with him, Jason said that he'd stay and help with the canning. Without Jason to watch Joy, she had to remain, too, and had to be consoled with the promise of a ride on Jack's horse.

Rid of the depressing presence of Birdie, Julie's mood lightened, as did that of the other members of the family. They worked happily together, and an hour before noon, all the jars were packed with juicy red tomatoes and waiting for the hot water bath. While the oven was hot, Julie stirred up a dessert she had always called Hurry-Up Pudding because it took only a few minutes to prepare. It was her mother's recipe, one she had written on the back of an envelope.

Julie had just slipped the pan in the oven when she heard Joy squeal. She hurried to the door in time to see Evan scoop the child up in his arms and step onto the porch. Joy clung to his neck and placed kisses on his cheek. He had a huge smile on his face, and something deep inside Julie trembled for a moment.

"If I'd known I'd get this kind of reception, I'd have come over sooner." His smiling eyes caught and held Julie's.

"Mornin'," Julie said shyly, wrapping her hands in her apron and stepping out onto the porch. *Oh, Lord! I must look a sight—my hair, my wet apron—* "Joe and Jack are out back . . . someplace."

"I saw them. I came over to make sure you didn't forget about tonight."

"I haven't forgotten." Julie pushed the damp hair from her face with the back of her hand. "We've been canning tomatoes."

"Joe said your . . . company went to town with Jethro."

"They'll be back soon."

Evan searched her face and found lines of fatigue. He wanted to touch her, but with Joy in his arms he could only caress her with his eyes.

"You don't have to hold her—"

"I know." He lowered the child to the porch and took a candy stick from his shirt pocket. "A sweet for a sweet pretty little girl."

"Ohhhh . . ." Joy squealed. Then, "Can Jason have one?"

"Joy!"

"I already gave Jason one."

"What do you say, Joy?" Julie prompted.

"Thank you. I'll give you another kiss if you want one." She looked up at him with a cocky little grin.

"Well, now, that's an offer I can't turn down." He squatted down and Joy planted a wet, sticky kiss on his cheek.

"Thank *you,*" he said and stood.

"Evan, I didn't know you were here." The screen door slammed when Jill came out of the kitchen. "Did Julie tell you that we got a breather from the witch and her brat?"

"Jill, for goodness' sake!"

"It's what she is. I hate her more and more. I think maybe Papa's beginning to think she's not all that grand anymore."

Julie turned to look at her sister. "Why do you say that?"

"For a couple of nights he's found something to do in the barn after supper. Last night he was sitting out there on a box, not doing anything."

"Maybe he was tired."

"Yeah. Sure. Evan, are you courting Julie?"

"For crying out loud! Jill—" Julie wished that a hole would open up and she could drop into it.

"I'm trying to, Jill." Sparks of amusement glittered in Evan's eyes as color rose up Julie's neck to flood her face. "Do you mind?"

"Heavens, no. I think she's taken a shine to you, too. Oh, gosh, I'd better get out of here. She's going to kill me after you leave. Come on, brat." Jill grabbed Joy's hand, jerked her off the porch and headed for the barn.

"I apologize for—"

"Don't. I'm glad she feels free to come right out and ask."

"There . . . isn't a bashful bone in her body."

"How is it going with Mrs. Stuart?"

"It's like a . . . standoff. She comes out at mealtime and that's about all. I don't know what she finds to do in that room all day. In the evening she sits with Papa on the porch."

"And fills his head with strange notions?"

"Yes. Did Joe tell you?"

"He told me. What's important to me is that you didn't believe her. It's hard to fight back against a woman, but I have a few cards up my sleeve."

Julie walked with him out to the fence where he had tied his horse.

"You're welcome to stay to dinner."

"Thank you, but I'd better get back home. Walter—" Evan stopped what he was saying and looked up at the sky.

Julie's eyes followed his, and then she heard the faint drone of an airplane engine.

"It's a Jennie," Evan exclaimed. "I'd recognize the sound of that motor anywhere." He shaded his eyes. "There she is!" He pulled Julie in front of him and turned her. "She's coming right over town."

The two-winged airplane descended and flew over the farm. The man in the open cockpit waved something red.

"Good Lord! It's Wesley!" Evan mounted his horse and raced out into the open pasture, waving his arms at the circling plane.

The horses in the side pasture neighed and ran the fence line. The chickens squawked, and the two big geese ran for the shelter of the lilac bushes. Joe and Jack came running out of the barn with Jason, followed by Jill and Joy.

"That's an airplane!"

"What's Evan doing?"

"Is it comin' back?"

"Will it hit the house?"

No one waited or expected a question to be answered. All eyes were on the plane and on Evan, who was now waving a white handkerchief. The plane soared over Evan and dipped its wings several times. Evan raced back to the house.

"He's going to land in the pasture," he said excitedly. "I told him the farm was south of town. He probably thinks that this is the place."

"Can we see the airplane?" Jason asked.

"Sure. Wesley is a barnstormer. That means he flies around the county putting on shows and giving rides."

"Rides! Do you think—"

"No!" Julie cut Jack off in midsentence.

"Ah . . . Sis—"

Evan was beaming down at Julie. "I want you to meet Wesley. He's quite a guy."

"Oh, I can't. Not like this!" With her hands in the pockets, she held out her wet apron.

"Then run put on a clean one. He'll be landing in a minute or two." He gave her a gentle push and she ran to the house.

Not until she opened the door did she remember the pudding in the oven. She removed it quickly, raced upstairs and slipped into a clean dress, poked at her hair with her fingertips and ran back downstairs.

Her father, with Birdie and Elsie, drove into the yard as she went out the back door. Julie ignored them and hurried to where

Evan and the rest of the family waited at the edge of the pasture. The plane was coming in slowly. It bumped the ground once, then settled down to a roll. Jason took a few steps toward the plane.

"Wait, Jason," Evan cautioned. "Wait until he stops and turns off the propellers. The blades can cut a man in two."

"How come you know him?" Joe asked.

"I met him in France. Wesley Marsh is one of the most skilled pilots to come out of the war."

"Have you been up with him?"

"Quite a few times. I had a letter from him a week or two ago. He said he was going to Colorado to put on a show and if he could find the farm he'd stop by."

The plane rolled to a stop, the engine was cut and gradually the propeller blades ceased to turn. The man who climbed out of the cockpit wore a helmet, a brown jacket and a red scarf around his neck. Evan, holding Julie's hand as if he feared she would run away from him, led the way across the field to meet the pilot. The family followed, Joy riding on Joe's shoulders.

Evan and his friend met each other with a hand clasp, then slaps on the back. It was obvious they were good friends and glad to see each other.

"I didn't have an idea I'd find you so soon." Wesley Marsh was a small, wiry man with thick light hair, a pug nose and bright blue eyes. When he smiled, he showed a mouth filled with gold-capped teeth.

"My place is a half mile over. I knew it was you when I saw the stars on the underwing. These are my friends, the Jones family. Julie, meet Wesley Marsh. He saved our bacon a time or two during the war by bringing in ammunition in such a reckless way the Germans didn't bother with him because they were sure he wouldn't make it and would blow himself up."

"How do you do, Mr. Marsh?" Julie extended her hand.

"Howdy, ma'am." His bright eyes went from Evan to Julie because Evan was still holding on to her other hand.

"The rest of the troop are Julie's brothers and sisters." Evan introduced them all and Wesley gave each one his attention and shook hands.

"My name's Joy," Joy declared from atop Joe's shoulders.

"And a pretty little girl you are, too."

"Wanta kiss?"

Julie groaned. Evan grinned and squeezed her hand.

"Why, shore, honey."

Joe stooped down, and Joy planted a kiss on Wesley's cheek.

"That was worth comin' down for, sugarfoot. Anybody else givin' out samples?" Wesley's laughing eyes went from Jill to Julie.

"That's all you're getting, jelly bean. When he lands after a performance," Evan explained, "the ladies swarm over him. He's getting spoiled."

"But I'm havin' a hell of a lot of fun."

"Can we look at the airplane?" Jason asked.

"Why, shore, come on over. I promise it won't bite."

Julie looked back across the field toward the house. Her father stood alone at the edge of the pasture. He looked so lonely, so left out. Julie tugged on Evan's hand and mouthed, "Papa."

Evan turned, whistled and waved for Jethro to come. Julie held her breath, then her father started across the pasture toward them.

For a half hour Evan entertained them with stories of Wesley's aerial feats, and Wesley patiently showed them the plane. He lifted Jason up to sit in the passenger seat while he explained that he would meet his wing-walker in Colorado. The man would walk the length of the upper wing, then climb down to the lower wing, then onto the wheels, before parachuting to earth.

"Anyone want to go for a ride?"

"Jack and I would like to try it," Joe said.

"Joe . . . please don't."

"It's the chance of a lifetime, Sis."

"I can take only one at a time."

Jethro stepped forward. "What's the cost for the boys to have a ride?"

"A couple cans of gasoline," Wesley said and grinned at Evan. Not wanting to interfere, Evan waited for the nod of agreement from Jethro.

After Joe was strapped in, the family moved back to the edge of the field. Julie's heart was beating like a hammer when Wesley spun the propellers. The motor purred and he climbed into the cockpit.

"I wish he wasn't going," she said.

"It'll be all right. Soon people will be riding in airplanes all the time. Wesley is good. He can land that thing on a dime . . . almost." Uncaring that Jethro was there, Evan took her arm and pulled her close to him.

It suddenly dawned on Joy that Joe was going up in the airplane.

"I don't want Joe to go. I'm scared he'll fall."

"He'll be all right, punkin." Jethro lifted her up in his arms.

The plane picked up speed and suddenly climbed into the air. Julie bowed her head and closed her eyes. *Please, God, bring Joe down safely*.

"They're circling around. They must be over town now." In her excitement, Jill clutched her father's arm, all thoughts of Birdie gone.

After two circles of the area, the plane leveled off and came down in the pasture and rolled to a stop. Joe jumped out and ran across the field.

"He said to stay clear of the propellers and to strap yourself in," he shouted to Jack, who had run out to meet him.

As soon as Jack was in the plane, it began to roll again, the start of another agonizing ten minutes for Julie. Joe was so excited he could hardly talk.

"It was great, Pa. You should go up. I saw the whole town and the river curling around it. It was quiet up there. The motor didn't even sound as loud. I was holding on for dear life . . . I don't know why, I wasn't about to fall out." He laughed. "I can't imagine a man getting out and walking on the wing while the plane's up there."

Julie wasn't hearing a thing her brother said. Her mind was on Jack up there in the sky without anything under him but that little old airplane.

"Don't worry," Evan whispered in her ear.

"I can't . . . help it."

"Why don't you go up, Pa?" Joe was saying.

"Go for a ride, Jethro," Evan urged. "You might not get another chance for a long time."

"Well . . ." Jethro grinned at Julie. "Why not?" He stood Joy on her feet when the plane came down and started across the field.

"Maybe he doesn't have enough gas to take him up," Julie said hopefully.

"He'll know if he has enough gas or not."

"You've known him for a long time?"

"A couple years during the war, and I've seen him a time or two since."

"It was great!" Jack's freckled face was split with a huge smile. "Great! I'm goin' to fly one of them someday."

"Me, too." Jason looked up at his brother. "Would my foot keep me from flying a airplane, Jack?"

"Naw. You don't use your feet. You could do it if anyone could."

"I can't play baseball, so I'll fly airplanes," Jason said as Jack looped his arm over his brother's shoulders.

When the plane came in after taking Jethro for a ride, Wesley cut the engine and climbed down from the cockpit. Julie was exceedingly glad all in her family were back on the ground.

"How come you didn't go up?" Julie asked Evan.

"I wanted the boys to go."

"It was wonderful for them . . . now that they're down," she added and smiled at him. "Thank you."

"Jethro seems to have enjoyed himself." Evan watched Jethro and Wesley come across the field, each carrying a gas can.

After Evan, Wesley and Jethro left to buy gas in town, Joe and Jack refueled the fires beneath the copper boilers. The jars of tomatoes were removed from the hot water and turned upside down on the porch to cool and secure the seal. A new batch of jars was set carefully on the racks in the boilers.

When Julie went into the kitchen, Birdie and Elsie were at the table eating from bowls of pudding covered with thick cream. Birdie had scooped pudding from the pan Julie had taken from the oven when she came in to change her dress.

"Where did Jethro go?"

"To town."

"He just came from there."

"Well, he went back," Jill said. "Shall I set the table, Julie?"

"Yes, please. Wipe the oilcloth with a damp cloth."

Jill wiped the table, sopping up cream from around Elsie's bowl. She ignored both Elsie and Birdie.

"You hate me, don't you?" Birdie said suddenly.

Jill said, "Yes," as Julie said, "No."

"Hate me all you want. Jethro would marry me in a minute if I wanted him to. Then, my girl, you'd be out of here on your ear."

She spoke to Julie, but a shrill angry cry came from Jill.

"You are mean and hateful! And . . . yes, I hate you!"

"Honey," Julie said calmly, "will you please go see about Joy? She's probably all sticky. Wash her off at the well."

"I . . . I . . ." Jill was so enraged she couldn't articulate what she wanted to say.

"Go on." Julie felt strangely calm. She put a cloth in Jill's hand and gently pushed her out of the kitchen.

"What she needs is a good slap now and then. When she's under my care, that's what she'll get."

Julie turned to look directly at Birdie. "She will never be under your care. Nor will Jason or Joy."

"Do you think Evan will marry you and take you and those kids to live in that hog pen with Walter Johnson? Jethro will never let that happen. He's beginning to understand just what kind of a man Evan Johnson is."

"With your help, I suppose."

"Of course. When I take over here, there will be some changes in this house. There will be no coming to the table in night-clothes, I can guarantee you that. And a decent cloth will cover the table at mealtime, not this filthy oilcloth. Jill and Joy will be taught to act like ladies, and those brothers of yours—"

The screen door was flung back and Joe came into the kitchen. He stood with his hands on his hips and looked from Birdie to Julie. His face was as angry as Julie had ever seen it.

"What about Julie's brothers, Mrs. Stuart?" he asked sharply.

"Don't talk to me in that tone of voice, young man." Birdie had been enjoying baiting Julie and had not expected to be confronted by her tall, blond brother. She was momentarily shaken.

"Mrs. Stuart is explaining how it's going to be when she takes over here." Julie spoke calmly, although inside she was raging.

"Tell me, Mrs. Stuart," Joe said softly.

"I'll tell you nothing. I'll talk to your father. It's strange to me that Jethro has two adult children still living at home, living off his toil, still eating his food. I would think the two of you would be ashamed." She stood. "Come on, sugar, we'll sit in the porch swing and wait for Jethro."

"Mama, she said she didn't have raisins, but she did. They were in the pudding."

"It's what we should have expected, sugar." Birdie shot Julie a private, tight smile and raised her brows.

Julie held her breath until she heard the front screen door close. She was too angry to cry. Strangely, she felt relief. Now things were out in the open, and she no longer had to suffer Birdie's little digs alone.

"Sis, what are we going to do? Jill's out in the barn crying. She and Jason want to leave home. Jack wants to come in here and strangle that woman!" Joe had a look of total frustration on his face. "Jack and I could leave. We could find work enough to get by. But we'll not go and leave you and the kids with her."

"Please don't even think of it. If we can wait it out, Papa will see her for what she is. That is . . . if—"

"She don't get him in bed. He'd marry her thinking he had made her pregnant."

"It's what I'm afraid of." Even in anger, Julie's face reddened at the subject.

"Evan said for us to hold off and not rock the boat for a few more days. He thinks something might happen by the middle of the week."

"What could possibly happen?"

"He didn't say. He just said things have a way of working out."

"You've talked to him about it?"

"Yeah. Quite a few times. Where do you think Jack and I go evenings? We can't sit on the porch. Papa isn't interested in playing cards. I've been saving money to buy a Victrola, but I don't want to buy it while she's here."

"A Victrola? We could dance to the music." Julie's face brightened with the thought of dancing with Evan.

"Evan has one. It's a small one that sits on a table. I saw one in the furniture store that is tall and has a place for records."

"I don't know what to do about tonight. I'll not leave the kids here with her and Papa. I'm afraid of what Jill will do, and poor little Jason is so unhappy. Elsie asked him if he was a cripple because he was a bad boy."

Joe swore under his breath. "I'll take them with me to watch Jack play ball."

"Do you think Papa will let you take the car?"

"If not, we'll walk. Jack and I can take turns carrying Joy on the way back. Or I could hitch up the wagon. That's how we got around before we had the car. You go and be with Evan. I'll take care of the kids."

"Oh, Joe. What would I do without you?"

"Right now you'd better get some dinner on. I'm sure Papa will invite Evan and Mr. Marsh to eat."

"Did you enjoy the ride in the airplane? I was so scared something would happen and you'd fall."

"It was just . . . great!" Joe's beautiful smile appeared as if by magic. "Evan is a swell guy. I'm so glad he likes you and that you like him. Some words passed between him and Mr. Marsh about giving us a ride. I didn't hear what was said, but right after that Mr. Marsh asked if anyone wanted a ride."

"When you go out, tell Jill to come help me."

"Don't worry about Mrs. Stuart, Sis. She'll not start anything with Evan and Mr. Marsh here. Don't let her get your goat."

"I won't, but I don't know about Jill."

"Shit," the man muttered and crawled out from under the thick bushes where he had concealed himself when the airplane had taken off the first time. He was hot and dirty, and besides that, he'd stirred up a hill of little brown ants and the little bastards were crawling all over him.

He laughed. The thrill of seeing the little blond rascal and Jill, the mama of her future little cousin, was worth the discomfort. He'd have the young filly and the family wouldn't kick up a fuss. They would make up a reason for keeping the baby. His offspring wouldn't be given away like an unwanted cat.

He watched the family and the airplane pilot walk toward the house. It was clear for him to get his horse and head back to town.

Chapter 22

IN THE LATE AFTERNOON, after the last of the jars of tomatoes had been lifted from their boiling bath, Julie carried a bucket of water to the room she shared with Jill and Joy, removed her clothes, washed and dressed for her outing with Evan. She would have preferred to get into the washtub, but not with Birdie in the house.

Evan and Wesley Marsh had not stayed for the noon meal. Evan had insisted that he had to get back home. Julie was sure he'd decided not to stay because of Birdie. The pilot told Jethro that he had to be in Colorado at a certain time and must be on his way.

The family stood at the edge of the pasture and watched the plane take off. Wesley circled the farm, dipped the wings and waved his red scarf. Then he shot almost straight up and rolled the plane over. They all caught their breaths. Evan laughed when Julie put her hands over her ears. He told them that the roll was just a sample of the stunts Wesley performed at the air shows.

During the noon meal, Joe had brought up the subject of taking the kids to watch Jack play ball and asked Jethro if he could take them in the car.

Before Jethro could open his mouth, Birdie said, "Jethro,

you promised to take me and Elsie to Spring Lake to watch the dancing."

"I did? Well, I guess I had forgotten about it."

"Oh, you! You've just got too much on your mind, what with supporting this big family and all. Can't they go in the wagon?"

"Don't worry about it, Mrs. Stuart, we'll get there," Joe said politely. Then, to his father, "Things look different from up in an airplane, don't they, Pa?"

"They sure do. I hadn't realized the river had so many turns in it and I could see from one side of the town to the other."

"I sure would like to learn to fly one of those things," Jack said.

"You'll have to finish school first."

"Jethro Jones!" Birdie expelled a heavy breath. "You went up in that rickety little old airplane? Why, it was old as the hills! It probably got all used up in the war. In Memphis they throw those things away. Oh, I'm glad I didn't know. I would have fainted dead away knowing that you were way up there."

Julie's eyes went from Jack to Joe to her father. Jack was trying not to laugh, Joe's face was expressionless, but his eyes twinkled at her, and her father looked down. He appeared to be embarrassed.

Birdie had given Elsie a large helping of pudding and the girl had eaten only the raisins out of it, leaving the rest to be thrown out to the pigs. Julie had caught Jason looking pointedly at his father to see if he would remark on it. When he said nothing, Jason had looked at him, his face tight, almost as if he faced an enemy.

My little brother is losing respect for our father and it makes me sad.

Julie had held her breath for fear something would be said about her going out with Evan. She didn't want her outing discussed by Birdie. She had been truly glad when the meal was over.

When Evan arrived, Birdie, in a thin, flowered dress and Elsie, dressed all in white, were seated in the swing on the front porch. Evan drove around to the back, where Jill stood holding tightly to Joy to keep her from running in front of the car.

Jethro came out onto the back porch in time to see Joy running to Evan and saw him scooping her up in his arms. Jill was laughing, something she never did in the house anymore. Jason, with a rope on Sidney, hurried to greet Evan. Joe and Jack stopped playing catch and joined the group.

A lump came up in Jethro's throat. He clenched his fists. Was he losing the love of his family because of his friendship with Birdie?

Julie came out of the house.

"Sis," Jethro said before she stepped off the porch. "Keep an eye on Jill like I told you."

Julie turned to look at him. Today she had felt sorry for him standing alone at the edge of the field, and now she almost disliked him for being so stupid as to let Birdie Stuart plant such evil thoughts in his mind.

"Papa, do you really think that the only reason a man would be interested in going out with me is so that he could be near my young sister? If you think that, it's not very flattering to me."

"I can't help worrying, knowing how Walter is around women."

"Evan isn't like Walter," Julie retorted angrily. "If you're worried about Evan having an interest in Jill, I think you should talk to him about it. Better yet, Mrs. Stuart should give Evan her reasons for thinking such a thing."

"Birdie has seen the sorry side of life and knows such things go on."

"I, too, know such things go on, but that doesn't mean that Evan is guilty."

"Come on, Julie," Jack called. "I don't want to be late."

"Don't worry, Papa." Julie stepped off the porch. "Go on and have a good time with your . . . lady friend and Elsie. Joe and I will see that no harm comes to Jill, from Evan or anyone else, if we can help it."

Jethro went through the house and was on the front porch when the car passed. The kids waved and he waved back, then went to sit down beside Birdie in the swing.

"I know that you're worried about Jill, Jethro, dear. I hope and pray that nothing happens to rob her of her innocence."

"On what do you base your suspicions about Evan, Birdie?"

"Several things. I know men, Jethro. Heavens, I've had to ward them off all my life."

"What exactly did Evan do to arouse your suspicion?"

"Well, I didn't want to say anything, but . . . at one of the ball games, I was at the water bucket and caught him staring at Jill. He said not a word to me until Jill went around the house and was out of sight. He was breathing hard—you know, like a man in . . . in lust—and, Jethro, an embarrassing lump appeared, ah . . . you know where. I grabbed Elsie and hurried back to be with the other women.

"After that I watched him, and believe me, Jethro, he couldn't take his eyes off Jill." Birdie dragged air into her lungs and sighed deeply. "I hated to tell you this but felt it was my duty. As the mother of a young girl, I would want to know if a man old enough to be her father was lusting after her."

Jethro didn't say anything for a long while. His mind was going in ten different directions.

"When are we goin', Mama? I want an ice-cream cone."

"Just be patient, sugar."

"I'll bring the car around." Jethro went through the house feeling empty and a little sick.

Julie got into the car and moved close to Evan to make room for Jack. His smiling eyes traveled over her face as she tucked her shoulder behind his. She was terribly aware of the warm solid body next to hers. His close scrutiny suddenly made it difficult to breathe.

"Joe and I hatched this up in case he couldn't use the car to take the kids to the ball game," Evan confessed.

"When was this?"

"Before I left this noon."

"Joe, you could have told me and relieved my mind."

"Sorry, Sis. I didn't think about it."

"Can I ride in front sometime? Pl-ease." Joy, standing behind Evan, put her hands on his shoulders.

"Sometime," Evan promised. "How about an ice-cream cone?"

"Yeah," Joy yelled and her small hands circled his neck.

"Evan, you shouldn't," Julie said.

"I brought money for all of us." Joe leaned over the seat and dropped a coin in Julie's lap. "Jack, can you be a minute or two late?"

"For an ice cream? Sure, if you're buyin'."

Evan loved being with this family. He stayed in the car while Joe and Jack went inside the drugstore to get the cones. He understood Joe's wanting to pay for the treat and teased that he could take them all to the picture show if he was so flush with money.

At each practice the crowds had increased, and tonight half a hundred people milled around the ball field. After the cones were passed around, Evan took a blanket out of the trunk of the car and spread it on the ground in the shade. Jill found her friends and eagerly began to tell about Wesley Marsh and the airplane. Joe spied Thad Taylor and went off with him, talking excitedly about the big event of the day. Joy and Jason sat on the blanket, leaving Julie some time alone with Evan.

"We're missing another picture show," he said, his eyes on her face as she licked the cone.

"I don't mind, if you don't."

"Being with you and the kids is treat enough for me."

Not knowing what to say, she looked out to see ice cream running down Joy's arm.

"Joy is going to be a mess."

"I came prepared tonight." Evan pulled a cloth out of his back pocket. "I'll wet it at the water cooler and she'll be as good as new. Hummm . . ." He leaned close to look into Julie's face. "I might have to use it on you, too."

It was at that moment that Julie knew for sure that she had fallen in love with him.

"Papa's home," Jill said as the car approached the house. "I guess they didn't go to Spring Lake."

Light glowed from the window of the room Birdie used, and as they stopped beside the porch, they could see Jethro sitting in the porch swing.

"Jack hit a home run, Papa," Jason said as soon as his feet hit the porch. "You shoulda seen it. Crack! I thought he'd broke the bat."

"The league will be here for a game next Saturday night and again Sunday afternoon," Jack announced. "Are you coming, Papa?"

"Of course, I am. I'd not miss seeing you play," he replied almost gruffly. Jethro rose from the swing and came to the edge of the porch.

Joe stooped to look into the car window. "Have a good time. Don't worry, Sis. One of us will wash Joy's feet before we put her to bed."

Evan moved the car to circle the yard and head back down the lane. Jethro was still standing on the edge of the porch when they passed.

"Is he still suspicious of me?" Evan asked.

"Yes, I'm afraid so."

"He was cordial today when we went for gas."

"Papa wouldn't say anything to you in front of a stranger."

"If he thinks I'm such a bad fellow, why is he allowing you to go out with me?"

Julie giggled softly, although the subject of the conversation was deadly serious.

"I asked him that, and he said I could take care of myself; but Jill was young, and a man with a glib tongue could turn her head."

"How, if you're out in the dark with a man who outweighs you by sixty or seventy pounds, can you take care of yourself?" Evan spoke angrily. "I can't believe that he's so completely taken in by Mrs. Stuart that he believes her stories. If he really thought that I was such a monster, he'd not allow me on the place, much less take his daughter out in the car at night."

"He's been awfully quiet lately. Jill and I think he may be regretting inviting Mrs. Stuart to come and stay."

"What are you doing sitting way over there?" Evan asked suddenly and reached for her arm. He gently tugged until she was close beside him. "We're on a date. Remember? I've been looking forward to it all week."

"So have I."

"Is there someplace you'd like to go?" They were driving slowly down the main street of Fertile. "We could go back out to Spring Lake."

"Is that what you want to do?"

"Not especially. I just want to be with you."

"We can't keep driving and using up gasoline."

"I'd like to get out on a country road somewhere and run out of gasoline." He laughed outright at her puzzled expression.

"Have you done that before?"

"Not on purpose." Evan drove out of town and took the road along the river. When they reached the bluff above town, he stopped the car. "Shall we sit here for a while?" he asked before he shut off the motor and turned off the headlights.

"It's pretty up here. I didn't realize there were so many lights in town."

Evan turned, facing her, and leaned his back against the door. He lifted her hand and held it in both of his. Julie was intensely aware of him, from the top of her head to the tip of her tingling toes. Her world narrowed suddenly to the small space in the front seat of the car.

"I hadn't intended to speak so soon, partly due to Jethro's suspicion of me, but I can't keep it to myself any longer," Evan spoke slowly, almost fearfully. "Julie, I've fallen in love with you. I've never been in love before. I didn't know what to expect. You're in my thoughts day and night. I live for the times I'm with you. It doesn't matter if your family is around or where we are. I just want to be near you."

His quiet words were so unexpected that Julie was incapable of replying. She sucked in a breath and tried to keep from shaking. Words formed in her mind and refused to pass her frozen throat. She closed her eyes. Her heart hammered against her ribs.

"Have I shocked you?" he asked after a long moment of silence.

"I . . . I don't know what to say." Her voice wobbled.

"You don't have to say anything. I thought it only fair to let you know how I feel." He moved his arm around her shoulders and pressed her to him. She went willingly and rested her head against him.

They sat in silence while his hand moved over her hair. When she spoke, it was in a soft whisper and her voice barely reached him.

"Evan, I . . . love you, too."

He held his breath until his chest hurt, then let it out in a long sigh of relief.

"Sweetheart. I didn't dare hope— Say it again. Are you sure?" His arms tightened until she was crushed against him.

"I love you," she said very carefully so that he would know

that she meant it. "I'm sure of it." She tilted her face to look at him and her arm crept up around his neck.

"Thank God!" he whispered fervently and lowered his mouth to hers. He kissed her without demand: her bottom lip first, then the upper one, his tongue stealing out to trace the sensitive curve. He kissed her again and again, not hard, not long, but gently, reverently, keenly aware of every lovely curve of the body pressed to his.

"Sweet, darling, beautiful Julie," he murmured when he could speak again. "I never expected to ever find such a treasure as you and to have you love me."

"Why not? You're a wonderful man. I can't believe you'd want me." She wanted to wrap herself around him. The feelings he awakened in her were so delightful they were almost scary.

"You're what I've looked for and was almost sure I'd never find."

He held her, warm and soft and infinitely dear, against him, lightly kissing her parted lips. Her breath was sweet on his mouth. There was no woman to compare with her. He laughed low and tenderly, unable to contain his happiness.

"I want to tell you everything about me. I want to know everything about you."

The hand caressing the back of his head stilled and then her fingers slid around to cover his mouth.

"No secrets tonight, Evan. Please. I just want to enjoy being here with you and hearing you say that you love me."

Her lips replaced her fingers and she kissed him urgently, almost desperately, while her fingertips stroked his cheek. When she freed his lips, he moved them over her face to her closed eyes and found the tears she was trying to blink away.

"Darlin' girl." He rocked her gently in his arms and kissed her tear-wet eyes. "Sweetheart, don't cry."

"I'm not crying."

"You are. Are you afraid to tell me about Joy?"

Julie thought her heart would stop. She felt as if the bottom had fallen out of her world. *He knew.* When she was able to speak, the words came out on a sob.

"How did you know?"

"My mother wrote often to me while I was in school and later when I went to France. She was terribly upset about what happened to you. Your mother had confided in her. She told me that at fifteen you'd had a terrible thing happen to you and that you had come through the experience with your head held high, not whining, but doing what had to be done. When your baby came, you were out in the barn all alone. Your mother passed Joy off as hers. She admired your mother and father for the way that they had handled things and you in particular. She never dreamed that I would come back here and fall in love with you."

"You've known all the time."

"I've never told a living soul, sweetheart."

"Joy may be . . . could be—"

"Walter's? My mother intended to tell you that it couldn't have been Walter who made you pregnant. I guess the time was never quite right. Because of an injury, Walter isn't capable of . . . the act it takes to father a child. He likes to talk dirty and threaten people. Trying to make up the loss of his manhood may be why he's so disgusting at times. I think he loved my mother as much as he could love anyone. He was decent to her and only to her."

Julie was very still, her mind flooded with unanswered questions. If not Walter Johnson, then who had attacked her in the woods, put the cloth over her eyes and thrown her to the ground? The threats he had whispered in her ear after he'd had his way with her had terrified her.

She had told only her mother. Then, when it became known to both of them that she was going to have a baby, they'd had to tell her father. That winter she'd stayed home on the pretext of caring for her ailing mother. It was a long, hard winter and they'd had few visitors, with the exception of Mrs. Johnson.

During the last month of Julie's pregnancy, her mother had taken to her bed with an ailment resembling influenza; and shortly after Joy was born, she had died. The general assumption had been that she died from complications of childbirth.

Joe had been fourteen at the time and Julie was sure that he knew her secret, but he had never mentioned it.

"Julie, honey. If I knew who it was that caused you so much pain, I'd kill him. I would never hurt you like that. You believe me, don't you?" His fingers lifted her chin so that he could look into her face.

"You . . . still want me?"

"Want you? God in heaven! I want to marry you and live with you for the rest of my life. I'd walk through fire to get to you if you called me."

"Evan . . . I never thought anyone would want me if he found out about Joy." Tears rolled from her eyes and wet both their cheeks.

"Ah, sweetheart. Don't cry. That little girl won my heart, too. I'll love her as if she were my own." He cupped Julie's chin in his palm and kissed her mouth, her wet cheeks.

"Hush, now, and listen. I have things to tell you. I want no secrets between us." He waited for her to become aware of the gravity of what he was about to say before he continued.

"Walter isn't my father." He watched her face and saw her mouth form a silent O, before she gasped.

"Oh, Evan!"

"I have his name because he married my mother before I was born. The man, or rather boy, my mother loved was killed before they could marry. Her parents got Walter to marry her to save her from disgrace. He was a poor fellow who had never dreamed he'd have a farm. They gave him the farm, which had been in the family before the Civil War, for as long as he lived, then it goes to me. Mother told me when I was ten years old and gave me a picture of my father.

"Ah, honey," he whispered and cuddled her close. "We've each got something to hide."

"You've had to pretend that he was your father all this time, and I've had to pretend that Joy was my little sister." Her arms hugged him to her.

"I'll not shame my mother's name by denouncing him now."

"Of course not!"

"Julie . . . guess what my real father's name was. James T. Jones," he said before she could speak.

"Could he have been related to my father?"

"No. He was from England. I looked the family up while I was there. They were a family of modest means, highly respected in their village."

"I worry that if someday Joy finds out that I'm her mother, she'll hate me."

"She won't," he said positively. "Jethro wouldn't tell her, would he?"

"No! He dotes on her. I think he loves her more than any of us. It may be because while my mother was so sick that I had to be with her, he took care of Joy."

"Will he let her go with you when you and I make a home together?" His words caused Julie to catch her breath.

"I'm sure he will, but it can't be anytime . . . soon."

"I know, sweetheart. I wouldn't ask you to come live with me while Walter is there. I plan to give him money to sign the farm over to me. A part of my grandparents' deal with him was that he could have the farm for as long as he lives. If I give him enough money, he might move somewhere else."

"I can't go and leave the kids. If Papa marries Mrs. Stuart, Joe and Jack and I plan to take them . . . someplace."

"Honey, I don't think we'll have to worry about Mrs. Stuart staying much longer. What I worry about is what lasting influence her time here will have had on Jethro."

"Oh, I hope she goes soon. Evan—"

He put his finger over her lips. "Enough about everyone but us. Sweetheart, this is the happiest night of my life. It's going to be hard to wait to make you mine."

"I'm already yours, my love," she said and lifted her face for his kiss.

"I'll be so gentle with you, honey. Will you hate being with me as my wife?" His hand slid down the side of her breast and over to cover its softness. "Considering what you've been through, I'll understand if you are afraid."

"My mother loved Papa. She told me that being with the man you love is one of God's gifts. She said that someday I would meet a man who would fill my life with his presence. I would love him and together we would have children. She didn't want what had happened to me to make our coming together as husband and wife an ugly thing."

"Julie, my sweetheart, my love, I'm overwhelmed." Joyous relief washed over him. "I thought that if I was lucky, you'd like me. And after you got to know me better, I might have a chance that you'd even love me."

She laughed happily. "You silly man. You made my heart flutter the night you came with Joe to play cards and caught me licking the fudge knife."

He laughed, and she felt the movement in his chest and placed her palm over his heart. They sat quietly holding each other, reveling in their newly revealed love. Finally Evan stirred and she lifted her head from his shoulder.

"I'd better check my watch and see what time it is. The moon went down a while ago."

"It did? I didn't even notice."

They sat for a while longer, exchanging lingering kisses and enjoying the miracle of loving each other. Then, reluctantly, Evan started the car and drove slowly down from the bluff.

* * *

It was an hour after midnight. Otto Bloom sneaked into the bushes beneath Amos Wood's bedroom window. He had several pebbles in his hand and tossed one of them at the windowpane. After three or four throws, the window slid up and Amos Wood motioned Otto toward the front porch.

"What's happened?" the banker said as soon as he stepped out onto the porch in his nightshirt. "This isn't the night the shipment comes down."

"No, it isn't th-that," Otto stuttered. "I need to borrow your car, Mr. Wood."

"What the hell for?"

Otto stepped close and spoke into the banker's ear for a minute or two. When he finished, Amos moved away from him and, in a low, angry voice, called him every obscene name he could think of.

"You're a goddamned fool!" he exclaimed. "I should have let Appleby keep your ass in jail until hell froze over. Take the car, damn you. And don't you forget that I will never admit to allowing you to take it. Understand?"

"Yes, sir. I understand. There's nothin' for ya to worry about, Mr. Wood." Otto bobbed his head up and down. "I know what to do." His head was clearing up fast, but he was still unsteady on his feet.

"You'd better. Now get on and do what you have to do, and get that car back here in an hour. Hear?"

Otto pushed the car out onto the street before he got in and drove away without turning on the headlights.

Chapter 23

JULIE LAY IN BED BESIDE JOY and hugged the little girl to her. What had happened tonight seemed unreal. Knowing her secret, Evan had fallen in love with her. It made him all the more dear to her. It was such a relief. Lord bless Mrs. Johnson for telling him.

What a shock it had been to learn that Evan was not Walter Johnson's natural son, as everyone believed. All this time she had thought that it was Walter who had come up behind her in the woods and violated her. If, as Evan had said, Walter was unable to perform the act that made her pregnant, then it had to have been someone who knew she came home from school through the woods that time of day. But who?

Julie hadn't wanted to sleep. She had wanted to stay awake and live over and over again every word Evan had said and feel again the kisses they had shared; but when the red rooster in the barnyard announced a new day, Julie woke with a start.

As she slipped out of bed and hurriedly dressed, she recalled that she and Evan had decided to say nothing to the family, just yet, about their plans to spend their lives together. She longed to tell Joe. He was the one who would be the happiest for her.

Her father, who usually milked the cows on Sunday morning, came into the kitchen as Julie was building the fire in the cookstove.

"Morning," she said over her shoulder.

"Mornin'. You were out pretty late last night." His voice was gruff, critical.

"Yes," Julie admitted. "It was late."

"Not a very good example to set for the young ones."

"They should have been asleep when I got home," Julie said calmly, determined not to let his grouchiness take the edge off her happiness. "Are you going to church this morning?"

"Planning on the whole family going."

"Mrs. Stuart, too?"

"She says not."

"I'll stay home and cook dinner. I don't think we should all go and leave a guest in the house."

"Why? Are you afraid she'll steal something?"

He went back out before Julie could reply. She looked after him, wishing things were different between them and that she could tell him of the wonderful thing that had happened to her.

Julie worked swiftly, pinching off dabs of biscuit dough the size of an egg, flattening them between her palms, and placing them in a row in the shallow baking pan. She shoved the pan in the oven, added a dozen cobs to the firebox because they made the fire hotter, removed a round stove lid and placed the big spider skillet over the open flame.

While placing the strips of meat in the skillet, she paused to think. Even if Birdie wasn't here, who would cook the breakfast, do the washing, mend, clean, and do all the other chores if she went to live with Evan? Jill was fifteen, the age Julie had been when she took over the running of the house, but somehow Jill seemed younger. Oh, there were so many obstacles to overcome before she could be with Evan.

Julie pushed the thoughts from her mind, and by the time the family had gathered, breakfast was on the table.

"Do you want to call Mrs. Stuart, Papa?"

"There's been racket enough to wake her if she wanted to come in." He took his place at the table. Behind him, Joe grinned and winked at Julie.

Birdie and Elsie came to the table when the meal was almost over. She apologized, saying that she had a terrific headache this morning. She and Elsie ate only the biscuits with butter and honey. Julie had taken the jar of strawberry jam to the cellar.

"Did you enjoy yourself last night, Julie?" Birdie asked.

"Very much. Jason, if you want more honey, I'll pass it."

"I heard you when you came in." Birdie looked pointedly at Jethro.

Julie chose to ignore the comment, and the conversation died from her lack of response.

Birdie had ceased in her pretense of helping after the meals. She and Elsie went to the bedroom. While Julie and Jill were washing dishes, Jethro came in with a chicken he had plucked and cleaned. It was in a pan with a cloth over it.

"I cleaned this last night, Sis. I was kind of hungry for chicken and dumplings."

"The chicken will have to boil for a couple of hours. If I go to church, it'll not have time to cook for dinner."

"I changed my mind about going. I'll watch it if you'll put it on. Joe can take you in the car. It's too hot for you to walk."

"All right. I'll make the dumplings when we get back."

An hour later, church and dumplings were the furthest thing from Julie's mind.

After she had dressed Joy and herself and was waiting for a grumbling Jason to change his shirt and pants, a car came down the lane from the road.

"Who is it?" Jill asked.

"I don't know."

A big touring car stopped beside the front porch. A tall man wearing a felt hat and a large tin star on his shirt pocket got out. Julie could see Evan in the front seat, but he made no move to leave the car. The officer paused to say a few words to Evan, then came around the car to the porch steps, where Jethro had gone to meet him.

"What's going on?" Joe asked from behind Julie. "That's Deputy Weaver. What's Evan doin' with him?"

"I don't know, but I'm going to find out."

Julie went out onto the porch and, ignoring her father and the deputy, went to the side of the car where Evan sat. Before she could say a word to him, the deputy grabbed her arm and pulled her away from the car.

"Keep away from my prisoner, miss."

"Prisoner? And . . . let go my arm."

Evan opened the car door.

"Stay put," the deputy barked. "Stay put or I'll put the cuffs on you."

"Papa, what's going on?"

Julie looked from her father to the sneering face of the deputy. The rest of the family had come out onto the porch, followed by Birdie and Elsie.

"You goin' to church with us, Mr. Johnson?" Joy yelled as she darted down the steps to the car.

The deputy caught her under the arms and roughly swung her back up onto the porch. Scared, Joy burst into tears.

"Get your hands off her!" Julie shouted, even as she heard a growl come from her father's throat. Jack swung Joy up into his arms and held her protectively.

"What do you think she'd do?" the boy demanded.

"He probably thought she was going to slip him a knife or a gun," Joe said dryly.

"I don't think you understand what's going on. I've got a job to do here and I'll not put up with a couple of smart-aleck, wet-eared kids." Deputy Weaver reared back and looked down his nose at Joe and Jack. "Keep your mouths shut unless I ask you a question. There's been a murder, and this man is my prisoner."

"Murder?" Julie's hand flew to her mouth and her eyes to Evan.

"Walter Johnson was killed last night, and it's my job to find out who did it."

"You . . . think . . . Evan did it?"

"Yes, I think he did it. He says that he was with you last night." Weaver's narrowed eyes focused on Julie's face.

"He was. He was with all of us until just after dark, then he and I went for a ride in his car."

"Where'd you go?"

"We went along the river, then to the bluff overlooking town."

"What did you do up there?"

"We talked."

"Talked? Bull-foot!" The deputy cast a disgusted glance back toward the car.

"What do you mean by that?" Jethro's irritation was evident.

"It means . . . well, never mind. What time was it when he left you here?"

"I'm not sure of the minute," Julie said trying to remain calm. "But it was shortly after two o'clock. I heard the clock strike when we were on the porch, and we stayed a little while after that."

"Talking? You must have had a lot to talk about."

"We did. Not that it's any business of yours," Julie added sharply.

"That remains to be seen."

He glanced over his shoulder as a car came down the lane and stopped. Chief Corbin Appleby got out and came to the porch. He nodded a greeting.

"She says he was with her until two o'clock." The deputy raised his brows in an insinuating way.

"Are you sure of the time, Miss Jones?"

"I'm sure."

"It was about that time, Chief," Jethro said. "I heard her come in."

"Then who came in a little after ten? I thought that was Julie; the boys had already gone upstairs." All eyes turned to Birdie. She put her hands to her cheeks, and her eyes got large and fearful. "Did I say . . . something I shouldn't have? Oh, Jethro, I'm sor-ry."

Julie turned on her, her eyes blazing with anger. "What are you trying to pull now, Mrs. Stuart? You didn't hear me come in at that time, and you know it."

Birdie's eyes became even larger and slowly filled with tears. "Oh, you're just so . . . mean. I don't know why you said you came in later."

"Ma'am." The deputy reached for Birdie's arm. "Let's go over here and have a little talk. Chief, see that this bunch stays away from my prisoner."

"I don't want to get Julie in trouble." Birdie threw a pleading look over her shoulder at Jethro and choked back sobs. She grabbed Elsie's hand and walked behind the chief's car with the deputy.

"Papa, you know it was around two when I came home, don't you?"

"I heard the car drive in and stop away from the house, and I heard the clock strike when you were on the porch."

"Is the time important, Chief Appleby?" Julie asked.

"Yes, ma'am, it is. Gus Keegan, who runs a joint down on the river, was out on his dock around two o'clock. He told the deputy he was fishing, but I know that he was pulling up a gunnysack full of bootleg whiskey out of the river. A car drove up and someone began to pull something from it. He thought it was thieves out to steal his whiskey. He yelled. The man got in the car and drove off, leaving the bundle on the ground.

"Gus walked over and discovered the body of Walter Johnson. He had been stabbed many times and his throat was cut. Whoever killed him must have been in a rage, because he was cut up pretty bad. Gus thinks the man was going to get him in the river, hoping the current would carry him downstream. Doc Forbes said Walter had been dead for four or five hours."

"Why does the deputy think Evan did it?" Julie asked.

"Because of the car. Gus said he had seen a car like the one that brought the body go by earlier in the evening and he thought it was the same one. The car he described was like Evan Johnson's. From a previous conversation with Johnson, when Weaver and the marshal went to the farm to talk to Walter, Weaver believes he wanted his father dead so he could have the farm."

"Can I go say something to Evan?" Julie asked.

"As far as I'm concerned it would be all right, but this is out of my territory, although Well's Point where the body was found is and I'm in charge of the investigation."

"Does Weaver know that?" Jethro asked.

"He was on hand and thinks he's my superior. Ah, hell, come on, Miss Jones, and speak to Johnson. You've made your statement."

Julie hurried to the car. The chief followed and stayed a short distance away.

"Evan, I'm sorry about Mr. Johnson." Julie reached her hand in and he clasped it tightly. She saw the deep tension in his face and took a deep breath that quivered her lips. Her eyes caressed his face. The look warmed him to his very soul.

"So am I. He was as ornery as the day is long, but he didn't deserve to die like that. Honey, I didn't want to drag you into this."

"I don't know what Birdie is telling the deputy. Did you hear her say I was home at ten o'clock?"

"I heard. Just stay calm and don't let the deputy get you mad. He's showing off. The marshal is a straight shooter. He should be here sometime today. What we've got to do is find out who around here has a car that would look like mine at night."

"I love you," Julie said on a breath of a whisper, and tears filled her eyes.

"I love you, too." Evan brought her hand to his mouth for a quick kiss, his eyes glued to her face. "Tell Appleby that I'd like to have a word with him."

Julie backed away and Corbin moved around to the car window.

"The tires on my car are special. Check the tread and compare them to the tracks made by the car that dumped Walter by the river."

"Have you mentioned this to the deputy?"

"No. He isn't interested in anything I have to say. You'll know if the tracks by the river were made by my car; they cut deep. Check along the side of the road where he pulled over to dump Walter."

Weaver and Birdie came around the end of the car. Corbin stood with his arms folded and waited to see what the deputy had to say about Miss Jones talking to Johnson. He knew from the look on the man's face that he didn't like it.

"I didn't want her near him. They could hatch an alibi for him." His tone indicated that he considered his experience superior to Corbin's. "Did you hear what he said to her?"

"Every word." Corbin looked him in the eye as he lied.

Birdie Stuart was dabbing at her eyes. Elsie was holding on to her mother's skirt. They went up onto the porch, then directly into the house. Weaver jerked his head for the chief to move away from the car.

"The woman says the girl was here before ten o'clock. She doesn't know why Jones is backing his daughter's statement. She's scared to death of Johnson. She says he has a terrible temper. She heard him say several times that he wished the old man was dead. While she was staying at her brother's, she was sent over to the Johnsons' with a pie or something. Johnson was in a fit of rage and threatened to kill Walter while she was there. He tried to bash in the old man's head with a stick of stove wood."

"You believe her?"

"Hell, yes. Why would she lie? She's got to stay here with these folks until someone in Memphis sends her a ticket to come home. She doesn't want them to know what she's told me. But she said she would swear to it in a court of law when the time came."

"Why isn't she staying over at her brother's?"

"Hell, I don't know. Family squabble, I guess."

"I don't think you've got enough to lock him up."

"I do. I'm going to hold him until the marshal gets here. I didn't like that arrogant, know-it-all son-of-a-bitch the first time I saw him." He yanked the car door open. "Get out, Johnson, and turn around."

Evan got out, turned and put his hands behind him. His eyes were on Julie. He shook his head ever so slightly, signaling for her not to make a fuss.

"Why is he doin' that to Evan? Papa, do somethin'!" Jill's voice was shrill and angry.

Julie stood dry-eyed, with her chin up. Her eyes clung to Evan. He was so handsome with his blond hair and dark brows. Their eyes caught and held. A wave of helplessness came over her. He had become everything to her. She had never really understood the magnetism between a woman and a man before. It was both wonderful and devastating.

"Just a minute." Jethro came off the porch. "Evan, don't worry about things over at your place. Me and the boys will see to them."

"I'd appreciate that, Jethro. If I'm not back after I speak to the marshal, would you or one of the boys go to the telephone office and have them call my lawyer over in St. Joseph? His name is Casper Jenson. Tell him to come over right away. I'm going to have to make arrangements for Walter, too, but I suppose that can wait." Evan turned to Corbin Appleby. "Chief, I'd like to talk to you as soon as we get to town."

"Hush your gabbing and get in the car." The deputy opened the door and shoved Evan down on the seat. He was in a hurry to leave. He started the car, turned around in the barnyard, but the chief's car was blocking the lane and he had to wait. He hung his arm out over the side and slapped the door to get Corbin's attention.

"Chief Appleby," Julie said, as he turned to go to his car. "Evan was with me. He couldn't have done . . . that. I don't know why Mrs. Stuart said what she did."

"I'll bring the marshal out to talk to you. He'll want to talk to Mrs. Stuart, too."

The group stood on the porch and watched the two cars until they were out of sight.

"Papa." Julie put her hand on Jethro's arm. "Why is Mrs. Stuart saying that I was home at ten o'clock?"

"I don't know," he answered tiredly. "Maybe she really thinks she heard you come in."

"Hockey!" Joe snorted. "I wasn't asleep at ten o'clock. I'd have heard Julie come in."

"Have you wondered why none of the Humphreys come over anymore?" Jack was still holding Joy, whose little face was still streaked with tears. "This and That won't even come play catch with me."

"I bet they're afraid *she'll* want to go back home with them. She hates Julie and wants to make trouble for her," Jill finished angrily, turning to glare at her father.

"What can we do, Papa?" Julie turned to the one on whom she had always relied in time of trouble.

"There's nothing we can do now, Sis. We'll wait for the marshal. Joe, you and Jack better get over to the Johnsons' and see whether the chores are done. Weaver's got it in for Evan, for some reason, and might not have given him time to pen anything up."

"Chief Appleby seems a decent sort." Jack set Joy on her feet.

"I'm counting on him not to let Weaver railroad Evan if he didn't do it."

"I'm going to ask Mrs. Stuart why she's lying." Julie opened the door to go in the house.

"Leave her be, Sis," Jethro said quickly. "You could just make matters worse." He avoided looking at his eldest daughter, stepped off the porch and disappeared around the corner of the house.

To keep from crying, Julie held her lips tightly between her teeth and swallowed the lumps clogging her throat. Fear for Evan had caused her heart to shrivel within her. She longed to crawl in a dark hole and cry. Instead, she went to the kitchen and tended the chicken she had put on earlier and, because she had to be busy, she stirred up a batch of bread dough and left it on the back of the stove to rise.

When she had run out of things to do in the kitchen, she sat on the back porch and worked the dasher up and down in the churn, trying to stave off the memory of the deputy putting the handcuffs on Evan. It was usually Jason's or Jill's chore to churn, but everything about this day was different.

Birdie and Elsie had not come out of the bedroom, Jason sat quietly in the shade with Sidney, and Jill swung Joy in the rope swing suspended from a branch of the oak tree. Julie had not seen her father since he left the porch after telling her to leave Birdie alone.

Julie worked the dasher and waited for Joe and Jack to come back from the Johnson farm. Her brain was full of turmoil. It was hard for her to comprehend why Birdie hated her and Evan so much that she deliberately lied about the time she came home last night. Was Birdie hoping to convict Evan of murder? Her father had known the woman was lying. Maybe now he would see her for what she was.

What Julie had expected to be one of the happiest days of her life had turned out to be the most miserable.

Chapter 24

CHIEF CORBIN APPLEBY CAME UP out of the basement of the courthouse after locking Evan Johnson in the holding room and walked down the street to the furniture store, where the members of the City Council were meeting.

Something about Deputy Weaver didn't sit quite right with Corbin. The man's determination to prove Evan Johnson guilty of Walter Johnson's murder without even considering that someone else could have done it and his unnecessary roughness were not the actions of an impartial officer of the law.

Evan, aware that for some reason Weaver had a grudge against him, neither resisted when Weaver shoved him or responded to the jibes made about his wanting his father out of the way so that he would inherit the farm. The only time Evan's anger flared was when the deputy referred to Julie Jones as a hot little piece of ass.

Corbin had jumped in to grab Evan's arm and back him away from Weaver, or he would have torn into him.

"Go ahead and hit me," Weaver had taunted, shoving his face close to Evan's. "I'll work you over with this billy club and throw your ass so far back in the state pen that hell will freeze over before you find your way out."

"That's enough, Weaver. You had no business making such

a remark about Miss Jones. I don't blame Johnson for resenting it. I resent it, too."

"So that's the way the wind blows."

"I don't know what you mean by that, and right now I don't care." Corbin stood nose to nose with the man, refusing to be intimidated.

Not wanting to leave Evan alone with the deputy, Corbin had hung around until he left.

"Do you have any idea who could have killed your father?" the chief asked when they were alone.

"He had a few drinking cronies. Some of them floated up and down the river from one joint to the other, and several lived here in town or down at Well's Point. I don't know of any who had a car like the one described."

"Did you pass by Gus Keegan's place earlier in the evening?"

"Is it on the way to the bluff?"

"If you took the river road, you went right by it."

"Then I guess we did. You can still check the tire tracks and see that we passed on by. Didn't you say that Gus said the car pulled off onto the grass close to the river? You can prove it wasn't my car if you can get out there before the tracks are erased. I'd not put it past Weaver to go out and destroy them. That's why I never said anything to him."

"Gus has blocked off the road until the marshal gets here. I'm going to a council meeting, then I'll hightail it out to your place and take a look at your tires."

"Appleby, why are you helping me? Why aren't you as convinced as Weaver that I killed Walter?"

Corbin looked Evan in the eye. He wasn't as tall as the other man, but he had the bearing of a man who had been in the military.

"A bloody, messy murder wouldn't be your style. You've been on the front lines and would know how to kill a man quick and easy. I think you'd know how to do away with him without a finger pointing at you. You could have hit Walter in the head one night, buried him in the woods or carted him over to the Missouri River—it's no more than fifty miles away—tossed him in and told folks he'd run off. No, I figured right away that you were too smart to stab a man fifteen times, then cut his throat."

"Thanks." Evan's shoulders slumped with relief.

"One thing puzzles me," Corbin admitted. "Why is Mrs. Stuart sticking her neck out to put a kibosh on your alibi and make a liar out of Miss Jones?"

"You'd have to know Mrs. Stuart to understand. You know what they say about a woman scorned. Mrs. Stuart came here looking for a man to take care of her and, as I was her brother's neighbor and eligible, she made a play for me and felt scorned because I wasn't interested. Since that time she has spread tales about me because I didn't respond to her advances and about Miss Jones because I was interested in her. This is get-even time."

"What's she doing at the Jones farm?"

"She had a squabble with her brother's family, turned her charm on Jethro Jones and got him to invite her to stay there. If the deputy is counting on her to be a reliable witness, he'll be disappointed."

"You're sure of that?"

"I'd stake my freedom on it. The woman is completely self-centered and suffering from delusions. She's an unconscionable liar as well. She has no compunction about telling a lie that would destroy a person's reputation."

Corbin raised his brows. "You've given Mrs. Stuart some thought."

"Damn right. When someone sets out to ruin the best thing that has ever happened to me, I'm going to fight back."

"Can't say that I blame you. I've got the only key to this place, so you needn't worry Weaver will come back and pound the life out of you."

"He'd have to have help. I know how to protect myself."

Corbin thought about the conversation as he entered the furniture store and walked quickly to the back, where he heard voices raised in an argument.

"I say he's guilty. It's as plain as the nose on your face, Ira. I took his measure the day he came back here, lording it over us small-town folks, acting as if he was doing me a favor to put a little dab of money in my bank." The banker had a big fat cigar in his mouth and was talking around it as he paced the room.

"I didn't see him that way. He stayed to himself, but that's his privilege," the mayor commented.

"So he didn't put all his money in your bank. Is that what's eatin' you, Amos?" Frank Adler, the druggist, asked.

"That's got nothing to do with it. That bozo we've got for a lawman doesn't know his ass from a dip of snuff. Deputy Weaver says Johnson did it and I believe him."

"Whoever did it did a good job. Doc Forbes said any one of the ten stabs would have killed him. The other five would have caused him to bleed to death eventually." Herman Maddock, the undertaker, tilted his chair back against the wall and folded his hands behind his head.

"Maybe we should let Evan Johnson out of jail and pin a medal on him." This came from the druggist again. "We're rid of the town bully. Harvey Knapp at the billiard parlor will be relieved to know that he doesn't have to contend with him. Emmet at the barbershop said they hated for him to come in and thanked God it wasn't very often. Almost every business in town has had trouble with Walter."

Corbin lounged in the doorway and listened to the exchange until he was acknowledged.

"Come in, Chief, and have a chair."

"Thanks, Mayor, but I can't stay long. It appears that you've already convicted Evan Johnson."

"Well, hell, anyone with an ounce of brains could solve this case." The banker snorted his disgust.

"Some people with an ounce of brains don't look beyond their noses, and they see only what they want to see," Corbin said, tight-lipped and sharp.

"Are you insinuating . . ." Amos's fat jowls were quivering.

"If the shoe fits, Mr. Wood, wear it. I'm getting a little sick of being referred to as a 'bozo' and as incompetent."

"Now, now." Ira Brady got to his feet.

"Well, that's too bad," Amos retorted. "You can move on anytime you feel like it."

"You'd like that, wouldn't you, Mr. Banker? Is there a reason why you don't want a lawman in town?"

"Now, you look here. I've been in this town a hell of a lot longer than you have." Anger turned the banker's face a dull red. He reminded Corbin of a puffed-up bullfrog.

"I've known from the beginning that you didn't want me here, and I'm wondering if it's just me or any lawman." Corbin hooked his thumbs in his belt loops and looked down at the shorter man. "I'm telling you now: You'll have to fire me to get rid of me."

"None of that, now," the mayor said hastily. "The council is very well satisfied with the way you're doing your job."

"Doin' what job? Did I miss something?" Ron Poole came in, wiping sweat from his forehead. "Gol-damn, it's hotter than a two-dollar whore out there."

"You didn't miss anything. Amos is running off at the mouth," Frank Adler said.

"What else is new?" Ron picked up a cardboard fan and fanned his wet face.

"Now, look here. I've got a right to express my opinion. I was elected same as you."

"Not same as me," Ron exclaimed. "I didn't threaten to foreclose on anyone's loan to get them to get out and work to get me elected."

"Mayor, the only report I can give is that Evan Johnson is in my lockup." Corbin, tired of the banter, wanted to get the business over with so he could get out of there. "I'm looking for an automobile that from the back would look like a Hudson sedan. Do you know of anyone in town who has such a car?"

"There aren't many big cars in town. I've got a Buick. What make is your car, Amos? It's a big one."

"Chrysler. And it don't look like no damn Hudson."

Corbin went to the door. "I've got a few more things to check out. I'll report back later, Mayor."

"You'd better leave the lookin' into this to someone who knows what he's doin'."

Corbin looked at the banker. "Weaver is a hotheaded show-off. The marshal knows what he's doin'. I'll talk to him when he gets here."

"I thought that was why we hired you—so that the marshal wouldn't have to run up here every time someone got a bean crossways."

Corbin left the room without retorting and heard Ron Poole say, "Why don't you get off his back, Amos, and let the man do his job?"

"Him and that Evan Johnson are two of a kind. He'll do everything he can to pin this on someone else. Mark my words."

Corbin's temper cooled on the way out to the Johnson farm. When he had come out to the farm this morning to bring Evan the news, he had been surprised. It was the most prosperous-looking farm in the area. The deputy had arrived soon after; and because the farm was outside the city, he made a big deal about taking charge.

When Corbin drove into the Johnson farm this time, one of the Jones boys was carrying milk up from the cellar and dumping it in the hog trough. The other had penned the chickens and had turned on the windmill to fill the water tanks for the stock.

"After what's happened, do you think there will be ball practice this afternoon?" Jack asked.

"I've not heard different. I know they want to get in as much practice as they can. The big games are next Saturday and Sunday."

"That woman that said Julie came in at ten is lying through her teeth." Joe followed Corbin to the shed where Evan parked his car. "Jack and I were awake and talking about Mrs. Stuart and trying to figure out a way to show Pa what a bitch she is when I heard the clock strike ten. I remember hearing it striking the half hour, too. Julie hadn't come home. I was asleep when she came in at two o'clock, but our pa doesn't lie and neither does Julie."

"Evan's had to put up with being Walter's son and being snubbed by folks, but we like him and think he's a square-shooter." Jack's young face was serious. "Me and Joe wouldn't let our sister go out with a man we didn't trust."

"I'd say that's about as good a recommendation as a man could get. Don't step on the tire tracks," Corbin said when Joe moved around Evan's car.

Corbin knelt down behind the car and looked closely at the tire treads.

"You're going to compare the tracks. By golly, that's a good idea." Joe stood at the side of the car with his hand resting on the spare wheel and tire that were locked into the indention made in the front fender. "Why don't you take the spare wheel and roll it down the road—"

Corbin stood. "Now, *that's* a good idea." He gave Joe a pleased grin. "Where are the tools?"

"Right here in this box. Evan keeps everything in its place."

Twenty minutes later the spare tire and wheel were loaded in Corbin's car.

"You don't think he did it, do you?" Jack asked as he led his horse to water.

"I'm supposed to lay out all the facts before I decide anything. Right now there aren't many facts that tell me that Evan killed his father. This tire will go a long way in proving if he is guilty or not."

"We'll tell Julie you're goin' to compare the tire tracks. We want to give our sister something to hold on to."

"Well, if you mention the tire, don't do it in front of Mrs. Stuart or anyone outside the family. It may prove Evan was there, drove up and dumped his father, and it may not."

"There are many places along the river to dump something. I don't know why Evan would be in such a hurry that he'd stop near Gus Keegan's place, when a mile down the road he'd be in the woods."

"You've got a point. But a mile down the road it veers off and runs a good hundred feet from the river. It may be that whoever killed him didn't want to carry him through the woods." Corbin left the two boys standing in the farmyard and wondered if Evan Johnson knew how lucky he was.

Julie was putting the noon meal on the table when Joe and Jack came home. After taking care of their horses, they washed at the pump in the yard. Jethro appeared from somewhere behind the barn and spoke with them before the three of them came toward the house. Julie went out onto the porch to meet them.

"Is everything all right over there?"

"It is now. The deputy didn't even give Evan time to check the cookstove or shut the doors. Chief Appleby came while we were there. He took the spare wheel from Evan's car and is going to compare the tracks with the tracks made by the car that dumped Walter. He said for us to not spread it around."

"He doesn't think Evan killed Walter," Jack said.

"Did he say that?"

"No, but we could tell."

"Papa, will you let Joe use the car to take some dinner to Evan?"

"Fix it up, Sis. The boys can take it."

It was a quiet meal. Even Joy was subdued. Julie asked her father if he wanted to tell Birdie that the meal was ready. He ignored the question and took his place at the table. The family had almost finished the meal when the bedroom door opened and Birdie and Elsie stood in the kitchen doorway.

Birdie had big tears in her eyes and her mouth quivered when she spoke.

"My child is hungry, Jethro."

"Then sit down and eat."

Joe looked first at Julie, then rolled his eyes to the ceiling.

"What'er ya lookin' at, Joe?" Jason asked.

"I thought I saw a rainbow up there," he whispered.

"I can do without." Birdie hugged her daughter's head to her side. Dainty, pitiful sobs came from Elsie. "But it breaks my heart when my baby cries for food."

"You're welcome to eat . . . both of you." Jethro lifted his head to look at her.

"Can . . . we take it to the bedroom? I know Julie doesn't want us at the . . . the table." Her voice dropped to a pitiful whisper.

Julie dished some chicken and dumplings onto a plate, laid a fork alongside it, got to her feet and handed it to Birdie.

"You hate me, don't you, Julie?"

"Yes, Mrs. Stuart. I do."

"I . . . did . . . what I thought was . . . right." Birdie turned pleading eyes toward Jethro. "You don't blame me, do you, Jethro?"

"You deliberately lied," Julie said staunchly. "I'll never forgive you for that."

"I'll leave as . . . soon as I can."

Julie remained standing until she heard the bedroom door close. She had not been hungry to start with, and now she felt nauseated.

"Don't you think you were a little hard on her?" Jethro spoke without looking up from his plate.

"Hard on her? She lied to put Evan in jail."

"Maybe she honestly thinks she heard you come in at ten o'clock."

"Hockey!" Julie's control broke and her voice rose. "She's lying, Papa. She wanted Evan, and because he didn't want her, she lied about him, trying to blacken his name by telling you that he was after Jill. Then this opportunity came along and she lied again, trying to get him convicted of murder."

Jethro looked up at his eldest daughter. "Lower your voice."

"You believe her?" Julie looked at him with disbelief.

"I think she's mistaken; that's different from outright lying."

"Then you think what she told you about Evan being after Jill is true?"

"I never said she told me that."

"What's this about Evan being after me?" Jill's puzzled eyes went from her sister to her father.

"Who told you, Papa? If it wasn't Mrs. Stuart, then who?"

Jethro got to his feet. "Dammit to hell! Don't you think I have the brains to figure out a few things for myself?"

It was so seldom that their father cursed that his children were shocked into silence . . . all except Julie.

"She's very persuasive. She's good at manipulating men to do and think what she wants."

"So you're an authority on men now," Jethro sneered. "How do you know so much? You've never been off this farm. Birdie has had to face the world . . . alone."

"I may be just a stupid country girl, but I'm smart enough to know that she's trying to break up this family. I'm . . . I'm so disappointed in you, Papa." To the surprise of everyone, Julie burst into tears and ran out the back door.

Jethro stomped out of the kitchen and went to the small front parlor, a room seldom used but kept ready for company. He sank down on the uncomfortable parlor chair, put his elbows on his thighs and his head in his hands. He was being pulled in two directions.

Julie had fallen in love with Evan Johnson. He had no doubt of that. They were an unlikely match, and Julie was headed for heartbreak. He doubted that a man with Evan's background was seriously interested in his eldest daughter. If he was merely amusing himself with her, as Birdie said, he was as low as a polecat, but it didn't mean he was a murderer.

Jethro sat with his head in his hands for a long while, conscious of the sounds coming from the kitchen. Julie was talking to Joe and telling him to be careful with the basket of food she was sending to Evan. After Joe left, Julie and Jill washed the noon dishes. Jethro lifted his head and looked intently at the flocked wallpaper on the parlor wall.

Birdie would never be able to take over and run the house as Julie had done all these years. Some women were not suited for hard work, and Birdie was one of them. But oh, God, she was such a soft, pretty woman.

A couple of hours later Joe returned from town after taking the dinner Julie had packed for Evan and leaving Jack at the ball field.

"I found Appleby just as he was going to the restaurant to get a meal for Evan. He let me go into the cell with him. Evan said to tell you thanks and for you not to worry."

"Easy to say." Julie looked in the basket to see that Evan had eaten all she had sent. "Did Chief Appleby check the tire tracks?"

"I asked him and he said that nothing had been decided on that yet."

"What's to be decided? They either match or they don't."

"I'm telling you what he said, Sis. He's bringing the marshal out this afternoon to talk to you and to Mrs. Stuart. Where's Pa?"

"He and Mrs. Stuart walked out to the orchard."

"The brat, too?"

"Of course. It's like that girl is glued to her."

"I thought Pa was beginning to wake up," Joe said tiredly. "But I guess I was wrong."

"Jethro, I just can't lie and say Julie was out until two o'clock when I know she came in at ten." They had stopped beneath an old gnarled apple tree.

"I don't expect you to lie, Birdie. I just want you to be sure that you heard her come in. I heard her come in a little after two."

"It couldn't have been one of the boys. I heard her voice on the porch."

"The marshal will be out this afternoon to take a statement, and you'll have to tell him what you told Weaver."

"Deputy Weaver was such a nice man. He was so polite and listened to what I had to say."

"Mama, a bug bit me." Elsie's whiny voice broke into the conversation. "Look at the red bump."

"Oh, darlin'. Mama will kiss it and make it well."

"I want some lemonade."

"Later, sugar. Later, Mama will see if she can get you some. Jethro, will you take me to the train station tomorrow so I can see what a ticket to Memphis would cost? I feel . . . that I'm not welcome here anymore."

"Birdie, I had hoped that you'd fit into the family and like it here."

"They . . . don't like me." Birdie's voice broke. "Julie wouldn't give me a chance. She turned Jill and Joy against me. Oh, Jethro—" She placed her face against his shoulder. "I don't want you to see me cry. I'm . . . I'm ugly."

"There, there." Jethro patted her on the back. "I'll never, never think you are ugly. Wipe your eyes. The marshal and Chief Appleby just turned down the lane."

Chapter 25

Jill, take Joy and Jason out back, please."

"But Julie, I want to hear what the marshal has to say." Jill's softly spoken protest was mild for her.

"Me, too," Jason said. "I won't say nothin'."

"I know that this is important to both of you, and you're old enough to understand, but I'm thinking about Joy."

"I'll keep her quiet," Jill hastened to say. "I promise."

"All right. Wash your face and hands, Jason. We don't want the marshal to think we're a slovenly family."

"What's that mean?"

"Come on," Jill said to her brother. "I'll tell you later."

Julie greeted Corbin and the marshal at the front door and stepped out onto the porch. Corbin introduced her to the marshal.

"Would you like a drink of cool water?" she asked after shaking hands with the big man.

"I sure would, ma'am." Marshal Sanford pulled a white handkerchief from his pocket and wiped his forehead.

Julie opened the screen door. "Come through the house to the back porch. It's shady there and usually cooler this time of day. Today we have a breeze from the south."

Joe brought a bucket of water from the spring and offered the dipper first to the marshal and then to Corbin.

"I don't know as I've ever tasted better water," the marshal said.

They were seated on the porch when Jethro and Birdie came across the yard. Elsie, as usual, was clutching her mother's hand. Both men stood. Joe was already standing at the end of the porch.

Julie introduced her father to the marshal. After the two men shook hands, Jethro introduced Birdie.

"This is Mrs. Stuart, Marshal."

"Howdy, ma'am."

"Hel-lo." Birdie kept her eyes on the ground, then looked up at the marshal with eyes wet with tears. "I'll just go to my ro-om and . . . get out of the way."

"I need to talk to you, ma'am."

"I'll come when you . . . you want me."

"Why don't you and the pretty little girl sit right down here on the bench?"

"But I . . . I'm takin' someone's seat."

"It's all right, Birdie." Jethro took her arm as she went up the steps to the porch. "I'll get a couple of chairs out of the kitchen."

"Well, now," the marshal said when they were all seated. "There is a nice cool breeze out here."

"Ya want some buttermilk?" Joy asked. "It's cold."

"No, thanks, punkin." Marshal Sanford reached out and patted the child's head, then looked directly at Julie. "We've got to get a few things straightened out. Miss Jones, you said you were with Evan Johnson until two in the morning. Is that correct?"

"Yes, sir. I'm never up at two o'clock in the morning unless someone in the family is sick. I couldn't believe how fast the time had gone by while I was with Evan."

"Tell me where you went, who you saw and anything else you can remember."

"We took the kids to the ball field. Our brother Jack is going to play on the Fertile team when the league comes to town. But first we went to the drugstore and got ice cream." Julie spoke slowly, carefully, not pleased that Birdie was listening to her tell about the wonderful time she had spent with Evan, but wanting to impress on the marshal that she was speaking the truth.

"Do you remember what time you and Johnson brought your brothers and sisters back here?"

"I'm not sure of the exact time. Joe, do you remember?"

"The practice ended when it was too dark to play. After that we stood around and talked with Thad Taylor. Joy was asleep in the car and Evan said we should probably take her home."

"By eight it's starting to get dark this time of year and by eight-thirty it's dark." Corbin spoke up for the first time. "If they stood around for a while, and I'm sure Thad Taylor will verify that they did, they probably got back here between nine and nine-thirty."

"How long did you stay when you came back here?"

"Only long enough to let the kids out." Julie glanced at Joe.

"Evan didn't cut off the motor," Joe said.

Julie told the marshal about driving through town, then out on the river road to the bluff so they could see the lights of town. She ended by saying, "It was around two when Evan brought me home. I swear it."

"Mr. Jones, Appleby says you can verify that your daughter came home at that time."

"I heard her come in at that time. I don't know if she had come home earlier and gone out again. After they came home from the ball game, I went out to the barn. I have a cow who is going to calf at any time."

"Well, now, Mrs. Stuart, you told the deputy Miss Jones came in around ten o'clock. Are you sticking to that?"

"I'd . . . rather talk to you alone, sir."

"I don't think that is necessary. It's nice and cool here on the porch. What time did you hear Miss Jones come in?"

"It's as I said, sir. I heard her on the porch at ten or a few minutes after. The car had come in with its headlights off. I . . . I think Julie and Mr. Johnson were having a . . . quarrel, because Julie's voice was raised."

"What did she say?"

"I couldn't make out the w-words." Birdie glanced at Julie's angry face. "I'm sorry, Julie. I hate having to say this."

"I just bet you do," Jill said nastily, then put her hand over her mouth when her father glared at her.

"Mrs. Stuart, you made some serious accusations about Mr. Johnson to the deputy. I would like for you to repeat them to me."

"I don't know what you mean, sir."

"Tell me about the threats you heard Evan Johnson make regarding his father."

"Well . . . like I told Deputy Weaver, I heard him say he wished he was dead. . . ."

"And," the marshal prompted.

"I saw him trying to hit him with a stick of stove wood."

"Anything else?"

"Not . . . that I remember."

"Didn't you tell the deputy that Evan was a seducer of young girls?" Julie asked. "And that he was going out with me so he could be near Jill and try and seduce her?"

"I . . . never said that! Oh, Julie, you can be so . . . mean." Birdie began to sob.

"Mama, Mama, what's wrong?" Elsie clung to her mother's arm and began to cry also.

"Ma'am, I want you to be very sure of what you say. If Johnson is charged in the death of his father, you'll have to go to court and testify."

"I just never wanted to hurt . . . anybody. They've . . . Jethro has been so kind to me. I just couldn't have lived with myself if I hadn't spoken up."

"You'll swear on the Bible that Miss Julie Jones was here at the farm at ten o'clock last night?"

"Yes, sir. I'll swear on the Bible."

Julie jumped to her feet. "How can you say that? You know it isn't true."

"I'm sorry, Julie. I'm just . . . so sorry."

The marshal stood. Birdie got to her feet and cowered behind him.

Jethro spoke to Joe. "Someone else is driving in. Will you see who it is?"

"It's probably Weaver," the marshal said. "I told him we would be here."

"Marshal, are you going to take her word or mine and my father's?"

"Seems to me that your father is backtracking a little, Miss Jones. You could have come home around ten when your pa was in the barn with his cow. Later you could have gone out again, walking around or sat on the porch. When you came in the house at two, you made enough noise that he heard you."

"You think that?" Julie gasped, then turned to Corbin. "Evan didn't do this terrible thing. He was with us from about six in the evening until two in the morning." Her eyes pleaded with Corbin to believe her.

The first that Julie was aware that a strange man had come around the end of the porch with Joe was when Birdie let out a little squeak and tried to get into the house through the back door. Jethro was standing there and took hold of her arms.

"What is it? Nobody's goin' to hurt you."

"Papa, Papa," Elsie screamed, then jumped off the porch and ran to the man who stood there with Joe. He scooped her up in his arms and hugged her. She put her arms around his neck. "I want to go home, Papa."

"I came to fetch you, honey." He set Elsie carefully on her feet but kept a protective arm across her shoulders. He removed his felt hat. "Which one of you gentlemen is Mr. Jones?"

Jethro stepped forward. "I'm Jethro Jones."

"I'm Robert Stuart, Mr. Jones. I've come to take my wife and daughter home."

Stunned, Jethro turned to Mrs. Stuart and saw her expression change in an instant from absolute fright to bubbling happiness. She jerked her arm free from his hand and ran down the steps.

"Bobby, Bobby, darlin', I'm so glad you found me. I've been so scared . . ." Birdie wrapped her arms around the man's waist and clung to him.

Jethro appeared dazed as he looked from Birdie to her husband. Mr. Stuart was a tall, thin man with sparse gray hair and a kind face. He was at least twenty years older than Birdie.

"Run along and pack your things, Birdie. We're catching the six o'clock eastbound."

"Oh, goody. I can't wait to get home." She stood on her toes and kissed his cheek.

"Go help your mother, honey." Mr. Stuart gave Elsie a gentle push. "The man who brought me from the train station is waiting in the car."

"I'll hurry, Bobby." Without a backward glance, Birdie flounced into the house.

After Birdie and Elsie had disappeared inside, Jethro introduced Mr. Stuart to Julie, then to the marshal and Corbin. After the introductions, Mr. Stuart put his felt hat back on his head.

"Thank you for looking after my wife and daughter. I hope Birdie didn't cause you any trouble. She isn't well, you know."

"No, I didn't know," Jethro said spiritedly. "What exactly is the matter with her?"

"It's rather hard to explain. This is the fourth time since we've been married that she's run away and taken Elsie. The other times she hasn't gone so far away from home. Birdie lives in a dream world where everything revolves around her. She probably told you that I was dead and that she had nowhere to go." He shrugged out of his dark coat and hung it on his arm. "I think it's warmer here than in Nashville."

"Are you from Nashville? Mrs. Stuart said she came from Memphis." Julie tried not to look at her father.

"We are from Nashville. Birdie tells different things at different times. I understand she has a brother living here. I never knew that. I was under the impression that all her family were dead."

"Are you saying that your wife is not always truthful?" Marshal Sanford asked.

"Sir, that is putting it mildly. I could put you in touch with a dozen people who would tell you that Birdie does not know, or care about, truth. She conjures up something in her mind and, I guess, to her it's true. Besides being a beautiful woman, she's a very good actress and can make people believe her."

"We are investigating a murder here and Mrs. Stuart has made some serious charges against a suspect. She says that she will swear to them in court."

"Marshal, no court in the land would take Birdie's word for anything after her past is exposed. She's my wife, and I know this to be a fact, that she will lie about anything. I'll take care of her as long as I'm able and provide for her when I'm gone; it's the price I'm paying for marrying her. My concern is for Elsie. She's the child I never thought I'd have, and I love her dearly. I'm determined that she will not grow up to be a woman like her mother."

"Then you'd better do something quick, mister," Jill said staunchly. "Elsie is well on her way to being the meanest brat we've ever seen around here."

"I hate her," Jason said. "She don't—"

"That's enough!" Jethro's stern voice cut off Jason's words.

"It's all right, Mr. Jones. You know the saying: 'Out of the mouths of babes . . .' "

"They were ill-mannered and I'll not have it."

"Sorry, Papa," Jill and Jason said in unison.

"Elsie isn't a perfect child, but she's my child and there is time for her to change her ways."

"How did you find out that Mrs. Stuart was here?" Julie asked.

"When she left I made the same inquiries that I've made the other times when she took Elsie and disappeared. The other times I found her within fifty miles of home. A Pinkerton agent found a few of the notices I had posted. He called on me and told me that a mother and daughter by the name of Birdie and Elsie Stuart were here in Fertile living on the Jethro Jones farm. It seems someone from around here had hired him to find out about her."

Evan hired a Pinkerton agent. He said he had a trick up his sleeve. Oh, my love, thank you, thank you.

"We'd better get along." The marshal stood. "Nice to have met you folks."

"Chief Appleby, can I speak to you before you go?" Julie asked.

Corbin nodded and stepped to the corner of the house.

"Does this mean that Evan can come home?"

"The marshal will decide that. But it looks good."

"How about the tire tracks?"

"The marshal and I found the tracks that passed Gus Keegan's place and the ones that returned. The tracks that we think were made by the car that dumped Walter's body were not made by Evan's car."

"Oh, thank heavens!"

"The right wheels were on the grass, but the left wheels were on the dirt road. I'm looking for a car that looks like the Hudson from the back so I can check the tread on the tires. The marshal and I traced the pattern made by the left wheel tracks just in case they get wiped out."

"Thank you. Oh, so much has happened today, it's hard for me to sort it all out."

"Evan told me about Mrs. Stuart and the trouble she's caused."

"She's the most evil, conniving woman I've ever met."

"She's that, all right."

"Did the marshal believe her?"

"If he did, he'd not let her leave the state."

Julie and Joe walked with Corbin and the marshal to their car and she asked the question she had been burning to ask.

"Marshal, can Evan come home?"

"I'm planning on it, Miss Jones. We don't have enough to hold him."

"Oh, thank you." Julie impulsively hugged his arm.

"Deputy Weaver won't like that one bit," Joe said.

"Deputy Weaver isn't the United States marshal."

"What time should Joe or Papa come get Evan?" Julie insisted.

"In a couple hours, missy." The big gruff man patted Julie on the shoulder as if she were a child. "Let's get goin', Appleby. If we stay here much longer, this girl will have me singing 'Yankee Doodle.' "

Julie laughed and hugged his arm again. She and Joe watched Corbin's car until it turned down the road toward town, then they walked to the back of the house. Jethro was sitting on the back porch with Mr. Stuart and Al Manson, the driver who had brought him from town. Joy was sitting on Mr. Stuart's lap.

"Elsie didn't like me. She wouldn't play."

"Honey, I don't think Elsie knows how to play, but that's going to change. I'm making arrangements for Elsie to go to a boarding school. She will see her mother every other weekend for a while. She'll have work to do there, and I hope she will learn to get along and how to play with other little girls. I blame myself for not realizing sooner what Birdie was doing to Elsie."

"Will she come back?" Joy asked. "I'll swing her in my swing."

"I don't think she'll be coming back for a long time. But it's nice of you to want to play with her."

Joe and the driver carried Birdie's trunk and suitcase to the car.

"I'm so glad to be going home, Bobby," Birdie gushed.

"Not as glad as we are," Jill whispered for Julie's ears alone, but her voice carried to Joe, who winked at her.

"It's too bad you don't have time to go over and meet Mrs. Stuart's brother, Wilbur Humphrey," Julie said.

"I'd have liked that."

"Bobby! You won't go *there*!" Birdie cried and grabbed his arm. "I don't want to go *there*. I want to go home."

Mr. Stuart freed his arm from Birdie's grasp, shook hands with Jethro and Joe and tipped his hat to other members of the Jones family.

"Thank you for looking after my wife and daughter. Are you sure I don't owe you something for their keep?"

"No, no." Jethro made a waving motion with his hands.

"You've all been so sweet. Oh, I'm going to miss you all," Birdie called from the back seat of the car.

As soon as Mr. Stuart got in, the car turned around in the barnyard before going down the lane. As it passed the house, Birdie leaned out the window and waved her handkerchief.

"'Bye, Jethro. 'Bye, Julie and Jill and Joy. 'Bye, everybody. 'Bye. . . ." She was still waving when the car turned onto the road toward town.

Julie looked for her father. He was going around the end of the house with his head bowed and his hands buried in the pockets of his overalls.

"Can you beat that?" Jill shook her head.

"No, I can't. I'm just glad she's gone. Let's clean Papa's room, Jill, and put his things back in it. It may make him feel better."

* * *

Deputy Weaver was leaning against the outside door of the courthouse when Corbin and the marshal reached it.

"Damn waste of time coolin' my heels out here waitin' for a *town cop* to come open a cell so I can talk to my prisoner."

"Your prisoner?" Corbin lifted his brows and frowned. "He's my suspect."

"Call him what you want. He killed that old man and I want to talk to him."

"So now you have a confession." Corbin's dislike of the deputy was growing.

"Give me thirty minutes alone with him in that cell and I'll have a confession."

"That might not be a bad idea, Marshal," Corbin said. "I was told that Evan was bare-knuckle champion of his division during the war and that, in a barroom brawl, he's a fightin' son-of-a-gun. He'd be no pushover for you, Weaver, even with your billy club."

The marshal was frowning at his deputy. "You know I'd never stand for that kind of monkeyshines."

"It's done every day, Marshal, you can believe it or not," Weaver said. "I, for one, don't believe in mollycoddling prisoners."

"Just because it's done, doesn't make it right. What'er you wantin' to talk to him about?"

"I've got two people who saw his car in town a little before two o'clock. Not that I think he'll admit it. But if he lies about it, he'll lie about other things."

"He had to come through town to take Miss Jones home. He hasn't denied that," Corbin said.

"What are your ties with him, Appleby? Why are you always defending him?"

"Why are you so determined to find him guilty?"

"Because he is. Mrs. Stuart said that she'd swear Miss Jones was home. His car was seen by Gus Keegan. A member of your city council came to me and said he was guilty as hell."

"Amos Wood, the banker. A shady character if there ever was one."

"You don't have Mrs. Stuart, Weaver. She's gone back to Nashville with her husband. The car Gus Keegan saw only looked like Johnson's, and Amos Wood has been sending moonshine whiskey downriver for a year or two. I'd not take his word for anything." The marshal's voice rose with his agitation. "We don't have enough proof to arrest the banker and we don't have enough to hold Evan Johnson. Turn him loose, Appleby."

"You . . . you don't mean that?" Weaver sputtered.

"I mean it, and you're off the case. Go down to the main office. I'll be there in a day or two." Marshal Sanford looked his deputy in the eyes. "You were a pretty good man until a few months ago, Weaver. What happened to you?"

The deputy gave him a hard look, turned and walked away. The marshal and Corbin watched him go, then went into the courthouse to let Evan out of the holding room.

Chapter 26

JULIE WAS DISAPPOINTED that Evan wasn't with Joe and Jack when they returned. She waited on the porch while they put the car in the shed.

Joe knew what she wanted to hear. "We took Evan home to do chores. He'll be over later."

"Was he all right?"

"Seemed to be. He went to the undertaker and made arrangements for burying Walter. Then he spoke to Reverend Meadows about a graveside service tomorrow morning. We got a lot done in a short time."

"We saw Miss Meadows at the preacher's house. She asked about you," Jack said. "Joe told her about Mrs. Stuart's husband coming for her."

"Is there any news about . . . about who . . ."

"Killed Walter?"

"We didn't get to talk to Chief Appleby. He was with the marshal."

"How did the practice go, Jack?"

"I hit another home run." Smiles lit up Jack's freckled face. "Doc Forbes said I have one of the best swings he's ever seen. Oh, guess what, Sis? The team is going to have shirts alike. Mr. Poole is trying to get the city to buy them; but if they don't, and he doesn't have much hope because of Mr. Wood, the merchants are all going to chip in."

"We'll be so proud. You've got to have a haircut before next Saturday, Jack. I wish we had a Kodak so we could take your picture."

"Evan's got a Kodak," Joe said.

"I'll ask him to take Jack's picture."

"He'll do it . . . for *you.*" Joe's eyes teased her and Julie's cheeks reddened.

"Joe said the witch is gone. How did Pa take it?"

"He walked off into the woods after Mrs. Stuart and her husband left. We haven't seen him. Jill and I cleaned Papa's room and put his things back in it. He may be ashamed for having been fooled by her."

"Men have been fooled by a pretty face before, huh, Jack?" Joe nudged his brother, his eyes still teasing his sister.

"Hush up, you two, and stop teasing. I think Papa gets lonesome."

"With all of us kids here? I don't see how anyone could be lonesome," Jack exclaimed.

"He's lonesome for someone near his own age to talk to and do things with." Julie grinned at her brothers. "I like intelligent conversation sometimes myself. I get tired of trying to talk to . . . dumb-bunnies."

"She means us, Jack! Sis is really feeling her oats." Joe spoke to his brother as if Julie wasn't there.

"Yeah, I hear that's what happens when the love bug bites."

Corbin and the marshal sat on stools in Sparky's Eatery and waited for Sparky to bring them a plate of food.

"Anything will do, Sparky. We haven't eaten all day."

"How about a plate of sausage and eggs?"

"Sounds good to me." The marshal placed his hat on the stool next to him.

"Weaver wasn't pleased with his dismissal. I hope that doesn't mean he'll be giving me problems here."

"He used to be a damn good man. Here lately he's been taking too much on himself."

"Do you think he's tied in with Amos Wood on something?"

"I'd hate to think so. I shouldn't have let it slip that I think Wood is mixed up somehow with bootlegging. This is confidential. . . ." The marshal looked to see where Sparky was and lowered his voice. "Bank examiners are interested in Wood's bank."

"He protects Otto Bloom, who is a low-life, wife-beating son-of-a-bitch if there ever was one. Bloom works at the bank and, from what I hear, he was a pretty good fellow when he came to town about ten years ago. He drinks like a fish now, and when he's drunk he's got no sense at all."

"Here ya are." Sparky placed the plates of food on the counter. "I hear ya let Evan Johnson out."

"News travels fast."

"Well, it isn't every day we have a murder right here in Fertile."

"Did you see Walter last night, Sparky?"

"I saw him outside as I was closing. Otto Bloom was with him."

"Were they drunk or just drinking?"

"Didn't seem to be very drunk, but no doubt they were drinking."

"That's the last you saw of them?"

"Yep. Wife is bringing out some biscuits."

It was dark when Corbin and the marshal knocked on the door of the Bloom house. Mrs. Bloom pulled back a curtain and peered out.

"It's Chief Appleby, Mrs. Bloom."

She opened the door a crack. "I'm not supposed to let anyone in."

"You can let us in, ma'am. Doc Curtis is going to lift the quarantine tomorrow."

"He never said anything to me about it. Buddy is asleep."

"We'll not disturb him." Corbin pushed gently on the door and the woman stepped back. He and the marshal entered the small neat house. "Mrs. Bloom, this is Marshal Sanford. We'd like to speak with Otto if he's here."

"Otto? Ah . . . he's not supposed to be here," she said and nervously looked away from the two men.

"But is he?"

"No. Buddy has been awfully sick."

"Mrs. Bloom, was Otto here last night?"

"Last night? Oh, yes. He was here all night." She nodded her head up and down.

"Sparky Yates said Otto was uptown around ten o'clock."

"He came home right after that," she said quickly.

"Thank you, Mrs. Bloom."

"Pleased to have met you, ma'am."

As soon as they were out the door it was shut.

"He's there," Corbin said after they stepped off the porch. "That woman is so scared of him she'd say anything he told her to say. I'll move the car up the street so they'll think we've gone and I'll slip around the back. He'll either come out or I'll see him through the kitchen window."

Corbin heard voices as soon as he stepped up onto the small back porch.

"I told them what you told me to say, Otto."

"You're a stupid slut, is what you are. Why did you say I came home after ten?"

"I had to. If you were seen in town, how could you be here?"

"You could have said Sparky lied, was mistaken or something like that. *He came home right after that,*" he mimicked in a high woman's voice. "I ought to knock your teeth down your throat."

"I did what you told me—"

"And it could get you in trouble." Corbin stepped into the kitchen from the back door.

"What the hell? Get out of my house!" Otto, barefoot and shirtless, turned to pick up an iron skillet.

"Go ahead. Give me an excuse to shoot you." Corbin's gun appeared in his hand. "Your wife and boy would be better off without a drunk like you. And stay where you are," he said quickly when the man began to move sideways toward his wife.

"What are ya . . . Ya've no right here."

"The marshal and I are going to talk to you."

"Well, talk, damn ya."

"Not here. Down at the courthouse. Get his shoes, Mrs. Bloom."

"Ya can't take me to jail 'cause I'm in my own house. That old quack that put a red sign on the door don't know beans from a bullfrog."

"He knew enough to keep your son alive."

"Kid woulda got well anyway. Mr. Wood said I could come back here. It'll be the same as last time. He won't stand for you keepin' me away from my job." Otto's hands shook when he put on his shoes. His eyes were bloodshot and he smelled like sour whiskey.

"He'll be welcome to what's left when we get through with you. Get a move on." Corbin prodded him to his feet and toward the front door.

"What'd'ya mean, what's left?" Otto was drunk, but not enough so that he didn't realize the danger he was in. "Go get Mr. Wood," he shouted at his wife, although she stood not six feet away.

"What are you afraid of, Otto? Why do you think you need Wood?"

"He'll not let you put me in jail. He'll have yore job for this. He said ya was nothin' but a know-it-all."

Mrs. Bloom followed them to the door.

"I told ya to get Mr. Wood. And, goddamn ya, ya'd better do it or ya know what you'll get."

"When will he be back?" The woman cowered out of reaching distance of Otto's fists.

"Maybe . . . never." Corbin dragged the words out and poked Otto in the back with the barrel of his gun. "You're going to look good in black and white stripes, Otto. They'll match the blue bruises you've put on your wife's face."

"Get Mr. Wood," Otto yelled over his shoulder.

Marshal Sanford was waiting in the front yard, and Otto was hustled off to the holding room in the courthouse.

At suppertime, Jethro came quietly from the room across the hall. His eyes swung around the dining room, missing nothing. His family was ready to take their places at the table, their eyes on him. All of them were worth their weight in gold to him.

"Something smells good. What'er we having, Sis?"

"One of your favorites, Papa: creamed chicken gravy over hot biscuits and sweet potato pie."

"Isn't that a little much for Sunday night supper? You shouldn't have fired up that hot stove."

"I wanted to. This is to celebrate . . . Evan's release," she added quickly and turned her back to ease the biscuits onto a platter and pour the creamed gravy into a large bowl.

"That's not all we need to celebrate, but we won't speak of it now."

With Julie's nod of approval, Jason took a biscuit from the platter and went to the door. Sidney was hunkered down on the porch but quickly got up to accept his treat.

"Sidney's got to celebrate, too."

During the meal Jethro asked Jack about the ball practice and Joe and Jack told once again about Evan making the arrangements to bury Walter.

"We'll all go to the buryin' out of respect for a neighbor," Jethro announced.

"Papa, I don't think Joy and Jason should go." Julie dipped into the crock of butter, then spread it and strawberry jam on Joy's biscuit.

"Jason will go to school. Joy can stay in the car."

"Sidney will watch her," Jason said.

"No. Sidney will have to look after things here while we're gone."

"And he will, Papa. Sidney's a good guard dog."

Julie lowered her eyes and thanked God that the family was back to normal after the recent days of crackling tension.

After the supper things had been cleared away, Julie washed Joy and put her in her nightdress. The child was wound up and talked constantly.

"Is Evan comin'? Will he take us for ice cream?"

"Evan is coming. You're not to mention going for ice cream. It isn't nice to ask for things."

"I'll be nice, Julie. I won't ask."

"You can stay up for a while. Papa and the boys are going to play cards."

With Joy out of the way, Julie hurried upstairs to wash and put on a fresh dress. She combed and pinned her hair, then slipped a sachet of rose petals into the bosom of her chemise. She returned downstairs to hear the complaints about who was going to be stuck with Jill for a partner. Joy sat on Jethro's lap. Joe was dealing the cards. He glanced at Julie with a wide grin.

"Evan's comin'. I heard the horses nickering."

"Go on out," Jack said with a smirk. "We know you're dyin' to see him."

Julie could feel the heat flood her face. She stepped out onto the back porch, agonizingly aware that her brothers were snickering and her sister giggling. Her heart hammered and there was a fluttering in the pit of her stomach that refused to go away, even as she pressed her hands tightly to it. Sure that her hair was smooth and her dress properly buttoned, she waited the few seconds for her eyes to adjust to the darkness.

Then she saw his white shirt. He was coming across the yard. She stepped off the porch. He stopped and held his arms wide. It was all the invitation she needed. She ran to him. Her arms went around his neck as he desperately hugged her to him, lifting her off her feet.

"Ah, sweetheart," he said between kisses. "Ah, sweetheart." It was all he could say. She was softer and sweeter than he remembered. His lips caressed her mouth gently, tenderly, for a long time. Then he drew back to look at her. "Nothing has changed? You still love me?"

"Of course I do. Why wouldn't I?" She cupped his cheeks with her palm.

"After all that's happened . . . I was worried that you might have a doubt about me and wonder if, after I left you, I went looking for him."

"If you had brought me home at ten, I still wouldn't have believed that you did that terrible thing."

"Even knowing what you know about his not being my father and that I had always hated him?"

"Out of respect for what he did for your mother, you never, never would have killed him."

"You have that much faith in me?"

"And much more."

"I've never told anyone about Walter and my mother, but I wanted you to know."

"No one outside the family knows about Joy."

"Sweetheart." His lips moved against her temple when he spoke. "All this time you thought Walter had done that to you?"

"He was the logical one. Papa thought so, too, but I told him no. I was afraid he would kill him or be killed. Are you sure it doesn't make you think less . . . of me? I'd be in disgrace if it ever becomes known, and poor little Joy would suffer the stigma of being a . . . a—"

"Don't say it." He put his fingers over her lips. "You and Joy, too, are very dear to me. I hope to give her a lot of little brothers and sisters."

For a minute Julie couldn't speak. He was the man she had dreamed about, a man who would love her and who would accept her child. Tears came, but she blinked them away.

"Will you ever tell her?" he asked gently.

"I don't know." Arm in arm, they walked toward the porch. "I saved you some supper."

"I can't think of eating when I have you here in my arms." He stopped and pressed gentle kisses to her face. "I thought about this today while I was waiting in the locked room at the courthouse."

"I thought about you, too. This has been a day to remember . . . or try to forget." She laughed happily.

"Joe and Jack told me about Mrs. Stuart's husband coming for her. How did Jethro take it?"

"At first I wasn't sure. He walked out into the woods, and when he came back, he went to his room. Jill and I had it ready for him. He didn't come out until suppertime, then he said the strangest thing. I said that we were celebrating because you were out of that locked room, and he said we had something else to celebrate, but we wouldn't talk about it. After that he acted like his old self. He and Jill are playing cards with the boys." Julie stepped up onto the porch, turned and put her arms around his neck.

"You're the one who started the detective checking on her, weren't you? You knew Mr. Stuart was coming."

"I *thought* he was coming. From the beginning, I suspected that there was something fishy about her. She didn't really want to disappear. If she had, she wouldn't have used her real name. The Pinkerton man said he thought that she was waiting for her husband to find her."

"She couldn't have married Papa, but we didn't know that."

"She has an unbalanced mind. Let's forget about her."

Their lips met in joint seeking. This time the kiss was deep and long. Her lips parted under the pressure of his and she felt the lightning touch of his tongue on her lips. One of his hands shaped itself over her breast, the other flattened against her buttocks and held her tightly against him.

"Someday soon, I'm going to touch you and kiss you anytime I want to," he said breathlessly. "I'll never get enough of you."

"I don't deserve you," she whispered.

"Yes, you do, and I deserve you, darling girl. I must have done something right, for God to bring me back here to meet you."

She moved her head to look into his face. Her hand covered the one shaped to her breast.

"I feel in my heart"—she pressed his palm more firmly against her breast—"that I've always known you." She brought her lips to his and kissed him with such sweetness that he felt a swell of love and joy wash over him.

"Julie, my sweet Julie. It's going to be hard waiting to take you home as my wife."

"For me, too." Her voice came against lips that were kissing hers. Finally she drew back, took a deep breath and asked, "What time is the service in the morning? Papa said we'll all be there except for Joy and Jason."

"You'll probably be the only ones there besides me. Walter didn't do anything to endear himself to his neighbors or the people in town. That's why I welcomed the suggestion from Reverend Meadows that we hold a graveside service."

"We'll be there with you. You won't be alone." Her arms slipped from around his neck, and she smoothed her hair and poked loose strands back into the bun at the nape of her neck. "Come in and eat—that is, if you can stand the teasing from Joe and Jack."

The minute they stepped in the door, Joy slid off Jethro's lap and ran to Evan.

"Evan, I'm not goin' to ask for ice cream. Julie said it ain't nice. She saved you some pie."

Evan scooped her up in his arms. "Well, I guess you'd better mind Julie."

Joy planted kisses on his cheeks and he tickled her ribs before setting her on her feet.

While he ate from the plate of food Julie set before him, the card game came to an end. Jethro and the boys lingered to talk to him. Julie took Joy up to bed.

When she came back down to the kitchen, the men were talking about the thing that was on everyone's mind: who had killed Walter Johnson.

"The thing that puzzles me," Evan was saying, "is who has a car that looks like mine from the back?"

"Could it have been someone who came to Spring Lake from out of town and got into a fight with him?" Jethro asked.

"That's a possibility. How could Walter have gotten way out there? His horse was tied up downtown."

"The marshal and Appleby are both good men. If the killer can be found, they'll find him."

"Walter was not a good man," Evan said. "But he didn't deserve to die like that. He was foulmouthed, but I've never heard of him actually hurting anyone except another drunk."

"He was good to his animals, I'll say that for him," Jethro said. "They were always fed and watered." Jethro got up from the table. "You'd better get to bed, Jill."

"What about school tomorrow?"

"Jason will go. You and Jack can go after the service."

Joe got reluctantly to his feet and smacked his brother on the back.

"Come on, Babe Ruth. I suppose we'll be run out of the kitchen every night from now on, so we might as well get used to it."

"Ain't fair," Jack complained. "We got to go to bed just 'cause they want to . . . court. Papa, make 'em go out on the porch." His bright blue eyes flashed over his sister's flushed face.

"It's too cold out there," Jethro said sternly, but he was smiling.

"They didn't seem to mind a while ago," Jack grumbled.

"Dumbbell," Jill said with disgust. "Remember when you wanted to get rid of me so you could be with Ruby May? She said you kissed her."

"Why, that little tattletale!" Jack glanced at his father to see his reaction, then bolted up the stairs.

"Up to bed with you . . . tattletale." Jethro chuckled and went to his room.

In the quiet kitchen, Evan and Julie looked at each other and smiled.

"I like being here," he said. "This is family life that I've not known."

"I like having you here. We're very plain people. I worry that we're too countrified for you. That . . . I am."

He reached for her hand. "Never," he said staunchly. "You're honest, innocent, unaffected. You and your family are what you are . . . not something you pretend to be. You accepted me for me, without judging me by Walter."

For a long quiet moment they gazed at each other.

"I never dreamed that I would fall so desperately in love. There is so much sweetness in you that I want to pull you into my heart and hold you there and keep you safe from hurt." He watched her face with anxious eyes.

"I love you."

"I never heard those words until you said them." He pulled her to her feet and held her as if she were about to be snatched away from him. "And I've never said them until I said them to you. I love you, too."

"I'm glad. So . . . glad."

Chapter 27

IT WAS A SURPRISING TURNOUT for a man so hated and feared. A group of twenty people attended the graveside service for Walter Johnson. Besides the Jones family, Roy and Thad Taylor and their father were there and also Ruth and Wilbur Humphrey and their older children. Mr. Oakley, the grocer, and his wife stood at the grave site. Eudora Meadows came with her brother, the Reverend Meadows.

Evan stood alone at the head of the coffin. Julie, wearing her dark cotton dress and small black hat, wanted to go to him but didn't think it would be proper.

The eulogy given by the preacher was short. He said Walter Johnson had lived in this area for almost thirty years and that he was a good farmer and always paid his bills. After that there was not much he could say except for a few words about the Creator. In a sweet soprano voice, Miss Meadows led the singing of "The Old Rugged Cross."

Joe, Jack, Jethro and Thad Taylor grasped the ropes that lowered the coffin into the ground. Evan threw in a handful of soil, then the grave was quickly filled with rich black dirt. When it was over, Evan shook hands with every person there and thanked them all for coming.

Eudora, friendly as always, hugged Jill and spoke to each member of the family, then turned her attention to Jack.

"What's this I hear about you playing on the baseball team? The youngest player, I was told, is the best hitter."

Jack grinned his bashful grin. "I . . . I don't know about that."

"I'm proud of you, Jack. When you're playing in Chicago or New York, I'll be able to say that I had that boy in my Sunday school class."

"How is your mother, Eudora?" Julie asked.

"She's about the same, thank you."

"Are you coming to the ball game, Miss Meadows?" Jill asked, then barged on ahead. "Oh, do come. We're all going. Evan's going to take a picture of Jack in his team shirt. We can come by for you if you don't have a way of getting there. Can't we, Papa?"

"Maybe Miss Meadows doesn't want to go, Jill." Jethro looked uncomfortable.

"If I come, my brother will bring me."

"You'll sit with us, won't you? All of us there for Jack will sit together so we can yell when he hits a home run."

"A home run against the league players?" Jack threw up his hands. "Sis, you're daydreaming."

"You'll hit a homer or I'll beat you up, Jack." Jill gave her brother a saucy grin.

Evan had made the rounds and now came to stand beside Julie. He took her hand and pulled it into the crook of his arm, wanting all those present to see that she was special to him.

Jethro fell in step beside Eudora. "We'll be glad to come take you to the ball game, Miss Meadows."

"Thank you, Mr. Jones. I can find my way there." Large brown eyes smiled up at him. "I may impose on your generosity to get home."

"I'll be glad to oblige."

"I must say hello to Joy before I go." Eudora went to the car, where Joy was standing up in the seat twisting the steering wheel.

"I'm drivin' the car."

"I see you are. How are you, Joy?"

"I'm nice. I don't ask Mr. Johnson for ice cream."

"That is being a nice girl. But you're always nice." Eudora glanced at Jethro and smiled. "Good-bye." He tipped his hat when she walked away with her brother.

"Jethro, wait," Wilbur Humphrey called out to him as he was getting in the car. "I want to thank you for taking Birdie and Elsie in. I feel ashamed for pushing her off on you, but my family was falling apart."

"She's gone now. Her husband came and took her home."

"I heard that he did. The news is all over town. He hired Al Manson to take him out to your place. No one likes gossip like Al. He's had the time of his life spreading the story."

"Her husband has far more patience with her than I would have had."

"She's always been strange," Wilbur said. "When she was a little girl, she made up things so she could get her way. I got many a whippin' over something she told. I hadn't heard from her for many, many years when she came here. Because she's blood kin, I had to take her in when she said her husband had died and she had nowhere to go. She lied about that. I know that now. I know that she lied about a lot other things, too." Wilbur shook his head. "Ruth was ready to pack up and leave me."

"Poor devil of a husband of hers has his work cut out for him." Jethro glanced at Julie and Evan standing apart talking earnestly to each other, then at Miss Meadows, who had stopped to speak to Joe. The two of them were teasing Jack.

Whatever had possessed him to think that Birdie Stuart would fit into his family? Thank God for her husband.

"I've got to be gettin' on, Jethro. I just wanted to be sure that there was no hard feelin's."

"Not on my side, Wilbur. Comin' to the ball game Saturday?"

"We plan on being there Saturday evenin' and Sunday afternoon. With Jack playin', we wouldn't miss it."

Jill got her lunch box and Jack's out of the car. "Jack and I are goin' on to school, Papa."

"Can I go?" Joy yelled.

"No. You're too little."

"I don't wanna be too little."

"Well, you are and that's that."

Evan walked Julie over to the car. When she was seated, he spoke to Jethro.

"I plan to stay on the farm, Jethro. I'm going to need plenty of advice, as I'm not much of a farmer."

"We'll be glad to help in any way we can."

"I'll appreciate it." He reached for Julie's hand. "I've asked your daughter to marry me. We don't plan on marrying right away, but someday you're going to have to get along without her."

"I knew that I couldn't keep her forever. She's entitled to have a home of her own."

"I wanted you to know that I love her and will take care of her."

" 'Preciate you tellin' me. We'd better be gettin' along home."

"Thanks for coming, Jethro. I'll see you tonight, Julie."

A pair of sharp, bright eyes followed Jill and Jack as they walked down the street toward the school.

There she is again.

Something about her called out to him as none of the others had done. She was pretty and feisty and . . . young. She'd never been broken into. He would be the first, just the way he liked it.

For days now the pressure had been building. When that happened, he slept restlessly, if at all. Afterward he would sleep deeply and dreamlessly. He was sure that of the five Fertile girls he'd had this year, only two of them had *caught*. The other three were still in town, but it was too soon to tell about the last two. He had no way of knowing about the other five from the surrounding towns.

Seldom did he get to see his children, and that saddened him. Usually the girls were hustled out of town as soon as it became known that they were pregnant. Only once or twice had he been lucky enough to see one of them with her belly swelled with his child. It irritated him that some of the girls didn't keep the children who had been created from the fruit of his loins.

He chuckled as Jethro Jones turned out of the cemetery and headed up the rocky road toward home. Joy was on the seat between him and Julie. She wouldn't be leaving town. He'd be able to watch her grow up, go to school. Someday she'd know who he was.

God, how I wish I could claim her.

"Marshal, I could find someone to go along with you—Sparky, Poole from the hardware or the older Jones boy." Corbin Appleby stood beside Marshal Sanford's big touring car.

"It isn't necessary. This fellow isn't going to give me any trouble." After checking the cuffs on his prisoner and the padlocked chain that went around his waist holding him to the seat, the marshal and Corbin stepped away from the car.

Otto Bloom had stood before Judge Murphy at nine o'clock that morning and been charged with the murder of Walter Johnson. The marshal was taking him to St. Joseph to await trial because the facilities at the courthouse were inadequate for holding a prisoner any longer than a day or two. He would be returned for the trial. By then Corbin hoped to have his jail built.

"You're doing a good job here, Appleby. I wish now I'd taken you on as a deputy."

"Thank you, Marshal, but Fertile is big enough for me."

"Will Mrs. Bloom be all right?"

"I think so. The house is paid for. Surely she can find enough work to feed herself and the boy. It'll take a while for her to get her confidence and self-respect back after ten years of taking abuse from this shit-head. I'll keep an eye on her."

"Keep your eye on Wood. This may curtail his bootlegging activities for a while. Once Bloom realizes he's not going to get any help from him, he may spill his guts about goings-on at the bank." They walked back to the car. "I'd better get going and get my prisoner over to St. Joe."

Corbin walked up to the car. "Otto, I want you to know, before you go, that in my book you are one lousy, heartless, shit-eatin' son-of-a-bitch." Corbin tried to look the man in the eye, but Otto refused to look at him. "When you're in prison fighting to keep your pants up, think of the nice little woman here in Fertile who cooked your meals, washed your clothes and kept your house neat as a pin. While you're getting slapped around, think of the times you hit her with your fist and kicked her."

Like a little cornered snake, Otto spat, but not on Corbin. He was too smart for that. His small eyes blazed hatred.

"Mr. Wood will get you. He's not through with you."

"No? But he's through with you, isn't he?"

Corbin stood in front of the courthouse for a few moments after the marshal drove away, then started across the street. The druggist, Frank Adler, stood in the doorway of his establishment. At times the man gave Corbin the creeps. He seemed always to be watching. When Corbin saw Evan Johnson's car coming toward him, he stopped and waited for him to pull up beside him.

"Burial over?" he asked.

"It's over. I was coming to see if you have any news."

"Plenty." Corbin opened the door and got into the car. "Otto Bloom killed Walter. Pull up over here facing the courthouse and I'll tell you about it."

"Otto Bloom, that skinny little wart that works at the bank?" Evan asked after he had turned off the motor.

"That's him. Last night we heard that he had been with Walter around ten o'clock. We went down to his house and picked him up. He was half drunk and cocky. He told his wife to get Amos Wood to come get him out like he'd done once before. A couple of hours went by and Wood hadn't come. He began to get scared and started throwing hints that Wood probably killed Walter.

"About midnight, the marshal told him that we had a witness who saw him throwing Walter's body out of a car. He broke down and confessed that they'd had a fight over a bottle of whiskey and he'd stabbed him . . . protecting himself, he said. He said Amos Wood lent him the car to take the body and dump it in the river. When Gus Keegan yelled at him, he got scared and drove off. We checked Wood's car. The back looks the same as yours and there were bloodstains on the floor in the back.

"It was pure luck that he confessed. We didn't have a thing on him until then. So far he hasn't said why Wood would go out on a limb for him. The marshal thinks it's something to do with the bookkeeping at the bank. It'll be looked into, so if you have money there, I'd take it out—quiet-like."

"Thanks, I will. I was sure someone Walter knew got in the first strike or he'd have put up a hell of a fight."

"Doc Forbes said it looked to him as if he was stabbed in the back and wouldn't have lasted more than a minute or two. When he fell, Otto, not knowing that, or too angry to care, stabbed him with a vengeance, then cut his throat."

"The deputy will be disappointed. He sure wanted me to be the one who killed Walter."

"Do you mind if I ask why you call your father by his first name?"

"No, I don't mind. I left here at age twelve to live with my grandparents in St. Joseph. I'd not been around him for many years until I came back last spring. I never thought of him as my father.

"Walter was in many ways a reprobate, a foulmouthed drunk

who enjoyed causing trouble for those who he thought considered themselves better than he was, but never did he mistreat my mother. All the while I was away, she would write and tell me not to worry, that Walter was looking after her, seeing that she had plenty of firewood, food and whatever she needed. My grandparents would send someone from time to time to make sure she was all right."

"Do you plan to stay here?"

"I've decided to stay and marry Julie Jones." His stern face softened and he smiled. "I have a house in St. Joseph, a big old Victorian thing, but Julie would rather be here near her family, and I want to try my hand at farming."

"Congratulations. I thought the wind was blowing that way even before Weaver took you over to the Joneses'."

"Yeah. Lord, I'm lucky that she even looked at me twice. Being the son of Walter Johnson was a lot to overcome."

Corbin opened the door. "I've got to get over to the mayor's office and give him a rundown."

"Say, Appleby. I heard that a collection was being taken up to buy shirts for Fertile's baseball team." Evan fished in his pocket and brought out some bills. "Add this to the collection, anonymously."

Corbin took the bills. "You sure?"

"Sure as rain. And if you run short, let me know."

"See you around, Johnson, and don't forget to invite me to the wedding."

"Your name will be first on my list. Thanks for not letting Weaver railroad me."

"I kind of wish I'd left the two of you alone in that locked room. I figure you would've taught Weaver a thing or two."

"One of us might not have come out alive."

Corbin saluted and stepped away from the car.

Evan stopped at the furniture store and paid Herman Maddock, the undertaker, for his services, then went by the doctor's office to find out if he owed anything there. Next he went to the bank. When he told the clerk he was closing out his account, Amos Wood got up from his desk and came to the teller window.

"Leaving town?" he asked with a smelly cigar clenched between his teeth.

"No. I'm staying. How about you?"

"Why in hell should I go anywhere?"

"You tell me, Mr. Wood." Evan then spoke to the teller: "I'd like the money in cash, please."

"That's a lot of money to be carrying around," the banker said.

"I won't be carrying it far." Evan counted out the silver dollars the teller placed on the counter and put them in stacks. "I'd like the rest in paper, or do you plan on my not being able to get out of the bank with all this silver?"

"Give it to him and be quick about it," Amos said and went back to his desk.

"Disagreeable fellow, isn't he?" Evan spoke loud enough for Amos to hear. "How do you stand working here?"

He didn't expect an answer from the teller, who sent nervous glances toward his boss, and he didn't get one. When the money was laid out, Evan counted it and put the bills in his pocket. Seeing that he was not going to be given a bag for the silver, he spread his handkerchief on the counter, piled the silver dollars on it and tied the four corners.

"It was a pleasure doing business with you," he said, scooping up the silver and heading for the door.

At the other bank he deposited the bills in the account he already had and left still carrying the silver dollars. On the way back to the farm, Evan recalled the words of his shrewd old grandfather, who had made a fortune in the lumber business:

Don't put all your eggs in one basket, son. Find a hiding place and keep your silver. It will always be good. One day these damn banks are going to go bust and you'll have something to fall back on.

Evan was slightly ashamed of being so happy after he had

just buried Walter. As he drove into the Joneses' farmyard to tell them the news that Otto Bloom had been charged with the killing, his head was filled with plans to modernize his farmhouse before he brought his bride home.

Chapter 28

THE NEXT FEW DAYS WERE THE HAPPIEST Julie had ever known.

Evan came over every evening. The family accepted him as one of them. He helped Jason get the cockleburs out of Sidney's thick fur and Jill with her history lesson. Joy climbed into his lap at every opportunity, and he played catch with Jack when Jack had exhausted his older brother.

Jethro and Evan sat at the kitchen table and made plans for sharing the work on the two farms, and Jethro advised about crops, hogs and cattle.

The best time of all was when Julie could steal away with Evan for a few minutes alone.

"I want you to come over to the farm," Evan said one evening, "but not until I clean it up a bit. The kitchen was Walter's domain and isn't fit for you to see right now."

"I could help you clean it."

"No, honey. When you see your future home, I want it to be clean, at least. You can fix it up any way you want to after we are married."

One night Evan brought his Victrola and set it up in the parlor. The room was small and only one couple could dance at a time, but everyone had a turn, even Joy and Jason. Jill danced with her two older brothers, her father and Evan. Joe waltzed with Julie. When they grew tired of dancing, they listened to opera music sung by Enrico Caruso, and Evan told them about seeing the famous husband-and-wife dance team of Vernon and Irene Castle.

"Do they still dance?" Jill asked.

"No. Vernon was killed in 1918 while training cadets to pilot planes during the war. A year later, Irene wrote a book, *My Husband.* I have a copy if you'd like to read it."

"I would. Do you have a book about Lillian Russell or Nellie Bly?"

"No. Someday you can come over and see what I have."

Later, when they were alone, Julie explained to Evan Jill's fascination with the two women.

"She likes to read and learn about people. I think she would make a fine teacher."

Saturday came, and everyone was excited about the game. The morning was cool, cloudy, with the promise of rain. Jack stewed and worried and watched the sky. By noon the weather had cleared. Julie fixed a good midday meal, but Jack didn't eat much.

"Ah, Sis," he argued, "my stomach is so fluttery, I'm afraid I'll throw up."

"I don't want you suddenly to get weak during the game. I'll take a few slices of buttered bread wrapped in a cloth, and if you feel weak during the game, I'll have Joe slip them to you."

Jethro had taken Jack to town that morning to get a haircut and to pick up his team shirt at Carwilde and Graham's store. The game didn't start until four o'clock, but by two o'clock Jack was anxious to go.

"Try and get a good parking place, Papa. Evan is coming for us at three, and by the time we get there, the good places might be gone."

Half the town was already at the ball field when Evan drove in and parked the car behind Jethro's. Jethro had found a place directly behind home plate. Jill jumped out, went in search of her friend Ruby May and found her talking to Joe and Thad Taylor. Joy spotted her friend Sylvia, and the two little girls sat down on the blanket beside Sylvia's mother. Julie and Evan got into the car with Jethro.

The teams were warming up on the field. The league team had full uniforms: white with red stripes. Fertile's team shirts were white with black stripes. The family was watching Jack as if he were the only player on the field. He stopped playing catch with Dr. Forbes when a player from the other team came up and shook hands with the doctor. Obviously glad to see each other, the two men acted like long-lost friends.

The game started with the visitors at bat. They scored two runs before Ron Poole gave up the pitching mound for first base and Wesley Philpot, a farm boy from south of town, came in to pitch. He struck out the next batter, and the crowd cheered.

When it was Fertile's chance at bat, the first two batters struck out. Jack came to bat and Julie held on tightly to Evan's hand. Jack failed to swing at the first pitch and a strike was called. He swung and connected with the second pitch. The ball sailed out into left field and he made it to second base. The crowd cheered, and those sitting in cars honked their horns. The next batter hit an easy ball to the pitcher, who threw him out at first base, so Jack didn't have a chance to score.

The town team didn't score a run until the fourth inning. Jack again hit a two-bagger, which brought in the man on third. But the inning ended without Jack being able to score.

"He didn't eat much dinner," Julie said worriedly. "I brought buttered bread. Do you think I should have Joe take it to him?"

"No, honey." Evan grinned over her head at Jethro. "He would be embarrassed to eat in front of the other players. He's doing all right. He just needs some help from his teammates in the hitting department."

The last half of the ninth inning started with the score six to one. A line drive put a Fertile man on first. The pitcher walked the second man at bat, then it was Jack's turn.

Julie could hear Jill yelling at her brother to hit a homer. She was still with Ruby May, Joe and Thad.

"Hit a homer, Jack. You can do it!"

Jack fouled the first two pitches. On the third pitch, the bat connected with the ball with a loud *crack!* The ball sailed out over the head of the left fielder, who had moved back when Jack came to bat. The ball went on and on, far across the boundary and into home-run territory.

The noise made by the happy crowd could have been heard for miles. Every car at the field that had a horn was honking, men and boys yelled and slapped one another on the back. Jack trotted around the bases, being congratulated by members of the other team. Not one of them had hit a ball so far.

In the car, seated between her father and Evan, Julie held her hands to her cheeks and fought back the tears that came to her eyes when she saw her brother coming around third base with a wonderful smile on his face. She knew how much this meant to him. Evan and Jethro got out of the car to go to the fence, the better to see Jack's teammates pound him on the back and congratulate him.

Jill was beside herself with excitement. She threw her arms first around Joe and then around Thad.

"I knew he could do it. I told you he could," she exclaimed excitedly, unaware that a pair of interested eyes watched her from a dozen yards away and narrowed when Thad Taylor hugged her and lifted her off her feet.

The game ended with a score of six to four. Although the town team hadn't won, it was Jack's day. Dr. Forbes introduced him to his friend from Tennessee, who was the pitcher for the other team.

Dude Merfield, a well-muscled man with long arms and legs, had grown up in the hill country above the town of Harpersville, Tennessee, Dr. Forbes's hometown. They had known each other since they were ten years old, when Dr. Forbes's sister, Jesse, married Wade Simmer, a hill man. The boys had played together every summer until Todd Forbes went off to school.

When the game was over, Dr. Forbes brought Dude over to meet the Jones family. Jack came along. He couldn't keep the grin off his face and didn't object when Jill threw her arms around him and kissed him.

"We would have skunked you, if not for your boy," Dude said to a proud, grinning Jethro.

"He's worked hard and he loves the game." Jethro put his hand on Jack's shoulder. "You did good, son."

"Did you hear me yellin', Jack?" Jill asked.

"You didn't need the bread and butter," Julie said with proud tears in her eyes.

"You can be sure that I'll be careful what I throw him tomorrow," Dude said.

Ron Poole brushed Jill aside to get to Jack. "I can pick 'em, can't I, Doc? I knew he had the right stuff."

Corbin Appleby came to congratulate Jack, as did the Humphreys, the Taylors and people he didn't even know.

Eudora Meadows came up to the group. "Brother had to go out on a sick call, and I didn't get here until just a little while ago. But I saw Jack hit the home run. Oh, my, I don't know when I've been so excited."

"We could have come by for you, Eudora," Julie said.

"I didn't expect Brother to be called out."

"We'll see you home. But first could you come out to the farm for a while? I promised Jack I would make fudge and Evan's going by the store to bring home soda pop. We're celebrating."

Jill wormed her way through the men gathered around Jack to reach Eudora.

"Miss Meadows, please come. Please, please," Jill begged, her arms around Eudora. "Evan brought over his Victrola."

Eudora laughed and returned Jill's hug.

"I'd love to," she said to Julie, "if you're sure I won't be intruding on your family celebration."

"Not at all. We'll be so glad to have you."

"Honey." Evan came up behind Julie and put his lips close to her ear. "We'd better forget about the fudge and the soda pop. Jack asked Jethro if he could invite the Jacobses and the Taylors to come out. It could be that Doc Forbes and his friend Dude will come."

"Oh, my goodness. I wish I'd baked a cake or something."

"I'll go by the drugstore and see if he'll sell me a couple gallons of ice cream. Go on home with Jethro and get things ready. I'll come later with the boys."

Julie turned so she could look at him. "I don't know what I'd do without you. But . . . isn't that much ice cream awfully expensive?"

"Am I going to be the head of our family, or not?" His voice was stern, his eyes loving.

"Part of the time," she replied sassily, then added, "when I agree with you."

The house seemed to be alive with people laughing and talking. Jethro came to the kitchen, where Eudora and Julie were dishing up ice cream, and said that the Jacobses had to go home to do chores, but Ruby May would stay and spend the night with Jill.

"Where's that fudge you were going to make, Sis?" he teased. "I'd rather have fudge than ice cream."

"You'd better watch out, Papa, or I'll rename you Elsie." The words just slipped out and she looked at him with alarm.

He didn't seem to hear what she'd said. He put his finger in the container and scraped ice cream off the side. Julie attempted to hit his hand with her spoon.

"That's not nice."

"She's hard to get along with at times, Miss Meadows. As soon as Evan gets out of her sight, she gets cranky."

"Call me Eudora, Mr. Jones."

"All right, Eudora. Call me Jethro, and you've got a speck of ice cream on your nose." He left the kitchen chuckling when she put the back of her hand to her nose.

The men and boys, lined up along the edge of the porch, ate ice cream out of bowls and teacups. Julie and Eudora sat on the bench with Myrtle Taylor and watched Joy and Sylvia on the floor beside them.

Julie's eyes went often to Evan. He smiled and talked and laughed as if he were having the time of his life. Jason was always near him, even now, as Evan talked to Dr. Forbes and his friend Dude Merfield.

"Julie, are you through with this?" Jill took the empty bowl from her sister's hand. "Evan said we could play the Victrola and dance, but first Ruby May and I had to gather up all the dirty dishes and put them in the dishpan to soak."

"Have you finished, Miss Meadows?" Ruby May asked.

"Yes, thank you."

Jill tilted her head toward Julie. "She's starting Evan out right."

"I never asked him—" Julie sputtered.

"He's crazy about her," Jill confided. "Someday I'm going to find a man who's crazy about me."

"Jill, there isn't room to dance in the parlor."

"Of course not. Papa and Evan figured it out. Evan will set up the Victrola out here on the porch and when it gets dark, Papa will bring the lanterns from the barn. Open the door, squirt," she said to Joy.

"Your Evan gets along well with the family," Eudora said.

"And I'm so glad they all like him. And he's about as fond of them as he is of me," Julie said with a little laugh.

"I'd not go that far. Every few minutes he looks around to see where you are. You're lucky, Julie."

"No one knows that more than I."

Thirty minutes later, Evan had carried the Victrola to the

porch and the lilting notes of "The Missouri Waltz" drifted on the evening air. Evan took Julie's hand and pulled her out onto the hard-packed earth beyond the porch.

"I've been wanting to hold you all day," he whispered in her ear and drew her close to him. They danced for a while, their steps matching perfectly. "Do you think anyone would notice if I kissed you?"

"Evan Johnson! Course they would. Don't you dare."

Julie looked around to see Jack and Ruby May, Joe and Jill, and the Taylors dancing. Then her eyes opened wide with shock.

"Evan, look. Papa's dancing with Eudora."

"So that's why he suggested we dance in the yard. It's a good sign, honey."

"She's such a nice person. I wish Papa would fall in love with her."

Dr. Forbes was looking at Evan's supply of records and when the music stopped, he replaced the record, carefully wound the machine and came across the yard to tap Evan on the shoulder.

"My turn."

Evan released her reluctantly. "Don't forget that she's my girl."

The music playing was "I'm Always Chasing Rainbows." Dr. Forbes was not as graceful as Evan, but Julie enjoyed the dance and the easy chatter. She danced next with Dude Merfield, and he told her that Jack had the potential to become a great ball player if he had the desire.

"Do you have the desire, Mr. Merfield?"

"No, ma'am. I've no desire to make a career out of playing ball. I like the game and I like traveling around with the league, but in a month I'll be going back to my regular job."

"Which is?"

"I'm a cartoonist. I draw pictures for newspapers."

"You're an artist! And you get ideas by traveling with the ball team?"

He smiled. "Not many people ask me that. But yes, I do."

"What does your family think about your travels?"

"I'm not married, ma'am. My brothers and sisters live in Tennessee, not far from where we grew up. My sister is a nurse. She works for Todd's father. She had worked for him for a while before she went to help out during the war."

"What an experience she must have had."

The dance ended. Julie was claimed by Thad, and Dude moved on to dance with Eudora.

By ten o'clock, Joy and Sylvia were asleep on a quilt on the porch and Jason dozed in a chair. Dr. Forbes and Dude were the first to leave.

"I sure did have a good time, ma'am," Dude said to Julie. "But that don't mean I'm goin' to go easy on that brother of yours tomorrow." He grinned and hit Jack on the shoulder.

After the Taylors left, Jethro announced that he would take Eudora home.

"Can I go?" Jason was ever alert to the possibility of riding in the car.

"No, you can't," Julie said quickly. "You're so tired you can't see straight. It's time you were in bed."

"I had a wonderful time, Julie. Oh, my, I've never danced so much. This is the first time since my school days, and that was a long time ago," Eudora said.

"Come out again. We all enjoyed having you."

"Thank you. I hate going off and leaving you with all those dishes to wash."

"Don't worry about that. I'll have Jill and Ruby May to help me."

Julie stood on the porch, leaning back against Evan. His arms were around her, his lips nuzzling her ear.

"Do you think she likes Papa?" Julie whispered, watching her father help Eudora into the car.

"It's obvious that she doesn't dislike him."

"Tonight he could see the difference between her and Mrs. Stuart."

"He'd have had to be blind not to see that." Evan's lips traveled from her ear to the line of her jaw.

"He deserves to have someone really nice."

"So do I." His hand moved up under her breast.

"Jill is crazy about her. Always has been."

"I'm crazy about you and have been since I saw you again."

"I worry about Jason, if Papa remarries."

"I worry that it'll be a while before we can marry."

"We'll take Joy with us. Do you think Papa would let us take Jason? Would you mind?"

"What's one more? We're going to have a dozen kids anyway."

"I had such a good time tonight. It wouldn't have been possible if you hadn't been here."

"I had a good time, too." Evan locked his arms around her and buried his nose in her hair. "But I wish you were going home with me."

The Sunday afternoon ball game was not as exciting as the Saturday night game. The league team won eight to three and left town on the evening train.

Jack didn't hit another home run, but he did have several base hits and earned the reputation of being the best ball player in Fertile.

Chapter 29

SEPTEMBER MOVED EASILY INTO OCTOBER and harvest time. The hay had been put up; the garden vines, dried long ago, were dotted with large yellow pumpkins. Apples had been individually wrapped in pieces of newspaper saved for that purpose and were stored in a barrel in the cellar.

Evan hired Ernie Hovelson, a man from town, to help with the harvest, and between the two of them, Jethro, Joe and Jack, when he wasn't in school, all that was left to be done on the two farms was to pick the corn.

Jethro counted out five rows and drove the team to straddle the middle row. It was called the down row. In years past, Julie sat with Joy on the wagon seat and drove the team. Her brothers picked on one side and threw the ears in the wagon, her father on the other. The down row was left for Jill and Jason to pick. This year, with Evan and his hired man to help, Jill and Jason drove the team after school, which let out at noon during harvest, and Julie stayed in the house to cook meals for the men.

The last day of the corn harvest was to be one the Jones family would never forget. The day was cloudy, a cold wind blowing from the northwest. It was dusk and in another half hour or so the last of the crop would be in the wagon.

Jethro told Jill that Jason could handle the tired team and

she could go to the house and tell Julie that they would be in for supper in an hour. Jill jumped off the wagon, wrapped her heavy sweater around her and walked across the field to the woods that separated the Johnson farm from theirs.

The man, who had tied his horse to a stump a half mile away and had come through the woods to watch the girl on the wagon seat, couldn't believe his luck. The tempting little vixen had been in his mind for the past several months and at last he was going to catch her alone. The temporary relief he'd felt after he'd had the girl at Centerville a few weeks ago had long since vanished.

One other time he'd felt like this, and that was while he was down south making plans to marry. For three weeks after seeing that girl, he'd not been able to think of anything but conquering her, going inside her, using her. He had ended up choking the life out of her. She had been an obsession with him as Jill was now.

He had no desire to kill again. He wanted a baby out of Jill. He had been careful not to relieve himself for a couple of weeks, waiting for this opportunity. He was sure that when he let go the fluid that carried his seed, it would be powerful.

The light in the woods was dim, but Jill could see clearly and was unafraid. She walked the path between the two farms made more distinct recently, since not a day went by that Evan wasn't at the Jones farm. She jumped over a pile of horse manure, then suddenly a steely arm snaked around her waist, jerked her off the path and dragged her backward into the woods. She let out a piercing scream before a hand was slapped over her mouth.

"I'll not hurt you if you're quiet." The words were whispered against her ear. The arm around her waist loosened and she lurched, but was held tightly against him by the hand over her mouth. A cloth was wrapped around her eyes. The instant the hand was removed from her mouth, she let out another scream, then her mouth was full of cloth and she was sure that she was going to die.

Jill's heart was whamming, but it didn't seem to be pumping enough air into her lungs. When he threw her to the ground, there was no doubt in her mind that he was going to kill her. He checked the blindfold to make sure she couldn't see and then flipped her over. He sat on her thighs, holding her hands out from her body, then drew them to the top of her head and tied something around them.

"I got to see your titties, pretty thing, before it gets too dark." The hoarse whisper again.

Jill felt his hands spread her sweater, rip open the bodice of her dress. A knife cut her chemise to expose her small breasts. She writhed and tried to hit him with her tied fists.

He laughed.

"Just as pretty as I thought. Now let's see what's under that skirt." He moved down, holding her legs apart with his. When he threw up her skirt, she could feel the cold air on her legs above her stocking tops. Finding a hole in the crotch of her drawers, he ripped them, exposing her most private parts.

Jill thrashed about and screamed inside, *Papa, help me!*

"Be still, damn you. As horny as I am, this'll only take a minute."

Jill's ears were ringing. Cruel fingers were inside her, pulling her apart. Panic consumed her. She screamed inside, kicked and tried to buck him off her. He laughed again, seeming to enjoy her struggles.

"You could learn to like this, little wildcat. I could teach you a lot of things."

He laid something long and hard against her breasts, nudged them with it, rolled it over them, then trailed it down to between her legs and began to push it into her.

She almost strangled on the gag that had been jammed in her mouth.

Help me! Please, God, don't let him do this.

Suddenly the weight was lifted from her. She heard a yell, a snarl, the stamping and whinnying of a frightened horse. A heavy boot hit her thigh and she rolled to get away from the struggling bodies beside her. Her clothes were around her waist, her bare thighs and buttocks scraped against twigs and stones. With her bound wrists, she tried to tear the cloth from her eyes, but it was knotted too tight.

"Goddamn you! Goddamn you!" an angry voice was saying. Then came a piercing cry of someone in pain, followed by the sound of dull thuds.

"Oh, my God!" Then, "Whoa, Ranger. Whoa, easy, boy."

Jill became vaguely aware that someone was trying to soothe a frightened horse.

Help me get away. Jill prayed with a grim, terrible strength of will and began to crawl as fast as she could away from the sounds made by the man and the horse.

"Jill, Jill, it's me!"

No! No! Get away! She struck out with her bound hands.

"It's Thad, Jill. Thad." She felt hands on her shoulders. "He'll not hurt you."

His hands untied the knot, pulled the gag from her mouth and unwrapped the cloth from her eyes. As soon as she could see, she threw her arms around his neck and sobbed, completely unaware of the naked flesh she pressed against him.

Thad held her to him for a long moment, trying to calm her.

"He'll not hurt you. He . . . may be dead. Ranger stomped on him. Are you all right now? We've got to get help." He untied her hands, pulled her to her feet and covered her breast with the sweater that hung from her arms.

Thad shielded her with his arms from having to see the man on the ground, and they hurried down the path. He stopped, put his fingers to his lips and sent out several sharp urgent whistles.

"Roy was coming along behind me. I guess he stopped to

see if Jack wanted to come. We were on our way to town and took the shortcut."

"Oh, Thad, he was goin' to . . . goin' to . . ."

"Don't think about it. I hear Roy comin'," he said when he heard the thud of horse's hooves and his younger brother came charging down the path. Roy pulled the horse to an abrupt halt when he saw them.

"What—?"

"Go back and get Jethro and the men. Hurry. There's a hurt man back there."

"What—?"

"Don't ask questions. Go!"

Jill and Thad stood in the path and waited for her father to come. She leaned against him. What had happened to her was all too real. A man had come out of the woods and attacked her. She wound her arms around Thad's waist and looked fearfully over her shoulder.

"He couldn't get up. He can't hurt you," he whispered. "Your pa and the boys will be here and take you home."

Minutes later, Jethro, riding with Roy on his horse, arrived and Jill flew into his arms.

"Papa! Papa! A man pulled me off the path and threw me down. If Thad hadn't come, he'd have—he was goin' to—"

"You don't have to say it, honey." Jethro tried to choke down his rage. He hugged his daughter—his feisty, mouthy little girl who meant the world to him—and silently swore that he'd kill the bastard that hurt her.

"Roy said there was a hurt man, is it . . . the one who did this?"

"Yeah. He's back there a ways. He—" Thad stopped when Joe, Jack and Evan arrived, all breathless from running.

"Take care of your sister, Jack." Jethro gently moved Jill to her brother. "There's a lantern on the wagon—"

"I brought it, Pa," Joe said.

"Light it, and let's go see the son-of-a-bitch."

"He may be dead," Thad hastened to say. "Ranger stomped him."

"If he isn't, he'll wish he was." Jethro was shaking with rage.

Jill and Jack stayed on the darkened path, while Joe, with the lantern, led the party to where a man lay not ten feet back into the woods. The light shone on his blood-splattered face and into thick blond hair. His eyes were open and he was breathing hard.

"Godamighty," Jethro gasped when he recognized the man. There were similar exclamations from the others.

Ron Poole, the owner of the hardware store, a member of the City Council, the organizer of the baseball team, lay in his own blood, looking up defiantly at the men who stared down at him.

"Did you know who he was, Thad?" Jethro asked.

"Not till after Ranger stomped him. I didn't tell Jill."

"You sorry son-of-a-bitch. I should kill you."

"Go . . . ahead. I'm goin' to die anyway." Blood came from the corner of Ron's mouth.

"No. You need to suffer for what you did to my girl."

Evan pulled Jethro aside. "We should try to keep him alive until Appleby gets here."

"Why? The sooner he's dead, the better I'll like it."

"For the record and for Thad's sake, Appleby needs to see him and hear what Jill has to say. We don't want someone like Weaver to try and pin a murder charge on the boy."

"I see what you mean."

"We can take a side board off the wagon and get him to the house. Meanwhile, send someone for Appleby and the doctor."

"All right. I'm just so angry, I can't think."

"Roy," Evan said, "lend Joe your horse so he can get into town and bring back Chief Appleby and the doc. Ernie"—he motioned to his hired man—"you and Thad go back to the wagon and bring a side board to put him on so we can carry him out of here." Jethro told Jason to drive the team to the edge of the woods so the wagon wouldn't be far away.

"Joe," Evan said when Joe was mounted on Roy's horse. "Don't tell them who it is if there's anyone around to hear. Have them hurry. We should be at the house by the time they get there."

Jethro was grateful that Evan took charge. So many questions roamed around in his mind. Julie had told him what Evan had said about Walter Johnson being unable to have intercourse. Could this son-of-a-bitch be the man who had raped Julie?

Evan squatted down beside Ron. He wrapped a black cloth he'd found nearby around his head to stop the flow of blood. The horse's hoof had scraped the side of Ron's head and his ear hung by an inch of skin. A short, thin-bladed boot knife lay in the grass not far from him.

Ron's eyes roamed. A broken arm was extended out from his body; his other hand clutched his side.

"I . . . coulda liked you, Johnson." Evan didn't say anything. "You stood out from these hicks . . . like a sore thumb."

"Better save your breath, Poole. You'll need it when we move you."

"Hand me that pig-sticker over there and I'll save you the trouble."

"No. It would be over too fast."

"Well, then I'll just make you mad enough to use it on me yourself."

"Go ahead and try."

"I hear that you're going to marry Julie Jones. When you take her to bed, remember that I had her when she was just fifteen. I'm the one who broke her in. I still remember how tight and sweet she was." He chuckled, and blood bubbled from his lips. "She was so scared, I came in her before I wanted to. Whataya think of that?"

"Not much. She told me that she'd been raped," Evan replied calmly.

"Joy is my kid. She'll never be yours."

"She'll be mine. Thank God she'll never know you."

"I wanted her to know. I was going to tell her someday."

"You won't get the chance now."

"She'd a had a little cousin if that damn kid hadn't come along. I been letting the pot boil for a couple of weeks and I was horny as hell."

"Bet your wife appreciated that."

"My wife!" His voice was filled with contempt. "That stupid woman fooled me; she knew she couldn't have kids when I married her. Ever since I grew up alone in that orphanage, I've wanted kids of my own. Well, I've taken care of that. I must have at least eighteen. When Ron Poole goes, there'll be part of him left. Good kids with sweet clean virgin mothers. I picked them young, broke them in myself. The more they struggled, the more I knew that they were fit to bear Ron Poole's children, to keep my line going."

"You're a peach of a fellow, Poole."

"Too bad about the one that got a look at me. She had to go, if I was to keep spreading my seed."

"Which one was that?"

"Doesn't matter. It happened down south. I been lookin' forward to Jill. Almost shot my wad as soon as I touched her." Blood slid from the corner of his mouth."

"You're sick, did you know that?"

"Maybe. But I figure I've got eighteen or more kids scattered around over the country. How many you got?"

"You'll not have any more. I doubt you'll last out the night."

"I want Joy at my funeral."

"You'll be in hell. Why should you care who's at your funeral?"

Jethro's head was pounding with all he had heard. He had to leave before he kicked the man to death. He began pacing up and down the path and finally went back to where Jill waited with Jack.

"I thought I told you to take her home," he said crossly.

"You didn't, Pa. You said stay and take care of her."

"Sorry, son." Jethro's voice softened. "I should have told you to take her home. It'll be a while before we can get him out of here. Tell Julie to fix a place in the barn. I don't want the bastard in my house."

"Roy came back and said it was Ron Poole. I can't believe he'd do such a thing, Pa."

"Some people have bad stuff buried deep inside. Are you all right, honey?" He put his hand on Jill's shoulder and peered into her face.

"Is he dead?"

"Not yet. You go on home with Jack. Julie will take care of you. The doctor is coming. Do you want to see him?"

"No! Papa, don't make me."

"You don't have to see him if you don't want to. Here comes Thad and Ernie with the board. Jack, take Jill to the wagon and help Jason get it home."

Light shone from the lanterns in the yard and in the barn when Evan, Ernie, Jethro and Thad walked into the yard carrying Ron Poole on the board. He was alive and cursing them every step of the way. Ron was a big man and they were exhausted.

Jack held open the barn door. He had forked fresh hay into the stall nearest the door. After lowering the board, they moved out of the stall. Ernie left immediately to go back to Evan's place to do chores.

Jack got his first look at the man who had tried to rape his sister.

He stood over him and spat. "I thought you were the nicest man in town, but you're nothing but a pile of . . . shit."

"Do me a favor, kid, and cut my throat. If you don't have the guts, get me a knife and I'll do it."

"I wouldn't give you a horse turd."

Ron's lips curled back away from his teeth. "Then get the hell away from me."

Joe came into the barn to get a sack to wipe down Roy's horse. "They're coming. I cut across the field."

A minute or two later, car lights came down the lane. Corbin Appleby and Dr. Forbes, with a bag in his hand, got out of the car. Jethro motioned them to the barn, where Evan waited beside Ron.

"No," Evan was saying. "Absolutely not!" He got to his feet to make room for Corbin and the doctor.

"What's he wanting?" Jethro asked.

Evan motioned him out of the stall. They moved down the aisle toward the door.

"He wants to see Joy."

"Jesus Christ." The words exploded from Jethro. "He'll tell Appleby and Doc."

"Better them than some others. They're good men. They'll not say anything if you ask them not to. Does Joe know what happened to Julie?"

"He knows."

"We'll keep everyone else out. I want to see Julie."

Evan walked toward the house. Jethro lingered in the doorway of the barn. It was strange being here in his own barn, hearing the murmur of voices as the doctor and the police chief talked to Ron Poole.

Julie had made coffee. Evan could smell it as soon as he opened the door. The table was set for supper, and only Joy was eating. The others sat with coffee cups in their hands, even Jason.

"Evan, Jason's got coffee," Joy yelled. "Julie said I was too little."

"And you are, sugarplum. But you're not too little to give me a kiss." Evan bent over and Joy planted a wet kiss on his cheek. He hugged her head to him while his eyes caught Julie's across the table.

"Are you all right, Jill?" he asked as he went around behind Jill and put his hand on her shoulder.

"I'm all right, or will be when *he's* out of here."

"What does Doc think?" Thad asked.

"I didn't stay to find out." Evan went around the table to Julie, put his arms around her and pulled her back against him.

"I was going to put supper on," Julie whispered, "but no one seems very hungry."

"It's been a shock to all of us."

Joe came to the door and beckoned to Evan. He spoke as soon as Evan reached the porch.

"Doc says it won't be long. He spilled his guts about Joy. He said if he could see her, he'd tell them about the other girls he'd raped. The bastard. I could cut his throat."

"What did Appleby say to that?" Evan asked anxiously.

"No deal. Poole wanted him to know about the other girls. Seemed to be proud of it."

Jethro came out of the barn and they walked out into the yard to meet him.

"He's gone. Something broke loose inside and blood gushed out all over."

When the doctor and Corbin came out of the barn, Jethro went to meet them.

"Chief, no one knows about Joy except Joe and Evan and of course Julie."

"Don't worry, Mr. Jones. What I heard in there will go no further."

"That goes for me, too." Dr. Forbes nodded.

"He told me quite a bit while we were up in the woods," Evan said to the chief. "I think he knew he was dying and wanted to inflict as much hurt as possible. He thinks he's got as many as eighteen children from young girls he's raped. The man had to be sick in the head."

"I couldn't believe it at first when Joe told me who he was. Is Jill all right?"

Evan answered, "It'll take her some time to get over it, but she's a strong girl."

"What I'd like to do is get the parties involved together and talk a bit."

"I'll go speak to Julie and see if she can get Jason and Joy to bed." Jethro turned toward the house, then back. "The Taylor boys are still here. You'll want to talk to Thad. He's the one who pulled him off Jill."

"We've got to decide whether or not to let all this dirty laundry out of the bag." Corbin looked searchingly at Dr. Forbes and at Evan. "And if we do, what will it do to a nice woman like Mrs. Poole?"

"I heard a yell. I didn't know what it was until I heard it again."

Thad was nervous speaking to the police chief and under the watchful eye of Dr. Forbes, who leaned against the doorframe with a cup of coffee in his hand.

"Then I heard her yell again. I hurried on down the path and heard a man's laugh. I turned into the woods and saw them. I just jumped off the horse and pulled him off her."

"Did you know who he was?"

"Not then. I didn't know it was Jill. He had wrapped a black thing around her head. I didn't have time to think about who he was or who she was. I was trying to keep him from cutting me with his knife."

"You managed pretty good. He must've outweighed you by fifty pounds or more."

"We rolled till we were almost under Ranger, and when he went to stab me with the knife, I bucked up and the blade went into Ranger's leg. It scared him and a hoof came down alongside of Mr. Poole's head. I rolled away. When I got to my feet to see what was going on, Ranger was still stomping on him.

"I really didn't care. I hoped Ranger would kill him. When

I saw that he wasn't going to get up, I got the horse away from him and went to Jill."

"Thank God you were there." Jethro's eyes were haunted, his face haggard. "I can't thank you enough for what you did."

"It ain't no more'n what any man would've done, Mr. Jones."

"I'm going to have to make a report," Corbin said slowly and looked at each one. "There are times when the truth hurts more than a lie. If it gets out that for years Ron Poole has been raping girls in this area, a lot of people will be looking at kids and wondering about girls who have gone away and returned with babies and tales about their husbands being killed. And folks will be wondering about Jill and watching to see if she's pregnant.

"The reason I came here was because the girl I was going to marry was raped and murdered by a man from Fertile. Tonight Evan told me that Ron bragged that he was the one who killed her. I despise the man. As far as I'm concerned, we could put a wire around his neck and drag him down Main Street. I'm thinking of the girls, the children and Mrs. Poole. It would be a living hell for that poor woman if it became known what Ron has done. She'd have to sell out and leave town.

"If you all agree, I'll say that Ron Poole somehow fell from his horse and the frightened animal stomped on him, then ran off. Thad heard him call when he went through the woods on his way to town and went for help.

"It was Doc's idea to do it this way," Corbin continued, glancing at the doctor, who nodded in agreement. "As soon as we decide if this is what we want to do, he'll go notify Mrs. Poole and send out the undertaker."

"It will go against the grain to see the son-of-a-bitch buried with a big funeral," Jethro said.

"We don't have to go to his big funeral, Papa." Julie covered her father's hand where it lay on the table. "I'm glad no other girl will suffer what happened to Jill. I don't care how big a funeral he has. He was an evil, mean man, and I can't be sorry that he's dead."

"If we all agree, that's the report I'll give to the council."

"It's for the best," Jethro said. Then: "What do you think, Thad? You're the man who brought him down."

"I'd hate to have folks talkin' about Jill and . . . wonderin'. . . ." Thad then spoke to Corbin. "I'd like for me and Roy to tell our pa. We've always been square with him, and him with us. I don't want to tell him a lie."

Corbin nodded and stood. "I understand your thinking. Tell him what we've agreed to. Doc, I'll stay while you fetch the undertaker."

"I've got to go find my horse." Thad reached for his hat.

"Take one of ours out of the lot," Jethro said.

"Thanks, but I'll ride double with Roy."

"When I see your pa, I'm going to tell him that he's got a right to be proud." Jethro held out his hand and Thad shook it.

"That goes for all of us." Joe extended his hand. "Our little sis is mouthy, but she's ours."

"Thank you, Thad." Julie kissed him on the cheek.

"Tarnation!" Roy said with disgust. "He'll be gettin' a swelled head sure as shootin', with all this kissin' and hand-shakin'."

Jill got up from the table and went to the tall boy. "Thad, can I kiss you, too?"

He grinned. "Why, shore, Miss Jill. I ain't gone plumb loony yet."

Later, when the undertaker arrived, Julie and Evan stood on the back porch and watched the activity going on in the lit barn.

"What do you think, honey? Are you satisfied with its being handled this way?"

"I'm glad I don't have to wonder anymore. I'm glad he'll never see Joy again. Lordy, when I started out on this day, I never dreamed it would end like this."

"If I hadn't been sure he was going to die, I'd have been tempted to kill him for what he did to you."

"It was a terrible experience, but I've got a sweet little girl out of it."

"Correction! *We've* got a sweet little girl."

Julie turned in his arms and looked up at him. "Evan Johnson, may I kiss you?"

"Why, shore, Miss Jones. I ain't gone plumb loony yet."

Epilogue

December 15, 1922

WELL, MRS. JOHNSON, WHAT DO YOU THINK?"

"About what?" Julie stretched, then snuggled against him. She hadn't been prepared for the warmth or the strength of his hard, muscular body, the long legs against hers or the enormous arms under and around her.

"About our getting married today. About being my wife. About what we just did."

"Oh, *that*." She pressed her nose against his neck. "I've not decided about *that*. Maybe if we did it again, I'd be able to decide."

"Ah, sweetheart, you are a treasure." He kissed her tenderly, nudging her lips, stroking them. "I thought you were afraid of me. I could feel your trembling and the frightened pounding of your heart."

"I wasn't afraid of you, my wonderful man," she whispered. "I was excited."

The loud clanging of a bell and shouts of male voices broke the silence.

"I thought they had gone," Evan groaned.

"Evan!" The shout reached into the upstairs bedroom. "We've got an old girlfriend of yours down here."

"Yeah, Evan, she wants to see you!" *Bang! Bang!*

"I hope they don't shoot someone," Evan whispered.

"Give us a dollar, Evan, and we'll take her away."

"A dollar! I'm not taking that witch away for a dollar!"

"Throw out five silver dollars, Evan, and we'll go home."

The bells clanged, then more gunshots. Evan swore.

"I'm going to smash your brothers' heads tomorrow for this and for putting that fresh cowpie outside the door for me to step in."

"Joe said This and That Humphrey and Roy Taylor put it there."

"And you believe him? Bull-foot! Jethro's in on it, too."

"You can pay him back when he and Eudora are shivareed."

"If those lunkheads don't leave soon, I'm going to start boiling oil to throw on them. I want to love my wife in peace and quiet," Evan complained, his lips nuzzling her breast.

"They'll get tired pretty soon and go away." Julie consoled him with small, quick kisses. "Isn't it wonderful that Papa and Eudora are getting married? She says they should wait at least a month. Her mother died only last week."

"Yes, wonderful. . . ." His voice drifted. Evan had difficulty grasping the fact that this woman was his wife. *Wife*. She was his, to love and to protect forever or until death parted them.

"Evan, Papa knew that we would take Joy, but he was a little hurt that Jason wanted to come live with us."

"Don't worry about it, honey. Jason will have two homes. When the newness wears off, he may want to go back."

"I thought of that. Jill has grown up since what happened to her in the woods. She's tickled that Papa is going to marry Eudora. Don't you think he seems years younger? He smiles all the time."

"That's nice," Evan murmured, his lips nipping at the smooth line of her jaw. Beneath her nightdress, his hand found her buttocks and pressed her tightly to the part of him that strained to go inside her again.

"Evan, did I tell you that I just love the new stove? The oven will hold a big, big turkey if you can find us one. Christmas Day I'll fix a dinner and we can have the whole family over here. That is, if it's all right with you."

"It's all right with me, love. Humm . . . you taste good, smell good." He pushed back her hair so that he could nibble at her earlobe and caress the soft flesh in the curve of her neck.

"Why do you suppose Mr. Wood sold the bank and moved away? Zelda wasn't happy about where they were going."

Evan grunted something about not caring where they went and continued to caress her.

"Did you know Shirley Poole's brother came to help her with the store? It was nice of Chief Appleby not to want her humiliated because of what her husband had done."

"Oh, yes, he's a great guy. . . ."

Julie wrapped her arms around Evan's neck and rubbed her cheek against his. "I'm so glad I've got you, Evan. I love you to distraction."

"It's about time you paid some attention to me." He placed a hard kiss on her lips.

"Did I thank you for the beautiful kitchen cabinet? It's got a tin flour bin and a place to roll out dough. I can put all the everyday eating utensils in one of the drawers. The beautiful silverware you got from your grandmother will go in the buffet along with the lovely dishes. Do you think we should use them for the Christmas dinner? They'll be pretty on the crocheted table cloth Mama—"

"Julie Janet Jones Johnson," Evan said in an exasperated tone, "if you don't run down pretty soon, I'm going to gag you."